Connie ②

Some Kind
of Miracle

Bernadette Carson

Copyright © 2007 by Bernadette Carson

ISBN 0-7414-4080-6

Published by:

PUBLISHING.COM

1094 New DeHaven Street, Suite 100
West Conshohocken, PA 19428-2713
Info@buybooksontheweb.com
www.buybooksontheweb.com
Toll-free (877) BUY BOOK
Local Phone (610) 941-9999
Fax (610) 941-9959

Printed in the United States of America

Printed on Recycled Paper

Published July 2007

Acknowledgments

Again my sincerest thanks to Leanne Cusimano ("Frannie Oliveri" in my novels). If I hadn't been inspired by Amore Breakfast and Leanne during my first Ogunquit visit, *Morning Glory* and this sequel might never have been written. Her enthusiasm, support and promotional efforts helped skyrocket *Morning Glory* above and beyond my wildest dreams. Thanks also to Leanne's parents, Phyllis and Tony Cusimano, who allowed me to enjoy fictionalizing them.

I'm hard pressed to find descriptive words for Donna and Gordon Lewis. It still amazes me how they opened their hearts and their home to me that very first day we met. I've been their house guest several times already and can honestly say I've never met two kinder, compassionate, energetic and civic-minded people. I consider myself privileged to know them.

Dr. Timothy Quinn (a/k/a "Tank" to his friends and "Dr. Timothy Quinlan" in this novel) is another Ogunquit shining star. I recall when he introduced himself at Amore Breakfast. He had heard I needed a doctor's help with *Some Kind of Miracle* and actually *volunteered* despite my warnings that he might be sorry. But that never happened. Tim's prompt responses were unparalleled and his enthusiasm for my work definitely fueled my writing.

Matthew Stewart, retired Detective Sergeant with the Maine State Police, helped me through *Morning Glory* and although I tested his patience then, he too *volunteered* to do it again! Without Matt's guidance, I could never have "murdered" anyone in my novels.

Special thanks to Ken Holmes and Jason ("Jake") Corbin, owners of The Admiral's Inn. When I introduced *Morning Glory,* Ken and Jason were kind enough to host my promotional week without charge. Now, for this sequel, they allowed me to use The Admiral's Inn in the worst possible way—all for the fun of fiction. Thanks also to bartender, Vic Guay, for making me feel welcome and allowing me to include him also.

Zackary Kaliher, State of Maine Child Protective Duty Worker, deserves special thanks also for his prompt and pleasant responses. Without his help, my plot would have been crushed from the start.

I can't forget Sharma Damren, Diane Moore and the entire Ogunquit Police Department for always answering my questions and giving me a warm welcome when I visit. Their kindness inspired me to create a short scene at the OPD.

Many thanks to Bill Frank, Esq. ("Bill Franklin" in novel), an excellent lawyer and old friend from my days with the Rockland County Attorney's Office in New York, for his guidance with Suzanne Oliveri, a principal character in this novel.

Thanks also to Leo Downey, owner of Ogunquit Sunrise Properties, Inc., and Bob Poliquin, Rentals and Property Management. Bob responded eagerly to my questions. His pleasant personality added him to my long list of Ogunquit friends.

Special thanks to Bill Carson, who spoke often of Ogunquit when we first married, insisting I'd love its charm. How right he was! If he hadn't introduced me to Ogunquit, there would be no *Morning Glory* or *Some Kind of Miracle.*

My character, Steve Lynch, was a pleasure to create. I simply visualized the real Steve Lynch and a smile stretched across my face. Hope my readers get to see him around Ogunquit. He really *does* have that dazzling smile!

And lastly, I could never forget the special person whose spirit and gentleness also inspired me to write this sequel. Mark Thallander, my "angel" whose friendship is one of my Ogunquit treasures.

Dedication

This book is dedicated to my family; my son, Michael Martorelli, his wife, Ellen and their four children: Andrea, Lauren, Michael and Vincent; my son, Frank Martorelli and Kristin, his fiancée; my daughter Bernadette Kilduff, her husband Danny and their three children: Brian, Jaclyn and James; my son Paul and his wife, Lauren, and their son, Matthew.

Stay happy, stay safe, my darlings. I love you all.

Chapter One

While enjoying a leisurely dinner and the company of good friends at Clay Hill Farm, Frannie Oliveri tried to ignore the weather. According to this afternoon's forecast, the worst wasn't due for a few hours, but icy rains had been pouring down on Ogunquit all week. Combined with the wind gusts expected to strengthen, the storm would attack tonight with a vengeance. Spring had arrived days ago, but Old Man Winter refused to relinquish his domain. She couldn't stop thinking of Benny. Would the howling winds and heavy rains frighten him?

Frannie threw out her hands and reached for her parka. "See what I mean?" she said to her friends. "Why did I get that stupid dog? I'll have to skip dessert, guys, and check on Benny. He might be scared out of his mind."

Benny entered her life only two months ago, but she was hooked the moment she first stroked his face. His coat was a blend of straw and silk, his color like a fiery sunset. Frannie remembered how her golden retriever had looked up at her with those sad brown eyes. With his head tilted, his body in a rhythmic vibration that made him sound motorized, Benny made his plea. She had scratched his ears playfully and kissed the top of his head. Never before had she kissed an animal—she could never get past that distinctive "doggie" odor—but with Benny, it seemed perfectly natural. A spontaneous reaction prompted by love.

When she finally pulled her Volvo onto the pebbled driveway, she was relieved to be home and safe. But after a week-long Caribbean cruise followed by two weeks with her sister in the California sunshine, home was not too appealing. Freezing rain lashed out and fell like bullets. She zipped up her parka and threw up the hood. Her fingers felt like icicle sticks and she silently cursed herself for never carrying gloves. The ocean was in a bitchy mood tonight and seemed to be at war with the wind. Territorial rights, Frannie mused. *Let them fight it out.* She couldn't wait to get inside and get a fire going.

Storm or no storm, she stopped dead when she heard Benny's incessant barking coming from the other side of the house. *How the hell did he get outside? Did I forget to lock the damn door? Did the storm fly it open? Wait, don't panic. If he wanted to, he could get back in the same way he got out.*

A comforting thought surfaced and a satisfied grin crossed her face. *Sure, I know why he's barking like crazy. He probably found something he wants to show me.* Her face soured at the image. *I hope it isn't a dead bird, or God forbid, a rodent of some kind. He might want to dump that in my hands like a coveted trophy. No—cats do that, right? Do dogs do that too?* Frannie sighed, resigned to the knowledge that she still had a lot to learn about living with a golden retriever. Visualizing what Benny might have in his mouth, Frannie reversed her steps, opting not to enter the house, but to go around and check Benny first. She covered her face with her hands to shield it from the rain and went to rescue her dog. Just in case her bizarre thoughts materialized, she didn't want to open the side door from inside, allowing him to drag in whatever unwelcome guest he might have.

For the five years Frannie had lived here in her oceanfront home, Mother Nature had never shown rage of this magnitude. When she had left Clay Hill Farm, it hadn't yet been this violent. Something made Her mighty angry tonight. Frannie glanced upward and hoped the storm wouldn't unearth an avalanche of stones or send branches crashing onto her house. Sputtering a string of obscenities she hadn't used for a while, she lowered her head, braced herself and went after Benny. She followed his sound and found herself approaching his run.

When she had bought her forty-year-old home, one of the features was a large fenced-in area that had served as a huge playpen for the previous owners' twin toddlers. Now it conveniently served as a run where Benny could enjoy himself barking at the occasional passing cars.

A gust of wind took Frannie by surprise and pushed her against the house. She grabbed the wooden railing attached to the three concrete steps outside the laundry room entrance. She called out his name, and when he didn't come running, she tried to whistle, but her trembling lips were in no mood. Again she called.

"Benny, get over here!" She clenched her teeth and silently resolved to find time for some necessary doggy training—obedience training. Like she had nothing better to do. In between overseeing necessary repairs, refurbishing three of her upstairs rooms, together with the upcoming season openings of her restaurants, Amore Breakfast and Amore Evenings, she couldn't imagine how she could squeeze in professional training for Benny. *I should have my head examined instead,* she thought, then pulled up her hood again and took off for Benny. Her face was so cold it felt as if it had fallen into an ice bucket.

The tall gas lamp at the edge of her property offered an umbrella of light—enough to see part of the run. And Benny. Her insides churned and she forgot all about Mother Nature's wrath. She stood frozen for what seemed an eternity at a sight she couldn't fathom.

Benny stood there, helpless, drenched and terrified, leashed to the fence. His bark diminished now to a mournful cry. Shock waves shot through her and mobilized Frannie into action. Benny's cries grew stronger when he saw her and Frannie's tears streaked down her face along with rivulets of rain. With a good grip on his collar, she led him to the back door that allowed entry through the laundry room. She climbed the three concrete steps and, with her one free hand, fumbled for the seldom-used key. When she found it and looked up, she realized she had no need for it.

The glass window pane was smashed.

Frannie's stomach turned over, shooting up a chunk of the roast duck she had devoured earlier.

But whoever had tied up Benny hadn't hurt him. *How touching,* she thought. *An animal loving sonofabitch who merely wanted to trash my house. But how the hell did he get past Benny? How did the bastard manage to get a leash on him?*

With one hand on Benny's collar and the other reaching for the cell phone in her pocket, she stood at the door, praying to God the thief was long gone. Her heartbeat joined the ominous sounds of a raging sky. She wanted to run to the safety of her car and drive far away from her home-not-so-sweet home, but her grip on Benny's collar was weakening.

It wasn't until she opened the door—with fear lodged in her throat like a steel ball—that she heard another sound. A cat-like sound. *Oh God, what the hell kind of animal is in there?*

Benny went flying in, barking like mad now, and led Frannie to the sound.

Chapter Two

Afraid to look and afraid not to look, Frannie took cautious steps through the laundry room and into the foyer. Recognition kicked in immediately when she spotted the huge pink bag on the dining room floor. The pieces began to fit. She dismissed the fear of finding an intruder and replaced it with another. With quickened steps, she entered her living room, freshly carpeted at forty bucks a yard and never gave thought to all the rainwater dripping from her hair and clothing.

She followed the meowing sound and her fears were justified. The pink bag she had seen already warned her of what she'd find. It also explained how Benny got tied up. Still, Frannie let out a gasp when she discovered little Heather, her cousin Suzanne's four-month-old baby, crying in her infant seat.

"Oh, my God! Oh, my God!" she cried out first, then, "Suzanne? Suzanne?" Panic played at her nerves and temporarily robbed her of clear thinking. She had wanted to comfort Benny and give him a good rubdown with his big thick towel, but he had already shaken off in the laundry room and came running at the sound of Frannie's cries.

"Suzanne, where the heck are you?" she called out again. Flames of anger stirred inside her just thinking about her scatterbrained, irresponsible cousin. Emotional Suzanne who could turn the most mundane incident into a major crisis. She had trouble taking care of herself, much less a baby. But when she had seen mother and baby together for the first time, Frannie thought she saw signs of change. Well, maybe not *change,* but hope for change. She recalled how she had studied Suzanne's face as she nursed her baby. Was that love reflected in her eyes? Knowing Suzanne, whose world revolved only around herself, maybe the unexpected pregnancy had been good for her after all, she concluded. Maybe little Heather would finally turn her mother into a mature, responsible adult. A little far-reaching for a twenty-five-year-old girl who behaved like the sky was falling if she chipped a nail.

The infant was screaming now, probably needed a diaper change or a bottle. Or both. *Oh, no, not me. I don't do babies,* Frannie thought ruefully. Beside the infant seat she found an insulated bag. She zipped it open and found the bottle. Warm? Cold? Who the heck knows? And wasn't she breast feeding anymore? She turned on the lamp so she could at least see what she was doing. Heating it up could take forever and God knows when she was last fed. She yanked the bottle cap off like a dentist pulling his first tooth and, with some trepidation, put the nipple slowly into the infant's mouth. Frannie felt a tug at her heart when Heather's tiny mouth grabbed that nipple and sucked as if she were a contestant in a baby formula competition.

While Heather sucked away, Frannie turned to Benny who stood ramrod straight, fascinated by this new whatever it was. "What about burping? Aren't they supposed to do that?" she asked Benny for lack of another pair of ears to listen. Benny recognized her questioning gaze, perked his ears, and gave her a *don't-ask-me* look. Heather gulped down the six ounces of formula so fast that she burped on her own, spilling some of the excess onto the three yellow ducks on her white sweater. She pulled out a wipe to blot her up, then grabbed another one for her diaper change. She and her cousin Suzanne had never been what you call *close*, but she was a relative, her father's brother's daughter, who popped into her life whenever she needed something. And Suzanne, being the materialistic person she was, always needed *something*. And Frannie, being Suzanne's only relative with a cash reserve and a generous heart, became an easy target.

Still, as much as she disliked Suzanne's attitude and lifestyle, blood is blood and she never turned her away. It's not as if she could have gone to her father for help. Apparently he hoarded all his money to keep his liquor cabinet well-stocked.

Okay. Now for the diaper change. She wrinkled her nose anticipating what she'd find in there, but compared to the gravity of a missing mother, she couldn't give much attention to a smelly diaper. "Suzanne, how can you do this?" she cried out, alarm building in her voice. She had been trying to think of some critical situation that made Suzanne leave the baby alone here in her house, but not a blessed thing entered her mind that could justify such negligent action.

Frannie spread the baby's receiving blanket on her couch and placed her on it. Heather was still so tiny she was afraid to hold her, but desperate situations call for desperate actions. She unsnapped the bottom of the white stretchie and gently pulled out the tiniest pink legs she had ever seen. Her thighs were fuller since she had last seen her, but still a little wrinkled. Funny, she mused, how we're born with these darn wrinkles and we die with them—and that's if we're lucky.

Seeing the baby content now that she'd been fed, Frannie threw the receiving blanket over her bare legs and reached for the phone on her coffee table. It occurred to her that since she hadn't found a note from Suzanne, she might have left a message. *Dear God, how can she do this? She may be self-centered but this is inexcusable!* No message.

Frannie went back to the first-time business of changing a baby's diaper. As soon as she released a few more snaps, the odor hit her. She grimaced and reached for a few more wipes. When she lifted the stretchie a little higher to keep it "out of harm's way," her gaze fixed on a blue sheet of paper, folded in half, and attached to the baby's undershirt by a long strip of white paper tape. She ripped it off, fearful of what crisis in Suzanne's life had led her to this insane act.

Impulsively, she tossed it on the coffee table until she had completed Heather's diaper change.

Frannie turned her head aside, took a deep breath and held it, bracing herself for the unpleasant odor. Her mouth remained closed, lips sealed shut. Armed with four wipes and a tube of Balmex, she tackled the job—even managed a smile—with surprising ease. Heather cooed her relief when Frannie strapped her into the infant seat again. "See, that wasn't too bad for either one of us, right, Heather? Hey, if I can clean up after Benny, I certainly can handle cleaning you. Your little bottom is a lot cuter than his."

Frannie could have sworn Heather understood because a flash of a smile curled her tiny lips. So pretty. "If that's what they call baby gas," she said aloud, "I say bottle it and sell it! But not to me. One dependent doggie is enough." She darted a look at Benny. Right now his wet smell made Heather's diaper seem like an exotic perfume.

Frannie used her pinky to gently stroke the softness of the baby's crescent-shaped brows. Barely visible if not for the lamplight, they arched over her midnight blue eyes like slices of moonlight.

Her face draped with dread when she eyed the blue note paper. *Crazy, self-centered sonofabitch. I could kill her for this!* She reached for the note, determined not to forgive her, no matter what it said. But Suzanne's message was brief:

"Frannie, please take care of Heather. Emergency! S."

Chapter Three

Suzanne Oliveri's nightmare had begun only hours ago when she came home from work shortly after six in the evening. With Heather asleep in her arms, she was greeted at her apartment door by her annoying neighbor, Martha Simone. "Someone was here to see you today, lovey." The woman's sly smile revealed that she had already formed answers to unasked questions.

"Really?" Suzanne responded with disinterest. She couldn't imagine who would come calling at her door or why.

Mrs. Simone sucked on her orange wedge waiting for Suzanne's curiosity to kick in. But curious as Suzanne truly was, she could tolerate neither sight nor sound of the woman whose life quest was to report with malicious overtones the comings and goings of everyone in the neighborhood.

"Mrs. Simone, I'm in a big hurry, so if you'll excuse me ..." She let the rest of her sentence hang and turned her key, anxious to get inside. Suzanne was well aware that this obnoxious woman was waiting for an invitation or an excuse to get inside her apartment. Each time she saw her she tried to inch her way in.

Martha Simone arched her eyebrows, giving herself a momentary facelift. "So you don't care ... fine by me. But if I had a tall hunk of a guy like that interested in me..." Her eyes danced with imaginary thoughts. "Those eyes of his were bluer than Paul Newman's. And if the diamond in his ear was real ..." She winked as though she'd like to devour this perfect catch.

Tall. Blue eyes. Diamond earring. No, no, no! Suzanne's legs turned rubbery. If it weren't for Heather in her arms, she would have collapsed. Steeling herself to keep her expression benign, she turned to the woman with one hand on her doorknob. "Did this person leave a name or a message?"

All Martha Simone's wrinkles swept upward like drawn drapes. Her mouth widened with her sweet tasting smile of satisfaction. "I asked the gentleman his name, or if he wanted to leave a card or something, but he just said he's a friend. An *old* friend."

"And what did you tell him?" *God, no, not something about the baby!*

"Me? Nothing. I had no idea where you were and if I did, do you think I'd tell a total stranger? No, lovey, I'm smarter than that." She gave her a complacent smile and tapped her temple, as though proud of her perceptive and intuitive mind.

Suzanne thanked her curtly, gave a dismissive nod and slipped inside, quickly locking the door behind her. Oblivious to the sheet of white paper that had been slipped under her door, she stepped right over it and went into the bedroom to settle Heather in her crib.

But she stifled a scream when she came back into the living room and spotted it. She recognized the handwriting from ten feet away. Numbed by the shock, she sat on the edge of her sofa and stared ahead unseeingly. She tried desperately to think of a workable plan to save her baby from the grips of her monstrous father.

And then suddenly it shot through her like a bolt of lightning. Yes, a desperate plan, but it had to be done. And she had very little time to pull it off.

It took Suzanne at least ten minutes of deep breathing to stop hyperventilating. *Why must emotions always take control of your body when it's most important to stay calm?*

The thought only frustrated and angered her, adding to her already harried state.

She had to make that call. And she had to do it now while Heather was asleep. But her mouth felt thick and dry as cotton balls and her stomach was shooting up warnings that she'd need to run to the bathroom real soon. She knew that her daughter's fate—and her own—depended on how she handled this call.

After gulping down half a bottle of water, she tapped out that familiar phone number and waited with a thumping heart until he picked up. "Tyler, I can't believe you're here in Ogunquit," she said as pleasantly as she could manage. She forced herself to obliterate the image of her last violent hours with him; to pretend they never happened. "Did you come to see for yourself if Ogunquit is half as beautiful as I said it was?"

Tyler's laugh was slight but its sinister tone came through loud and clear. Her sugar-coated friendliness didn't fool him for a minute. *She's probably still scared shit of me,* he thought. He remembered well the hatred in her eyes when he left her in an alley with the garbage and the rats. "Yeah, yeah, your picturesque little town is pretty, all right, but you know me. I'm not into pretty and quiet. I like New York's crowded streets, the noise, the traffic, the smells, the skyscrapers. I'm a city boy, through and through."

The sound of his voice repulsed her. It made her crazy to think she had allowed him to father her child—not that it was intentional. It seemed incomprehensible that a child as sweet and precious as Heather was born of the seed of this low-life degenerate. "Yes, I guess you are," she answered, but thought, *probably born and bred in the sewers.* She couldn't keep the edge out of her voice. "So city boy, what are you really doing here?"

"I came to take you home, baby. This is no place to live your life. You're much too young. New York is where the action is. You lived there long enough to know that. What the hell do you do with yourself here? Listen to the ocean? It looks like Deadsville to me."

"That's because it's still March. In a couple of months, it'll be just as busy as your hot and crowded New York streets."

"Well, listen, baby, I didn't travel six hours to compare New York to Ogunquit. It's apples and oranges anyway. I came here to apologize for going nuts on you that last night."

"Coming from you, that's nice to hear. I'm sure apologies don't come easy for you. But you weren't exactly a saint before that either, Tyler. No girl wants to be some guy's punching bag every time things don't go his way."

"Ah, so I roughed you up a little now and then. But before that last night, I never really hurt you, did I?"

"Well, no permanent scars, I guess. Not on the surface anyway," she said blandly, as though time had withered the memories, but her insides were burning. She vividly remembered the pain; the discolorations that covered her body like snake skin. Even when she wasn't the cause of his anger, she was the one who got the brunt of it. And once his anger sated, he always feigned remorse and showered her with loving words until he got her back to bed. The flashbacks shot through her like tongues of fire. Suzanne couldn't figure out sometimes who she hated more—Tyler Keaton or herself for allowing it all to happen. "What happened to your new girlfriend? The one you dumped me for?"

"I didn't dump you for her. I dumped you because you were getting to be too much of a smartass. Wasn't I the one who took you in, gave you a job and a place to stay? I treated you like a f---in' princess, didn't I?"

"In the beginning, yes," she admitted, but thought to herself: *And I fell for it like every other naïve jerk who goes to The Big Apple with empty pockets and big dreams.* "I'm curious, Tyler, how did you find out where I live?"

He roared with laughter at her question. "Are you kidding? You, of all people, should know better than to ask such a stupid question. You couldn't hide from me in all of New York City if I wanted to find you, but here in your own little home town … that took me less than five minutes." He paused and lowered his voice to that sexy, throaty tone that used to melt her down. "But hey, baby, why the hell are we talking on the phone? I'm coming over. We'll have ourselves a nice little reunion party, you, me and my bottle of Jack Daniel's."

She had to make snap decisions but panic consumed her and she couldn't think straight or fast enough. "No, not here, Tyler," she blurted out. "It's been a long time for us and I want it to be special. These walls are like paper. That woman you met—my nosy neighbor—will have her ears glued to the wall."

He laughed. "So we'll give the old bird a few thrills. Who cares?"

"I do. Look, I have a better idea. Where are you now?"

"I checked in at a place called The Admiral's Inn. Wanna come here? I've got a nice clean room and they have a great bar."

The Admiral's Inn—no way! Suzanne had met the owners briefly, but she was particularly familiar with Vic, the bartender. She'd been there several times for his famous Cosmos and didn't want to chance being spotted with Tyler. "I don't think so," she answered quickly, not knowing what alternative she could offer, but words spilled out anyway. "They're expecting a pretty bad storm tonight."

He laughed. "Are you telling me you're still scared of a little thunderstorm? Then why don't you get your pretty ass here in a hurry. Just come around the back of the inn. I've

13

got my own private entrance and I'll be waiting at the door. It'll be my pleasure to help you out of your wet clothes." He made the same guttural sound that used to make her come running and sickened her now.

Her eyes widened when he mentioned the private entrance. She knew exactly where he meant. During the off season, Vic had given her an impromptu tour of the renovated rooms. This particular room had not only its own entrance, but a fireplace and a private little deck. *Perfect,* she thought.

She took a few silent seconds to organize her thoughts. A screw up is the last thing she needed now.

Tyler misinterpreted her hesitancy and softened his voice. "I can hear you thinking, baby, and I don't blame you. But it's gonna be different this time. I promise. We're doing real good now. Money's pouring in faster than I can spend it. The bar and the tables are full ninety percent of the time. So if singing is what you really want, you've got it. You'll be our first lounge act. How does that sound?" He paused while she digested it all, then added, "I mean it, baby, I guess I didn't know how much I needed you until I lost you."

Before that last night, before she knew she was pregnant, she would have melted like ice cream under a summer sun. But it was all so different now. She felt like a dam was about to burst inside her, but she squeezed her eyes closed and tightened her lips. She could cry tomorrow and all the following tomorrows, but now was not the time for tears.

Suzanne let out a long sigh of feigned resignation. "Okay, Tyler, it's no use. The plain truth is I should hate you, but don't. I guess I never stopped loving you, even after what you put me through that last night—*It was a miracle I didn't lose the baby, you bastard*—I found myself making excuses for you and blaming myself for provoking you. So if you're ready to take me back, I'm ready to try again. Things haven't been working out too well for me here. And if you'll let me sing in your lounge, well, honey, I'll have the best of both worlds."

"Now you're talking, baby, but we're wasting time. Let's enjoy tonight, then tomorrow, as soon as we open our eyes, we can take off."

"What about my car? It's ten years old but still running. I'd like to take it." Her mind was already racing ahead to New York and how she could possibly escape him there. Once she worked out a plan, she could drive back to Maine, pick up Heather and get as far away as possible.

"Are you kidding? We'll dump it somewhere. No woman of mine is going to run around in a ten-year-old car."

Another pause. Without her car it wouldn't be so easy to escape him. But if she could abandon her baby, she certainly could abandon her car. She felt her stomach sink at the thought of what she planned to do. "I need some time, Tyler ..."

"For what?"

"Well, I have to pack some stuff ..."

"Forget it. I'll buy all your clothes from now on, baby."

"But you know how I am. There's a lot a stuff I want. Things my mother gave me... you know, sentimental stuff. I'm just talking a couple of hours, Tyler."

"Fine," he said, his voice growing impatient now. "I'll wait for you at the bar."

The bar was the last place she wanted him. For sure the alcohol would loosen his tongue. She couldn't give him the opportunity to mention her name, if he hadn't already. "Never mind," she said. "I'll come there now. I'm too anxious to see you. I can always come back later. If the storm gets too bad, I'll do it early in the morning before my witch of a neighbor sticks her nose out her door."

15

"Why should you give a damn about her?"

"I don't," she answered. "I'd just rather not deal with her. She annoys the hell out of me." But she did give a damn about Martha Simone. The fact that she could identify Tyler left Suzanne extremely uneasy. And she needed to know ASAP how he found her apartment. Whoever he spoke to obviously hadn't mentioned the baby because Tyler seemed totally clueless.

But, on the other hand, Tyler had always been shrewd as a fox and lethal as a rattlesnake.

Chapter Four

The roads were deserted and the rain blinding, but no match for the tears that flooded her eyes and streamed down her face. Suzanne drove towards her cousin's home, agonizing over what she intended to do. She had spoken to her briefly that morning and Frannie had casually mentioned that she and her friends had a six o'clock dinner reservation at Clay Hill Farm. It was only 7:15 now and chances were good she hadn't returned yet, but would soon. *But what if they cancelled because of the weather?* she thought. *If she's home there's no way she'll let me run off and leave Heather with no explanation.*

But Frannie's Volvo was not in the driveway when she pulled her Honda in. "Thank God," she murmured, then cringed to think she was thanking God for the chance to abandon her baby.

Only five minutes later, she shivered uncontrollably from the cold and the shock of what she had done. But Heather had been sleeping through most of the night these past weeks and she prayed that this night would be no exception. After using her coat to protect the baby from the rain, her wet clothing clung to her like an icy blanket, but her fears were more chilling than any rain the heavens could pour down.

Somehow she'd have to figure out how to make a quick call to Frannie later to be sure she had come straight home and Heather was safe. She also had to keep Frannie from alerting the police. But even if she did, the Ogunquit Police Department would have enough on their hands tonight to bother looking for her. It would be different if the baby were missing, she reasoned, trying to convince herself and lessen her problems.

She tried to stay focused on driving as she drove at a snail's pace towards The Admiral's Inn. Visibility was practically nil and the last thing she needed was to end up in a ditch. She absolutely had to get to Tyler. For the past year she had psyched herself to push memories of him from her mind, but tonight they all surfaced like a tidal wave. His presence had never been more threatening than tonight.

Suzanne hadn't seen or heard from him since that night in New York when he beat her, raped her and threw her out on the street. With thirty-eight dollars and a nearly maxed-out credit card in her pocket she had headed for The Port Authority to catch the next bus home.

But thinking back to that desperate night eleven months ago, Suzanne remembered vividly her trepidation. Home in Ogunquit, Maine had not conjured up images found on Christmas cards. Not since her mother died. Home had become a sorely neglected house where every room was in disarray. Home was where the smell of beer, cigarettes and sweat had replaced the tantalizing aroma of her mom's beef stew simmering on the kitchen stove. Home was where weeds had invaded the front lawn and her mother's flower garden had died with her. As a child, after she and everyone else tired of the snow and long, cold winter, a welcome springtime would wake up the town she had loved. The sun would shine down on Ogunquit blanketing it with lush greenery and bursts of colorful flowers. But once Suzanne's home had fallen under the total control of her alcoholic father, it had become a clear reflection of its sole occupant who used grief—or the pretense of grief—as his excuse to destroy himself, physically and emotionally. Only the yellow dandelions offered an incongruous touch of sunshine to the house across from All Saints Church where the blinds were always closed and darkness prevailed.

Suzanne had never been able to save her father once he had again succumbed to alcoholism. To imagine he could love his daughter more than his precious booze had been a childish unrealistic dream. A painful dream. She had tried for two years until she could no longer stand the sight of him. She left for New York City with lots of dreams and little else. And then, when she couldn't have been any more vulnerable, she met Tyler Keaton, who showered her with attention. Until the novelty wore off. Then she had become nothing more than one of his possessions.

After four years of abuse and dead dreams, home had become hope. That night, on the long bus ride back to Ogunquit, Suzanne had fed on the memories of her life as it used to be; when they were a family in the true sense of the word. Until *Death* paid a visit and claimed the lives of both her parents. No matter that one continued to breathe.

And now, after more than a year of freedom from Tyler's control and brutality, he was here in Ogunquit. She had wished him dead many times before, but never to be compared to the death wish she had for him tonight.

*   *   *

There were only four cars in The Admiral Inn's parking lot when she arrived and it looked like the entire area had lost electricity. The streetlights were out and the Inn itself was totally dark. At 7:40 in the evening, it was highly unusual that not a single window was illuminated by lamp light. She pulled up right alongside the small wooden deck that adjoined Tyler's room.

With chills rippling through her body and a pounding heart, she knocked on his door.

A wide satisfied grin crossed his face when he saw her. He pulled her inside more like a fisherman reeling in his prize catch than a man reunited with his lost love. "What the hell happened to you?" he asked, seemingly amused. Her hair was drenched and stringy. What was left of her eye makeup formed dark circles under her eyes. Her lips quivered at the sight of him. Fear gripped her. Fear for what she had done and for what she was about to do.

He peeled off her wet coat and let it pool at her feet. His arms went around her for a few warm-up kisses before he threw her on the bed, but he stopped and pulled away. "You're clothes are soaking wet, too. Where the hell were you? And why are you crying?"

She skipped over his first question and answered the second. With a forced smile, she said, "I'm crying because I can't believe you're here and want me back. I thought I'd never see you again."

His curious gaze relaxed into a smug smile. "Well, I'm here now, baby. And don't you worry; I'm never letting you out of my sight again."

Bile shot up in Suzanne's throat as his hands worked to remove her damp clothes. Her body shivered at his touch, but Tyler merely laughed, mistaking her revulsion for desire. *The stupid bastard actually believes me!* But she remembered well how to feed his narcissism and use it as a defense mechanism. Sometimes it had worked and sometimes it had not. It blew her mind to believe she had once loved this abusive egotist and it made her crazy to think of him being only minutes away from Heather. No matter what it took, she resolved, she'd never let him near her baby.

With that driving force pounding in her mind, she fell onto the bed with this man she loathed.

Chapter Five

Frannie stared at Suzanne's note and felt a wave of nausea. *Frannie, please take care of Heather. Emergency! S.* Shivers of fear rippled through her body. She wasn't sure what frightened her more, the desperation of the words in Suzanne's note or her scrawled, erratic handwriting, as though she were racing with time. This was not the writing of a young woman in control. It looked more like the writing of a young mother whose hands trembled with fear. But on the other hand, this was *Suzanne.*

Memories of madness flashed before her eyes— memories that allowed an agonizing moan to escape. The only time in her entire life she had felt *real* fear was when she started to suspect her cousin Carl was a deranged killer.

Now, looking at Heather, some of that fear surfaced. Frannie's first instinct was to call the police; her second instinct was to call her uncle—Suzanne's father—but her fingers seemed to have a will of their own. They tapped out the numbers for her dear friend and business partner, Glory English.

Glory answered on the first ring, her voice a clear reflection of an upbeat mood. "Hey, what's going on? We've been playing telephone tag since yesterday. If we're going to make those menu revisions, we'd better get together—"

"Glory, stop! Listen to me ..." Frannie said, interrupting her friend's stream of chatter. Only minutes ago she would have considered the subject a top priority, but now the incongruity of business details versus an abandoned baby and a missing mother triggered an emotional rush. Her voice cracked and her words tumbled out in a flash flood of sobs, but she sucked them back and started again. "*Listen* to me, Glory. Something's wrong here ... very wrong." Her gaze flew to the baby who slept peacefully, her lips puckering gently. *Thank God she's too young to know what's going on,* Frannie thought. *So oblivious.*

Glory's lighthearted tone disappeared instantly with the realization that Frannie was crying. At first she thought the sound was laughter. Frannie was gifted with an innate ability to see humor in any situation. Laughter, not tears, came easy for her. "Oh, dear God, what?" she mumbled in a breathless whisper while her heart raced.

"Believe it or not, I came home tonight and found little Heather here—"

"Who?"

"Heather. My cousin Suzanne's baby."

Glory hesitated, sure she misunderstood. "Heather and Suzanne? Are they still there?"

"No, not *they,* just Heather. Let me explain. As I started to say, because of the weather, I came home tonight a little earlier than planned. I was concerned about Benny, thinking how the storm would frighten him. But when I got home I found him tied up outside in the pouring rain." She paused for a deep breath. "Glory, I never tied him up out there by his pen. I left him in the house. I knew right then and there that someone had broken into my home, someone who probably knew how to gain Benny's confidence. I couldn't imagine that he'd allow himself to be tied up by a stranger without a fight."

Glory was already full of questions, but she didn't want to interrupt.

"Anyway, when I freed him to bring him inside through the side entrance, I found the window smashed."

"Oh, no!" Glory gasped. She threw a hand to her mouth to stifle her sound. "I'm sorry. Go on."

"Don't go losing it on me now," Frannie warned. "I need you to help me stay calm and figure this out."

In the few seconds she had been talking to her friend, Frannie managed to pull herself together. She was not the type to panic easily or overreact to a situation. Life in general had taught her early on to toughen up, not to dump your whole heart, your whole soul, on one person. Never again would she set herself up for such heartache. She was only twenty-eight when she found out Wade was a bigamist. After three years of marriage—or what she thought was a marriage—she was shocked and devastated to discover that her hard-working, forever-on-the-road husband, without a home-cooked meal, without the warm embrace of his loving wife, was actually a son of a bitch with another wife, two kids and a dog. All tucked away in a Cape Cod cottage in Rhode Island, complete with white picket fence.

Later, much later, Frannie decided that Wade had done her a favor. She resolved to put it all behind her and make herself number one in her life. Determination had fueled her desire and earned her the success she now enjoyed as sole owner of Amore Breakfast and co-owner of Amore Evenings. She and Glory had just celebrated Amore Evenings' first year mark and business had been even better than they had hoped.

"Let me get back to Suzanne," Frannie continued. "I know you never met her, but do you remember what I told you about her a few weeks back when I needed to vent?"

"Yeah, pretty much. She's all into herself and all her problems are catastrophic, you said. You didn't trust her and hoped she wouldn't neglect the baby. I warned you about her when we talked. She sounds like one who would dump her troubles on you on a regular basis, I said, and would always be looking for a handout. You're a tough businesswoman,

Frannie, but when it comes to matters of the heart, you're a soft touch. Watch out. What's she up to this time?"

Frannie's voice cracked again. She couldn't help herself every time she glanced at Heather. "I haven't the faintest idea! All I know is she left Heather here—a four-month-old baby, *all alone*. She had already befriended Benny the two times she was here, so he probably offered no resistance when she went to tie him."

Glory blew a frustrated sigh. "I can't get it through my head that she *intentionally* left her baby alone in your house. Why? What could possibly make any mother do that to her own infant?" she asked, incredulous and angry.

"Glory, I feel exactly the same, but you're not letting me finish. She left a note taped to the baby's undershirt. All it said was 'Frannie, please take care of Heather. Emergency! S.' She underlined the word *please,* put an exclamation point after *emergency,* and signed it only with the initial S. If you could see the handwriting, you'd know she was in a big hurry or big trouble."

"Or both," Glory offered, then paused, still searching for possible explanations that could diminish the urgency of the situation. But nothing could. Not when a home is broken into and a baby is left alone inside. "Who else did you call?"

"No one yet. I was going to call the police, but hesitated in case this was just one of Suzanne's insane stunts. It would not surprise me if she showed up at my door, laughing and saying something like 'You'll never guess what happened!' Once I get the police involved, they'll probably call Child Protective Services, who might take the baby away from her—and maybe she'd deserve it, but I'm not ready to make that decision alone. I wanted to call my parents, but they'd be scared out of their minds. Right now I can't deal with their emotional reactions and Heather too."

"Frannie, I'm having the same thoughts. Don't do anything yet. I'll be there in ten minutes. Do you need anything for the baby? Formula? Diapers?"

"No, don't stop for anything in this storm. We have enough to make it through the night. I just fed her and there are three cans of ready-made formula in her diaper bag and a few diapers. Just come and help me make some decisions. Then we'll both need a crash course in handling a baby if Suzanne doesn't show up soon."

Chapter Six

Suzanne wasn't the only one on a mission that night. Short, stubby fingers had fired up Tyler Keaton's computer hours earlier. The tropical scene on the fifteen inch screensaver cast a turquoise glow in the small windowless room. The intruder needed certain information, but had no idea whether or not Tyler's computer or anything within the confines of the claustrophobic room would yield that information.

Nevertheless, the dark eyes had stayed fixed on the screen while the right hand worked the mouse and the arrow keys. But after almost an hour's search, nothing in any of the files revealed—or even remotely hinted at—what the person intended to learn.

In frustration, the stubby fingers had pushed aside a tray of papers and suddenly something caught the intruder's eye. The small stick-on note had something scribbled on it which was nearly undecipherable. But the dark eyes widened as they studied the writing on the little yellow paper. RM3 was clear enough, but the shadowy figure's brows furrowed into one, resembling a caterpillar crawling across the olive-skinned face. The remaining letters were anybody's guess. TAL? TAI? Whatever the hell that means. Probably nothing related to the business at hand.

Only one thing about it was bothersome. It was written in red ink. On the desk was a New York Giants mug that held a bunch of pens, but on the desk itself was a red Bic pen. It could only be assumed it was the last one used.

The stubby fingers then returned to the keyboard and clicked on Google to feed in various combinations of the letters. Like a damn *Scramble* challenge. It was a long shot and could have taken forever.

But the intruder was soon pleasantly surprised when its fingers had fed in only the letters TH.

A sardonic smile crossed the olive-skinned face. *Well, now, aren't computers wonderful!* The dark eyes lit up like flashlights at the five words that appeared in the box below.

"The Admiral's Inn, Ogunquit, Maine."

Now the RM3 made sense. Room 3 at The Admiral's Inn.

Bingo!

Chapter Seven

Glory showed up prepared to stay the night. Or longer if necessary. She dumped her overnight bag in a corner and went to see Heather first. Child abuse stories had filled her mind as she drove. She looked over the sleeping infant for telltale signs but found none. "When you changed her diaper, you didn't see any bruises or anything, did you?" She didn't like thinking that, especially since Suzanne was Frannie's relative, but when you're looking at possible child abuse, those sensitivities are cast aside.

Frannie was quick to allay her suspicion with a dismissive hand wave. "Hey, my cousin may not get a Mother of the Year award from what I've seen so far, but to think *abuse* is pushing it." *Who am I to judge what is or what isn't?* she asked herself. With the help of her therapist, she had learned to deal with the guilt about Carl. At least she steeled herself to think about it less and less. But deep down Frannie knew she'd never totally forgive herself for not noticing his madness before he took the life of Paula Howard, an innocent Alzheimer's victim—kidnapped and tormented Glory, along with two teenagers, Sara Baisley and Tim Waite. They had all come within seconds of death until Paula's younger sister, Allison, burst onto the scene. Allison, who plotted with Carl the death of her own sister, had long suppressed the guilt of her unspeakable crime, concentrating only on the six million dollars she would inherit upon her sister's death. Then, like a tsunami, the guilt came without warning and flooded her. But her guilt soon settled with an inexplicable calm. Allison paid for her sins the only way she knew how. She had shot him dead before he could kill his three victims, then turned the gun on herself.

Glory busied herself starting a fire on the hearth while Frannie sat in silence, deep in thought. "I can read right through that expression, Frannie."

Frannie came out of her ruminations with a half-smile. "You always could. But we both can take credit for that gift." Her smile faded. "If you think my mind was on Carl, you're absolutely right. But what I'm really thinking is: What the heck is wrong with my family? Is there something in our blood that can cause two cousins to go crazy? It's surreal!"

Glory replaced the screen on the fireplace and sat next to Frannie, grabbing her face to turn it towards her. "Now, wait just a minute," she said with a disciplinary tone. "First of all, need I remind you that Carl was not your blood relative, but a foster child who was later adopted? I'm not going to sit here and let you go off the deep end. You're the one who always has it together—the one who takes on everyone's problems. The eternal optimist, everyone calls you, right?"

Frannie responded with an arched brow and a dubious smirk.

"Don't give me that look. It's true, isn't it? If you fall apart, it'll start a chain reaction." She paused for a sincere smile. "You know sometimes I think your success as a restaurateur is not only your fabulous food, but your personality. People love to talk to you, to confide in you. You're like Ogunquit's Oprah, for goodness sake!"

"All right, all right, don't get carried away—" She stopped to stand up and get a better look at Heather, who stretched her little legs and arms, but never opened her eyes. Her gaze returned to Glory. "Yeah, I won't be too modest. You'd see right through me anyway, so yes, that's true for the most part, but I myself don't have that same strong confidence anymore. Misjudging Carl really did a number on me. I keep saying what if this, what if that ... If only I had

29

noticed his problem and helped him, maybe he and the Howard sisters, Paula and Allison, would all be alive today. And look at the pain it caused Alex—losing two sisters weeks apart."

"Don't waste your thoughts on Alex. He's doing fine now. He has me to share his future with; he has your friendship which means a lot to him, and he has my dad. They've become so close—I'm so grateful for that. But hey, how did we get on all that again? Suzanne is the reason I'm here. No," she corrected herself, "*you're* the reason I'm here. Not even for Heather. She's safe here with you."

"I'm worried, Glory. Really worried. While half of me is cursing her out, trying to convince myself this is typical of Suzanne's theatrics, the other half is getting sicker by the minute." She paused a moment, then lifted her eyebrows and tried for a positive attitude. "But then, look at it this way: Maybe she knew where I was. Maybe she knew I'd be home soon and decided to leave Heather here before I showed up. That way she could avoid a confrontation. For all I know, she could have taken off for a Vegas weekend with her latest boyfriend!"

Glory listened, observed and smirked. She had no doubt Frannie's harsh words were nothing more than a shield to mask her fears. She let her rant on a little more until she ran out of steam. "You don't really expect me to believe that, do you? I know you don't believe it."

Frannie responded with a deep sigh and an eye roll.

"At least she thought to tie Benny up. That shows some responsibility—some concern for her baby's safety." Her hand went up before Frannie could give her an argument. "Not that I condone what she did. Taking off without waiting for you. That's unforgivable." She furrowed her brows thoughtfully.

"What bothers me is *why* she had to take off." Frannie stood up and paced the floor with her arms folded. "I'm going to call Land & Sea. For all we know, maybe that was her emergency—unexpected hours. Maybe she was afraid she'd get fired if she didn't help out." Her eyes brightened with hope as she made the call, but Glory sensed that Frannie's wishful thinking would fizzle out and wash that smile off her face.

And it did. She put the phone down and turned to Glory. "All I got out of him was that she worked her regular shift and left."

They fell silent for a few moments, each with their separate but common thoughts. Glory went from the club chair to the floor where she could get a closer look at Heather. The more she stared at the sleeping infant with the rosebud cheeks and heart-shaped lips, the more inconceivable it was that any human being could abandon her—especially her mother. "I guess you don't believe the Vegas theory any more than I do, huh?"

"Not for a minute. I didn't show you her note yet, did I?" She went to the coffee table where she had left it and handed it to Glory. "Take a look at that handwriting. Doesn't it scare you?"

Chapter Eight

Glory made two cups of hot chocolate and brought them into the living room. "Thanks. This is going to be a long night," Frannie said. "I have a tough choice to make but the decision has to be mine alone, and I think I have to go with my gut feeling." She scooped out some of the marshmallows and put them in the saucer, then sipped the soothing sweetness. "At this point, calling the police is not an option. My cousin is not technically *missing*. She left a note—in a hurry, yes—but a note asking *me* to care for her child. A *babysitting request*, you could say if you wanted to play it down," she told Glory. "Maybe a friend of hers had a serious accident. Maybe this. Maybe that." She gave a who-knows shrug of her shoulders. Together the two friends came up with several scenarios that could have prompted Suzanne's actions. But the more time that passed without Suzanne showing up or calling, the more their fears silently escalated. Frannie had said she'd wait until morning. If there's no word from Suzanne by then, new decisions would be made. For now, they wait.

For two hours, they talked nonstop, moving away from the problem that remained prevalent in their minds. Frannie spoke about Suzanne, and how little she really knew about her, except for what she'd exhibited since she had moved back to Maine. The cousins saw little of each other over the years, had nothing in common. Frannie was fifteen years older, and even if they had been closer in age, their choice of friends would have differed sharply.

"Suzanne was a looker and knew it," Frannie said. "I think in her case it was a disadvantage. She thought her face and body could buy her anything she wanted in life. After two years in college, she took off for California, thinking she could flash that big smile and maybe spend a few hours in the sack with the right guy, and she'd have instant success." She shook her head, still in disbelief that Suzanne, who had a brain if only she'd used it, had allowed herself to be so damn star-struck. Her eyes gazed upward with the memory. "My poor aunt. She went nuts. As if she didn't have enough to cope with married to an alcoholic."

Their conversation drifted. They reminisced about how their friendship had begun. How Glory had left New York in search of the real father she never knew existed until after her parents died. How the shock of that knowledge had crushed her after loving Steven English, the only father she knew, for thirty-five years. How emotionally raw she had been at the time, still hurting from the pain of her husband's betrayal. She never had a clue about Jason. Wherever he said he was, she believed without a second thought. It wasn't until that night—that horrible night—when he had come home unexpectedly early. She had thrown her arms around him and smiled, asked if he was hungry. "Want pizza?" she had said. "No, Glory, I want a divorce."

It was like the sky had opened up and it never stopped raining after that. She thought nothing could be more painful than the aftermath of divorce. Of loving someone who only pretended to love you back until he was ready to make his move. Until he and his new love were ready to start their lives together. They were both sorry for the pain their spouses would feel, he'd said, but they'd adjust eventually. Dr. Jason Vance and Marilyn Stillwell, his medical supplies salesperson, were moving on from business to pleasure.

"Our husbands both did us a favor, Glory. Not that they were thinking of our happiness at the time," Frannie said with a bitterness that would never completely disappear.

"That's for sure. I wish I could have known then what the future held for me here in Ogunquit. I could have saved myself a lot of grief. I don't know how I got through those days—and nights—they were the worst. Between all those tears and sleepless nights, I had bags under my eyes the size of Texas."

Frannie darted her a look. "You didn't exactly have smooth sailing here either for a while." Neither of them needed to be reminded how Carl Duca had impacted both their lives.

"Yes, but in the end we were all survivors, thank God. And look what I found waiting for me here in Ogunquit." She shook her head and smiled, still considering it all almost miraculous. At least finding Dan Madison, the father who gave her life, bordered on miraculous. For a father and daughter to find each other after thirty-five years—two people who never knew of each other's existence, Glory figured there had to be some divine intervention to make that happen. When she started her search, she hadn't even known his name. "Every time I think back to that day on the bench in Perkins Cove when I first spoke to my dad, I'll never forget that feeling, that instant, soaring love we shared. No matter how long I live, it'll always be one of my most treasured memories."

"Too bad his family had given you such a hard time," Frannie said. "It took a lot of control on my part to stay out of it, but I was seething every time you told me how they treated you. I wanted so badly to go shake some sense into their empty heads."

Glory waved it off. "Hey, I'm past all that now. I can understand why they went ballistic when I showed up. It was tough for them to accept that their father had a daughter from an old summer romance. They all thought it was scandalous and didn't want to share his love. For me it was different. When he told me I had two sisters and a brother, I was excited—couldn't wait to meet them. Growing up an only child was lonely for me. I always envied all my friends who had siblings." She cringed remembering how her father's family had so cruelly rejected her, but quickly chased the memory away. They had flooded her with their remorse, begged her forgiveness. A wounded heart, alone and aching for the love of family, offered no resistance. Today they treated her as though she had always been part of their family.

"I know we promised each other that we'd try not to talk about Carl. It's painful for both of us, but a thought just came to me. Isn't it ironic that Carl could be credited for getting your dad's family to accept you? Not that it ever entered his mind, of course, but it just happened that way. If he hadn't abducted you, Sara and Tim, that family's icy hostility might never have melted. Isn't it horrible how you don't realize how much people mean to you until you're about to lose them?"

"It all happened for a reason, Frannie. Look at me and Alex. I had my doubts about him, too. All those whispers about his wife's death—how maybe it wasn't an accident. Even you were caught up in all that gossip. But it was Alex who taught me to trust again, to love again."

"Yeah, he won me over in a heartbeat. Once we joined forces that night to find you and the kids, his integrity—not to mention his love for you—came through like a burst of sunshine." Her smile disappeared in an instant. "Too bad he had to lose both his sisters. It will always kill me knowing they died as a direct result of my cousin Carl's tormented mind."

"Frannie, you have to let that go. Sure, I suffered through those hours of hell with Carl, but I chase the memories away as soon as they surface. I count my blessings instead. Alex and I have a love for each other and a friendship we never knew was possible. And my dad—talk about miracles! To watch him fighting for his life right after we found each other—twice, no less—first the accident, then his heart attack—" The memory brought tears to her eyes. She paused for a deep breath. "Don't you remember how I felt the night of the accident? It was as though someone had dumped a mountain of guilt on me. All I kept telling myself was if he hadn't told his family about me, that argument would never have started, and he never would have left the house angry. Mixing anger and motorcycles can be just as lethal as alcohol and motorcycles."

"Yes, I know you had guilt. Plenty of guilt. But nobody died, thank God. With Carl, it was different ..."

Moments before midnight, Heather broke through their somber mood with a healthy cry. They both bounced off their chairs and knelt down on the floor, one on each side of her. The two women looked at each other blankly. Neither one had ever spent five minutes alone with a baby.

"Just feed and change, right?" Glory asked.

Frannie shrugged and gently took Heather in her arms. "Guess so. It worked the first time." She didn't say so to Glory, but she could probably juggle six raw eggs with more confidence than this. She watched Benny pick himself up and disappear in the bedroom. He wanted no part of this scene. And morning was still hours away.

Chapter Nine

It was past midnight when Tyler Keaton's sexual appetite finally sated. Suzanne had never felt dirtier in her life. Well, maybe that last night in New York, but if she lived another fifty years she'd never forget tonight. There was no physical abuse this time because she had given the greatest performance of her life. She had suffered through sexual acts repeatedly with the pretense of pleasure while wishing him dead so she could be rid of him forever. It seemed surreal now that for a few months in the beginning, she had loved every intimate moment in his embrace.

In the darkness, she fumbled her way to the bathroom. Her hands found the bed again and she ran her fingers along its edge until she reached the footboard. Not that she could see it in the inky blackness, but she knew there was a chair to the right, alongside the window. Flashes of lightning lit up the sky for split seconds and thunderous sounds of the treacherous storm put horrifying images in her mind: driving home to call Frannie and pack, but smashing into a tree instead. If she died, would they investigate until they found Heather's father and give her to him? *God in heaven, no. I can't let that happen.* She shook the thought away but another took its place. A vision of Frannie's house, with Heather alone and helpless inside, being uprooted and whipped away into the sea. Silently she prayed for the storm to ebb so that she could drive home without getting swept away.

When she opened her eyes again, she realized she had fallen asleep. She hadn't thought she could sleep in her emotional state, but her body had succumbed after all. Electricity hadn't been restored and she still couldn't see the time on her wristwatch, but the sky was definitely calmer. The sounds of the wind had subsided and the smothering darkness was lifting.

Tyler was still snoring away and she was grateful that some of her prayers had been answered. He never made it to the bar and if his habits hadn't changed he'd be conked out until noon or later. Not that she would let him sleep that long. She had to get him up and out of Ogunquit before they could be noticed. There was no time to waste.

The relentless rain continued as she drove but at least visibility had improved. Trees were down everywhere and hopefully the roads she had to travel were clear. She had intended to call Frannie the moment she was back in her apartment, but was now having second thoughts. *What could I possibly say to convince her to go along with my plan and not breathe a word to anyone? There's no way in hell she would. How could she explain my absence and why I left Heather?*

There were no answers and Suzanne knew she couldn't make that call. Instinctively she turned the car around.

She was taking a big chance, she knew, but had to make sure Frannie was home. At least she'd know Heather was safe and would be well taken care of. When she got close enough, she cried tears of relief to see two cars in the driveway—Frannie's Volvo and Glory's Lexus. Thank God, she thought, no other cars present. Maybe they hadn't alerted the police yet.

Suzanne remained dry-eyed for a while, relieved that Heather was in good hands, but burst into tears again when she entered her apartment. She had always complained it was too small, too run down, too depressing. But now it suddenly looked like paradise about to be lost.

She cried endless tears while she threw some clothes into her small suitcase, then stopped. "I can't do this! I can't do this! Please God, give me another way …"

For more than a half hour, Suzanne cried, hoping for some kind of miracle that would offer a solution. But nothing came to her. She took a few deep breaths, accepted her decision as the right one—the only one—and continued packing. Without Heather, she could fit all she needed into an overnight case; two pairs of jeans, one long loose skirt, four stretch polos, a nightshirt, a handful of underwear and an extra pair of shoes. A compact life. And without her daughter, a meaningless life.

She caressed Heather's framed 4" x 6" photo and wrapped it securely between her packed clothing. An agonizing cry escaped Suzanne's lips as she called out her daughter's name. To muffle the sound, she bit down on her finger.

Ten minutes later, in her robotic state of mind, she picked up her overnight case and keys, then quietly locked the door behind her. *This separation will only be temporary,* she kept repeating to herself. *I'll be back for Heather. I'll take her somewhere so far away he'll never find me and she'll never know I had left her.*

Driving back to The Admiral's Inn, she concentrated on what she could do—or not do—to slowly let Tyler lose interest in her without provoking his temper. She remembered how, in the beginning, he loved not only her face and figure, but her wittiness and sense of humor as well. He also liked that she wasn't prudish or wimpy, had sharp eyes and ears and knew how to handle herself in the company of his friends and acquaintances. In his smug and possessive way, his pride was transparent.

Well, that could change. For openers, she could gain weight, neglect her appearance and be downright boring, not to mention a less enthusiastic sexual partner. But those changes would have to be subtle or she might end up half-dead in the alley again. And if she could manage to let him *want* to be rid of her, without him realizing she had orchestrated it, he'd have no reason to come after her again.

He could easily replace her, especially if his lounge was now as successful as he had boasted tonight.

*   *   *

The parking lot at The Admiral's Inn looked like a swamp. She climbed up the concrete steps and ran along the wooden walkway that extended along the rear of the inn. "Damn!" she yelled when she reached Tyler's room. She found the door wide open banging against the inner wall. It was the least of her troubles now, but she silently admonished herself for not closing the door securely in her haste to run out. The carpeting was sopping wet and her feet felt as though they were being sucked into the ocean floor. "Stupid son of a bitch!" she mumbled, seething and hating him more than ever for showing up without warning and causing this crisis from hell.

She shook his leg. "Tyler, get the hell up. How could you have slept through this?" She slapped his leg again, gave the door a shove with her hip, then locked it. "Man, some things never change," she said, thin-lipped and fuming. She moved from the foot of the bed to the head. Just as she was about to give his shoulder a good shove to wake him up, she instinctively jumped back and away. Her hand was wet and sticky. And dark. She stared at it, refusing to focus on the images it provoked. Instead, she slowly lifted the shade. Daybreak painted a dark gray hue on the window. Her gaze went down to her hand again and dizziness enveloped her.

Ice blue eyes stared up at her like glass marbles. A mournful sound shot up in her throat like a volcanic eruption. She tried to breathe, but her breaths were short and shallow. Instinct to save a life made her reach for the knife that protruded from his chest. And instinct made her pull away. Her hand opened wide and her fingers stiffened like an open umbrella. Their rigidity formed a haunting silhouette against the window pane.

In concert with her pounding heart, her head hammered. Her bulging eyes felt as though they would pop out of their sockets. Fear rendered her silent and a surge of panic filled her. Her brain seemed to battle its own raging storm inside her head, denying her the ability to think.

Suzanne would never know how long she stood there staring at death, but when her thought process began to function again, she found herself in her car, driving mechanically, with no destination in mind, no plan.

And she remembered. She would always remember the sight of him. The unmoving, unseeing eyes. And she would never forget—never be able to wash away—the feel of his blood on her hand.

Drive. Just drive. Get out of Ogunquit. Get out of Maine. Get out of New England.

Suzanne Oliveri, who tonight had abandoned her infant daughter, had left fingerprints, hair and who knows how much other evidence, hadn't even called 9-1-1. She had just run out and away from the scene of a crime. A horrific, brutal crime.

Then in the corner of her eye, something caught her attention. A stupid, mundane problem. A problem so ludicrous that it triggered a fit of laughing.

The Honda was almost out of gas.

Suzanne Oliveri thought she would die laughing.

A violent roar ripped through her hysteria unlike any sound she had ever heard before. Then, in one horrifying split-second, her car plunged downward, lost in the roar of collapsing steel, stone and earth. Everything went black, then white and luminous, like rays of the sun on an avalanche of snow. Death hovered over her, about to snuff out her life like the fiery flash of a serpent's breath.

Chapter Ten

At 6:45 in the morning, Heather's cries brought both women to their feet. Glory slipped out of her pajama bottoms and stepped into her jeans. She poured the formula into the baby's clean bottle, rinsed the can and threw it in her bag. "Just to be sure I don't screw up and bring back the wrong kind. While you feed her, I'll run out for more formula and diapers."

"You don't have to go *now*, the minute you open your eyes. Make a pot of coffee for us—give yourself a chance to wake up."

"No, I'll do that when I get back. It's no big deal. How long can it take me—ten minutes?"

"About. I'd go myself, but I have to make those calls right after Heather's fed and changed."

Glory scrunched her face. "Are you kidding? How can you even *say* that? Why in the world would you hesitate to ask me such a small favor? This is your best friend, here, remember?" She tapped her chest, as though proud of the title. "Besides, what if the phone rings?"

Frannie nodded in agreement. "I know. But I stared at that phone all night long, waiting for it to ring. My mind went wild imagining the worst. Every damn day we turn on the TV, we see one horror story after another. As if we don't have enough trouble looking for terrorists, we have to watch for all our own predators who walk the streets waiting to attack."

Glory didn't bother to comment, just threw her a *no-one-would-argue-with-that* smirk. She grabbed her jacket and bag, then paused at the bedroom door. "Frannie, don't make any calls until I get back. *Please?* We waited this long, what's another ten minutes? I want to be here with you."

Frannie looked at her with questioning eyes. "Don't worry, she said, "I'm not going to crack up. I have no time to waste on emotions."

That put a smile on Glory's face. "Ten minutes, okay?"

"Fifteen, tops."

The phone rang in nine. Its sound pealed through the quiet tension. Her heart hammered. It had to be Suzanne. Who else would call her at this hour? She grabbed at it and screamed into the mouthpiece, releasing all her bottled-up fear and anger. "Suzanne! Where the hell are you?" Her tone demanded answers but relief flooded through her momentarily until she caught the full name on her caller ID. *Oliveri, Gerald,* not *Oliveri, Suzanne.*

"That's what I want to know. Where the hell is she, that whore?" This from Suzanne's father—Frannie's Uncle Jerry—whose voice revealed that he'd already had his morning wake-up drink.

Her gaze darted over to the infant seat, to be sure Heather was okay. The last thing she needed was for him to hear a baby crying. "What makes you think I'd know where she is, Uncle Jerry? And do you realize what time it is? Some people sleep this early in the morning." She couldn't keep the bite out of her tone. She was so ashamed of what he had become. The complete opposite of her gentle and loving father—although even her dad hadn't always been a model husband and father. But that was another story.

"I don't give a shit who's sleeping!" he snarled. "If she had shown up last night when she was supposed to, I wouldn't be calling you. But she's an unreliable, selfish little bitch. I'm ashamed to call her my daughter."

Frannie rolled her eyes. It would take control to suppress all the things she wanted to lash out in Suzanne's defense. *Talk about the pot calling the kettle black.* "I have no idea where she is, Uncle Jerry. I'm sorry." *Well, at least that's true.* She hit the *off* button but knew it would ring again. Her uncle, under the influence, would not be easily dismissed. Glory walked in as the phone rang. Her eyes went wide and she dumped the two large plastic bags on the floor behind her. Frannie shook her head as she answered it, dismissing Glory's apprehension.

Jerry Oliveri was ready for round two. "Who the hell taught you your manners? Don't you ever hang up on me again!"

Frannie clenched her teeth and felt her jaw tighten, but kept her cool when she spoke. "I didn't hang up. I simply said I have no idea where she is. Look, Uncle Jerry, I can't talk to you now. I have guests in my house—"

"Oh, it's too early for phone calls, but not too early for guests? How many 'guests' do you have there? What the hell's going on—an orgy?"

She threw Glory a frustrated look. "I'm going to hang up now and please don't call again because I won't answer."

"You won't answer? *You won't answer?*" He repeated it as though her words shocked him. "Is that the way you show respect for your uncle?"

"Respect has to be earned, Uncle Jerry. No matter who you are or how old."

"Well, you listen to me, you little shit, I want you to ride your ass over here and give me the fifty bucks she was supposed to bring last night—no, on second thought, from you, make that a hundred. And if you don't show up in one hour, I'll be knocking your door down, I'm warning you."

Frannie didn't know how a visit from him was possible. He had lost his license years ago. But she wasn't taking any chances. "I'll be there this morning, but I can't promise to get there in an hour."

"Then you better put a bonus on that C-note. If you have money to blow on 'guests' you can help out family. And I'm family!"

Don't remind me, she thought, then hit the *off* button again and turned to Glory. "Am I already guilty of omission? Did I have a legal obligation to tell him what's happening here?"

Glory looked her friend in the eye. "Frannie, I don't think there's a court in the country that would consider him a *responsible* next-of-kin." She made a hand gesture towards the phone still in Frannie's hand. "Make your calls."

Frannie had long ago committed to memory Detective Sergeant Tony Gerard's cell number. Some things you never forget—you never *allow* yourself to forget, she thought as she tapped out the numbers. A smile of relief crossed her face when he answered.

Next she called her father, the other Oliveri brother, the good one, the sober one. But the one whose temper will hit the ceiling when he hears what's happening. Or not happening. She could hear him already: *And you waited until now to call me?*

She was right. Almost verbatim. "I'd better put up the big pot of coffee. They'll all be here within minutes."

"Who's all?" Glory asked. "Your parents and Tony Gerard?"

"That's it, as far as I know," Frannie answered with a shrug, but her mind was already worried that CPS would be called in. Child Protective Services. *God, I hope not.*

Chapter Eleven

Detective Sergeant Tony Gerard hadn't wasted words when Frannie called. Once he got the gist of her problem—especially when he heard a baby was involved—he was on his way.

Benny raced off the braided rug in the bedroom and nearly collided with Frannie when the doorbell rang. She mumbled her annoyance with a few choice words which Benny totally ignored. The rain was still falling steadily, but with the violent winds finally gone, everyone breathed a sigh of relief.

In the vestibule, Tony hung his raincoat on a wall hook. Frannie was full of apologies. There was still that sliver of hope that nothing was wrong and she had allowed one of Suzanne's "emergencies" to grow out of proportion. She could walk through that door any minute and laugh at this scene. But even that remote possibility wouldn't excuse her. "Thank God you're here, Tony. I'm so sorry I had to drag you out—"

Glory grabbed a hand towel from the bathroom and threw it to Tony. He and Glory exchanged a look acknowledging Frannie's harried state. He tried to relax her with a smile. "It's what we do, Frannie. With no time off for inclement weather. Besides, after last night, this is nothing. The cleanup will be hell, though."

Tony went first to take a quick look at the sleeping baby and the women assured him they had found no evidence of physical harm. At his insistence, since his pants hadn't escaped the rain, they sat at the kitchen table. Glory poured each of them a mug of coffee and placed before Tony a paper plate with two chocolate-covered biscuits. He tried to ignore them since he was here on business—serious business—but the temptation was too great. He took a hearty bite.

He lifted his gaze to Frannie, and was just about to speak when she stopped him. "Before you say anything, I just want to let you know that my parents are on their way. Is that okay with you? I'm a little nervous about my uncle—Suzanne's father. He called earlier looking for her, but I said I had no idea where she is—which is technically true." She looked at him and hesitated. "He's a hopeless alcoholic, and—"

Tony raised his hand. "Wait, Frannie. First things first. I have to tell you that I called CPS. Any time a child is involved, it's my duty to inform them. They're already on their way."

Frannie's face dropped. "Oh, no. I was afraid of that." She raised both hands upward in frustration. "This could all be for naught, you know. You don't know my cousin. She's a little flaky." The moment she said it, she regretted it. "She's a good mother, but new at the job ..." She stopped herself, knowing she couldn't fix it up. In those few words, she had already painted a vivid picture of her cousin.

Tony glanced over at the baby again. Frannie had lifted the infant seat and brought her in the kitchen. "Now don't think of CPS as the enemy here," he said. "They're not the big bad guys whose only purpose is to take children away from their parents or family. I'm assuming you want Heather to stay with you until her mother is found?"

"Of course! But I'm also worried about her grandfather. I started to tell you about him before. Sure, he *is* Heather's closest relative, but if any agency or court decides to make him her temporary foster parent, that would completely destroy my faith in the law. And don't try to tell me these injustices haven't happened before. I've seen plenty on TV and read plenty of stories that made me sick to my stomach."

"I'm not going to say any such thing," Tony countered. "But you're jumping ahead, fearing the worst. Let's stay focused. I need to ask you some questions about your cousin first. Are you okay?"

Glory cut in to offer some assurance and confidence for Frannie. "She'll be fine, Tony. Give her a minute. The thought of her uncle possibly getting custody of Heather scares her to death."

Frannie drew a breath and exhaled. She gave him an apologetic smile. "I'm okay, Tony. Glory's right. I'm worried about Suzanne; it's been too long now—but mostly I'm worried about this poor innocent baby. What'll happen to her?" Her words came out choked on tears, but she quickly composed herself and looked straight into Tony Gerard's eyes. "Okay. What do you want to know?"

Tony took another bite of his biscuit and washed it down with his coffee. "Plenty. But first let me get back to your fears about CPS. If the baby's grandfather is in fact an alcoholic, they'd never place the child with him. Get that out of your head. With the exception of the baby's father, you'd be the likely candidate to be granted custody, after the CPS checks you out, of course. Just knowing you as I do, and looking around at your home, I see no reason in the world why they would reject you."

"What about my restaurants? Both are scheduled to open Friday. Glory can manage Amore Evenings without me for a while, but Amore Breakfast is open from 7:00 until about 2:00. I have to be there. Will CPS allow me to bring her every day? I can easily put up a crib in my office and I'll have plenty of help—starting with my mom."

"That'll be fine, I'm sure," Tony said. "Plenty of foster children are sent to day care also, so that's another option. Once it's checked out and approved—no problem."

"No, I want her with me where I can keep a close eye on her." She paused, tipped her head and darted her eyes sideways. "And what if they find the father?"

Tony was slow to answer. "Well, that would be a new ballgame."

The conversation froze at that point because the bell had rung again. Benny came flying out, his barking drowning out all other sounds. Four soaking wet people were at the door this time. Two were Frannie's parents, Tess and Sal Oliveri, and the other two, a man and a woman, were strangers.

Child Protective Services. Who else? Frannie thought. She steeled herself to stay in complete control and make a good impression. These were the people who controlled Heather's fate.

Chapter Twelve

By the time all four shed their wet outer clothing, the vestibule floor had enough water to accommodate a school of fish. Glory and Tess worked together to mop it up and Sal volunteered to help with the coffee and cake. Since the recent weather had trapped Tess indoors for days, she had baked to pass the time and distract herself from the depressing weather. She had no idea at the time that her crumb cake would be consumed here at her daughter's and used for such grim purposes.

The moment Tony introduced the two Child Protective Service workers, Frannie's apprehension eased. She had created a different picture in her mind—the "big bad guys," as Tony had surmised. But Sandy Lawson's bright smile and wholesome good looks reminded her of a young Sally Fields and as soon as she spoke, her pleasant personality came shining through. Will Barker, was older—somewhere in his forties, Frannie guessed—and seemed more reserved; soft-spoken. But his quick smile too was suggestive of a gentle and caring man, and if she had read him correctly, he was the right guy for the job.

While Tony remained in the kitchen with Frannie, the other five gathered in the living room, all shoeless. Will and Sandy both knelt down beside the sleeping infant for a cursory examination. She appeared healthy and content, but a complete workup would follow if temporary foster placement became necessary. They spoke briefly about last night's storm and their concerns about its aftermath.

Tess Oliveri could not equate the storm to the situation at hand. With wrinkled brows, she waved her hands like windshield wipers. "Wait. Stop. The weather means nothing compared to the safety of my niece and her baby. We need to talk about that." Her voice broke up and she started to cry. Her husband's arm went around her, but she brushed off his comfort. She wanted answers.

Sandy Lawson led her to the sofa and sat down next to her. "Look, Mrs. Oliveri—Tess, right? Do you mind if I call you Tess? And you can call me Sandy, okay?"

Tess acquiesced with a quick nod followed by a wave of her fingers indicating that Sandy should forget the amenities and get on with whatever information she was about to provide. She steepled her fingers over her nose, as though that gesture could put a plug on emotions. But anxiety and fear prompted her body to rock back and forth.

"Tess," Sandy continued, "first you, your husband and daughter should understand that we don't foresee a problem with Heather. Look at her ..." She extended an arm towards the infant seat. "She *is* safe, so don't upset yourself further about her. We'll speak to Frannie in a few minutes when Tony is through, but from what I see—and hear—your daughter would most likely be approved as Heather's temporary foster parent."

Tess sniffed away her tears and nodded, taking comfort in the fact that Heather would not be given to strangers should this crisis with Suzanne continue. "Well, that does make me feel better, but the baby needs her mother ..." She paused and swallowed hard. "And what about Suzanne? God knows what kind of trouble she's in!"

Sandy was about to console her further, but Sal cut in. "Now Tess, you have to calm yourself and let these people do their jobs. They shouldn't have to waste precious time dealing with the emotions of family members." His voice was slow and even when he started talking, but ended laced with anger and impatience.

Will Barker had been busy pulling forms from his briefcase to start the voluminous paperwork required for this case. He put it aside and stood up, resting a hand on Sal Oliveri's shoulder. "You too need to calm yourself, Mr. Oliveri. In stressful situations, we all get emotional; it's natural. But as we all agree, the safety and welfare of Heather and Suzanne are top priority. That's what we need to concentrate on. Sandy and I—and certainly Tony—need your cooperation so that we can gather as much information from you as possible to help us find Suzanne. Okay? Can we count on you guys?"

Tess and Sal nodded in unison. Both mumbled their apologies; their faces draped with remorse for their outbursts. Glory broke the mood. "C'mon, Sal. I thought you volunteered to help serve the coffee and cake?"

In the kitchen, once he had allayed her fears about Heather's placement, Tony continued questioning Frannie. "Now, when we spoke on the phone, you skirted the issue of the baby's father. Did you not want to get into that until I got here or were you trying to tell me Suzanne actually doesn't know who the father is?"

Frannie made a face that simultaneously answered his question and apologized for her cousin's irresponsible behavior.

He gave her a slanted look. "Are you sure she doesn't know? That would take a lot of sleeping around. Still, she can pin it down if she wanted to."

Frannie shrugged. "Probably. But she never told me who she was involved with in New York, nor would I ask. It's none of my business," she said, then quickly added, "Well, *now* it's certainly my business, isn't it?"

"And the business of Child Protective Services, as you already know. They'll search way back—from before Heather's birth—before Suzanne's pregnancy. They'll find the baby's father. If I were a betting man, my money would be on them. They're damn good at what they do. Trust them, Frannie. Everyone concerned has a common goal."

Frannie heaved a sigh. "I know. I'm just a little crazy right now. I try to pretend that Suzanne pulled one of her worst stunts, and I try to cover up my fears by cursing her out." She shook her head, thinking about it deeper and deeper. "But Suzanne would never do this. She may be a little dizzy, but the bottom line is she loves her daughter. I'm convinced she's in trouble. *Major* trouble," she said, wiping the corners of her eyes.

Glory stepped into the kitchen and excused herself for interrupting. "I'm sorry, Tony," she said, then turned to Frannie. "I just wanted to say that I have no problem staying here with you until we hear something, or for as long as you need me. If that's okay with you, I'll run home now for a few things."

"Wasn't Alex supposed to come back from Jersey today or tomorrow?"

Glory put a hand on her hip and glared at Frannie. "Under the circumstances, life as usual is temporarily on hold. Besides, I just spoke to Alex. He's the one who suggested it!"

Frannie managed a smile. "Sure, then. That'll be great. Otherwise my mother would insist on staying and I don't want her to leave my dad alone."

"Okay, now," Tony continued when Glory left. "I want you to tell me everything you can about Suzanne. Who her friends are—male and female—who she likes or dislikes. I understand she works at Land & Sea. Is she particularly friendly with anyone there—do you know?"

Frannie curled her brows thoughtfully. "If she had— oh, God—I mean *has*—a particular friend, like a special guy she was interested in, she never mentioned him to me. But that doesn't mean one doesn't exist. Suzanne is *friendly* with a lot of guys." Her face soured for a second at the memory, but the scowl faded instantly when her thoughts came back to the present. She wouldn't care if Suzanne walked through that door with an entire football team trailing behind her, as long as she was alive and well.

"What kind of car does she drive? Does she own or lease? And where is it now?"

"She owns an old Honda Civic—a '96, maybe '97— I'm not sure of the year. And where is it now, you want to know." She fingered her lips while she pondered. "That's a good question …Wherever she is, I guess."

"When did you last speak to her?"

"Early last week. Tuesday night to be exact. She called me."

Tony's arched brows asked the question for him.

Frannie sighed. Suddenly she wanted to protect Suzanne from any scrutinizing of her unfavorable characteristics. "She called to ask if I could lend her some money—fifty dollars until Friday night. I gave her a hard time because she only said she 'had some unexpected expenses' and I didn't want to let her off that easily."

"Why? Does she do that often—borrow money?"

"Well, that depends on what you call often. A few times … a little more than a few … I don't know, maybe five or six times."

"And does she pay you back?"

"Sometimes yes, sometimes no."

"And you don't ask if she doesn't return your money?"

"There again, it depends on my mood. Sometimes I get tough with her. It's hard for me to listen to her hard luck stories when her nails are always done and she always manages to buy for herself whatever is trendy. But then I look at the baby, and my heart melts a little." She shrugged an apology before he could say anything.

"Did you make any calls to anyone—her boss, maybe, to ask when she last worked?"

"Yes, that's the only call I made. But he barely spoke to me. I could hear all the noise in the background—they were probably so busy he cut me off before I could ask anything further. They don't like their wait staff to get personal calls. All he said was Suzanne worked her regular shift and left."

"Doesn't she have a cell phone?"

"She did. Some guy she was seeing had given her his spare to use, but when they broke up, he took it back." A sickening thought sent that rock-hard lump up her throat again. "She had hinted around for money to buy one, but I refused to get suckered into that, too." Her voice quivered. "If I hadn't been so damn stubborn about it, maybe she'd be able to call me and tell me where the hell she is and why."

"Forget it. How could you have known? She may be out somewhere partying while you're making yourself sick." He squeezed her hand. "Let me look into this while you talk to Will and Sandy. I promise you I'll keep you posted."

Frannie stood up and gave him a quick hug. "Thanks, Tony. You're an angel. I can't believe we're going through another horror story."

"It's not a horror story. At least not yet, and chances are, never will be. Hang in there."

She smiled. "I'm hanging."

Heather began to squirm just as Tony left. All eyes turned to her, anticipating the sweet sound of her infant cries. She didn't disappoint them. She wailed.

Sandy and Will washed their hands before approaching the baby, then Sandy gently lifted her and looked at

Frannie. "She'll need a crib, of course. We'll arrange for that today. But for now, can you spread a clean sheet or something so Will and I can look her over?"

"Sure," Frannie answered and promptly went to her linen closet. She smoothed out the sheet on her bed and stood by as Sandy undressed Heather. "Can you tell me what you're looking for? There are no signs of abuse, I can tell you that. There isn't a mark on her."

"Oh, that's not all we look for," Sandy said. She reached for a baby wipe, a clean diaper and the tube of Balmex. "Ah! See? She pooped. That's good. We need to check that it looks normal; that there's no diaper rash—or any other rash, for that matter." Will silently examined Heather's hands, feet, hair and scalp before Sandy completed her task. "Do you know the name of her pediatrician?" he asked.

"Yes, Dr. Smallen in Wells."

"Fine. We'll get in touch with him today. By tomorrow—I hope—we'll have a placement specialist here to conduct a home study."

Frannie took a quick look around her to see what they'd object to. Benny?

Will gave her a relaxed smile. "Don't worry. All family members should be as qualified as you. We'd have less job-related heartaches. Once you're formally approved, there'll be a few rules to follow, but nothing you can't handle." His face went serious. "I should warn you, though, that a diligent search will be made for the baby's father—"

"And that would be a whole new ballgame, I know. Tony already warned me."

Chapter Thirteen

Kim Haggarty was noticeably shaken when Tony Gerard introduced himself at her doorstep. She had never met the detective, but his name and face were certainly familiar from newspapers and TV news coverage. It seemed whenever and wherever a crime erupted, he'd be at the scene, surrounded by reporters throwing questions.

Kim's husband, Greg, who was outside replacing a fallen window shutter, had stopped immediately when Tony's car pulled up. He wiped his hands off with the rag tucked in his back pocket and shook Tony's hand. Kim opened her mouth to introduce them, but Greg waved her off. "Tony Gerard," he said. "I recognized your face." His gaze was a mix of admiration for Tony's reputation and concern for the purpose of his visit. "Come in, Sergeant," he said and the three of them settled in the living room. Tony shot a glance at the two children in the adjoining den whose attention was being completely absorbed by a Disney classic, *Finding Nemo.*

"Oh, don't worry about them," Kim said with a nervous smile. "They won't move a muscle when that's on." She cleared her throat and rubbed her fingers absentmindedly. "It's our pleasure to meet you, Mr. Gerard, but as you can probably tell, we're a little apprehensive ..."

Assured now that the four-and-five-year-olds would not interrupt, Tony got right to the point. "Mrs. Haggarty, you babysit for Suzanne Oliveri's little daughter, Heather, correct?"

The whites of her eyes made a full showing and she shook her head, afraid for him to continue. "Oh, my God, don't tell me ..." She couldn't finish the chilling thought.

"No, let me go on," Tony said, his tone assuring but his thoughts similar to hers. "Heather is perfectly safe. She's staying with Frannie Oliveri, Suzanne's cousin. It's Suzanne who brought me here. We haven't been able to locate her and I'd like to ask you a few questions. You might have been the last person to see her last night when she came for Heather."

"Oh ... My ... God," she repeated, this time with emphasis on each word. Both hands crossed her mouth now.

"Mrs. Haggarty, did you happen to notice if anyone was with her, maybe waiting in the car?"

She frowned and shook her head ruefully. "Oh, no, I'm sorry, I didn't. I just give the baby to her, exchange a few necessary words about when she had her last bottle and diaper change ... that sort of thing, and she goes on her way. Besides, with all that rain and wind, even if I had thought to look, I'd never be able to recognize a face, if that's what you need to know. Everything was black and scary out there." Her mouth began to quiver and she darted a look over to her children who were still glued to their movie, oblivious to the stranger in their home. "What's going on, Sergeant? How could Suzanne be missing if Heather is okay, as you say? How did she get to Frannie's and why?"

"The 'why' is what we're trying to find out. All I can tell you is that Suzanne brought her there, left Frannie a note asking her to babysit. Said she had some kind of emergency."

"What emergency? What did she tell Frannie?" She didn't wait for an answer, but quickly pulled her cell phone out of her pocket. "Do you mind if I call Frannie myself? We know her pretty well. Greg and I take the kids often to Amore Breakfast." She gave an incredulous look. "This is insane! She's supposed to open for the season this weekend and we were planning to take them Saturday. That poor woman."

"That won't be a problem. With or without Heather, Frannie still plans to open on schedule. We're all hoping by that time, Heather will be safe in her mother's arms again. But if you want to call Frannie just to hear for yourself that the baby's okay, go right ahead." He smiled to lighten the mood. "She might be a little busy. Caring for an infant is totally new to her and, of course, she's concerned about Suzanne."

"I want to offer to watch her. Not for the money, we just want to help, right, Greg?" she said looking up to him.

Greg squeezed her shoulder but spoke to Tony. "Sure. If Frannie needs us until Suzanne shows up, we're here for her, Sergeant." He said it with a polite smile, but his eyes communicated that he sensed something was terribly wrong. Tony's eyes neither assured nor denied Greg's silent questions.

Chapter Fourteen

Later, after everyone had left, Glory and Frannie were playing with Heather while watching the news on TV. They were shocked at the devastation in the wake of the storm. Homes and buildings had collapsed, along with a small bridge. In one area—ironically *Lake Street*—only the roofs of cars were visible and most of the homes were deeply immersed in water. Sidewalks and streets had vanished under the rush of raging waters. Emergency workers and volunteers used boats to rescue stranded and desperate residents on streets that had formed a river. An overpass had collapsed, and from what they could determine so far, at least two cars were crushed under the rubble. The newscaster appeared grim when she reported that authorities feared all occupants would be found dead.

Compared to what they had seen, Frannie and Glory agreed that they were extremely fortunate. Miraculously, Frannie's house had only minor damage, and when they finally got through to the right person, they were informed that despite fallen branches and flying debris, Amore Breakfast and Amore Evenings looked structurally sound. Glory had decided to wait for Alex before checking both restaurants for flooding or other related damages.

Their conversation waned and both seemed lost in their thoughts. Up until the wee hours of the morning, both had truly believed—or had made themselves believe—that Suzanne would come storming through the front door with a hell of a story to tell. But now, after all these hours, they were both hard pressed to think positively. Between the storm's devastation and all the crazies who either live in or pass through every town, there were plenty of haunting images to fill their minds.

Glory's cell phone rang and she jumped up to answer it in the kitchen. "That was Alex," she said when she came back. "He's on his way. Depending on what tie-ups he finds when he reaches the area, he should be here in an hour or two. And he's coming straight here. Do you mind?"

"Mind? Are you kidding? Right now we need all the friendly support we can get. And you never know. We might be able to pick his brain and come up with something new for Tony to check out."

The sound of wheels on gravel stopped them short. "Who the heck is that?" Frannie said aloud. Curious, they both went to the window. "Damn! It's my uncle!"

Glory, acting on impulse, scooped up the infant seat and brought Heather into the bedroom, not to hide her but to protect her from the sound of her grandfather's anticipated anger.

Jerry Oliveri rang the bell with one hand and pounded at the door with the other.

Stunned by his unexpected presence, Frannie had to make a split-second decision. Her first instinct was to ignore him and hope he'd go away, but there was no chance of that with two cars sitting in her driveway. Her second instinct was to say Suzanne had a chance to go away with friends for a couple of days and she had volunteered to babysit. She considered that idea about two seconds before she rejected it. Knowing her uncle Jerry, he'd run to the nearest lawyer trying to find some way to sue her for lying about his daughter and withholding information. It would have little to do with concern for his family and lots with whatever money he could squeeze from his successful niece.

When in doubt, go with the truth, she decided.

She sucked in a deep breath and braced herself. As much as she abhorred her uncle, she wasn't looking forward to telling him that his daughter was missing and might be in danger. Maybe long before years of alcohol consumption had burned his brain and turned him into a bitter, angry man, he'd had the capacity to love. Maybe somewhere buried inside him …

The thought died an instant death when she opened the door.

He looked like hell and smelled worse. His breath reeked of alcohol and cigarettes. The woman who clung to him like a snake in sunlight appeared to be a perfect match for him. Wearing a plastic raincoat with huge daisies and a matching hat, only her face was visible, but that was enough. The wide-brimmed hat had apparently not helped her escape the rain. Mascara dripped into the many crevices of her skin, which was already burdened by more layers of makeup than a corpse ready for viewing. All this punctuated by two smears of red on bony cheeks and matching blood-red lipstick.

What the hell's going on?" he barked. "You were supposed to be at my house an hour ago with my money!"

Frannie felt the heat rising in her cheeks. "Now, hold it right there, Uncle Jerry." She hated using that title. It suggested affection and/or respect, neither of which applied. Worthless son of a bitch would have been a more appropriate title. "Since when is *my* money *your* money? And what gives you the right to barge into my house uninvited?"

He jabbed a finger at her nose. "Whether you like it or not, I'm family, and I've got a good thirty years on you. *That* gives me the right." With a defiant snarl, he walked right past her and plopped down on her sofa, slapping the cushion next to him with an invitational smile. His lady love took her place beside him. He never bothered to remove his yellow rain slicker, nor did she part with her matching set.

Looking at the ravaged face among the daisies, Frannie imagined a skunk in a field of flowers.

Now she—this nameless intruder—dared to point a finger. "You should show your uncle a little respect. Shame on you!"

Frannie was dumbfounded by the woman and the whole scene. She wanted to yank them off her sofa and throw them out. From behind the unwelcome guests, Glory stepped out of the bedroom and threw a warning glance to Frannie. She put a finger to her lips and Frannie got the message. Calm down; don't get argumentative. God forbid they put on a good performance for CPS and make *you* look like the monster ...

Her arm made a machete-like sweep in front of them. "All right, both of you, cool it. Hear me?" She turned to Skunk Lady using a pointed finger as they had. Maybe it was the only language they understood. "I don't know who or what you are nor do I care. As far as I'm concerned you just drove him here." Again she pointed rather than say *my uncle*. "But I have some urgent family business to discuss and perhaps you shouldn't be here. I can drive him home later." She feigned a thank-you-for-coming smile and nodded towards the front door.

Jerry stood up, his face reddened with anger. Glory, still at the doorway behind the sofa, cringed and covered her ears. This was what she was afraid of. She slipped back into the bedroom ready to soothe Heather in her arms at her slightest whimper.

"Who the hell do you think you are? I never realized what a disrespectful brat my brother raised! How dare you insult my friend like that? There's nothing you can say to me that she can't hear. Now give me my money and we'll both be out of here. We've got better things to do than sit here and be insulted." Skunk Lady stood up beside him wearing the same indignant expression he wore.

Neither one had taken a step to leave. Instead, both heads turned, Jerry's eyes blazing. In the bedroom, Heather let out the loudest cries Frannie had heard since she found her last night. Maybe she sensed her grandfather's presence or heard his nasty voice. "That's her kid!" he yelled when he walked in and grabbed Heather from Glory's arms.

"Hey! That's no way to handle a baby!" Glory retaliated and tried to take her back.

"You mind your own damn business. What the hell are you doing with my granddaughter and why were you hiding her? And where's my daughter?"

"If *she's* your business," Frannie said, thumbing towards Skunk Lady, "Glory sure as hell is mine. Now give Heather to me and let me calm her. She's probably scared to death at the sound of your angry voice. I'm not telling you anything you want to know until you do."

Jerry clutched the baby while Frannie and Glory stood like bookends on opposite sides of him. He remained adamant and stone-faced.

Frannie threw her hands up but stayed close. Just in case. "Fine," she said with a shrug. "But if you want to leave here with what you came for, Heather stays in my arms, not yours." On those words, she gently took Heather from him, cradled and rocked her.

"Why don't you let me hold her while you two talk?" Glory offered and took the baby back to the bedroom, knowing that the conversation to follow would surely turn eruptive—or heated, at least.

"Sit down, *Uncle*," Frannie said, her tone mocking the title. "I have something to tell you." He and his lady were quick to notice the serious edge to her voice. They both sat back down on the sofa, he on the edge of the seat.

He glared at her with slitted red eyes. "I don't like the look on your face," he said, still holding on to the anger that shielded his weaknesses.

"Suzanne left me a note last night." She repeated the words without preamble.

"What kind of emergency? Where did she go? Let me see her note," he demanded, on his feet again.

"I don't have the note. I gave it to a detective friend of mine who's helping us find her. And I have no idea where she is. I already told you exactly what she wrote."

He shot her a sour look. "You called a detective before calling me—her father? Who the hell gave you that authority?"

Frannie raised her brows and crossed her arms. "Suzanne did when she wrote that note specifically to me. You didn't expect her to trust *you* with her baby, did you?'

"I'm her grandfather!" he shot back.

"How unfortunate for Heather—and Suzanne," she said sarcastically. "But I'm happy to say that all the *other* things you are would immediately disqualify you as Heather's caregiver."

He lifted a hand and Frannie thought he was about to strike her, but he snarled instead as though she wasn't worth the effort. He stood silently in thought a few seconds, then gave her a condescending smirk. "You know what I think? I think this is all a lot of bull you and she cooked up." He shook a finger in her face. "She's shacking up with somebody, isn't she? That's why she never brought my money! Sure, why should she give a shit about her father when she's got—"

This time Frannie's temper boiled over. "Are you out of your friggin' mind? If you had any sense you'd realize no sane person would create *that* for a cover story! And why is it always about what Suzanne and other people can do for you? What the hell did you ever do for Suzanne—or Aunt Laura, for that matter? Everything always had to revolve around you. Then after Aunt Laura died, you forgot about Suzanne completely and drowned yourself in alcohol. Who was there to comfort her? You were useless and selfish, so Suzanne did the best she could." As the words poured out, Frannie realized that she was defending her cousin like a loving mother would defend her child. She never knew she had it in her and hoped to God she'd have the chance to be more patient with Suzanne. Maybe with a little affection and guidance from someone who really *cares* about her, she can straighten out and reshape her life.

"It's none of your damn business how I live my life, so don't try any of your soap box sermons on me. Just give me that kid—*my grandkid*—and some money to buy the stuff she needs, and we'll get the hell out of here. Four or five hundred should do for now."

Frannie looked at him as though he were totally out of his mind. Her words spilled out with a laugh. "Are you crazy? What did I just say? Grandfather or not, you could never take care of Heather."

"I ain't gonna take care of her. Eloise here had kids. She'll know what to do."

Skunk Lady who now had a name sprang to life with a wide-eyed look of unexpected shock. "Hey, babe, that's going too far. I don't mind a little cooking now and then, but you ain't dumping no screaming kid on me. No way!"

Frannie and Glory exchanged a glance. Jerry and Eloise's reactions were so predictable it was almost amusing.

"Forget it. Don't bother to argue and waste my time, both of you. I wasn't finished explaining before you interrupted with your nasty remarks. Child Protective Services was already here early this morning. Heather will stay here with me and they're sending a team to do a home study. That will officially make me Heather's temporary foster parent until Suzanne—or the baby's father—is found."

"And who's looking for Suzanne? That bitch is gonna get a good piece of my mind when she shows up. Some nerve she had taking off before bringing me my fifty bucks! What the hell is fifty bucks to her?"

"To Suzanne, maybe it's food for her and the baby." *So okay, I'll forget the nails and the new sexy clothes.* "But to you, it's probably a bottle of booze. And that's why, *my dear uncle,* you'll never get custody of Heather. So if you were thinking you could get a windfall of cash from me or CPS—now or later—you can kiss that thought goodbye."

He stormed away, Eloise on his tail. Before he slammed the front door on his way out, he balled his fist and screamed. "If she doesn't show up real soon, I'm getting me a lawyer! I'm warning you!" Glory shook her head in disbelief after they left. "The man is crazy!" she said, then laughed. "How did he get into your family?"

Frannie sighed ruefully. "My dad said he always was a troublesome kid; always had a chip on his shoulder. But as he got older, instead of mellowing like many do, he got worse and worse ..."

"I'm going to prepare Heather's bottle and feed her. Maybe she'll settle down, now that they're gone."

"Good. 'Cause I still haven't taken my shower and after my uncle's visit, I suddenly feel dirtier."

"Frannie, before you go in, I sort of hate to bring this up now, but our restaurants are scheduled to open next week..."

"And we won't miss a beat, I promise. It's great that Alex will be here. He'll be a big help to us—especially to you at Amore Evenings. Heather will be with me at Amore Breakfast every day. I don't want her out of my sight." Before heading towards the bathroom, she stopped to gaze lovingly at Heather in Glory's arms. "Let's hope we won't have to worry about that. Maybe this beautiful little girl will have her real mommy back soon. Miracles happen."

"Truthfully, Frannie, do you really think we need a miracle?"

"Absolutely. But for now, I'd settle for a phone call from Tony."

Chapter Fifteen

In the midst of all the emergencies that had erupted as a result of the storm, Tony Gerard made a quick stop at the State Police barracks. He poured himself a much-needed cup of coffee and sat at his desk, rethinking Suzanne Oliveri's disappearance. His instincts rejected the theory that this could be a preplanned adventurous getaway, as Frannie had suggested. Something told him if she didn't turn up real soon—like today—this case would escalate from an attempt to locate to a missing person. He was not at all pleased. All he had was lots of speculation and little facts.

He picked up the phone to arrange for an investigative team, but he suspected that in the aftermath of the storm, manpower would be stretched thin. He wasn't about to ask other municipalities for help because they'd have to deal with their own emergencies. All police, fire and emergency workers were out there risking their lives to save others, and private citizens were volunteering en masse to join the search and rescue effort. Tragedy had sobered the faces and attitudes of everyone. Ogunquit particularly, where merchants had been occupied with thoughts of how to make this season more successful than the last, had immediately changed their priorities. How can we help? they'd asked. And for those who needed help most, their friends and neighbors were there for them. Even for those few who harbored resentment against each other, those barriers of hostility were gone. Tragedy has only one positive impact, Tony mused, it brings people together.

Like 9/11.

Although it had rained the whole week before, it wasn't until last night that fierce winds had joined the steady downpour, turning it into a violent storm that claimed four lives. Two elderly people, a sister and brother, were swept away by floodwaters only minutes before rescuers would have reached them. In separate incidents, the other two had been fatally struck by flying debris.

At this point it was still highly possible that Suzanne had been a victim. Her body could be found sometime soon. Or maybe it would never be found. She could have died as tragically as the elderly siblings.

But Tony had no intention of making that assumption. Since Suzanne had abandoned her baby in her cousin's house, and disappeared before the storm strengthened to a life-threatening level, the circumstances were deemed suspicious and warranted a thorough investigation.

Land & Sea had severe flooding and would not re-open for several days. Attempts to locate the owner and employees had been difficult. When finally all but one had been contacted, the results were fruitless. No one knew, no one heard, no one noticed. All that they had confirmed was that Suzanne had worked her regular shift yesterday and left.

His partner, Detective Pat Carney, stepped in his office, surprised to see him. "Hey, Tony, I didn't expect to see you here. You've been all over the place this morning, like me and everyone else."

"And last night too, but I won't be here long. I needed a bathroom and coffee real bad." He lifted his cup. "As soon as I finish this, I'm out of here."

Pat had been assigned to track down Jocelyn, Suzanne's co-worker at Land & Sea. If they were friendly, Suzanne might have mentioned something, either confidentially or casually, that could help their investigation. "I take it you haven't found Jocelyn yet, right? That would have been the first thing out of your mouth," he said with a smile.

"Not directly, no. Neither she nor her car is anywhere around. But I did speak to her neighbor." She referred to her notes. "A Mrs. Lillian Douglas—a pleasant woman somewhere in her sixties, I'd guess. Anyway, she said chances are Jocelyn might have gone to her parents' home to help them out. But the parents live up in Kennebunk, and, of course, electricity is out."

"No cell?"

She wrinkled her nose. "No. You know how a lot of older people are—they're resistant to change and have no patience for learning how to make use of 21st century technology."

Tony smirked. "Tell me about it! My parents are always telling me how simple and uncomplicated life used to be in their time." His smile faded quickly and his face grew serious. With his elbows leaning on the desk, he cupped his chin and took a decision-making moment. "Look Pat," he said, "why don't you and Jesse take a ride there? I hate to see the time wasted if we don't get any useful information, but it's a step we can't pass over."

Tony's cell phone rang. He glanced at the caller ID and signaled Pat to wait. As he listened, his lips parted and he shot up out of his chair. "What? Oh, jeez, this is gonna kill them," he said ruefully. "But thanks, Willie. I'm on my way." He flipped the phone closed. "Talk to you later, Pat. I'm out of here."

"Why? What happened?"

"The Townline Drive overpass just collapsed. And a Honda went down with it."

Chapter Sixteen

It was a hell of an inconvenient time for a murder. Tony Gerard had been at the Townline Drive collapse site only fifteen minutes when a phone call sent him racing over to The Admiral's Inn.

When Tony arrived, a crime scene unit had already begun sealing off the area with the familiar yellow tape. It had only been nineteen months since the last murder case in Ogunquit; when Paula Howard was drowned by Carl Duca.

Although the search for Suzanne Oliveri had ended tragically, he still needed to know what caused her to abandon her baby. What was her *emergency*? He wasn't buying any theory related to her irresponsible behavioral pattern. From what he had learned so far, that didn't apply to her baby. She was a loving and attentive mother.

Officer Corrine Hart, one of the two initial responding officers, waited while Tony parked his car. They went through the motions of exchanging pleasantries, although with an air of formality.

"Okay, what do we know?" he asked.

"At 9:10 a.m. one of the owners, Ken Holmes, called 9-1-1," Corrine began, referring to her notes. "He reported that the housekeeper, Anna Gurski, had made the discovery. She's an elderly woman and pretty shaken up. We have someone with her in the TV room behind the bar out front."

"Is the owner on the premises?"

"There are two owners, Ken Holmes and Jake Corbin, and the bartender, Vic Guay. Jake was out of town and only Ken and Vic were on the premises yesterday and last night, although when they were first questioned, both said they had no clue as to what happened. Only that when the victim checked in, he said he'd probably be staying only one night."

"And what did we find out about the victim?"

"According to our New York contact, it seems Keaton's been a loser most of his life, but no criminal record. Always trying to make a fast buck, but never succeeding. Until he hit it off with this lounge he co-owns in Manhattan, *The Bird's Nest.* Apparently he inherited some big bucks from an uncle who died in a nursing home and he sunk it all into this business. It wasn't doing well at first, but it is now—or had been."

"And the nature of his business in Ogunquit?"

"We didn't get that far yet. Sorry."

"Any witnesses?"

"None. Eleven guests are registered in six rooms; five occupy the second floor front rooms, six guests on the first floor, left side, with Keaton in the rear." Although it was a sight that couldn't be missed, she extended her arm in that direction. Several officers were manned outside to protect the integrity of the crime scene. "Everyone claimed to be sleeping and neither saw nor heard anyone or anything. All individuals, guests, both owners and the bartender are secured and separated, and are now being held in the inn for questioning. All unauthorized and nonessential individuals have been removed from the scene." She rattled it off like a prerecorded message, her eyes never leaving her note pad.

Tony nodded, acknowledging the information with the same formality it was delivered. He and Corrine hadn't even exchanged a quick glance. Their jobs brought them together often and there was no way they could avoid speaking, but their conversations were limited exclusively to police business. Only bittersweet memories remained of their two-year love affair that ended abruptly and left two hearts wounded. *Never again.* Those were the last personal words he said to the woman he had planned to marry. He repeated those words to himself every time he saw Corrine, just in case the sight of her weakened his resolve.

She started to walk away and he stopped her. "One more thing, Officer Hart ..."

Corrine raised her brows in question but her eyes were fiery. Addressing her as "Officer Hart" was a direct hit that Tony instantly regretted, but he couldn't pull back the words. "What about cars in the parking lot? Anyone pulling out or in when you and Officer Walker arrived on the scene?"

"No, no moving vehicles," she reported, and flipped through her notes again. Not that she needed to refer to them, but it enabled her to avoid his gaze. "There were six cars in the parking lot. They were all checked out and found to belong to the owners, the bartender and the guests." She slipped her pad back in her back pocket. "Anything else, *sir?*" She emphasized the "sir" as a subtle counterattack for the "Officer Hart."

A slight smile sneaked around the corners of Tony's mouth but he twisted his lips and fingered his chin, feigning deep thought. "No, not for the moment. Thank you, Officer."

"My pleasure, Sergeant Gerard," she answered, her voice dripping with sarcasm.

He decided to give her the last word and go visit the corpse with the butcher knife stuck in his chest.

He covered his feet and hands with the prerequisite latex gloves and booties and entered the room. Police photographers were clicking away at the bloody body of New York resident, Tyler Keaton. Technicians from the Medical Examiner's Office were performing their gruesome tasks. Every move was documented, every sample logged and tagged.

In accordance with police procedures, the officers assigned were carefully observing all actions to ensure that no evidence was contaminated.

Deputy Chief Medical Examiner Joseph Conway continued his work while Tony questioned him.

"Time of death, Joe?"

"Judging by the body temperature, the state of rigor and lividity and the condition of the exsanguinated blood, I'd pin it down to between 5:00 and 8:00 a.m."

"Any other wounds—defense wounds?"

"No way. This guy never knew what hit him. You can be sure he was in dreamland when the knife went through his heart."

Tony nodded. "Well, that answers my next question. So there's nothing to suggest the body might have been moved after death?"

"Not likely," Joe quickly answered. "There's no blood trail, no abrasion marks on his heels, no drag mark impressions into the carpet … no nothing." He pointed to the doorway. "That entire wet area of the carpet was caused by rain coming in. The housekeeper had reported that she found the door unlocked and slightly ajar." His finger directed Tony's attention back to the bed. "So this is where he got it and this is where he stayed. When we arrived on the scene, his body was slightly slumped over, facing left, towards the window. I'd say when the blade penetrated, he clutched his chest, struggled for breath and keeled over."

Tony turned next to Dave Porter, one of the CSI technicians, and his former Little League coach decades ago. "And what do you have for me, Dave? Anything good?"

Dave grinned as though he had dug up a treasure. "Damn good—if the samples we collected are the right ones. If they are, I'd say we have enough evidence to make your star shine a little brighter, Super Sergeant. One thing's for certain—our killer stormed into this room with a vengeance and only one thought in mind—to shove that butcher knife into the guy's chest."

"Any good prints?" Tony asked. "Any luck with the weapon?"

"We've got several prints, but nothing on the weapon. The killer obviously wore gloves because you'd have to have a damn good grip on that thing in order to cause penetration like this. So, assuming he—or she—wore gloves, all the other prints found in the room are probably not our killer's. Let's face it, you don't walk into a guy's room packing an eight-inch butcher knife unless you intend to use it. And if you intend to use it, you don't leave your prints around first." He raised his brows and tipped his head, as though waiting for Tony to agree.

Tony put his hands up, fingers extended. "Hey, you'll get no argument from me. But what about hair?"

"We've got plenty of those, but I can tell you now that they're not all from the same person. This room is used actively, I understand, and although it's cleaned daily, vacuum cleaners don't pick up everything, as you know." Dave paused and grinned at him. "Now here's the kicker: I can tell you this guy went out in glory because we found several long hairs on the bedsheets. Traces of semen also. So maybe we have a female killer this time. The last few were men, so it might be a refreshing change."

"Oh, I've had my share of female killers. And let me tell you 'refreshing' is not a term I'd use to describe them." He smiled at Dave, then shook away the memories of heinous crimes committed by women. "So, what else you got? No signs in the room of struggle or theft?"

"No, like I said, the guy never knew what hit him and his wallet was found in his pocket with $532 in cash."

*　　*　　*

Tony asked a few more questions and walked over to the front of the inn where he positioned himself at the reception desk. He called for Ken Holmes, the owner on duty at the time Keaton checked in. The guy's hand was ice cold when he shook it and he appeared upset. Understandable for a guy who probably sunk a small fortune buying and renovating the place.

The sun was trying to make a comeback after a week's absence, but the clouds were still fighting for their air space. Every time a stream of sunlight managed to flash through, The Admiral's Inn looked like a commercial for a cleaning product. The wood floors and windows sparkled, the wallpaper made you think spring and the lace curtains were reminders of your grandmother's house when you were a kid.

Poor guy, Tony thought. Every new business wants publicity, but a *murder?*

"Did you personally handle Tyler Keaton's check-in?"

"Yes. He had made the reservation online. When he arrived at 3:15, I showed him the room. He said it was fine, and I left him."

"Was there any other conversation that you recall?"

Ken took a moment to ponder the question. "Nothing important. Just a little small talk …"

"Like what? Tell me what you remember."

"I asked him if he had a good trip here; how was the weather in New York, and I said I was sorry that he had chosen to visit Ogunquit at the worst possible time—that we were expecting the worst of the storm."

"And did he reply?"

"Nothing much ... just said it didn't matter." Ken shrugged, wishing he had more to offer. "Apparently the guy wasn't here on a pleasure trip."

"Anything else you recall hearing or observing?"

Ken drew a breath and searched his memory once more. "Jeez, if I had known the guy would end up dead— *murdered*—I would have paid more attention, but I honestly don't think he said anything more, and I never laid eyes on him again after I showed him to his room."

Tony skipped over the other owner, Jake Corbin, who had just returned from New Hampshire and had nothing to offer to the investigation. He continued questioning the others and was getting no place fast until he reached Melinda Frawley, a guest who had been sitting at the window while her husband took his usual afternoon nap. She was delighted to tell her story since she was the only guest who had seen Keaton.

"I didn't know what to do with myself," she said. "The rain wouldn't quit, my husband was sleeping and I had already finished my novel, so I just sat there looking out the window. I remember seeing this guy wearing a navy blue windbreaker and jeans get into his car."

"Were you able to identify the car—color, make?"

"I don't usually, but it was a classy-looking car, so I did notice. It was a Thunderbird. But I didn't get a good look at his face. He had pulled the hood up. It was pouring out there."

"Did you happen to notice what time it was?"

Mrs. Frawley's eyes brightened. "I sure did. It was exactly ten to four. That I remember because I was going to put the TV on at four o'clock to watch Oprah."

He had put off questioning Anna Gurski, the house-keeper who had found the body, until they were able to calm her a bit. She was now as calm as could be expected and wanted to help in any way she could, she said.

Tony pulled up a chair and sat facing her. He spoke to her in the softest voice he could manage. Her hands were shaking and she rubbed them continuously.

"Mrs. Gurski, I promise you this won't take long. Just answer my questions to the best of your recollection. If you don't remember, just say so. Okay?"

"Okay," she said, biting her lips now, along with the hand rubbing.

"What brought you to Mr. Keaton's room and at what time, if you recall?"

"It was nine o'clock, give or take five minutes—I was working the first floor, but most of the rooms were still occupied. It was hard to tell—I think some of the signs—you know, the ones that say "privacy" on one side and "please clean room" on the other—anyway, when I got to his room, I noticed that the door wasn't locked. It was closed, sort of, but not all the way, so I knocked and called out, 'Housekeeping,' but no one answered. So I opened the door…Oh, my God, my God," she wailed suddenly, "How am I ever going to get that sight out of my head…never, never…"

Tony waited and offered her comforting words, but just as he thought he'd have to give up for the moment, Mrs. Gurski came across. She opened her mouth, sucked in a deep breath, and gave him one of those inside hand waves that says, I'm okay; come back. "I can wait, Mrs. Gurski, if you need more time," Tony whispered.

"No, no, I'll be fine. I want you to catch that … sorry, I don't like to use bad words, but I'm sure thinking of some good ones!"

Tony smiled at her warmly and she eased. "What did you see when you walked in? What was the first thing you noticed, do you remember?"

"I saw the man sleeping in the bed—at least I thought he was sleeping. Ordinarily, I would have closed the door and left immediately, but I noticed that the carpeting was sopping wet. At first I figured that was because the door wasn't completely closed, but then I saw that this big stain came from around the bed, near the window. Then I thought the rain was coming in from somewhere—how come this guy slept through it all, I asked myself. That made me think maybe he had a heart attack or something, so I went to look…" Mrs. Gurski squeezed her eyes closed and covered her mouth, then shook it right off and continued. "Well, you know what I saw, Sergeant. I was so scared I couldn't even scream for help. I just ran out of there and kept running until I found Mr. Ken."

After he had concluded his questionings, Tony had only crumbs to work with. Tyler Keaton had come to Ogunquit on a mission. He had planned to stay one night and didn't give a damn about a threatening storm. And he left at 3:50. To do what? Where was he going or who was he going to meet?

That was the million dollar question at the moment. He had no answers yet.

Yet being the key word.

Tony was on his way back to the crime scene when the dispatcher put a call through.

"Sergeant Gerard, this is Officer Paul Laverty, Ogunquit P.D. We're at the Townline Drive collapse site. The emergency crew pulled up the Honda. We can't believe it ourselves, sir, but the girl is still alive. Medical personnel are on the scene and a 'copter is on its way to transport her to Maine Medical Center."

"I'm on my way," Tony said and shoved the phone back in his pocket. He took a few seconds only to assign an officer to replace Corrine. "Let's go, Corrine," he said, crooking a finger and walking with a quickened pace. He called her by her first name intentionally, setting aside their personal problems for now.

Corrine recognized the urgency, and she, too, forgot all about the little game they had been playing. "Where are we going?"

"I'll tell you on the way." Tony wasn't quite sure whether finding Suzanne alive was good news or bad. He hated to raise the family's hopes for a moment and have them plunge downward the next.

In the car, Corrine sat silently awhile waiting for him to speak. "Well, when are you going to tell me what's going on?"

Tony shook his troubling thoughts away. "Now. We've got a murder and a collapsed overpass hitting us back to back. But there's a bright side. No fatalities yet. Paul Laverty called in to report that they found Suzanne Oliveri still alive when they brought the car up." He glanced over at her. "Unbelievable, isn't it?"

Corrine was stunned for a moment, then her mouth flew open and, unthinkingly, she squeezed Tony's arm. "Oh, Tony, that certainly is unbelievable! I hope to God she makes it."

Tony smiled his agreement, warmed by the hope for Suzanne's survival and the touch of Corrine's fingers.

Chapter Seventeen

Ogunquit Police Officers Matthew Stone and Ron Taylor tried a second time to reach Jerry Oliveri. This time someone came to the door. They stepped inside without waiting for an invitation.

"What the hell do you guys want?" he snarled, stunned and indignant by their presence in his living room. He hated the sight of a police uniform; blamed them for losing his driver's license.

"Mr. Oliveri, I'm afraid we have bad news for you," Matt Stone began. "You might have heard that the Townline Drive overpass collapsed earlier this morning. About an hour ago, emergency workers at the scene sighted another car—a third car— crushed under all the debris. It wasn't visible at first, but it's been identified now. It's your daughter's car, sir. I'm sorry."

Jerry Oliveri's bloodshot eyes stared at them in disbelief. For a long moment he showed no other reaction. His gaze went from one to the other, squinting as though he were trying to wake up from a bad dream.

Then, like a raging fire out of control, it surfaced. "What the hell are you telling me, that Suzanne's dead? That can't be! She's alive, isn't she?"

"She was when we left the scene, sir, but her injuries are extensive, I'm afraid." Matt Stone shook his head and lowered his gaze. He never saw it coming, but Jerry Oliveri's punch in the face staggered him. Blood gushed from his nose.

No, that ain't true!" Oliveri screamed. "That ain't true! Get the f--- out of my house!"

Officer Taylor reacted. "Son of a bitch!" he yelled and yanked out his cuffs.

Oliveri had run into the kitchen screaming every profanity ever known to man. With a second blow he punched a hole in the wall, then smashed his bottle of vodka against the kitchen counter.

Ron Taylor was about to subdue Oliveri but Matt stopped him. "Hold it, Ron. He'll run out of steam. Some people react to shock in crazy ways."

"Hey, I feel sorry for the guy, too, but that doesn't give him the right to assault an officer."

"I know," Matt countered, still trying to soak up the blood with both their handkerchiefs that were already saturated. "But I went to school with his daughter, so for her sake …. Look, why don't you go grab me a towel out of the bathroom? When he calms down I'll get some ice."

But Jerry had already calmed down. The anger his denial had fired was reduced to tears. The two officers gave the grieving father a few moments alone. They just watched as he leaned over the counter with his head cradled in his arms, quietly at first. Then came the sobs. Loud, mournful and agonizing sobs, as he cried out his daughter's name and begged her forgiveness, then lifted his head and looked at the officers with remorse. "Take me to her … take me, *please…*"

Chapter Eighteen

For a Sunday, it was an unusually busy day. But then again, *unusual* was too bland a word to describe the day's events. Frannie was fighting away flashing images that shivered her bones. Suzanne dead under a fallen tree; Suzanne alive but trapped in some obscure location where she'd never be found; Suzanne drowned by rushing waters that took her body out to sea for its creatures to feast on; Suzanne, unconscious or dead in some fleabag motel brutally beaten by a lunatic who salivated at the sight of his victims' begging and suffering.

Frannie squeezed her eyes shut, remembering the horror of Carl, her cousin with the entertaining sense of humor. He's a million laughs, people said. But Carl entertained himself a hell of a lot differently.

Heather opened her eyes wide and their deep blue brilliance seemed to illuminate her pink skin. Frannie's dark thoughts were immediately obliterated as she watched her. "Glory, look at her! I think she actually smiled. C'mere, maybe she'll do it again."

Glory stood over Heather waiting for the smile that never came. But watching Frannie's face was a love story in itself.

Frannie caught her staring. "Why are you looking at me with that smirk?" she asked, although she knew the answer. Both women could read into each other's minds so well it was spooky.

Glory laughed. "You are *so* transparent. In one glance anyone would see how much you love her. Aren't you the one who said 'I don't do babies'?"

"I never said I was incapable of *loving* babies. I only meant how would I find time for that whole domestic scene while I run two restaurants that are open seven days a week?"

Glory jabbed a finger in the air. "In season. And now with my help."

"Yeah, yeah. So what would I say to my kid, if I had one—see you in January? How could I possibly handle a child?"

Glory gave her a sideways glance. "You'll soon find out."

Frannie raised her eyes to heaven. "Oh, don't even say that, Glory. I'm still clinging to the possibility that she'll walk in here all smiles with some bizarre story to tell us or stuck somewhere in her car, without a cell phone. If I dwell on anything else, I'll go crazy!"

Glory heard the quiver in Frannie's voice and let it go, but her friend had to face the possibility that her cousin could be dead. As the hours passed, that *possibility* had escalated to a *probability.*

That crunching sound of tires on gravel interrupted and sent their gazes to the window. Alex. Glory ran out, arms open wide, and welcomed him. Frannie stayed back to give them a few private moments, but they both came right in.

Alex approached Frannie with concern written all over his face. They had become such good friends from the night they joined forces to save Glory, Tim and Sara. Seeing him now was a surefire tug at her heartstrings. He opened his arms and she let him wrap them around her and Heather. She cried a little but broke away smiling to show off her baby cousin.

"Oh, she's so beautiful, Frannie. How's she doing, okay?"

"She's a perfect little baby. No trouble at all. Not that Glory or I have ever had another baby to compare her to."

From the corner of his eye, Alex stole a glance at Glory, trying to read her thoughts, then turned to Frannie. "Have you guys heard anything new since my last phone call?"

Frannie folded her arms and paced the floor, her eyes cast downward. "Not a word. They say no news is good news, but don't believe it. It's agonizing. We've been going through hell just sitting around and waiting."

"Well, your wait might be over, Frannie," Alex said, standing at the living room window. "I think Tony Gerard is pulling up in your driveway. It looks like him."

Tony had his hands full with the murder investigation, but didn't want to send someone else to inform Frannie. He approached her house once again, but this time with more trepidation than before. Experience had taught him that in grave situations, people react to the word *alive* with such joy that they refuse to accept anything negative. They convince themselves that if they don't think about them, they won't happen. Period. He blew a sigh wishing life could be that simple.

Earth would be heaven.

"Oh, dear God, I hope he has good news," Frannie said. Her hands trembled as she reached for the doorknob to let him in. "Oh, no!" she cried the moment his eyes met hers. Her hands flew to her mouth. Tony hadn't said a single word, but his long face was a definite prelude to bad news. He drew a breath before he spilled out the devastating news. "I'm so sorry, Frannie, but you might have heard about the overpass collapse we had earlier over on Townline Drive," he said, glancing over to the TV screen. "Well, I've just been notified that Suzanne's car went down with it. It was completely hidden by all the rubble at first and they just discovered it now." He chose not to mention yet that her packed bag had been found, with only her clothes and a crushed baby photo.

Panic ripped through Frannie's body. She neither screamed nor uttered a sound. Only her eyes revealed the terror running through her veins. Alex and Glory stood behind her, as thought anticipating her collapse and ready to break her fall.

"No, hold it, Frannie," Tony said. "Don't think the worst. Let me finish." He sat beside her while Glory tried to summon up the strength to fight her own emotions. Frannie was a strong and independent woman, but life was dumping overwhelming challenges on her; first her bigamist husband, then Carl, now Suzanne. "She's alive. No one expected her to survive an accident like that, but she was alive when they pulled her out of the wreckage. I have to warn you, though, that her injuries are extensive."

Frannie ignored the warning. A smile exploded across her face and happy tears blotched her cheeks.

Tony had seen Suzanne when they cut her out. He couldn't share Frannie's joy.

She literally dragged him into the living room where Frannie and Glory had been sitting with Alex and Glory's dad, Dan Madison. "Hey, guys! Suzanne's alive. Tony said they pulled her out and she's alive! Is this a miracle, or what?"

Standing slightly behind her, Tony communicated the gravity of Suzanne's condition with one grim look. His lower lip protruded as he shook his head. Everyone was standing now, waiting for more details. They, too, wanted to magnify the positive and suppress the negative.

Frannie took Heather from Glory's arms and smothered her with kisses. "Your mommy's alive, little princess. She's alive!" Then she turned to Tony again. "Where did they take her? I'm so excited I forgot to ask."

"When I left, they were transporting her to Maine Medical Center in Portland."

"Were they able to determine the extent of her injuries, Tony?" Alex asked. "I know they won't have a full picture yet, but an educated guess, maybe?"

"Severe head trauma to begin with. Nobody likes to guess. It'll be a while before we get a full diagnosis and prognosis."

Frannie's euphoric face grew serious, then slightly confused. "Gee, Tony, I have to get there, but what about Heather? Can I leave her with Glory? Would that be okay?"

"I'll talk to Sandy, but I'm sure it'll be fine."

"It better be fine, 'cause I'm the only family she has."

"Not true," Tony said. "Her dad is being driven there as we speak."

Frannie did a double take. "Are you serious? The only time my uncle Jerry looks for his daughter is when he wants something. And that's usually money for booze."

"Well, I don't know the guy, but when he was told about the accident, he took it pretty bad. Very bad, actually, the officers reported."

Frannie found that hard to imagine and the cynical smirk that curled her mouth confirmed it. "Boy, never thought he had it in him," she said. "Miracles never cease, huh?"

Glory slipped her arm through her father's and kissed him on the cheek. "Don't talk to us about miracles. We've already been there, done that, right, Dad?" Dan Madison smiled down at the thirty-six-year-old daughter he'd met only nineteen months ago. He stroked her hair and kissed her forehead.

Alex lowered his eyes, but no one noticed.

Chapter Nineteen

While Frannie prepared to leave for the hospital, she rattled off to Glory reminders about Heather's care. Alex had turned the TV back on so that he and Dan could get an update of local news. Suzanne's rescue had probably been covered already, but would certainly be rebroadcast throughout the day.

But a different scene splashed across the screen, prompting shocked reactions from both Alex and Dan. "Frannie, Glory, you'd better come in here." Alex called out.

When the ladies joined them, all four stood staring at the TV screen in disbelief, listening intently to the reporter detailing the events of a murder scene at The Admiral's Inn. Tony Gerard of the Maine State Police was in charge of the investigation, she said.

"Holy shit!" Frannie cried out. "Excuse me, guys, but this is too much to take in one day. Ken and Jake are my good friends. They just reopened the place and were doing so well. What the heck is this going to do to them now?" She stopped to listen further, then said, "But Tony was just here. Why didn't he tell us?"

"I guess he figured we'd find out soon enough," Dan offered. "And he knew you have enough of your own problems now."

*   *   *

Frannie had driven to Portland many times before, but the distance had never seemed longer. Her cell phone never rang, so no news is good news, she concluded, then reconsidered. If Suzanne didn't make it, they probably wouldn't call. They'd wait until she arrived. She tried to pray but couldn't concentrate. Too much was happening too fast. And she had too many people to pray for—Suzanne, Heather, Jake and Ken for their new troubles, and the poor guy who got killed at The Admiral's Inn. Whoever the murdering bastard was, why did he have to pick their place to murder him? The victim was a New Yorker. Why did he follow him to Ogunquit and knock him off here?

Her friends' problems had to be put on the back burner of her mind when she entered the medical center. To think that only yesterday her most pressing problem was working out the menu revisions with Glory before Amore Breakfast and Amore Evenings reopened on Friday.

Chapter Twenty

Tony returned to The Admiral's Inn to oversee operations and ensure that the crime scene remained fully protected. He and Corrine separated with a nod and a quick hand wave. A hell of a lot different from those nights they couldn't let go of each other.

He cast an observant eye over the entire area, checking primarily for crowd and media control, two ever-present conditions that stretched thin his investigative team. But it was always anticipated and handled. A juicy murder story in a quaint tourist town had great shock value. The public stayed glued to their TV sets and bought up all the newspapers.

The puzzle pieces began flying around and a few slipped into place almost effortlessly. The first came in the form of a phone call from his partner, Pat Carney, who had gone off in search of Jocelyn Carter, Suzanne's co-worker at Land & Sea. He should have trusted his instinct and stopped her when he learned that a Honda went down with the Townline Drive collapse, but he went flying out instead. Her report no longer mattered now that Suzanne had been found, but Tony didn't know if word had reached her yet. "Hey, Pat, how's it going? Look, I should have called earlier—"

"Forget it. I heard—first about Suzanne—is she still hanging on?"

"As of ten minutes ago, yes."

"Oh, God, the thought of that poor baby never knowing her real mother ..." She shook the thought away. "Then I got the call about The Admiral's Inn. Jeez, with all this storm damage, we need that like a hole in the head."

"I don't think Ken and Jake are too happy about it either. After that first great season, this could drag them down."

Pat had a more optimistic view. "No, I don't think so. It could work in reverse. Who knows? The Admiral's Inn could become a tourist attraction."

Tony laughed at the absurdity. "Sure, every Halloween the place will be mobbed."

"But seriously, Tony, let's get back to business. I picked up some interesting information from Jocelyn Carter. She told me that Suzanne had been involved with a guy in New York—"

"That's pretty obvious. She came back pregnant—" He stopped short and slapped his forehead. "Son of a bitch! Don't tell me—Tyler Keaton, right?"

"Well, technically, she said 'a guy named Tyler' but that's enough, I guess. She stressed, however, that Suzanne swore up and down that he's not the baby's father."

"Jeez, I can't believe I never made the connection. Why the hell didn't I see it?"

"There you go again, Tony, beating up on yourself. I can hear the anger in your voice. Why must you always be perfect? We're only humans and humans make mistakes. And this is not a mistake anyway. We get so many visitors from New York, why should we have known to connect the two cases? If Jocelyn hadn't mentioned the name *Tyler* I never would have—"

"Pat, in our business we can't screw up. Simple as that. Mistakes can be deadly."

Pat decided to accept defeat before she went too far. "Okay, you win, Tony," she said, but thought maybe if he wasn't such a stubborn perfectionist, he wouldn't have lost Corrine. He may be a damn good cop, but has a lot to learn about human weaknesses and the rewards of a forgiving heart. "So what's next?" she asked him.

Tony was glad to dismiss the subject. In his opinion, argumentative discussions about personal character traits were dangerous ground and should always be avoided. "Try to reach Lt. Andrew Donovan in New York. He's with the 21st Precinct. He owes me a few favors and I need a few fast answers. Patch me in when you get him on the phone."

"You got it. Anything else, boss?"

"Yeah. One more thing—Sorry. I didn't mean to snap at you."

"Ah, that's okay. These broken romances can turn the best of us into nasty sons of bitches."

Tony laughed with her and instantly relaxed, even though her words had hit their target.

Chapter Twenty-one

Frannie had been so consumed with worry about Suzanne's chances of survival that her uncle Jerry never entered her mind.

Now that she had arrived at Maine Medical Center, she stiffened and braced herself. The last thing she needed was another bout with his obnoxious behavior.

At the reception desk, she was directed to the family waiting room where someone would eventually advise her of the patient's condition.

The room was large and brightened on one side by a wall of windows. Most people were seated in the front rows, hoping and waiting for good news. Anxiety was evidenced on most adult faces; boredom and restlessness on the children who waited with them.

Jerry Oliveri was not among them.

Frannie spotted her uncle seated alone in the back row against the wall. He hadn't noticed her yet; he sat leaning forward with his head in his hands. *He's probably hung over and wishing he could run out and find a bar,* she told herself, trying to let her disdain for him take the lead.

But her heart won instead when he reached in his back pocket. He pulled out a handkerchief and covered his mouth. Tony had said that her uncle had taken it bad, but after their earlier confrontation she found it difficult to visualize. But here he was, sobbing and biting the handkerchief to muffle the sounds.

She might hate him again tomorrow, but today, at this very moment, her heart melted. The ugly cloak of alcoholism had been lifted and there before her eyes sat a broken man, fighting another battle with grief.

Frannie's arms were around him before she knew it. For one long silent moment, she held him as he rocked with the pain of grief and probably regrets. She wiped away her own tears and whispered to him. "She'll be okay, Uncle Jerry. She's young and strong and that's in her favor." *Clichéd words, yes, but if they help* ... "Has anyone spoken to you yet about her condition?"

He shook his head and held his gaze on the tile floor. "Nothing more than I knew when they brought her in."

"Look, there's a machine over there," she said, pointing. "Why don't I get us both a cup of hot coffee? I'll be right back."

She returned with the two steaming cups and a package of Drake's crumb cake, thinking he'd probably wave it away. But he fooled her and ate it all in seconds. *God only knows when he ate last*, she thought.

They sat together in almost total silence for more than an hour, waiting. There was so much she wanted to say to him—comforting words, assuring words—but lack of privacy held them inside her. Instead, she stroked his back every now and then. The gesture seemed perfectly natural until her thoughts snapped out of the moment and flashed back in time. Only hours before she had hated him with a passion. Now she saw him so differently—a helpless old man, broken apart into little pieces. If his daughter didn't make it, and he continued his love affair with the bottle, no one will ever be able to put him together again.

Like Humpty Dumpty, Jerry Oliveri sat on a wall.

A young doctor with an engaging smile approached them. Both Frannie and her uncle rose out of the seats as if the President of the United States had walked in.

He shook both their hands and introduced himself. "Mr. Oliveri, I'm Dr. Timothy Quinlan, the trauma surgeon who will coordinate your daughter's care. Let me first say that Suzanne's injuries are quite serious, but not without hope."

Both Frannie and Jerry exhaled a sigh of relief and looked up at him, wide-eyed.

"Here's what we found so far. She has a ruptured spleen, a femur fracture and a head injury. The emergency squad did stabilize her at the accident scene, but she'll need immediate surgery. Someone will be here shortly for your signature, sir. I understand she has no husband, correct?"

"No, no, I'll sign," Jerry quickly answered. "But tell me, Doctor, what do you intend to do to my daughter?"

"Well, she needs a spleenectomy—that means we remove the spleen, of course. We also have to insert what's called an intramedullary rod to fix the broken femur, and burr holes in her skull to relieve the subdural hematoma. In layman's terms, that means to relieve the pressure on her brain."

Frannie was afraid to ask in her uncle's presence, but they both had to know. "What are her chances of surviving all that, Doctor?"

"Good. I don't have to tell you—no one knows these things for certain—there are often complications—but if everything goes well, we should see a huge improvement within a few weeks."

Relief overwhelmed them. Despite the doctor's warning, his words had given Frannie and Jerry more hope than they had expected.

Jerry raised a finger and spoke in a gentle voice. "Doctor, before you go, can you tell me where the chapel is?"

"Sure," Dr. Quinlan answered. "It's on this floor, just past the elevators on the left. You'll see the sign directing you." He started to walk away and turned back. "And by the way," he said with a smile that illuminated his face, "say one for me."

"You bet I will! You're operating on my daughter!"

Frannie raised her eyes to heaven. This was so out of character—so unlike the man she knew before that she prayed it would last. Maybe it took something like this to wake him up. She only hoped Suzanne lived to see it and that her uncle had the strength to battle his addiction. "Wait for me, Uncle Jerry. I'm coming with you."

Chapter Twenty-two

Tony sat alone at a table where guests are usually served breakfast at The Admiral's Inn. He faced the window and gazed at the passing cars on Route 1, but his mind was sharply focused on the day's events. He didn't like the way things were shaping up. The second puzzle piece appeared to be another nail in Suzanne Oliveri's coffin—and it in no way related to her medical crisis.

The more he learned, the more he couldn't avoid connecting the two cases. It was as though if he plugged them together, all the facts would explode in his face. He would have no choice but to deal with them. It might almost be better for Suzanne and her family if she died of her injuries rather than face murder charges.

And Tony had a strong, nagging feeling that's where this mess was headed.

Lieutenant Donovan of the New York Police Department apologized for the delay in returning Tony's call, but he had been involved with a street gang war that left two teenagers dead and a twenty-four-year-old police officer fighting for his life.

"Hey, don't apologize to me, Andy. As they say, 'you're preaching to the choir.'"

"So how are things up in Maine—calm and peaceful? I sure could use a Maine vacation. My wife and I haven't been there in a few years. I miss Ogunquit. Just the thought of it relaxes me."

Tony laughed. "Well, it's not so calm and peaceful now. We've been hit with a powerful storm that did plenty of damage, and right in the middle of that, we had a missing young mother—from Ogunquit—who was later found trapped in her car. We had an overpass collapse and she went down with it. But believe it or not, she's still alive!"

"Wow! That *is* unbelievable. I hope she makes it."

"Wait … it gets better—or worse, I should say. In the middle of that, some guy gets offed in his room at a newly renovated place, also in Ogunquit, The Admiral's Inn."

"Man, that's what I call trouble in River City. Ogunquit, yet?" He said it as though it were unimaginable for the charming seaside town where people from everywhere flocked to temporarily escape the horrors of the real world.

"Yes, Ogunquit," Tony reiterated. He didn't bother to get into the fact that they'd already had a murder only nineteen months ago. "And here's the kicker—what would you say if I told you I think the young mother—her name is Suzanne Oliveri—might have been the assailant? And oh, by the way, did I mention she got him with a butcher knife in the middle of his heart?"

"Holy shit!" And here I was thinking you guys were busy pulling cats out of trees or helping old ladies cross the street."

Tony's laugh was laced with good-natured sarcasm. "Yeah, right. Maine breeds only angels. Just keep in mind, wise guy, that the victim was a New York resident, and the suspect lived with him in your great big sour apple."

"Okay, truce. I know you're only pulling my chain like I'm pulling yours, but nobody calls my city a sour apple, okay?"

"My humble apologies," Tony said, half-kidding, half serious. "The whole country has a soft spot for New York. You guys are the ones who have to look at that hole in your skyline, although we all feel it—always will."

The memory of 9/11 silenced their banter and Tony cleared his throat to switch to business. "Look, Andy, here's what I need: See what you can dig up for me about the victim, Tyler Keaton." He provided the lieutenant with all the personal stats he'd need to investigate. "I particularly need to know if anyone knew the girl was pregnant and by whom."

Donovan sounded surprised. "You don't know that?"

"No, not for sure. All we know is she was pregnant when she returned to Ogunquit. She gave birth to a baby girl seven months later and refused to name the father. Just today we learned from her coworker that—and I'm quoting—'she swore up and down that Tyler was not the father.'"

"Sounds to me like the lady doth protest too much," Donovan said.

"I agree."

"Did she make any kind of statement?"

"Nah. She's out of it. Personally, I think she needs a miracle." Tony blew a breath. "Andy, see if you can find any friends Suzanne might have confided in. Anyone who might be able to fill in some blanks."

Donovan was silent for a moment. "I'm thinking of a young mom slicing into a guy with a butcher knife. Jeez! Did she really think she could get away with that? She must have had a hell of a motive!"

"She did. Assuming Keaton's the father, I don't think the guy knew he had a daughter."

"That's motive enough for me. Let me see what I can find out. I'll get back to you ASAP."

Chapter Twenty-three

After Frannie left for the hospital, Dan lingered awhile longer, talking with Glory and Alex. No one was optimistic about Suzanne's chances and looked ahead to Heather's fate—and Frannie's fate—should Suzanne die.

"Do you think Frannie would want to legally adopt the baby?" Dan asked his daughter.

"That's hard to say, Dad. To 'want' is one thing; to 'do' is another. I think she's already more attached to Heather than she realizes. For someone who jokingly says, 'I don't do babies,' you should see how affectionate and protective she is—"

"We've all witnessed that," Dan agreed. "She already has that maternal instinct, whether she wants it or not."

Seated next to Glory on the sofa, Alex took her hand and held it. "No one would disagree with that, but for Frannie to be tied down with a baby on a permanent basis … I don't know if she could handle it. She's a really busy lady, and ambitious. She has enough responsibilities now with the two Amore restaurants, and my guess is there are more in her future."

They tossed the subject around a few more minutes, but Dan noticed that Alex had never let go of Glory's hand. He suddenly felt in the way and stood up. "Glory, now that Alex is here to give you a hand, I'll get back to Louise. Needless to say, she offered to help you and Frannie in any way she can. So did your sisters and brother. Just give any one of us a call should you need us, okay?"

"No, it's okay, Dad. Thank them all for us. But for now we're in good shape." She kissed her father on the cheek and walked him to the door.

Alex waited until Dan pulled out of the driveway, then cupped her face in his hands. He gazed deep into her eyes for a long moment. "And how are you holding up, Glory? I'm worried about you. I know how you are—you'll try to be a rock for Frannie, and you'll hold all that tension inside."

"Don't waste your worries on me, Alex. I'm not fragile, like a piece of fine china. Between you, my father and my therapist, I've developed a tough skin. Once you've had a madman shove a gun in your face, it can't get much worse."

Although she said it with a forced smile, Alex cringed. It made him crazy every time he allowed the image to take shape, but Glory actually went through it. No, a lifetime of therapy couldn't possibly erase that horrific memory. He wished he had the power to help her forget, but all he could do was listen when she needed to talk about it. Maybe if she spit the memories out often enough, she could eventually expunge them all. Then maybe—just maybe—his love would help her heal.

A long shot, but possible.

He smothered her face with kisses—soft, gentle kisses, brushing her hair, her eyes, her mouth, her nose, her neck. A breath caught in her throat and she shivered when his fingers stroked her spine.

Glory broke away and placed both her hands on his chest to put distance between them. "Alex, I've missed you too, believe me, but ..." She widened her eyes and, with a forlorn look, extended a hand towards the bedroom where Heather slept.

"I know, I know ... That wasn't my intention at all. I just got carried away—as usual—once I had you in my arms." He raised his hands in surrender and sat down on the club chair. "If only you could shake all those other crazy thoughts out of your head and marry me. I told you, you'll never have to worry about me taking off on you like Jason did. That'll never happen, I promise."

"Oh, Alex, it's not that. Please … I know you've been patient, and God knows I *do* love you, but today especially, I can't think of my own problems. If Suzanne doesn't make it, that poor baby will never feel a mother's love." Her voice cracked as she said it. She hadn't been thinking of her own mother, but that face she missed so much flashed vividly in her mind. She looked at it every day in the two 5" x 7" framed photographs that hung on her bedroom wall; one of her mom with Steven English, the man she knew and loved as her father; and one of her mom with Dan Madison, the real father she had never known for thirty-five years. The photo was taken right here in Ogunquit at the Howard family's Ratherbee estate—Alex's family, all of whom were gone, and not all by natural causes.

Alex broke through her flashing memories with an ear-to-ear smile. "Sweetheart, you're absolutely right. This is not the time to discuss our own problems. Sometimes when I think about how much I love and need you, I can get pretty selfish and self-absorbed. What I should be doing is helping you and Frannie, any way I can. So c'mon, give me something useful to do." He crossed his arms and grinned playfully.

"Well, actually, Alex, since I have Heather now, I'd feel a lot better if you would go alone to check on the restaurants. Who knows what time Frannie will be back and in what condition? If the situation is bad, I won't be able to leave her and go with you."

"Fine. I should have thought about that myself." He shook his head and stood up, eager to help. "Too bad I didn't because I could have asked your dad to come along."

Glory dipped her head and gave him a sidelong glance. "I think my dad left abruptly in order to give us some time alone."

Alex raised a finger. "Ah! I knew I loved the guy for a reason." He kissed her again, long and lingering, tasting the sweetness of her mouth. Then he stood back and teased her. "See? I kept my hands in my pockets this time so I can get out of here."

Glory laughed and teased him back. "I'm not so sure that's where I want them, but for now, keep them warm until I can put them to better use." She handed him his jacket, then patted him on the behind to send him on his way.

She stood at the window when he left, watching the rivulets of rain creating silvery scallops on the glass and listening to their lulling sounds. But last night their raging sounds were so terrifying, they filled her now with ominous thoughts. She compared them to all the maniacal people in the world. Monstrous leaders whose insanity caused and continue to cause the death of millions. Like the quiet drizzle of rain compared to a violent storm, those mass murderers had once been angelic newborn babies, sucking innocently at their mothers' breasts. If we could have known, could we somehow have suffocated their rage?

Glory sighed. *Ludicrous*, she thought. As if we mortals could predict the future.

She shivered and rubbed her arms, waiting for the sun to break through again and warm her, both mentally and physically. The house was chilly and quiet—too quiet. She wondered how long it would take to hear from Frannie. An hour at least, allowing the drive to Portland and the chance to speak to a doctor.

And that's if Suzanne is still alive. The thought alone chilled her and goose bumps roughened her skin. She pulled Frannie's small blanket off the sofa and tossed it around her shoulders. If only Heather would wake up, she thought. One smile from that precious baby could snap anyone out of a dark mood.

And then, without warning, Glory's eyes filled with tears. She let them go and cried aloud without really knowing what triggered the outburst. Heather? Suzanne? Jason? The loss of her parents? The thirty-five years she'd lost with Dan, her real father? Or was it still the flashbacks of that night in hell with Carl Duca?

Maybe all of the above.

Maybe Alex was right. Maybe Jason's betrayal had scarred her so that she was afraid to plunge into marriage again. Was that it?

Or was it all about Alex? Was he the crux of her indecisiveness? Why had she refused to set a date to marry him? She loved him, no question about that, even though it had surprised her as well. After loving Jason so completely for twelve years, she never would have believed she could fall for someone else so hard and so soon after their divorce. So why was she making excuse after excuse to stall the wedding?

For a half-hour she listened to the quiet, stared out the window. The raindrops had diminished—first to a faint drizzle, and then nothing more than a mist.

The phone never rang. She held it in her hand and shook it, as though she could will it to ring. "C'mon, Frannie, call me … tell me she's okay; tell me Heather won't lose her mom."

Then came the racking sobs that shook her shoulders, releasing a flood of tears. It was as if she had broken through a brick wall in her mind, releasing all the emotions she had locked away. And ironically, it was Heather, the most innocent of all, whose only communication was an occasional smile or a clutch of your finger. Holding her so often since last night had brought that brick wall down spilling out all those pent-up feelings. Two years after they were married, she and Jason decided to begin a family. But after a year of disappointment, she finally convinced him that they should both be tested. She was devastated to learn that Jason's weak sperm sharply reduced their chances. She was equally devastated to witness his indifferent attitude. He shrugged it off as though it were some event they might have enjoyed, but no big deal if they missed.

Now, in two more months, she would be thirty-seven. Although lots of women have babies later these days, she was well aware that having a first baby at her age added certain risks. After the first crushing blow when she learned it was practically impossible for her and Jason, time and a successful career as a food columnist had clouded over that longing for a child.

That was until she held Heather in her arms and all those old feelings surfaced. She knew now that she'd be willing to take the risk. Thousands of women my age give birth to their first babies, she reasoned.

But the real reason she had put off marrying Alex had also surfaced.

Alex didn't want children. He had made that clear several times and she had listened and accepted. Everything he had said made sense, she had to admit. Alex was forty-nine now, so much older than she, and much too old to become a first-time father. At his age, he should be a grandfather, not a father. It would be selfish to start raising a family at his age. It wouldn't be fair to the child or children, he'd said.

Glory could come up with no defense to Alex's argument. He was absolutely right and she had decided to once again throw herself into her work. Between her food column and managing Amore Evenings, she had plenty to keep her busy.

That's what she kept saying to convince herself that becoming parents was out of the question for her and Alex.

Heather's little fingers wrapped around her pinky told her otherwise.

Chapter Twenty-four

Frannie had thought—and certainly hoped—no other stressful situation would ever compare to the night Carl abducted Glory and the kids.

But she was wrong. Waiting through Suzanne's surgery had paralleled that horrific night.

Her cousin's condition was critical when they wheeled her into that operating room, but there were no other options. Without immediate surgery, Suzanne would not survive.

While Frannie and her uncle sat and waited, barely talking, a team of doctors and nurses worked tirelessly, under Dr. Quinlan's watchful eyes, to save Suzanne's life. Six agonizing hours later, Dr. Quinlan walked into the waiting room specifically provided for families of surgical patients. Frannie stood up first and got a strong grip on her uncle's arm. Just in case. She lifted her eyes to meet the doctor's gaze. Her stomach plummeted at the thought of what he might say.

Dr. Quinlan pulled off his green surgical cap and spoke directly to Jerry. "Mr. Oliveri, your daughter came through the surgery very well, considering the extent of her injuries. For a while it was touch and go." He made the could-go-either-way gesture with his hand. "That's not to say she's out of the woods yet—we're a long way from that, but her age and general physical condition are in her favor."

Frannie hadn't intended to interrupt, but she impulsively tugged at her uncle's arm. "See? I told you her age was in her favor," she said to him, then apologized to the doctor for interrupting. "How soon can we see her, Doctor?"

Jerry cut in before Dr. Quinlan could respond. "I'm more interested in knowing what to expect, Doc. Is she gonna come out of this okay? And how long will her recuperation take?"

Dr. Quinlan gave him a thin-lipped smile with cautious overtones. "I'm not God, Mr. Oliveri. It's much too early to tell. I'm sure you're aware that occasionally even when the surgery is successful, complications can occur. But we'll be watching her very carefully. You can count on that."

"What kind of complications, Doctor? Can you tell us?" Frannie asked.

"Well, for instance, Suzanne lost a lot of blood. That presents the danger of hypovolemic shock. That's primarily why she's being sent to ICU. This type of surgery also runs the risk of seizures, but let's not worry about anything that may never materialize. As I said, she'll be monitored very, very carefully here. I'm sure you're familiar with this hospital's excellent reputation. Suzanne is in good hands." With a squeeze of Jerry's hand, he sealed his words of assurance.

"Just one more question, Doc," Jerry said, still visibly shaking. "When will she come out of the anesthesia? Will she be able to talk to us a little?"

Dr. Quinlan inhaled and exhaled quickly, then shook his head. "That will be awhile, I'm afraid. Suzanne had to be put in what we call a medically-induced coma." The doctor saw four eyes widen simultaneously. He put a hand up. "Now, wait. Don't let the words frighten you. Let me explain. In the presence of severe head injury, this procedure is done basically to allow the brain to heal."

"How long does this medically-induced coma last, Doctor?" Frannie asked.

"Usually between one and two weeks. Family will be allowed brief visits, but don't expect a response for a while, okay?"

"Thank you, Doctor. Yes, we understand. Thanks for everything you've done for my cousin and for being so patient with our questions."

Dr. Quinlan gave her a mock salute and a wide smile. "It's what we do here. Feel free to contact my office whenever you need to. I'll return your call as soon as I can."

Her uncle was so shaken up after the doctor left that Frannie couldn't be sure of its cause. Relief perhaps? The culmination of all these tense hours? Or was it all those hours without a drink? If he got through a trauma like this without one, maybe there's hope?

For Suzanne's sake and for Heather's sake, she liked to think positively. One thing that was glaringly noticeable all these quiet hours—her uncle Jerry hadn't cursed or snarled or shown the slightest trace of anger.

"C'mon, Uncle Jerry. You must be starving. And so am I. Let's go down to the cafeteria. My treat."

Her uncle nodded and for a split-second she could have sworn she saw a hint of a smile. It may be short-lived, Frannie thought, but for now she considered it a hopeful sign.

Chapter Twenty-five

When Frannie arrived at 6:30 a.m. for Amore Breakfast's opening day, Tess Oliveri's car was already parked. *Ah, mothers,* she thought with a proud grin on her face, *what would we do without them?*

She unlocked the seat belt and pulled Heather's infant seat out of her Volvo. This was day one of running a nonstop business where the boss never got to sit down and rest her aching feet or enjoy her own breakfast while it was still hot.

But Frannie wasn't complaining; she loved every crazy busy minute. She loved seeing old friends again, both year-round residents and tourists who came back to Ogunquit again and again. Now, even though Tess was here to help, she had no idea how she could run her business and take care of a baby. She certainly couldn't tie up her mother's time, from 6:30 a.m. to 2:30 p.m., seven days a week.

"How's it going, guys?" she called out to her kitchen staff.

"Bring the baby over, Frannie," one of them called out. "We're dying to see her."

But her mother's arms were already outstretched to welcome little Heather. "First come see how nicely your father and I set up her crib and dressing table in your office. I bought her a beautiful baby comforter with matching bumpers."

Frannie laughed and teased her mother. "I love your enthusiasm, Mom, but I hope you still have that energy by closing time. Heather's a good baby, but a lot of work. I think you'll be looking to steal a nap in that crib yourself."

"You don't have to tell me that. I raised two babies myself, remember?"

"Sure, when you were in your twenties, Mom."

Tess waved off her daughter's playful warning. "Ah, I can handle it. I'm not over the hill yet."

Amore Breakfast was only into its first hour of business and already she had to tell people they'd have at least a half-hour wait.

"I'll take a counter seat whenever it's available," a man's voice said over her shoulder.

"Name, please?" Frannie asked, her eyes fixed on her clipboard.

"Steve …Steve Lynch."

Frannie's eyes lit up and she instinctively hugged her old friend from California. "Steve, what a surprise! When did you get in? How long will you be here this time?"

"A week—ten days, maybe a little longer. But I'll be back in July to stay the whole summer."

"Wonderful!" she said, then glanced around and gave him a forlorn look. "Gee, I'd love to talk to you but …" She finished with a shrug that said it all.

"Not to worry. I'll eat now and come back later when you're ready to close. I heard bits and pieces about what's been happening in your life. I'm shocked and so, so, sorry. I'd like to hear from you how things are going. Will you have time for me?"

"For you, Steve, even if I didn't have time, I'd make time. You're on my top ten list of nice guys."

Steve gave her another quick hug. "The feeling is absolutely, positively mutual," he answered. "Now let me get out of your way. I'll grab a mug of coffee and go sit on the porch. I'll chew someone else's ears off for a while."

"No one would object to your company, Steve. Even if they don't feel like talking to a stranger, you'll wow them with your 24-karat smile."

*   *   *

Hours later, after Amore's staff had served 375 breakfasts, Frannie took time out to enjoy waffles and blueberries while talking to her friend. "Did you give someone your order, Steve?"

"Are you serious? After that huge Crack o' Dawn omelet I had here this morning, I'm good until dinner."

"So you're going to sit here and watch me stuff myself?"

His gaze darted to the display case adjacent to the counter seats. "Well, I've had my eye on that Morning Glory muffin. I tasted it the last time I was here and even that was outrageously delicious, so I can't resist."

"Good choice," Frannie said and asked one of the waitresses to bring him one.

Steve bit into the moist muffin, then examined it as though he had to see what ingredient made it taste that good. "Now tell me how your cousin is and how you're doing with the baby," he said. "Where is the baby, by the way? I'd love to see her."

"My mom took her for a stroll along Shore Road. She wanted to sit by the water at Perkins Cove since the weather is so great today. Heather is a happy baby, thank God. Otherwise I don't know how I'd manage. Like today, for instance, I'll take the baby home when I close up here so my mom can have a break. But then tonight, she and my dad are sitting again so I can go to Portland and check on Suzanne at the hospital. From there I'll go straight to Amore Evenings. Tonight's our season opening there, too."

Steve threw her a look under wrinkled brows. Half admiration, half concern. "Gee, Frannie, I hope you don't intend to keep up that pace every day. I don't mean to sound insensitive, but last I heard Suzanne is still in a coma. Do you have to go every day? And Amore Evenings, too—can't Glory handle that without you for a while?"

Frannie scooped up the last of the tiny blueberries in her dish and held the spoon in midair. "In answer to your first question, I don't *have* to go every day, but I do. I'd only be restless worrying about what's going on anyway. And besides, I drive my uncle there." She paused to swallow the spoonful of blueberries. "As far as Amore Evenings is concerned, yes, Glory can manage alone, but it does get mobbed at times. She really needs my help. The place is half mine anyway, so I *should* help."

"I'm sure she understands your situation," Steve offered.

"She does. And she helps me too—big time."

"And what do the doctors say about Suzanne? Are they optimistic?"

Frannie tipped her head. "If all goes well, they anticipate she'll come out of the coma in a week or so. But so many things can happen, it's scary."

Steve had begun to say something but was stopped by the sound of Frannie's cell. She answered it and listened to the caller. Her face grew taut. "I'll leave now. Thank you," she said, then turned to Steve. "I'm sorry. I have to go. Suzanne had a seizure."

Chapter Twenty-six

For the first time in his law enforcement career, Tony dreaded pursuing an arrest. He had known from the beginning that crime lab results would bring him to this point. He had hoped for the long shot chance that the hairs found in the bed, and between the deceased's fingers, belonged to some other woman. But from the moment he learned they had been lovers—had lived together in New York—there was little room for doubt. Several of the hairs were found to be root hairs, consistent with head hairs. In all probability they were yanked out in the heat of passion.

And root hairs, unlike all others, can provide full DNA.

And yet, there was still the slightest chance she could rise above suspicion. All that had been established with the hair samples was the fact that she had been present at the scene. That didn't prove she killed the guy.

But that hope for her innocence was short-lived. Prints found in the pooled blood at the scene had later been identified as Suzanne's. That moved her from suspected lover to suspected murderer with bullet-like speed. She'd need a hell of a good lawyer to explain that one—not that it hadn't been done before.

He did not look forward to Suzanne's arrest. Nor did he look forward to notifying Frannie and her uncle that her case would be presented to a grand jury for indictment. If he thought it would ease the blow, when that day comes, he'd like to tell them this made him feel more like a snake than a detective doing what he had pledged to do; that at times like this he hated his job; that justice and the law don't always move in the same direction. But in the end he would tell them that all evidence points directly at Suzanne. The Attorney General's Office would have no problem getting the indictment and ultimately winning their case. *Chalk up another one, guys.*

But then, you never know, Tony thought, thinking back to other cases that had looked like slam dunks for the prosecutor but ended up with a not guilty verdict.

Chapter Twenty-seven

Frannie wanted to run up the stairs rather than wait for the elevator to make all its stops, but considering her uncle's physical condition, she doubted he would survive climbing four flights of stairs.

She hoped that Dr. Quinlan was still in the hospital so they could have him paged, but she breathed a sigh of relief when she spotted him at the nurses' station.

The doctor saw their anxious faces coming towards him. "We have her under control now. It's okay."

"What happened, Doctor?" Frannie asked.

"She had a seizure. It's a common problem with comatose patients. I put her on Dilantin, which is an effective drug to control seizures. Most patients respond well to it, so let's hope Suzanne does, too."

Jerry pointed a finger at the doctor, as though he'd follow up with a threat. "And what if she doesn't?"

Frannie grabbed his finger and held it tight. "Uncle Jerry, *please try to stay calm,*" she said, fighting the urge to scream at him. "Let the doctor finish talking."

Dr. Quinlan waved it off. "That's okay. He's upset. I understand." He turned to Jerry and lowered his voice. "Mr. Oliveri, I was about to explain that we're sending Suzanne for an MRI of her brain to determine the cause of the seizure. In some instances, when a patient has several seizures, additional surgery is required, but right now that's not the case for Suzanne."

"And the test will tell us all that, right?" Frannie asked.

"Yes."

Frannie continued her questions. "When will she get the MRI and when will we know the results? If she needs another surgical procedure, do you anticipate any problems?"

Dr. Quinlan smiled and raised his eyes to heaven. He answered slowly, spacing his words for clarity. "I don't anticipate problems, but that doesn't mean we won't encounter any. We're scheduling the MRI now. She'll probably have it done within the next hour or two. And you won't have to wait. We'll have the results as soon as the test is completed."

"And why did she have this seizure?" Jerry asked, his accusatory finger pointed again. "Is this because you guys fooled around and put her in a coma?"

"Uncle Jerry, stop it!" Frannie's embarrassment overwhelmed her. "How can you talk to the doctor like that? He's doing everything he can to help Suzanne. Are you crazy?"

With one empathetic look to Frannie, Dr. Quinlan excused himself and walked away briskly.

In the waiting room, Frannie ignored her uncle. There were other people sitting there watching CNN and she wasn't about to start arguing with him. He'd obviously been drinking again. She thought she picked up the scent when he got in her car. It was stupid to think he could stop abruptly and stay off it. Not without help. She couldn't imagine him agreeing to attend Alcoholics Anonymous meetings, but without them, he doesn't stand a chance.

She sat there with her arms crossed, her eyes fixed on the TV screen. Her uncle skipped three chairs and assumed the same position.

Two hours passed and still no word.

Finally, Dr. Quinlan came walking towards them. Her uncle had dozed off and she decided not to wake him. "What happened, Doctor? Do you have the results yet?"

"The test wasn't done yet, I'm afraid." He paused. "Perhaps you'd better get your uncle. He'll probably get angry if you leave him out."

Frannie blew a defeated sigh. "Doctor, when he's drinking—which is most of the time—*anything* makes him angry."

When she shook her uncle's arm, he woke up startled and frightened. His hands covered his face protectively. As he approached the doctor, his mood was passive, dulled by sleep.

"Mr. Oliveri, your daughter has had several seizures since we last spoke. She has a condition called status epilepticus, which is extremely serious if not controlled."

Jerry's eyes were suddenly alert. "What are you saying, that she could die?"

"That's what we're trying to avoid. We've had to sedate her heavily. She's being brought in for the MRI as we speak, and I've also ordered an EEG, a brain wave test."

"Does that mean you have to do that other surgery?"

"Not if we don't have to. We're hopeful that once we find the cause, we can control her seizures with medication."

"Thank you, Doctor. I guess I'd better call my mom. She had offered to stay overnight for Suzanne's baby. I didn't want her to, but now I guess she has no choice."

Dr. Quinlan shook his head sympathetically. "This is tough for you. I'm sorry. And don't you have a business, too—a restaurant?"

Frannie gave him a rueful smile. "Two of them. And they both opened for the season today. Yes, it is tough. I can't be everywhere at the same time ... but hey, you're a busy man. Go, Doctor," she said with a wave of her hand, "let us know the minute you have the results of the MRI."

"Absolutely. Take care."

Jerry sliced the air with an arm. "What are you complaining about? My daughter's the one with the troubles, not you!"

Is that the same daughter you called a whore last week? Those were the words she wanted to scream at him but she bit down on her lips instead.

Chapter Twenty-eight

Sara Baisley pulled out a chair and sat next to her boss. "Man, this was one heck of a night. I barely had time for a bathroom break."

Glory gave her an understanding smile and a *hang-in-there* squeeze on the arm. "Look on the bright side. If tonight was a sample of what lies ahead for Amore Evenings, we'll all be sitting pretty."

Sara yanked out a wad of bills and held it up proudly like a trophy. "You can say that again. If Tim and I do as well with tips this season as we did last year, we'll not only be able to finish college without a cash flow problem, but we can stash some away, too."

Pride and affection filled Glory as she watched Sara's delighted expression. She and Tim were a pleasure to watch. Both nineteen years old and deeply in love, they had much to look forward to and were truly each other's best friend. More importantly, they appreciated everything and took nothing for granted. Glory and the teenage couple had formed an unbreakable bond when they nearly died together at the hands of a twisted mind gone mad. Carl Duca had come within a hairsbreadth of savagely killing all of them.

Tim came out of the kitchen with a triumphant smile. He gave Glory and Sara a thumbs-up gesture, then reached across the table to shake Glory's hand. "Hey, congratulations, boss lady. What a night! Did we break any of last year's records?"

"Could be. We'll soon find out. Alex is in the office tallying up the receipts. Thank God we had him here tonight because I totally panicked when I heard Frannie couldn't be here." Her contented smile faded to sadness. "I feel so bad that she had to miss tonight's opening. We were both so excited about it."

"Have you heard from her again since she called about the seizure?" Sara asked.

"No, she said she'd call when they get the results of the MRI."

The gentleman in charge of the cleaning crew interrupted their conversation. "Excuse me, Miss English, but I think we're about done. If you'd like to check around before we leave to see if there's anything else you need ..."

Glory smiled at the elderly man. "No, thank you, Eddie. After last season, you've already proved your worth. I'm sure everything's fine."

Eddie took a moment to ask Glory about Frannie and Suzanne. As she briefed him and thanked him for his concern, Alex walked towards them, beaming. He presented Glory with the ledger book. "Take a look. The total will knock your socks off. And can you imagine if you didn't have to turn all those people away?"

With his hands, Tim shaped a megaphone around his mouth and mimicked an auctioneer. "Amore Three! Do I hear an Amore Three?"

Everyone laughed, basking in the euphoria until Glory's phone rang. "It's Frannie," she announced and wagged a finger. Everyone fell silent. "What's up?" she asked when she picked up.

"No, nothing bad. I just wanted to catch you so you wouldn't worry needlessly. Suzanne is pretty much stabilized and I'm exhausted. I've got to get my uncle home."

"How's he been behaving through all this?"

"Sometimes he looks like a lost soul, pathetic, and sometimes he goes a little nuts, to put it mildly, like he did tonight. The staff here politely *suggested* that we leave and get some rest. Anyway, I spoke to my dad and he's going to meet us at my uncle's house. He'll stay with him for the night."

Glory grimaced, listening. "Oh, your poor father."

"Yes, I don't like the idea either, but he can handle him better than I can. As long as it doesn't become an ongoing burden for my dad. But today with the seizure on top of everything else, it's been rough on my uncle. He tries not to show it, but I can imagine what's going through his head. Who knows what's in store for Suzanne now? I'm really worried. It's a nightmare ..."

Glory hesitated, then asked, "You don't think they'll try to connect her with this murder, do you? Just because she knew the guy—"

"Glory, she didn't just *know* the guy. She *lived* with him. All you have to do is count on your fingers, it's easy to figure out he was Heather's father. The father she refused to name. No question about it—I smell serious trouble. Once the police found out she lived with him in New York, the dots were connected. That's why I put the call in to Bill Franklin. I should have called him right from the start, but I didn't want it to look like her own family thought she'd need a criminal defense lawyer."

"You haven't heard from him yet, right?"

"Not yet. But I'm sure I will as soon as he checks his messages. Right now there's no immediate urgency, as far as I can see. While she's still in a coma, the police can't question her. And even if she comes out of it tonight, Dr. Quinlan would never allow her to be questioned that soon."

"Yeah, that makes sense," Glory said, then brightened her tone. "So, okay. I'll come down to Amore Breakfast in the early afternoon when it calms down and we can talk, okay?"

"Fine."

"Frannie, wait. I feel so awful for you. How can I help? Do you want me to stay at your house tonight? At least I can get up for Heather so you can get a few hours of uninterrupted sleep."

"No, I'll manage. Stay with Alex. You'll have enough to handle with Amore Evenings, especially with the weekend crowd."

"True, but at least I don't start at 6:30 in the morning."

"Glory, don't—I'm too drained to argue—more mentally than physically. Just tell me quickly before my uncle comes out of the bathroom—did everything go okay tonight? I wanted so much to be there, for your sake and mine."

"Well, don't waste your worries on me. We did fine. We were jammed all night, but thanks to your training, everything went smoothly. Now that Alex is here, he's a big help, so don't worry about Amore Evenings for a while. You have enough to handle."

In one way it was a relief for Frannie to know Alex could help Glory manage Amore Evenings. With this Suzanne nightmare going on, she could use the breathing room. But a part of her didn't want Alex stepping into her shoes. The restaurant was half hers and she didn't want it slipping out of her control. This was the feeling that had haunted Frannie when she and Glory had begun their partnership.

She swept the thought out of her mind, dismissing it as totally insignificant. Isn't it strange, she thought, how quickly some problems dissipate in the face of a *monumental* one.

Chapter Twenty-nine

Tony had just stepped out of the shower when his doorbell rang. Ten at night was not a time for casual callers. On second thought, he could not recall a single instance when friends or family stopped by without calling first.

He checked from his bedroom window to see who was at his front door.

Corrine.

He let the towel pool at his feet, didn't bother with underwear, and slipped into sweatpants.

Barechested, he opened the front door and stared at her for a moment. Once he opened that storm door to let her in, he knew what would happen. But she was here; she had made the first move.

Corrine opened the outer door herself. "Well, don't just stand there. It's freezing out here!"

When she stepped inside, Tony resisted the urge to take her in his arms and forget the argument that had destroyed their relationship two months ago. But in the morning it would still weigh heavily on his heart and mind.

"I'm sorry to stop in unexpected like this," she began, her voice softened, "but it was an impulsive decision. I heard you were feeling lousy about the Keaton murder case and its connection to Suzanne Oliveri. I wouldn't want to make that arrest either."

"It's not only because of my friendship with Frannie—it's the baby, and Suzanne herself. She's had a tough life since her mother died. I'm still hoping something will clear her, but it doesn't look good." He turned towards the kitchen. "C'mon, I'll make us a cup of decaf."

They each took a stool on opposite sides of his kitchen counter to play it safe for as long as they could resist touching each other. Their relationship was fraught with problems, the last one a culmination of many. They needed to talk. They had a lot more obstacles between them than a kitchen counter.

"How is she? Frannie, I mean."

Tony shrugged. "Not good. The lab results shocked the hell out of her. But compared to her uncle—Suzanne's father—well, let's say he went crazy when he heard. Frannie tried to calm him down. Not that she was successful ..."

"He's a longtime boozer, though, so I can imagine how he reacted." She went palms up and glanced sideways, as if to say she was glad she hadn't witnessed it. "And he wasn't exactly a model father, I hear."

"I think that's part of the reason he's taking it so bad. Guilt for turning his back on her for years. As far as Frannie is concerned, though, she's an intelligent, level-headed woman. If I have to arrest her cousin, I think she'll realize— after the shock settles—that I had no choice." He paused for a moment to convince himself, then forced a smile. "Not that I expect her to send me roses..." He sipped his coffee and continued to avoid Corrine's eyes. He was melting fast and the hot coffee had nothing to do with it.

Corrine kept her gaze lowered and her hands occupied by making pleats in a paper napkin. "So what do you think, Tony? Any chance Suzanne will come out of this?"

"Out of the coma or a murder charge?"

"Both, I guess."

"Her doctors are optimistic about her recovery—we didn't get into how long and if she'll recover a hundred percent. So often there are unforeseen residual damages, that no one knows anything for sure at this point."

Corrine frowned and shook her head. "But God, think about what she'll wake up to—being a prime suspect for murder. In a way she's better off in the coma. Ignorance is bliss."

"If she killed the guy, it'll be no surprise."

"And you're convinced she did it, aren't you, Tony? Not that I can blame you. The stupid girl left so much evidence. To me, it sounds like your classic case of a crime of passion. The killer is blinded and driven by revenge. He— or in this case, she—becomes so obsessed with the need to avenge her lover's betrayal that only his death can satisfy that obsession."

Tony made no comment. His sips at the coffee mug filled the silence.

Corrine looked him in the eyes and gave him an uneasy smile. "I don't have to worry about you going nuts like that, do I?"

A smile curled the corners of his mouth. "For a cop, you watch too many movies. That's an unfair analogy."

She rolled her eyes upward. "Tony, I didn't mean for you to take me literally. It took a lot for me to shake off what happened between us and come here like a puppy dog, so cut me some slack, okay?"

Tony arched a brow. "I did. I let you in, didn't I?"

Corrine reached across the counter to slap him but he caught her hand in mid-air. "I don't know why I bother with an arrogant bastard like you! Who the hell do you think you are? I didn't come here to kiss your feet. I just thought we might be able to talk like normal people, but I—"

She never got to finish her sentence. Acting on impulse, Tony slipped off his stool and pulled her in his arms. His mouth never gave her a chance to say anything more.

*   *   *

Hours later, when the fire between them had finally burned out, Corrine propped herself up on one elbow and played with the hairs on his chest. "So now what? Do we put everything behind us like it never happened? Is that possible, Tony?"

Tony drew a long, deep breath and took a pensive moment. He put her head back down on his chest and stroked her hair. "Truthfully? To be honest, Corrine, I'm not sure. I wish it were possible to completely forget, like it never happened, because I sure as hell do love you—"

"And I love *you*, Tony. That's why this is all so crazy—"

He put a hand gently over her mouth. "Stop. Let me finish. I was hurting so bad—so disappointed in you. Maybe if you had told me first ..."

She sat upright and crossed her arms. "Oh, yeah, right! Like you would have given me your permission!"

"Corrine, when you're engaged to marry someone, you don't go sneaking off with an old boyfriend on a date!" Just thinking about it started Tony's blood boiling again.

"I told you, it wasn't a *date*! I hadn't seen him in years. Our lives are miles apart, but he was only passing through Ogunquit on business and wanted to say hello to an old friend. What's wrong with that?"

"Not a thing," he said sarcastically. "Just your typical traveling salesman story."

Corrine got out of bed and started to dress. "You know, I give up. You just insist on making something out of

128

nothing." She snapped her jeans and lashed out at him. "What was I supposed to do, say, 'sorry, but I have a jealous boyfriend, so hello, goodbye and good luck'?"

"No, but how about, 'sure, I'd love to see you. I'll bring Tony along so you can meet the guy I'm going to marry.'"

"Oh, give me a break! Like that could have been a nice, cozy congenial evening."

"It could have been unless you and your old lover boy needed privacy to reminisce."

"That's exactly what we wanted to do—catch up on our lives and talk about old friends, but you had to make something ugly out of it." She was fully dressed now and still blowing off steam while he remained in bed with his arms crossed under his head. "You know what your problem is, Tony? You've been a cop too long. You're too damn cynical. Instead of seeing everyone innocent until proven guilty, you're ready to crucify them unless and until they can prove to you they're innocent. Well, honey," she said, the term of endearment devoid of affection, "I'm not about to about to kiss your ass and beg your forgiveness when I didn't do a damn thing wrong!"

Tony was still in bed, staring at the ceiling in the same position, when he heard his front door slam and the roar of her car engine. He remembered every stinging word she said and probably always would.

Corrine had swallowed her pride—big time—to ring his doorbell tonight. As angry as he was these past two months, the anger couldn't overcome the love. He had tried so hard to keep visualizing and remembering the shock of seeing her with him drinking and laughing in that restaurant. Surely the memory would destroy his painful feelings, he thought. But nothing worked. And yet, although he had ached for her every minute of every day, he never made a move to reconcile their differences.

But she had. It takes a special kind of love to do that, he realized.

And you blew it, Detective Sergeant Anthony Gerard, a/k/a Jackass.

Chapter Thirty

Glory's luxury apartment, conveniently located above Amore Evenings, had been designed to offer the ultimate in comfort and tranquility.

Ironically, it had been designed by Carl Duca.

The thought entered her mind often enough but Glory had taught herself not to entertain it. Carl Duca, the building contractor with the comedic flair who differed sharply from Carl Duca, the deranged killer.

She sank into the plushy sofa, put her feet up on the ottoman, and rubbed at the soreness. Alex was suddenly there. He brushed her hands away and massaged her feet. "Better now?" he asked after awhile.

Glory's eyes were closed, her head thrown back relaxing from the foot rub. "Much better," she said, then reached for his hands. "Come, sit next to me. I need to cuddle. You know how I love to lean my head on your shoulder."

Alex gladly complied with her request. One hand went around and rested on her shoulder and the other tipped her head against his chest.

They sat that way for a few minutes, drinking in the quiet intimate pleasure. He kissed her forehead. "I couldn't wait to get my arms around you tonight."

"And I couldn't wait to get in this position."

"I can think of a better one," he said and nibbled on her ear. "I hope you're not going to tell me you're too tired."

Glory laughed and kissed the tip of his nose. "Now why would I say that?" she teased. "We're not even married yet."

He pulled away slightly, his smile washed away. "That was a poor choice of words, sweetheart. You know that's my sore spot." He tried for another playful smile, but the mood had passed. "I'm pushing fifty. Time is not on my side."

Glory resisted the urge to say, *Why should it matter? You don't plan to have children.* Instead she said, "Oh, stop it. You just turned forty-nine. Don't age yourself."

Alex threw his hands out. "Oh, so big deal. Fifty is one whole year away." He turned to her and searched her eyes. "You know what I mean, Glory. I want you with me every day and every night. At our ages, the way we're living is ridiculous and you know it. Putting on this pretense because of your father's archaic ideals—"

Glory sat up and squared her shoulders. "Now wait a minute, Alex. Now you're touching *my* sore spot. My father may be old fashioned to you, but that doesn't make him wrong. Don't fault him for believing in family values and tradition. There was a time, if you'll recall, when living together was unheard of unless you were married. And frankly, Alex, I don't like the condescending tone I hear when you talk about my father."

Alex's old anger flared. *"What* condescending tone? Hey, I may not always agree with his attitudes, but I like the guy and I respect him. But still—I don't have to agree with him. He's entitled to his opinion and I'm entitled to mine. I do admit, though, that I don't like when his attitude affects your decisions when I know damn well that your attitudes were once the same as mine. That was before your father came into the picture."

Glory's mouth fell open. She stared at him in disbelief. "So that's what this is all about—you're actually jealous of my father! How can you say you like him and respect him when what you're really feeling is jealousy?"

He stood up and pointed an accusing finger at her. "Okay, so if you want to label what I feel as jealousy, fine. But I have one question and I want the truth: Before you got so chummy with your father, weren't we planning to get married and wasn't I going to leave New Jersey and move in with you until the wedding?"

Glory was silenced by his flare-up. This was the most blatant display of temper she had ever witnessed. Remembering the old stories, it scared her.

He slammed a hand down on her coffee table. "Answer me! Weren't those our plans?"

"Yes, Alex. I admit they were, but right now those plans are past tense."

Chapter Thirty-one

For the first time since Amore Breakfast opened for business, Frannie didn't want to be there. She had dragged herself out of bed this morning after only a few hours sleep and couldn't imagine how she'd get through the day.

For most tourists who didn't know her heartaches, how could she make conversation with them—wear a smile bright as a neon sign and pretend not a blessed thing was wrong? And for the locals—her friends who would offer her support and sympathy—how could she stay dry-eyed?

News of Suzanne's involvement with the murder victim was plastered across the morning newspapers along with photos of both Suzanne Oliveri, a prime suspect, and Frances Oliveri, the benevolent cousin who opened her home and heart to care for the infant daughter of the alleged murderer. And who just happened to be cousin to Carl Duca, the man who drowned Paula Howard, a helpless Alzheimer's victim.

What a story!

Admittedly, years ago, the part of Frannie that had once yearned to be a reporter, would have loved writing up a story like this. She would have salivated over every juicy detail. *Who ever dreamed I'd be mixed up with murder, not once, but twice!* She gave her head a good shake just in case it *was* a dream and she could breathe a sigh of relief. No such chance.

When she walked into Amore Breakfast, Frannie was surprised to see Glory working with the kitchen staff. "What the heck are you doing here at this unearthly hour?"

Glory scrunched her face, waiting for an amiable scolding. "Dicing vegetables?" she offered, as though she needed a valid excuse to be there.

Frannie gave her a slanted *you're-hopeless* smile. Her question had been rhetorical; the moment she saw Glory she knew why she had come.

"Where's the baby? Why didn't you bring her?"

"She was still sleeping and since my mom had slept over last night, she told me to leave her. She'll bring Heather in later."

Frannie busied herself with the routine tasks of setting up Amore Breakfast's business for the day, trying not to get on the subject of Suzanne's possible arrest. But she could feel Glory's eyes boring down on her from behind the partition that separated the dining room from the kitchen. She put a hand up to ward off her questions. "Not now, Glory. You know as well as I that in fifteen or twenty minutes we'll have every table occupied and a full-page waiting list."

Glory came around to the counter where Frannie pretended to focus on an invoice from yesterday's mail. Her gaze remained fixed on the sheet of paper. "Don't start, Glory. I know you mean well—you want to help, but this horror is so overwhelming it's choking me." She grabbed at her throat as though she could purge it out, then pushed the papers aside. "I'm sorry, friend," she said, patting Glory's hand. "I didn't mean to bite your head off."

"Hey, forget it. I'm not that sensitive. You can vent your fears and frustrations on me anytime. When you're ready to spill it all out, I'm here—or a phone call away."

Glory's smile of assurance comforted Frannie and she smiled back. "See? You always say I've got it all together; I'm totally in control. Look at me now. I'm not as unbreakable as you think. This situation is killing me." Her hands and gaze flew upward, as if she were pleading to God for help. "Suzanne may be a scatterbrain, but I don't care what forensic crap they have—my cousin is no killer!"

Glory sighed, searching for comforting words. "There has to be some explanation…"

"I'm sure there is, but she's laying there dead to the world—can't say a word to defend herself—and they're going to throw the book at her!"

Two cars pulled into Amore Breakfast's driveway and Frannie instantly pulled herself together to greet her first customers. An unexpected smile crossed her face and it felt good to be temporarily cocooned in the safe familiarity of Amore Breakfast.

She spoke pleasantly with the customers as she seated them, handed them menus, and introduced them to Donna, their waitress. Glory had returned to the kitchen and Frannie went directly to her. She pulled the string to untie her Amore apron, the gesture meant to chase Glory out of the kitchen. "Go home and relax, or do whatever you have to do. You'll be on your feet all night. You don't have to waste your energy here. Besides, I'm sure Alex wants to spend some private time with you. You know how I feel about that—I don't want him to build any resentment towards me for unnecessarily monopolizing you."

Like he resents my father, Glory thought, but this was no time to get into that shocking revelation. "That'll never happen, Frannie. Don't worry. Alex is not in my apartment waiting for me."

The tone in Glory's voice instantly alerted Frannie. She curled her brows in question. "Why? What's going on? Where is Alex?"

Glory shrugged, feigning indifference. "I have no idea. Probably back at Ratherbee. The realtor was supposed to meet him there this afternoon, but now I don't know what he'll do. It took him so long to finally take the plunge and put it up for sale. Although it had a lot of bad memories, it had plenty of loving family memories too. He grew up in that house so maybe he'll want to keep it for himself. Or maybe he'll want to get rid of it now so he'll never have to be near me again."

Frannie took a moment to study her friend's troubled face. "Are you telling me that you two broke up?"

"Looks that way," Glory answered and continued snapping the ends off her asparagus spears.

The news stunned Frannie and she saw the pain in Glory's eyes, despite her attempt to mask it. But the cars and the walkers from nearby motels were starting to pour in now and there would be no opportunity for the two friends and partners to share their heartaches. Frannie gave Glory's shoulder a quick squeeze meant to convey they'd talk later. "Sorry, Glory," was all she managed to say before she picked up her clipboard and stood at the front door waiting for the next wave of guests. Her smile widened when she spotted her friend walking towards her. She turned towards the kitchen and called out, "Hey, Glory, come out here. Wait till you see who's here!"

Steve Lynch with the dazzling smile and blonde hair highlighted by the California sun hugged his two friends. "What are you doing here, Glory?" he asked, kissing them both on the cheek. "I thought your time would be strictly devoted to Amore Evenings now."

"It is, but you know how we all feel about Amore Breakfast. It's that sense of home—the warmth—the friends—whatever. It's like a security blanket for some of us."

"Glory, why don't you take that corner table and keep Steve company while he eats his breakfast? And take that damn apron off! You're not working this morning. I'm in charge here and that's an order!"

"Oh, yes, please do join me, Glory," Steve pleaded with sincerity. "We have so much to catch up on. I haven't seen you guys since last summer."

Glory gave them both an affectionate grin and surrendered her apron. "Okay, let's go, Steve. My appetite just returned for one of Amore's delicious breakfasts."

Chapter Thirty-two

With mixed feelings of reluctance and relief, Sal Oliveri had left his brother to struggle alone with his physical and emotional traumas. He had sat up with him for hours last night, speaking little and watching helplessly while Jerry suffered with what looked like restlessness caused by fear for his daughter.

After several cups of coffee and all the encouraging words he could think of, he accepted that his words were falling on deaf ears. Though he had tried to deny it himself, he knew that his brother had tuned him out. Deep down Sal knew that his brother's anxiety could not be attributed solely to his daughter, but the need for alcohol. What Sal had witnessed were the early signs of withdrawal. And he had little hope that Jerry would get past it.

Alcohol was neither offered nor mentioned last night. Jerry's alcohol dependency had long ago become an explosive subject to be avoided at all costs.

And the costs were high.

Even Sal tried to ignore the problem, pretending it didn't exist. He worked hard at trying to con himself into thinking that his brother simply enjoyed his drink. Period. He refused to acknowledge that Jerry was an alcoholic. Once he labeled it as such, he'd have to equate it with a terminal disease because Jerry never had the strength of character to fight his way through any problem, much less one as devastating and challenging as alcoholism. It was always easier for him to reach for the bottle and temporarily drown his problems.

When Sal opened the door of his own home, he was glad that Tess had stayed overnight at Frannie's. Ordinarily he would miss her if she left him for more than a few hours, but this morning he needed some alone time.

Mechanically he went into his den, picked up the TV remote, then tossed it aside. With his elbows propped on his knees and his head braced in his hands, Sal cried his heart out. He cried for his brother—the brother who used to be his best friend—the brother he had lost to the bottle. And he cried for himself, for he too lacked the strength of character to help his brother out of the darkness of his addiction.

Chapter Thirty-three

Sal Oliveri had unknowingly escaped meeting Eloise Farrell, a/k/a Skunk Lady, by minutes. She was about to put the key in the lock when Jerry opened the door with a swift pull.

He looked at her with disdain. "What the hell are you doing here so early?" he snarled, snatching the key from her fingers. Eloise gave him a perplexed look that quickly switched to indignation. "What's eating you?" she asked and reached to retrieve the key.

Jerry pulled it away. "This is *my* key, not yours," he said, shaking it at her before shoving it in his pocket.

"But you gave it to me!" she retaliated and stepped inside, throwing her coat on the sofa along with a paper bag. "Look what I bought us," she said, wide-eyed and smiling now, trying to bribe him into a better mood. "Tomato juice and limes. I thought a good Bloody Mary would start off our day nicely. I know you're on edge—nervous about your daughter, so this will calm you down," she said, lifting the large tomato juice can like a prize trophy. She walked into the kitchen and looked at him blankly. "Where's the vodka?" she asked, knowing the liquor bottles had always been a permanent fixture on his kitchen counter.

"Gone. I ain't got no more," he grumbled.

She shot him a *what's-gotten-into-you* look, but didn't pursue an argument. She knew well where her bread was buttered and if she played her cards right, this house and everything in it could be hers. She heaved a sigh and put her hand out, palm up. "So give me some money. I'll pick up another bottle."

"I ain't giving you no more money. Why don't you spring for a bottle once in a while?"

For a moment she forgot to think of the big picture and snapped back. "Me? No way, Jerry, my boy. Where I come from the men pay for everything. They know how to treat a woman—it's called *respect*." She put her nose in the air and raised her eyebrows. A strong nod of her head punctuated her words like an exclamation point.

Frannie's words had haunted him, but they came in handy now. "Respect has to be earned, my dear miss high and mighty, and you've got to go a long, friggin' way to earn mine!"

"Well, look who's talking! You sonofabitch, you're nothing but a waste. Who the hell needs you!" She grabbed her coat and stormed out with the can of tomato juice tucked possessively under her arm.

Once she was gone, a new wave of panic shot through him, like zigzagging bolts of lightning. It so possessed him that he gasped for breath. He ran outside and put his hand up to stop her just as she was backing out of the driveway.

Skunk Lady rolled down the window.

Jerry reached in his pocket and peeled out three twenty dollar bills. "Here," he said. "Get two bottles."

She eyed his trembling hand and a satisfied smile curled the corners of her mouth.

Again, she put her hand out. "What about my key?"

Without a word, he fumbled in his pocket again and handed it to her.

Chapter Thirty-four

With trepidation, Tony Gerard pulled into Amore Breakfast's parking lot. It was nearly lunchtime and he had already skipped breakfast, so his stomach was gurgling for attention. After the long winter while Amore was closed, he had a strong, sudden craving for one of Frannie Oliveri's delicious breakfast creations. He could almost taste the melt-in-your-mouth waffles drizzled with maple syrup and piled high with blueberries.

He tried to convince himself it was only the incomparable food that led him to the popular Shore Road restaurant. But this time it was more than that.

He had to see Frannie.

Not that he could have a private conversation with her, but he needed to see her reaction—how she would greet him—if at all. As the lead detective on the Keaton murder case, some of the news media had portrayed Tony as the heart-of-steel super cop who will probably charge that defenseless single mother the moment she wakes up. Her horrific accident and subsequent coma bought Suzanne plenty of sympathetic supporters. He was in no position to publicly admit he was one of them.

As far as Frannie was concerned, she's a level-headed intelligent person. If and when he reaches the point where he has to arrest Suzanne, she would, hopefully, understand and accept that he had no choice.

Emphasis on *hopefully.*

By the time Frannie noticed him walking towards the porch entrance, he was only about thirty feet away. She was chatting animatedly with a few guests like she didn't have a care in the world. But the moment she spotted Tony, her face dropped.

He stepped onto the porch anyway. She was smiling again, answering the tourists' questions—where to dine— what to see. When he caught her eye, he gave her an uncertain smile. The kind that asks for understanding. She didn't say a word at first and certainly didn't crack a smile. Tony shrugged his shoulders and his facial expression asked the question: *Well, am I unwelcome here now?*

With so many people within earshot there was little Frannie could say. She heaved a frustrated sigh. There were so many words bottled up inside her, she needed to vent in the worst way. But she couldn't and Tony used the crowd of people to his advantage.

"Are you alone, Sergeant? Is a counter seat okay?" Except for the formality of *Sergeant* rather than *Tony*, the words were innocuous, but their icy coating was not.

"Sure. Preferred, actually."

Despite her frosty greeting, Tony's eyes gazed at her with a friendly softness. She heaved a sigh to blow out her icy shield. "I'll say one thing for you, Sergeant Gerard— you've got guts."

"Maybe so," he conceded, "But it's my case and I've got a responsibility. I had hoped you'd understand that. Do you think I like playing the heavy among family and friends?"

"No, I'm sure you don't. Just promise me you'll stretch this out as long as you possibly can. Maybe with more time to investigate, you'll come up with the real killer."

"Those are my exact intentions, Frannie, believe me."

He helped himself to a cup of coffee from the urn and took it out on the porch. Sunlight splashed across his face offering welcome warmth and he felt mentally relieved now that he had spoken to Frannie.

An older woman, pushing seventy or maybe more, he guessed, was seated in the left-hand corner of the porch. With her carrot red hair and a red sweatshirt, you couldn't miss her if you wanted to. Tony felt her eyes on him and he couldn't imagine why. When two seats opened up between them, the woman quickly slipped into the seat next to him.

"Excuse me, you're Mr. Gerard, aren't you?"

He gave her a curious look and nodded.

"I used to know your grandmother, rest her soul. Long time ago." She waved away the years. "Before she met your grandfather."

Tony managed an amiable smile. "Oh? Did you go to school with her?"

"Oh, no, she said," with a slightly indignant frown. "Your grandmother was four years older." She paused for a cursory glance at the people around them. Although they were all involved in their own conversations, they were certainly too close for comfort. "Look," she whispered, "I'd like to talk to you. Do you think we could step off the porch for a minute?"

Tony hesitated. He had no idea what she wanted to discuss and thought he'd better bow out gracefully. People often cornered him with complaints about what they considered to be crimes or injustices against them.

But her face revealed no traces of anger or frustration. He glanced over at Frannie in the doorway. "Well, I wouldn't want either of us to miss being called for a seat inside."

She placed one hand gently on his and used the other to cup over her mouth. "Trust me. It's important, I think."

He walked with her around the side of the building, hoping she wasn't another complainant who thinks he could cure all the ills of the world.

Her eyes bounced around for one more check, just in case someone was lurking around the corners. Feeling safe now, she smiled and drew a breath. "Okay, Mr. Gerard—is it okay to call you mister? I know you're with the State Police, but I don't remember your title."

"It's Detective Sergeant. Most people call me 'sergeant,' but that's okay." Tony never thought hearing someone address him by his official title would be offensive until Frannie used it moments ago. "What's on your mind, ma'am?"

"I hope this doesn't get me in trouble," she began, her tone admonishing, not remorseful. "Because I could have kept my mouth shut and no one would know the difference. Keep that in mind, okay?"

Tony nodded his agreement. "Okay, just tell me what's bothering you. But first tell me who you are."

"My name is Martha Simone, Mrs. Simone, but I'm a widow. I live in the apartment next door to Suzanne Oliveri."

Tony's attention piqued.

"Two people knocked on my door last week—from your office, I guess—asking me about Suzanne. If I had seen her recently or talked to her ... you know. Well, I had already heard about the murder and that horrible accident. Once I heard *murder* that was it for me." She sliced the air with her hand. "Hey, I live alone and I'm scared. I didn't want to get involved ..."

"Mrs. Simone, I understand, believe me. Fear stops many people from speaking up. Why don't you try to relax and tell me what you need to say. I think you'll feel better."

She gave him a thin smile. "Well, I don't even know if this is important or not, but this poor fellow who was killed at The Admiral's Inn last Saturday night—or Sunday morning, whatever it was ... Well, I spoke to him last Saturday afternoon, only hours before she murdered him with that knife!" Her hand went to her chest and she winced, as if she could feel the pain herself.

"We don't know that for sure, ma'am. Not until it's proven in a court of law."

Nonplussed and wide-eyed, she stared up at him. "Well, according to what I read in the newspaper and saw on TV, it sure looks that way!"

"How something *looks* is often not what it *is*, Mrs. Simone," he quickly answered. "Tell me how you spoke to Mr. Keaton—exactly when, if you remember, and what transpired between you. To the best of your knowledge."

Martha Simone threw her gaze upward and gave it her best shot. She repeated the brief exchange she had with the decedent, then gave him a smug smile. Martha was proud of herself and somewhat relieved for recalling details and doing her civic duty. If they took her picture and put it in the newspapers, well, that would be good too, she thought and grinned.

"How did you know the gentleman actually was Tyler Keaton? Did he introduce himself?"

She fingered her cheek while she ruminated. "I really don't remember to tell you the truth ..." Her face suddenly brightened. "His picture was in the paper," she said defensively.

"Yes, it was," he acknowledged, calmly writing his notes. "And is that why you believe Suzanne Oliveri murdered Mr. Keaton, Mrs. Simone? Did you read in any newspaper that Suzanne actually killed Tyler Keaton?"

She hesitated. "Well, no ... but ..." Anger filled her now. "Well, you've got a hell of a nerve, Mr. Gerard! I take a chance like a good citizen—get myself involved in a murder investigation, and suddenly I'm the one getting interrogated?" She waved a finger at him. "For your information, I'd bet my last dollar that she killed him. I can't tell you exactly why, but I caught the look on her face when I mentioned her visitor. She looked like she saw a ghost, then tried to cover up real fast." She shook her finger in his face again. "But I saw through her. Her eyes gave her away. Eyes don't lie."

Tony didn't like where this was going but held his impassive demeanor. "When was that?"

She folded her arms tightly across her chest, main-taining her indignation. "Sometime between six or seven. I'm not sure exactly," she said, refusing to look at him. Her penciled eyebrows stretched upward as far as her skin would allow. "I was watching the six o'clock news, like I do every night."

"And how did you happen to speak to her?"

Her eyebrows fell but her arms remained fixed in their defiant position. "My window is right above the parking area. I saw her drive in and waited for her to come up." She pursed her lips and scowled, remembering. "She's another one … like you. I tried to be neighborly and tell her about this guy who came for her and she brushed me off. Hey, I know she's in bad shape now, but let me tell you—that girl's an iceberg. Not sociable at all. You never see any emotion on her face." She unfolded her arms and used her finger again to drive in her point. "But when I told her about her visitor—especially when I said he had eyes like Paul Newman and a diamond in his ear—she jolted like she was struck by lightning. Without a doubt, this guy was no friend, like he said he was."

Tony thanked her politely for the information and she softened.

Later, while he ate the blueberry-topped waffles he had been craving, he watched Frannie going about her business. As always the food was hot and delicious, but today, although they had spoken peacefully, Frannie Oliveri was still troubled by his presence.

The pattern continues, he thought as he picked up his check. *Add another one to the list of Women against Gerard.*

Chapter Thirty-five

The Madison family had made Saturday evening dinner reservations to celebrate the second season opening of Amore Evenings. Dan and Louise were first to arrive. Glory went to greet them looking as cheerful as she could manage. She had prepared herself for their innocent inquiries about Alex, and sure enough, it was Dan who immediately asked for him.

"He had to see prospective buyers for Ratherbee. They came to Ogunquit unexpectedly and wanted to see it," she explained, hoping neither one could read her face. She never was good at lying and felt as conspicuous as Pinocchio with his long wooden nose.

"But the realtor always handles that alone, doesn't he?" Louise asked curiously.

"Ordinarily, yes. But Alex insists on being present. I think he wants to meet any and all interested buyers. He's adamant about that. He doesn't want it to fall under the ownership and control of anyone who won't love it and care for it as his family did. He refused to sign the realtor's agreement unless they stipulated to that condition. "She shrugged and smiled as if his absence were no big deal. "C'mon, I'll show you to your table myself. Then make sure you come find me when the rest of the clan shows up in case I miss them."

"Your brother and sisters are on their way," Dan said. "And Amy is bringing her new guy. She can't wait to show him off to us." He laughed, then shook his head. A proud grin crossed his face. "To me and Louise she'll always be

150

our baby, but I think I might be walking her to the altar too someday soon."

The word *too* stabbed Glory like a knife in her heart. But she swallowed hard and let it pass. This was neither the time nor the place to drop that bomb on her family. They adored Alex.

And so do I, she thought as she escorted her dad and his wife to their oceanfront table.

Sara and Tim crossed each other's path in the dining room. They were both carrying trays of food. Indulging in conversation, however brief, was out of the question. They had both noticed Dan and Louise's radiant smiles when they came in. They obviously didn't know yet.

The young couple exchanged a worrisome glance. They had learned about Glory and Alex's breakup as soon as they arrived for work that afternoon and were shocked out of their minds. Glory and Alex had become role models for them and dear friends despite their age difference. Apparently the older couple's love and admiration mirrored theirs because they had asked Sara and Tim to be best man and maid of honor at their wedding. Sara had screamed with delight and Tim couldn't stop pumping Alex's hand. "After what we went through—all of us facing death together— Alex and I agreed that no two people were more suitable," Glory had said.

Sara had hugged them both. "Well, that sure makes a hell of a lot of sense to me!"

Now, in disbelief, she stole a glance at Glory, busy greeting her guests. But tonight her face was shaded with sorrow. If anyone who knew her well took a good hard look, they would easily see that her smile was forced—that *for business only* smile, as Glory herself had tagged it.

Sara felt an aching tug at her heart. She could only imagine what Glory was suffering. A chill went through her at the thought of what she'd feel if she and Tim broke up.

She ran into Tim again at the kitchen door. He was coming out with another full tray and she was going in. "We have to do something, Tim," she said.

Tim didn't have to ask about what. He just nodded his agreement and went off to serve his waiting guests.

Amore Evenings was in full swing when Frannie arrived. She thanked God for her parents. Between Heather and Benny, they had plenty to do. They weren't Heather's grandparents—only great-aunt and great-uncle—but to anyone's observation, their affection for the baby was as strong as any grandparent.

It took an inner strength she never knew she had to conduct business in both restaurants and pretend life was a bed of roses. She could see pity in the faces of many who knew her troubles, had caught their silent stares, but no one had said a word. For that she was grateful.

While she spoke to the people waiting in the bar area for their table, someone tapped her on the shoulder. "Steve Lynch! Why didn't you call for a reservation?" She glanced again at her waiting list. "I'm afraid we can't seat you for at least forty-five minutes."

"That's fine. No problem. I didn't make a reservation because I couldn't be sure what time my sister and her husband would arrive. They flew in from Dallas and by the time they drove from the airport to Ogunquit … well, anyway, they're settled now at Sea Chambers. I told them to stay put and I'd call if we can get a table within a reasonable time." He shrugged and smiled pleasantly. "If not, I had to stop by anyway if only to wish you and Glory the best of luck for your second season."

"Thanks, Steve, you're a doll. Your visits are always a pleasure. Why don't you call your sister and tell them to come down in a half-hour. I'll squeeze you in somewhere."

"Great," he said, then whispered discreetly. "I know you can't talk now, but if you need me, call me at my cottage or on my cell, okay? Just remember I'm your friend—and Glory's too." He glanced around the dining room. "Where is she, anyway? I want to say hello."

"She just took a call in the office."

"Alex?"

"No, I'm afraid not."

Chapter Thirty-six

When his secretary, Joan Banks, followed him into his office, Tony was still fighting a brutal headache. She began to ramble on about an office problem. With his head throbbing, Tony had no patience to listen and play arbitrator.

He put a hand up. "Hold it, Joan. I woke up this morning with a bitch of a headache and right now it hurts just listening to you." He squinted his eyes, pulled an Advil bottle out of his desk drawer and swallowed two. "Now lower your voice, speak slowly and try to put your story on fast forward."

Joan looked like a pot about to boil. She sucked in a breath and folded her arms across her chest. "Never mind. I can see you're not in the mood to listen, so I won't bother."

She left in a huff before Tony could attempt to apologize and listen to her problem. Halfway down the hall she turned and called back, the anger in her voice still piercing. "And Tony—when those Advils kick in, call Lieutenant Donovan in New York."

Tony's attention piqued and his headache was momentarily forgotten. "When did he call?" He had hoped to hear from him sooner, but understood that Andy Donovan had a heavy caseload himself. Tony had decided, however, if he didn't hear from Andy today, he would have to push a little and call himself.

"Ten minutes ago." Joan gave him a look that silently said she noticed his headache had suddenly vanished. He was ready to conduct police business. But not hers.

Tony arched his brows in hopeless resignation. He wasn't scoring points with any of the ladies recently; first Pat chewed him out, then Corrine told him off, then Frannie told him plenty with her icy greeting. Now his secretary was as bitchy as last week's storm. And she wasn't about to cool off until she spilled out whatever was eating her.

While Tony waited for Andy Donovan to pick up, he clung to the hope that Andy would have some new and promising information that could clear Suzanne Oliveri. So many times something comes out of left field and turns everything around.

"Sorry I couldn't get back to you sooner, Tony..." Andy began.

"Forget it, Andy. We're all on overload. So how did you make out with my Keaton guy and the girl, Suzanne Oliveri?"

"Well, as far as the pregnancy is concerned, if anyone knew about it, we haven't found that person."

"Yeah, that's what I thought you'd say. She couldn't have been more than two months pregnant when she took off for Maine. Chances are if she never planned to tell him about the baby, she would never have confided in someone else. Too risky."

"I take it the lab didn't come up with anything conclusive yet on the paternity issue?"

"Not yet, but that could take weeks. I really hoped you guys might have found someone who could tell you about their relationship and what people generally thought of the girl. She's still in a coma and her cousin—who's a good friend of mine—is just about tolerating me right now because she's afraid I'll arrest Suzanne sometime soon. And to tell you the truth, Andy, if it comes to that, I won't be too crazy about myself either. This is one suspect I don't want to nail."

"Well, hold it a minute, Tony," Andy said, taking heed of his friend's mood. He knew well how that hard shell police officers supposedly develop can melt down instantly. The toughest part is not to let the meltdown show. "Let me go on," he continued. "We did find two such people. One is his partner, Cody Griffin. According to him, among people, Keaton treated his girl Suzanne like a queen, but everyone suspected he abused her physically. But no one knew for sure, though. The girl never said a word. He said he had no clue why she took off on Keaton so suddenly. She stuck with him while the going was rough, Griffin said, and she could have reaped the rewards if she had hung on. Their place took off like a rocket, he claimed."

Tony paused to digest the information. "So I take it this Griffin guy is sitting pretty now. I assume their partnership agreement automatically transferred ownership to the surviving partner in the event of death—particularly since there was no surviving spouse?"

"It does. It *did,* I should say."

"And what do you know about him? Anything?"

"I didn't dig that far. I'll have to leave that to you guys up in Maine."

"Yeah, hey, no problem, Andy. I appreciate what you did already. But what about the other person? You said there were two."

Andy Donovan blew a sigh so heavy it came through like static.

"Was that you?" Tony asked. "It sure sounded like a defeatist sigh. Like the kind that's followed by a negative story." He tried to laugh but knew it wouldn't fool Donovan.

"I guess it was a defeatist sigh," he went on. "Sight unseen, you probably like this Griffin guy, right? He's big on motive, yes, so he could take the heat off Suzanne Oliveri. But unless he hired a pro to do the job, you're barking up the wrong tree. The guy was in the lounge all night with wall-to-wall witnesses. It's not as if he could have slipped out and come back unnoticed. Not with the victim in Maine at the time."

"So maybe he did get some goon to finish him off. Why not? But let's get back to the other person—"

"Okay. But you won't like this one. Her name is Lily Santos, a thirty-two-year-old single parent who's employed as a waitress. She was a waitress there for five years before Keaton and Griffin took over and they kept her. Apparently she and Griffin clashed. He wanted to fire her but Keaton disagreed. Not because he favored her in any way, but he didn't want to rock the boat with any more new untrained employees than was absolutely necessary. Lily knew her way around and the customers liked her."

"So give me the punch line. Why wouldn't I like her?"

Donovan heaved another sigh. "Because apparently there's no doubt in her mind that Suzanne was abused. She was always black and blue—at least she was during the warm weather months when you couldn't hide it under winter clothing. Even then, she said, it was noticeable if she wore something low-cut, and Suzanne loved her sexy clothes, she added. If anyone asked her what happened, she'd make up all kinds of stories—the standard cover-up accident stories abused women give. Sometimes she'd say it was a reaction to medication and quickly brushed off the subject. Lily Santos laughed when she told me that, remembering when Suzanne pulled that excuse on a guy she later found out was a doctor. He wanted to know what kind of medication caused it. Then she went serious again and said anyone could see by Suzanne's reaction that she was lying. She thought the regulars assumed she was physically abused so no one asked anymore. Suzanne could sing, she said, but she couldn't act."

"Oh, really? Did she sing there at his lounge?"

"No, but she bugged Keaton about it; wanted him to give her a chance at least. Keaton kept putting her off. Griffin was willing to try her out, but Keaton was adamantly against it, always saying he didn't want to rock the boat."

"So now Suzanne has two strikes against her—maybe three. One, she had his baby and never told him; never let him know she was pregnant when she left. Two, he beat her up regularly. That alone is strong motivation as we see every day. And three, he refused to give her a chance at a singing career when even his partner was willing." Tony paused, thinking about how this would be presented in court. "Boy, the AGA who gets this one will love it. I can see the theatrics already."

"It *is* strong motivation, Tony. You can't deny that."

"True, but it's still possible someone else had stronger motivation. Like Cody Griffin, for one. And maybe once we start digging, we'll pull a few more suspects out of their holes."

"I hope so, Tony, for your sake as well the girl's. It's got to be tough looking at a young woman like that—mother of an infant—and not want to help her. But you've got to look at the other side of the coin. Maybe she'll wake up like a bitch on wheels and you won't be so compassionate."

Now Tony's laugh was genuine. "I guess if she's proven guilty, I would feel better knowing for sure she's not as helpless and innocent as she looks in that hospital bed. I think, though, that I want to see her cleared more for her baby and for her cousin Frannie Oliveri—the woman CPS appointed as temporary foster parent."

"Oh, yes, I remember you telling me her story awhile back. Let's hope this one has a happier ending. It'll be rough for the baby too as she grows up, living with the knowledge that her mother murdered her father."

Tony pondered that a moment, then said, "She'll be okay. If her mother dies or lives to be convicted and incarcerated, Frannie Oliveri would adopt her, I'm sure. She'll be in good hands. Nothing like some of the heartbreaking stories we see in Family Court."

"Amen," Andy quickly said.

Chapter Thirty-seven

The temperature had reached sixty-eight degrees when Frannie closed Amore Breakfast for the day. Her parents were planning to visit Suzanne today, so they could drive her uncle. She welcomed the reprieve. It was so depressing to stare at her cousin day after day waiting for her eyes to open and worrying that they never would. There were so many questions spinning in Frannie's head that only Suzanne could answer. When she was alone at her bedside, she'd ask them aloud, wondering if she could hear. She'd whisper little pleasantries about Heather. *Don't worry—she's happy, she's healthy and we're all smothering her with love. When you open your eyes you can see her again.*

Frannie tried planting any seeds that might bring her to consciousness. And yet, she almost dreaded the moment she opened her eyes and became cognizant of where she was and why. She shivered thinking of how her cousin would react when she awoke to the knowledge that Heather's father had been murdered and she was their number one suspect.

And would she be surprised and shocked? Frannie prayed that she would. While in the depth of her silent world, Suzanne could remain innocent in Frannie's mind. Once she could speak coherently, her family might not want to hear what she had to say. She knew that nagging feeling troubled her parents, although they tried hard to appear optimistic and supportive of her innocence. Uncle Jerry, on the other hand, refused to believe his daughter was capable of murder; not premeditated, not in the heat of passion, by irresistible impulse, temporary insanity, or anything else they might label it.

On that—and little else—she and her uncle agreed.

After her parents left for the hospital Frannie dressed Heather in a new outfit she had picked up in one of the Main Street shops. It was a perfect day for walking and she wasn't about to hide behind closed doors. She preferred to walk the village proudly, like she had every confidence this huge black cloud would pass as soon as her cousin could speak. With that positive attitude, she decided to visit some friends who owned businesses in the village. It had been a long winter and today it was great to see all the shops and restaurants alive again. Smiling friendly faces and warm hugs were just what she needed to boost her spirits. Besides, she wanted to show off her precious baby cousin. Heather had captured Frannie's heart so profoundly it was almost frightening.

The baby was smiling more and more the past few days and today, while Frannie walked her, she actually giggled. Leaning over the hood of the stroller, Frannie made funny faces and laughed with the baby. *If anyone is watching,* she thought, *they'll think I'm a nut job.*

But she felt good. Pushing Heather in the stroller and looking down at her beautiful baby face filled her with unparalleled joy. She had no idea she was capable of this much love. In the early years of her marriage, she had looked forward to being a mom, but no more than two, she had told her husband. He agreed wholeheartedly. Only problem was, while he was still married to her, he had them with someone else.

It's all past tense. Dead and buried. She repeated the words aloud, only this time with a wide smile because she was singing them to Heather, making up words to an old tune as she went along.

She made The Village Food Market her first stop and treated herself to a cup of Randy's and John's New England clam chowder. As always, it was thick, creamy and fresh—

just the way she liked it. Along with the comfort food, as anticipated, the guys gave her the hugs and kind words she had needed.

She stopped next at On The Main where Rick and everyone there fussed over Heather and offered themselves for whatever help Frannie might need. From there, she crossed over to Beach Street and stopped at Spoiled Rotten. Michael and Toby stopped what they were doing and sat with her on the front porch. Frannie loved being surrounded by the colorful spring flowers that attracted tourists to its doors and she was able to keep a close eye on Heather who was asleep in her stroller. Although she stayed only ten minutes, her conversation with Michael and Toby had been uplifting.

She made one more stop at Revelations, the gift shop on Shore Road near Amore Breakfast. Again, she was welcomed with arms open wide and sympathetic eyes. She embraced them all and assured these dear friends that she was "hanging in there" and would certainly call upon them to help, if necessary.

Although she had many friends at Five-O she would love to visit, she was glad it wasn't open yet. Since it opened, the Shore Road bar/restaurant had become another favorite spot for Frannie. Great food, great friends, great place to meet new ones. Frannie knew that once she started talking to Donato and Jeff, a brief visit would be impossible.

As Frannie continued her walk along Shore Road, she already felt a hundred times better than when she left her house. As she had hoped, the short visits proved to be a dose of good medicine. Nothing like *love* to take the bite off your heartaches, she thought.

To make her outing perfect, she wished she could have also enjoyed a long invigorating walk along The Marginal Way. Year after year, she never tired of the magnificent views from the rocky path high above the ocean.

But that pleasure would have to wait for another day. Today the Ogunquit Police Department would be her last stop.

Finally, she reached the station, walked up the ramp with Heather in her arms. Ellie Peterson and Maureen Spencer, who handled all the secretarial and clerical work for the department, both stood up and greeted her warmly. Maureen, the senior secretary who had passed the twenty-year mark with the OPD, stepped away from her computer. "Frannie! What a surprise!" she said impulsively but her expression quickly faded from pleasure to pathos. "Oh, this has to be little Heather." Maureen pulled the blanket away from the baby's face and peeked in at her. "Oh, God, she's so beautiful ..."

Frannie beamed. "She sure is, isn't she? I thought I'd take her out for some fresh air while the sun is shining. Can you believe I walked here all the way from my house? Don't ask me why. I get crazy ideas sometimes."

Maureen lifted a brow. "Well, if Amore Breakfast and Amore Evenings are examples of crazy ideas, come teach me how to go crazy too."

Ellie closed out her document and joined the conversation. "Ah, don't listen to her, Frannie. Maureen is never going to leave the OPD. She said she wants to be waked right there on that huge oak desk."

"Bet your sweet behind, wise-ass. They don't make 'em like this anymore, and I'm not trading it in for a chunk of metal." Maureen sealed her statement with a pound on the desk. *My territory, my property,* her clenched fist proclaimed. The banter exchanged between the two secretaries clearly reflected the sincerity of their friendship. Although decades apart in age, when Ellie's husband was killed by a roadside car bomb in Iraq, Maureen became Ellie's second mother and a second grandmother to her three-year-old son. Every one of them, from the OPD chief on down, became brothers and sisters to Ellie from the day that news crushed them all.

Ellie went to the coffeemaker and poured herself a cup. "How about you, Frannie? Are you coffee-logged from Amore or would you like some?"

"Actually it's a rare occasion when I can sit and sip a cup of coffee at Amore. It always ends up getting cold."

"Then here you go. Relax and enjoy it," she said, handing her a cup. "Regular, milk and no sugar, right?"

Frannie jabbed a finger in the air. "Yes, good memory. You can work at Amore anytime." She sipped it slowly, savoring the rich mellow taste.

Maureen heaved a sigh and crossed her arms. "How are you *really,* Frannie? To look at you, no one would believe what's been going on."

Frannie drew a breath and exhaled slowly. Her gaze settled on her feet as though something about them was more important than the question posed. "I'm doing okay. Between Heather, the trips to the hospital and my two restaurants, I'm too busy to think much. My attention is always needed elsewhere. That's good, I guess."

Maureen studied Frannie a moment and heaved a sigh. "I wish I had some encouraging words for you. There doesn't seem to be a damn thing you can do until your cousin comes out of that coma. The only one who can really defend Suzanne is Suzanne."

"Absolutely. But in the meantime we retained Bill Franklin to defend her."

"Oh, man!" Ellie threw in. "He's supposed to be great but *very* expensive." She wanted to ask who was picking up that tab, but couldn't be that pushy. It certainly wasn't coming from Suzanne or her father, although he did own a house.

Frannie easily read her thoughts and shrugged. "It won't be easy but it has to be done."

Maureen squeezed her hand. "Listen ... seriously, Frannie. If you need us, if there's anything at all we can do to help—especially with this beautiful baby—"

Frannie laughed. "You can't imagine how many people have offered to help with her." She put her pinky at Heather's hand and the baby grasped it. "In the three days since we opened, I'd venture to say dozens of people have offered. So far between my mother and Glory, we're doing okay. But thanks. Just keep your eyes and ears open."

"We certainly will. How is Glory, anyway?" Maureen asked.

Frannie rolled her eyes. "Don't ask. She was so looking forward to Amore Evenings' opening weekend, but she ended up working through it like a zombie. She managed to fake her way through, though."

Maureen and Ellie both gave her a curious look, waiting for the *why*.

"She and Alex Howard broke up."

The *why* remained fixed on their faces.

"She didn't tell me why and I didn't ask."

Actually Glory had told her but she wasn't about to share Glory's secrets with anyone else.

Chapter Thirty-eight

"Okay, what's going on?" Dan Madison asked his daughter the moment he kissed her hello. He had made an impulsive decision to pay her an unexpected visit.

Glory threw her head back and sighed. She gave her dad a half-smile and a look of defeat. She had intended to call him yesterday, but found another excuse to stall every time her hand reached for the phone.

"About what?" she said, still stalling. So far she hadn't devised a plausible story for her breakup with Alex. There was no way she would consider telling him the truth. It would hurt her father terribly. This was one of those cases where a lie—or an omission of truth—was an absolute necessity.

She decided to settle for a half-truth. "Come in the kitchen, Dad. I just put two slices of bread in the toaster. Want some? A sandwich?"

"No, I'm good. Louise and I just had lunch before I left. I smell fresh coffee, though. I'll have a cup." He put his jacket on the back of a kitchen chair and sat down. "And why are you eating toast at one o'clock in the afternoon? No Amore Breakfast this morning?"

Glory recalled her friend's benign admonition. "No. Frannie scolds me sometimes when I show up there for breakfast and end up working." She smiled gently as she explained. "It gives her a guilt trip to see me work for nothing. She can't get it through her head that I enjoy being there. So many great people come in and out every day. I love meeting them and socializing a little. And if I'm willing to help out during that early morning rush, why should she feel guilty?" Glory shrugged it off, as though she couldn't understand Frannie's attitude but would try to accept it.

She popped her toast, spread orange marmalade on it and poured two mugs of coffee. They were both silent at first, sipping their coffee and watching the ocean rush in. Glory took small bites of her toast, like someone who eats to live, not lives to eat. *So unlike her,* Dan thought, *this daughter of mine with the insatiable appetite.* He stirred an Equal packet in his coffee and stirred it much longer than necessary—like chocolate pudding he couldn't allow to lump. The few seconds of silence hung awkwardly between them.

"As far as Frannie is concerned, sweetheart, you have to look at it through her eyes. Amore Breakfast is her baby— hers alone—and she probably wants to maintain complete control. Because you own Amore Evenings jointly, your presence every morning at Amore Breakfast might make people assume you have a monetary interest there as well. I imagine that would offend Frannie, and I can understand it. As far as you helping her out … don't worry about it. She's done a great job running her business for years before you two met, so if I were you, I'd focus on your column and Amore Evenings."

"I do," she was quick to say. "But I like being busy. If I can give each of them some time, why shouldn't I?"

Dan blew a long breath and a hint of a smile filled his cheeks, as if pondering how to gently answer her question. Although it was more of a statement than a question. He blew at the still-steaming coffee, then sipped it. "Glory, look at it this way: Your *Glorious Cooking* column is well-established. I'm not at all suggesting that you slack off on that, but what I *am* saying is you should concentrate mostly on Amore Evenings. That's *your* baby now. Using the same principle you would on an infant or child, you have to love, nurture and guide it until it can stand on its own. Amore

Breakfast is all grown up now, so to speak. Amore Evenings, though, is still in its infancy." He looked her in the eye to check her reaction. "Does that make sense? Am I getting through?"

Glory lightened the mood with a genuine, affectionate laugh. She leaned over and gave him a peck on the cheek, then wiped off the smear of marmalade she had left there. "Yes, daddy dear," she said teasingly with eyes reflecting her love. "You're coming through loud and clear. To sum it all up, what you're trying to say is mind your own business—*literally*!"

"You got it!" he said, and they both laughed this time.

Glory finished her first slice of toast but abandoned the second. Her face grew serious again. "Okay, Dad. I get the message. I can't say that interpretation never entered my mind, but I really thought Frannie objected because she didn't want me working for nothing, but I guess that's secondary. From now on I'll be strictly a guest when I go there unless Frannie asks for my help."

"Good girl," Dan said, then walked over to the floor-to-ceiling window as though he needed a clearer, more unobstructed view of the rocky shoreline. He kept his gaze fixed on the mesmerizing sight and pressed on. "I don't know how we got on that, Glory, but I think you know why I came here. I heard about you and Alex. Do you want to talk about it?" His hand went up before she could respond. "It's your personal business, I know, but you're my daughter and I love you. If you hurt, I hurt. I'm here to listen if you want, if not …" He threw his hands out and shrugged.

Glory displayed no emotion, just sipped her coffee and nodded, silently acknowledging his love and support.

Dan brought his coffee mug to the kitchen sink and kissed her on the cheek. "Okay, sweetheart. I understand. Guess I'm stuck mall shopping with Louise this afternoon."

Glory pulled at his shirt just as he was about to leave. A rush of tears welled in her eyes. "Dad, wait. Don't go. Sit," she said, patting the leather seat of the chair he had vacated.

Dan gave her a sideways smile. "Sit? What am I—a dog?"

Glory's tears melted to laughter. "Oh, Dad, promise me you won't die and leave this earth before I do because since I found you, I can't live without you."

"Ditto," he answered. "Now talk to me. You'll feel better."

Chapter Thirty-nine

Sara Baisley never had trouble falling asleep. She could sleep for ten hours straight through if her schedule allowed—which it usually didn't. But tonight her mind was working overtime hoping for a brainstorm. There had to be some way she and Tim could play Cupid and help patch up whatever it was that drove Glory and Alex apart. After all, as their maid of honor and best man, wasn't that their responsibility? Or was that responsibility now defunct since the wedding might never take place?

At first Sara had suspected their rift was probably caused by some stupid little incident that had blown out of proportion. And now neither one would budge an inch. But in rethinking, Sara frowned on that assumption. Glory and Alex were long past that age of immaturity. At least she hoped that was the case.

Unlike Sara, Timothy Waite fell asleep the moment his head hit the pillow. Even if something bothered him at night, unless it was something catastrophic, he'd close his eyes and deal with it in the morning. Or not at all.

He picked up his cell phone without bothering to check the caller ID. "What's the matter?"

"What do you mean 'what's the matter'? Since when do I need a reason to call you?"

"Since you're calling when you *know* I'll be sleeping but you don't care." Tim tried to fake annoyance for having his sleep disturbed, but Sara's voice never annoyed him. He had been crazy about her the day they met and nothing would or could ever change that.

"Oh, stop sounding like an old man. It's not even midnight yet."

"Okay, okay," he said in his groggy but amused voice. "I'm sorry I sounded like an old—but hey, what am I crazy? You wake me up and I'm the one apologizing?"

Sara giggled. "Okay, I'm sorry I woke you up. We're even. So can we talk now?"

"Ah! Now back to where we started … what's the matter, Sara?"

"We have to do something about Glory and Alex. This rift between them might be over something minor; something fixable, but you know how stubborn people can get sometimes. Neither one wants to be first to give in and the results could be disastrous. Look at our parents—how they didn't talk for years. If we hadn't nearly died together that night, they probably would still be enemies!"

"But we don't know for sure that it's something trivial between Alex and Glory. Suppose it's something bigger, deeper? As close as we are to them, whatever their problem is, they'll have to work it out together. We don't really have a right to interfere."

"Okay, fine. Maybe that's so. But sometimes you have to be sure that's how the injured party wants it. Remember the summer before our senior year when Brianna Haines got pregnant? Some of us, myself included, never said a word to her. We all pretended nothing was wrong. She never spoke about it so neither did we. Much later, after the baby was born, she admitted she was crushed that her friends avoided her. She needed us then more than ever and we abandoned her because we thought we had to *mind our own business.*"

Tim was silent, remembering. Too late now, but Sara was right. Brianna's pregnancy had been ignored as though no one noticed the bulge in her belly and how it would reshape her life plans. "Okay, Sara, I get your point. So now what? What's going on in your head and what's my part in your scheme?"

"I'd much prefer that you call it a *plan,* not a scheme."

Tim rolled his eyes and grinned. "Semantics, Sara. Okay, what's your *plan*?"

Chapter Forty

Robert John Butler stood behind the bar where he had been earning a decent living for the last seven months. He enjoyed his job; loved talking to the customers, constantly meeting new people. But Rob felt certain it was simply a matter of time before he'd be headed for Iraq. He would have to complete months of grueling training here first, of course, but at least he would be safe in his own free country. Once they shipped him off to Iraq, though—or any other war-torn country, he might never come back. He knew that, had battled with it, listening and watching the massacres night after night, horrified like all other Americans.

Still, some compelling force told him this was God's plan for him.

He had already given notice to his employer and good friend, Frank Marsh, and this would be his last week working. Next Monday morning he would go down to the recruiting office and enlist.

Robbie was a likeable guy who easily made friends. He wore a perpetual smile on his face and never took anything too seriously. But he resolved that before he left for basic training, he had to make two important visits. His grandpa's heart was hurting bad. Robbie's smile was shaded with sadness knowing Grandpa Dennis would live in fear every single day that his grandson spent in Iraq. Robbie hoped the training would keep his head clear and his body ready. No sense dwelling on something over which he had absolutely no control. But some nights, those suppressed fears invaded Robbie's dreams. He'd wake up with a pumping heart and a body soaked with sweat.

He promised himself that he'd spend a couple of days of real quality time with Grandpa Dennis before he left. Just in case any of those dreams—those nightmares— come true.

Wanda Prewitt, the high school teacher he never lost touch with, was number two on his list of priority visits. She was probably no more than one hundred pounds and just about five feet, but to Robbie she was ten-feet tall and a powerful force. In his mind's eye he easily visualized Ms. Prewitt shaking a finger at him. The image moved his smile to laughter. She was relentless in her quest to fire up some ambition in him. He let his mind drift to those pleasant memories …

"There's a whole world out there, Robert Butler, and without a proper education, you'll never realize your full potential. Wouldn't you like to get an exciting job and travel all over the world?"

Robbie would pout and exaggerate his disinterest. "But why would I want to, Ms. Prewitt? Maine is my home, the land I love," he said with a hand over his heart. How he loved to tease her! The woman had a genuine affection for him and he loved her for it. Teasing her was the only way he could tell her without saying the words. "Besides, teacher dear," he had said tipping his Red Sox hat in a gesture of respect, "I have no desire to be a world traveler. We've got more beauty and rich history to explore right here in our good old United States. Just think about how many tourists we get here in Ogunquit. We take for granted what we have here, but don't people come from all over to enjoy our little seaside town and eat lobster dinners? And I've already traveled plenty. I went out west, down south—all over." He had grinned complacently as though he had already achieved his lifetime goals.

Ms. Prewitt sighed, folded her arms under her breasts. "Some day you're going to be sorry you never listened to me, Robert."

Robbie patted her shoulder affectionately. The smile never left his face when he and Ms. Prewitt had these little chats. "Hey, you may be right, Ms. Prewitt, but I promise you this: if later on I do get the feeling that I wasted my life, I'll come from wherever I am to find you. I'll be man enough to tell you face-to-face that you were right. Okay?"

Reminiscing about Wanda Prewitt always gave Robbie a warm, nostalgic feeling. She had a way about her that boosted his confidence. Hell, he would need that where he was going. Well, she always wanted me to get myself a good education, he thought with a thin smile. *Wait till she hears how I'm getting it.*

To his own surprise, Robbie had no problem risking his life to defend his country; he was proud to do it. But he was going to be careful as careful can be. He'd need eyes all over his head to stay alive and safe. And maybe an angel on his shoulder.

*   *   *

Grandpa Dennis was waiting behind his storm door when Robbie pulled up the driveway. He was wearing the saddest smile Robbie had ever seen. The kind that you force when trying to appear brave, proud and strong while your heart is so full of fear you're afraid it will burst.

He popped the trunk open and carried in his grandfather's new flat screen TV, glad that installing it would keep their minds off his imminent enlistment.

"You can do this later, after breakfast, Robbie. Aren't you hungry?"

"Yeah, but I can wait if you can. I'd rather do it now so we can relax and do something else after breakfast. Whatever you'd like, Gramps."

"Okay, fine. It might be better if we go later. Maybe the rush might calm down a bit at Amore Breakfast."

Installing the television had worked temporarily to keep his grandfather's emotions at bay, but Robbie caught sight of his quavering lips while he cleaned up the packaging and threw the debris into the empty carton. Their eyes locked for that split-second and that's all Grandpa Dennis needed. Quickly and with an embarrassed laugh, he brushed away the tears that welled in his eyes. Robbie understood his pain and blinked back a few tears of his own.

"I knew this day would come. I tried so hard not to think about it, but it never left my head." Grandpa Dennis struggled to hold his smile. "It's funny," he continued, "we old folk lose so much memory as we age, but the things we *want* to forget, we can't."

Robbie grabbed his grandfather for a quick hug of assurance. "C'mon, Gramps, don't make it worse than it is. I haven't even signed up yet. And you never know—I could break a few bones in basic and get to hang around in the States awhile longer." When his attempt at levity didn't work, he softened his voice. "Grandpa, don't make yourself crazy with worry. Plenty of our troops come back after their tour, alive and healthy."

But so many don't, Dennis thought. He had an ache in his heart that he hadn't felt since that horrible day nine years ago when he and his Hannah—gone five years already—learned she had terminal cancer.

"And about your age—you have to quit thinking of yourself as an ancient old man with one foot in the grave. What are you—sixty-seven, sixty-eight, right?"

"Pushing sixty-eight."

"Big deal! I'll bet among the seniors in your club, you're one of the kids."

Dennis gave Robbie a slanted look while a smile tugged at the corners of his mouth. The kid was not entirely wrong. Some days, depending on which group of seniors he mingled with at the center, he did feel like a kid. But younger ones were joining up every day … "You're trying to make me laugh, I know. But Iraq is no laughing matter."

Then, instantly realizing he should be showing his Robbie pride and confidence instead of fear and pessimism, he managed a huge smile. "C'mere, you big lug." He pulled him by the shoulders and wrapped his arms around him. Dennis held his optimistic smile but his arms gripped Robbie in the tightest bear hug his strength would allow. No words were necessary to convey its meaning. *Come back to us. Don't let those crazy bastards get you.*

"Will you send me a letter once in a while?"

"Sure, but e-mail would probably be better. Maybe I can e-mail my letters to you through my parents' computer. They can print them out and give them to you."

Dennis pouted his lips and nixed the idea. "No way. 'Mail delivery' might take too long. I made up my mind before you got here that I'm buying a computer and I'm going to learn how to use the damn thing. There are plenty of classes offered for seniors. So by the time you're ready to e-mail your first letter, you can send it straight to your grandpa. I'll be a whiz by then."

Minutes later, as planned, they turned onto Ogunquit's Shore Road and into Amore Breakfast's parking lot. Robbie was immediately impressed with the homey little restaurant that looked like it was cut out of a storybook. Painted white with red shutters and red window boxes filled with geraniums, its wholesome charm alone was inviting. People sat at checkerboard tables on its open porch drinking coffee and soaking up the atmosphere.

"I can't believe you've never eaten here!" Dennis said, truly surprised. "The whole world goes to Amore Breakfast. It's a not-to-be-missed highlight for all visitors to our area."

Robbie shrugged. "You have to remember I work nights, gramps, so I tend to sleep right through breakfast."

Grandfather and grandson exchanged a knowing look. *Those days will soon be gone.*

"Well, you're in for a treat, Robbie. The food is the absolute best, the service you get with a smile, and the owner has a personality that makes people feel like family. I'll introduce you to her. She's a real doll, and she's single. If I were a little younger ..." He left the thought suspended.

Robbie's brows shot up and he grinned like a fox. "You'd what?"

"Don't give me that look. I'm old, but not *that* old!"

When they walked inside to be placed on the waiting list, Frannie greeted them in her usual congenial style. With her ever-present clipboard tucked under her arm, she smiled warmly at Dennis. "How many today, Dennis?"

"Two, Frannie." He edged his way closer to her and said, "I know you're crazy busy—as always—but I want to introduce you to my grandson, Robert John Butler." He beamed at Robbie, his face radiant with pride. With an exaggerated wave of his hand, he presented him as though he were a world-famous celebrity, worthy of the utmost respect.

Robbie laughed, cast his eyes upward and shook his head. "The way he introduces me sometimes, I can almost hear the drumroll."

"Well, I *am* proud, *damn* proud," Dennis said in defense. "My Robbie is going to enlist next week. He wants to be a U.S. Army soldier and do his bit in Iraq. So shouldn't I be proud, Frannie?"

At the sound of that dreaded word, *Iraq*, Frannie's smile faded. Fear clutched her heart as she stared at this handsome young man with the lovable grin. *It's like throwing him to the lions!* But in his eyes, she saw no fear and her emotions shifted to admiration and respect. Struck by an irresistible impulse, she clapped her hands for attention. The porch was crowded with people drinking coffee while they waited for tables, and inside others were enjoying their breakfasts.

"Hey, everyone," she called out. "Excuse me for interrupting, but I want to introduce this young man to everyone here. His name is Robert John Butler, and he plans to enlist next week to serve us all, most likely in Iraq. So, with your permission, I'm going to put his name first on my list for a table. I'm sure none of you will mind. If he can risk his life for us, it's the least we can do, right?"

Applause thundered and cheers were shouted from all. Grandpa Dennis lost it. Overwhelmed by emotion, he cried openly, but his proud smile lit up his face.

Robbie stood there, shocked, but so deeply touched by the support. He swallowed hard. When everyone rose to their feet, though, still clapping, he couldn't hold back. He allowed a few tears to sneak out. People actually waited in line to shake his hand.

Later, after Robbie had finished every bit of his *In Your Teeth* omelet and Dennis his *Southwestern,* Dennis waved at Frannie and circled a finger over their dishes. She came right over to their table. "Forget it. No check for you guys," she said adamantly, then turned to Robbie. "You're our hero, Robbie. I'm happy to do it."

"But let me pay something, Frannie," Dennis insisted. "He's the one who's enlisting, not me."

She pointed a finger at him. "Right, but first of all, you brought him here, and secondly, without you he would never have been born. So that earns you a freebie too. Case closed."

"Can't argue with that," Dennis answered. They both thanked her again and Frannie hugged Robbie once more. "Good luck and stay safe. Our love and prayers are with you." Then, as she stepped away, she added, "Dennis, you're lucky to have such a fine young man in your family. I wish he were part of mine."

Chapter Forty-one

Dan Madison stared at the phone before replacing it on its charger. Trouble lines creased his face.

"Why did you hang up?" Louise asked. "Didn't she ask to speak to me?" She took a moment to study her husband's face. "What's wrong?"

Dan shrugged, but the gesture belied his look of concern. "Nothing's wrong," he said, forcing a smile. "That was my first question to her. Everyone's fine, she said, but she had to speak to both of us. Today, she said." His brows furrowed. "But she sounded so serious. Like she had something real heavy to discuss."

Louise's hand flew to her cheek. "Oh, God. I hope she isn't in some kind of trouble." She reached for the phone.

Dan put a hand over hers. "Don't bother. She's on her way over."

"Maybe she's in some kind of financial mess and needs our help."

Dan shook his head. "I doubt it. God bless that enterprising daughter of ours. She has a good head on her shoulders when it comes to business. Her three boutique shops are all operating in the black, doing very nicely." Pride brightened his face. "Unless she's been lying to us, which I also doubt."

"Gee, Dan, I hope she isn't planning a move to California. Every time she flies out to visit her San Diego friends, she comes back on a high, bragging about that city and its great weather. More than once she casually mentioned the idea about opening another boutique there, starting another chain."

Dan slipped his hands in his pants pockets, then wrinkled his nose to nix the idea. "Nah. She enjoys visiting there with her California friends—the ones who own condos here in Ogunquit—but I don't think she'd want to move there permanently. Her roots are here. Her family is here. Anyway, why are we knocking ourselves out trying to analyze her motive for visiting her parents? In a few minutes she'll be here and we'll find out what's on her mind." He laughed at himself while he prepared a fresh pot of coffee. It wasn't like him to overreact. Vanessa's serious tone was not necessarily an indication of trouble, he told himself. But he remembered her last remark, the line he had not repeated to Louise: "Put on a pot of coffee, Dad. The *big* pot," Vanessa had said.

Louise filled a dish with oatmeal-raisin cookies, a stock item in the Madison home that ran neck-in-neck with chocolate chips. "I hope she had lunch already because we don't have anything exciting to eat." She took another look in her refrigerator. "I could whip up an omelet, maybe."

Dan pulled out three mugs from the cabinet and put them on the table. "Don't sweat it, Louise. Why do you think every time our children come you have to feed them?"

Louise shrugged and smiled. "Who knows? That's what mothers do, I guess. It's like a bribe to get them to visit more often."

Dan smiled at his wife, but a sense of foreboding filled him. Somehow he sensed that Vanessa would have no interest in food today. Not even a cookie.

*   *   *

Vanessa threw her jacket on the coat tree in the entrance hall and walked straight to the kitchen. "Nobody's here, right?"

Dan and Louise exchanged a quick glance that mirrored their concern. "No. Just me and your father. Why?" Louise asked her daughter.

Vanessa kissed them both, as always, then grabbed the pot and poured coffee for all of them, avoiding eye contact with her parents.

Louise repeated her question. "Why is it so important for us to be alone?"

Vanessa sucked in a deep breath. "Because I need to talk to you both in privacy and uninterrupted. If the phone rings, can you let voice mail take it, please?" Her gaze went from her mother to her father who could no longer tell themselves this was just a casual visit.

"Vanessa, you're scaring me," Louise said. "What's going on?"

The coffee cups remained untouched while a heavy silence fell over them.

Vanessa squeezed her mother's hand, then reached across the table for her father's as well.

"I'm sorry if I upset you guys," she said, then looked at Dan. "Dad, I told you it's nothing bad about me or Todd or Amy or Glory, so don't start thinking dark and deadly thoughts." She inhaled deeply again, then exhaled slowly. "At least I don't think it's bad." She stirred the coffee and fixed her gaze on the dark swirls. "Bear with me. This is not easy," She bit her lip but the catch in her throat sent a rush of tears to her eyes.

Dan leaned across the table and held her hand between his. "Sweetheart, we're your parents, not your executioner. Whatever it is, we're here to help you. You've always made us proud and there's nothing you can tell us now that will make us love you less. So c'mon, as long as you're here and healthy, it can't be that bad." He gave her his sunniest smile while Louise dabbed at her eyes. She had no idea yet why she was crying, but if the problem brought her strong-willed, independent, thirty-two-year-old daughter to tears, it had to be monumental.

"I'm in love!" Vanessa blurted out. The emotion she had tried to suppress exploded like an erupting volcano.

Relief washed over Dan's and Louise's faces. They had hoped she would someday meet someone special. But their relief clouded quickly. They both realized that Vanessa's news should bring joy, not tears. There had to be a "but" coming.

"With a woman!" Vanessa cried out, then buried her face in her hands.

A soulful, involuntary cry escaped Louise's lips. "Oh, no. P-l-e-a-s-e, no!" In one fleeting moment, she mourned for the bride she would never see walking down the aisle on the arm of her father; for the grandchildren never to be born.

Dan was stunned into silence. It seemed like an eternity had passed before he found his voice. He got up slowly like a man who carried a heavy burden. But when he stood up, he held himself ramrod straight. For years he had a small, nagging feeling this day would come. There were always signs. Signs he ignored and swept from his mind. He cringed with guilt thinking how his daughter had probably suffered trying to live a life that so sharply contrasted with the one that possessed her physically and emotionally.

But how could he have introduced that sensitive subject? It was a long shot, anyway, he had convinced himself. Vanessa was simply too involved in building her businesses. She had always been energetic and ambitious, had lots of friends, she assured them, but no special relationships. Dan and Louise had assumed that Mr. Right had not yet entered her life, but hoped he would sometime soon.

While Vanessa still had her head cradled in her hands, unable to lock eyes with her parents, Dan lifted his wife's chin with one finger. He gave her a long, hard look to control her emotions. A display of grief is the last thing their daughter needed. Louise sniffed her tears back inside and nodded, steeling herself to be strong for Vanessa.

Dragging her chair closer, Louise wrapped her arms around her first-born child, kissed her tear-stained cheeks, then blotted them gently with a paper napkin. "I'm sorry, Vanessa, I didn't mean to react that way. It was a shock, yes, but my tears are for you, not me. I know how hard it was for you to tell us. It must have been hell to try to hide your true feelings all these years." She held her face with both hands, forcing her daughter to meet her gaze while Dan stood behind them fighting his own emotion.

Her mother's words brought fresh tears to Vanessa's eyes. "I'm sorry, Mom. I know how you dreamed of me marrying some prince charming and giving you grandchildren—"

Louise put a hand over her daughter's lips. "No, stop it, Vanessa. Don't think that way. Sure, that's true. Your father and I both looked forward to being grandparents and spoiling your children. But what we want most of all—what we've *always* wanted most of all—is your happiness. Don't ever feel you have to apologize to us for anything that feels right to you. Our love is unconditional and nothing can ever destroy that love. Do you understand?"

Vanessa hugged her mother and this time her tears were mixed with joy and relief. From her mother's shoulder, she looked up at her dad, who hadn't yet spoken a single word. Her gaze pleaded for his understanding.

He smiled gently and put his arms out wide. Vanessa jumped to her feet and hugged him tighter than she had ever hugged him before. "I love you, Dad. I love you both so much."

Dan brushed the hair away from her face with his fingers. "Not nearly as much as we love you, sweetheart," he said. "Now why don't we sit down and drink our coffee while you tell us all about your special friend. I'm sure you'll want us to meet her soon."

"Well, her name is Wanda Prewitt—"

"Wanda Prewitt?" Dan cut in. "You don't mean Amy's high school English teacher?"

"That's her, Dad. We've been committed for almost a year now. She's really something special, and so is our relationship. We truly care *for* each other and *about* each other. You and Mom only knew her as a teacher. But I want to bring her here so you can both know her as the wonderful person she is. Would that be okay? Can you guys handle it?"

"You'll have to give us a little time to get used to the idea. But yes, I think we can," Dan said, then gave her a bright smile. "And who knows? Maybe someday you'll adopt children and we can still be grandparents."

Vanessa beamed. "That's the plan, Dad. That's the plan."

Chapter Forty-two

Tony dreaded the long drive to New York with only his thoughts for company, but caseloads were particularly heavy and no detective or officer could be spared.

After their last conversation, Andy Donovan had assured Tony that both Cody Griffin and Lily Santos would be on the job after four o'clock at The Bird's Nest, the lounge now owned exclusively by Cody Griffin.

Cody wasn't in yet when he arrived but he found Lily Santos rearranging table setups. Andy hadn't mentioned how attractive she was—not that it was relative to Tony's investigation—but then again, maybe it was. She placed the pile of cloth napkins down on the table when Tony introduced himself and fingered his business card. "What can I do for you, Sergeant?" she asked, eyeing him cautiously. "We have several large groups coming in tonight and I'm sort of busy now."

"I won't take up much of your time. I'd like to ask you a few questions concerning your deceased employer, Tyler Keaton."

"I've already spoken to detectives—"

"Yes, I know, but since I'm in charge of the investigation, I have to ask my own questions."

Tony pulled out two chairs and made a hand motion for her to sit. Lily looked at the chair as though it were an animal trap or a hot seat, but she reluctantly sat down. "There's not much I can tell you, Sergeant. Mr. Keaton was murdered in *your* state, not mine."

"My questions won't pertain to the murder itself, Ms. Santos, but Mr. Keaton's life was here in New York City, and as I understand, most of his time was spent here in his place of business. Would you agree with that?"

She shrugged. "How can I know that for sure? I don't keep tabs on when and where other people spend their time."

"No one expects you to." He cleared his throat. "Let me rephrase the question. During your working hours was Mr. Keaton usually here?"

Lily Santos propped an elbow on the table and assumed her thinking position. Her chin rested on her clenched fist and her eyes stared ahead, not focused on anything in particular. Tony's polite patience did not go unnoticed by Lily. She smiled at the drop-dead gorgeous detective and wondered if he was married. Or if he cared that he was married. The absence of a wedding band on his left hand was not indicative of his status. "I'm sorry, but I was trying to remember. I think it's safe to say yes, most of the time—or maybe all of the time—he was here. Except for a short vacation once in a while—a few days here and there. He liked to go to Atlantic City often—that I know. He and Mr. Griffin used to cover for each other whenever they had to be away, for business or pleasure."

"Do you happen to know who he vacationed or traveled with?"

She shot him an indignant look. "That's none of my business. I would never dream of asking."

Tony gave her an apologetic smile. "Understandably," he said, looking around at the informal but tasteful décor and furnishings. "But people who work together, particularly in a small, intimate environment like this, tend to overhear conversations without intentionally *trying* to hear."

Lily pursed her lips and paused. "I'm thinking," she said as though she had to phrase her words carefully, then took a deep breath. "The guy loved his women. I can tell you that. But he liked to wine, dine and dump—and I'm leaving out one activity you can figure out for yourself." She wrinkled her nose. "No one ever lasted too long—until he met Suzanne Oliveri." She threw him a hooded-eye look, as though introducing a troublesome subject.

"Tell me your impression of their relationship. What you observed or overheard."

Lily opened her mouth to speak, then hesitated. "As far as what I overheard— well, since you're investigating a murder case, I wouldn't want to misquote anyone. But my impression? That I can tell you in one sentence: Tyler Keaton was a jealous, possessive, control-freak and Suzanne hated it."

"How do you know that? Did she confide in you? Were you friends?"

Lily laughed but with a sour tone. "Are you kidding? Tyler had her under his thumb 24/7. I don't think she had any friends of her own. He never gave her the opportunity. If she went for a damn haircut he wanted to know when she'd be back and if she was five minutes late, he'd call her. He'd say something like, "I was worried about you, babe." But no way was he worried—at least I don't think so—he just didn't want her out of his sight. She'd socialize with some of his friends, the regulars here, but never alone, never without him, as far as I could see."

"But you couldn't know that for certain, could you?"

She forced a polite smile. "Sergeant, you asked for my impression, based on my observations, and that's what I'm giving you."

Tony raised a hand. "My apologies, Ms. Santos. You're absolutely right. But try to think back—can you recall any incidents that formed the basis of your impression? I'm not expecting you to remember direct quotes. Just anything you recall."

Lily took another deep breath. Her smile was rueful this time. She wished she could simply lie and say she never saw, heard or surmised anything between the two that could have culminated into murder—more specifically the murder of Tyler Keaton with a red-hot finger pointed at Suzanne Oliveri. "I've been following the story. I know Suzanne had a bad accident and was lucky to come out alive. I know she's lucky she's in a coma and doesn't know what's going on. But when she wakes up … oh, boy!" She paused to shoot him a disapproving glance. "Do I think she had motive to kill him? Hell, yes. But do I think she did it?" She twisted her lips and paused again, revealing her uncertainty. "I don't know. She was a little on the wild side—no, I shouldn't say *wild*—more like a party girl." She erased that one too with a finger wave. "No, a nicer way to describe Suzanne would be *extroverted.* She liked her good times but I can't see her as a killer." She shook her head in disbelief, more confident now.

"Killers come in all different kinds of packaging, Ms. Santos." He took a moment to jot something down in his notebook, then continued. "What did Suzanne do to occupy her time while Tyler was away—" Tony saw that *how-the-hell-should-I-know* look again and quickly rephrased his question. "I mean, did she hang around here, work here?"

"Well, first of all, most of the time, he dragged her with him. When he didn't or couldn't, he kept tabs on her, called her on her cell all the time. That I know for a fact because she'd be blowing steam complaining out loud or mumbling under her breath that he was always checking up on her," she said, then laughed. "I remember her lashing back at him one day, saying, "Would you like to come in the bathroom with me, too? Maybe I might escape down the toilet bowl."

That got a chuckle out of Tony. "And how did Keaton react, if you remember?"

"Oh, I remember. He said, 'Don't give me any ideas.'" She smiled at the memory but it quickly faded. She shook her head as if to say the man was impossible and she didn't know how Suzanne put up with him.

"Why do you think she stayed with him so long?" Tony asked, anticipating the answer he already knew.

She gave him a sidelong glance and stood up. "Look, Sergeant, if you don't mind, I have to get back to work, so if you have more questions, you'll have to follow me around."

"Hey, no problem," he answered and stood up, too. For someone who was reluctant to talk, she had opened up plenty.

"The other detective—the one from the 21st Precinct—asked the same question and I'll give you the same answer. If you had seen some of the battle scars on her face and body, you wouldn't ask that question."

Tony nodded. "And she never said a word about his physical abuse?"

Her eyes widened. "Oh, never. He would have killed her for sure."

He moved with her to the next table. Lily twisted and swung the napkins around, creating red cone shapes with a flash of her hand. "Tell me about the relationship between Tyler and Cody. Did they get along fairly well?"

She pondered the question a moment, then shrugged. "Considering Tyler was a hothead and Cody had his own idiosyncrasies, I'd say they got along fairly well. They had occasional clashes like I imagine any business partners would, but I never witnessed anything that got really out of hand."

"How would you define Cody's idiosyncrasies?"

"He's a stickler for detail, very conscientious, on your back about every little thing. Unlike Tyler, who was lackadaisical and a procrastinator. Everything can wait until tomorrow or the next day ... you know the type."

"So you would say Cody was the more responsible partner, better equipped to handle the business, is that correct?"

"For the most part, yes, but when it came to PR, Cody couldn't shine Tyler's shoes. He knew how to charm the ladies and treat all the men like they were his best lifelong pals. You know—everyone got a bear hug or a back slap. Yes, Tyler sure knew how to pass the bull around."

"How do you think Cody felt about Tyler's popularity with the patrons?" Tony remained professionally impassive, but was inwardly amused by some of her mannerisms and facial expressions. Whenever a question required more thought, her lips would twist sideways. When she shaped her answer to her satisfaction, she'd nod first, then punctuate it with a jab of her finger.

For his last question, though, she put down her handful of silverware and crossed her arms. "Look, this is tough for me. Cody and I have a relationship going. I don't want to say anything derogatory about him. In the beginning, he and I were like oil and water. He was too damn fussy—wanted to change every little thing that I'd been doing without a problem for years before him. Eventually we reached a compromise. Since then, he's been good to me." She gave him a broad complacent smile. "He appreciates my worth now." She dropped her smile and continued. "But he was good to Suzanne too. He liked her voice and wanted her to sing. Thought it would bring in a nice crowd. But Tyler wouldn't hear of it. Didn't want men gawking and lusting after her." She shook her head and sneered. "Stupid ass, he was." She blew a sigh. "But maybe it was better that she didn't. With his temper I could just imagine what would have happened if some guy made a flirtatious or off-color remark. We would have had fists flying for sure."

"One more question and then I'll let you go. How long have you been romantically involved with Cody Griffin?"

191

The sneer snaked around her mouth again. "Romance had nothing to do with it. It just happened. And only a few weeks ago, actually. I was in a pretty down mood—crying—and he tried to comfort me. Before we knew it—" She threw her hands out in defeat.

"I see," Tony said and paused to scribble again in his notebook. "Do you want to tell me why you were crying?"

"Because that sonofabitch Tyler wanted to pick up where we left off three years ago, and I wasn't going to take any more of his crap. Once I got to know him better, I wanted no part of him—nothing personal, I mean. He had plenty to replace me, so he didn't care. Otherwise, it wouldn't have been so easy. Once Suzanne came into the picture, he didn't bother me for a while. Then one day, out of the blue, he comes up behind me and wraps his arms around my waist. Can you believe he expected me to sleep with him by day while he slept with Suzanne by night? No way was I going to do that!"

"Did you tell him that—refuse him?"

"I sure did. And he threatened to fire me, the bastard!"

*   *   *

Tony questioned the kitchen staff next, although he had predicted the results of those interviews before he stepped inside the swinging doors. Every one of them received him politely with apparent respect for his authoritative position in the investigation. But even if he were not a seasoned detective, he would have recognized the commonality in their reactions. As informally as he had posed his questions, all their faces went taut, their demeanor noticeably strained. All were too quick in their responses and all seemed to echo each other. As anticipated, Tony concluded that they had either been briefed by their surviving employer, or had made a concerted decision to play deaf and blind.

Cody Griffin, conversely, welcomed Tony like some kind of super cop who would find his partner's killer. Griffin's handshake was too strong, too long. The man was also too eager to cooperate, too in awe of Tony's position as lead detective on the case and too distraught to be believable.

But every now and then over the years, Tony's vibes had been proven wrong—not often, but enough to keep him from getting too cocky. He had humbled himself enough to keep an open mind before drawing premature conclusions.

It was Cody who asked the first question went they settled in his office.

"I don't mean to tell you how to do your job, Sergeant, but isn't it highly unlikely that someone in the New York area would be your guy? Why would he go all the way to Maine to kill Tyler? And how would he have known where to find him up there?"

Tony answered his questions with only a transparent smile and raised brows.

Cody apologized with a quick laugh. "Oh, I'm sorry. You should be asking the questions, not me." He leaned back in his swivel chair and crossed his arms. "How can I help? Ask your questions. I want to do whatever it takes to get the bastard who killed my partner."

"Tell me what you know about Tyler's personal life before and after you met him. For the two of you to form a partnership for this business, you had to know each other fairly well."

Cody steepled his fingers and rubbed them together while he pondered the question, then leaned forward and placed his elbows on the desk. "I would venture to guess, Sergeant, that whatever I can tell you about Tyler, you already know."

"That's a reasonable guess, but why don't you tell me anyway."

"Well, you probably know that Tyler was bounced around in foster homes most of his life. His father took off before he was born and his mother stuck it out for four years before she also abandoned him." Cody's gaze rested on his pen, which he twirled repeatedly. "He was still a teenager when he had to fend for himself. He was bound to tangle with the wrong people once in a while. But he'd never been in serious trouble, I'm sure, because the SLA would never have approved our liquor license." Cody paused and raised his brows questioningly, as though asking if he should continue. "I get the feeling you learned all about Tyler's background on day one of your investigation. Am I right, Sergeant?"

Tony cracked a smile. "How did you meet Tyler? When and where?"

"Right here. We were regulars who came here for a drink or a meal or both. We struck up a friendship right out there at the bar," he said, pointing. "Actually, we didn't have much else in common, except that we had the same taste in women." His sly smile held silent implications.

Tony let that one pass for the moment. "We understand that Tyler had worked as a bouncer in various places here in New York. Is that correct, to your knowledge, or are you aware of any other kinds of employment he might have mentioned?"

Cody's head pulled back as he darted Tony a perplexed look. "I don't mean to be rude, Sergeant, but aren't those redundant questions? Haven't they already been answered by your initial investigation, whether by computer searches or by other individuals' statements?"

"You'd be amazed, Mr. Griffin, how many different answers we get to the same questions. And even when the answers coincide, there's usually some slant or interpretation of facts that differs from the others. Sometimes we find gold buried in the mud. That's why we never stop digging."

Tony wrapped up his little speech with a smile that said no further explanations would be forthcoming.

Cody sighed and threw his hands up in surrender.

"What prompted the two of you to buy this place?"

"The guy who owned it had it up for sale for quite a while but could never get his price. According to what he told us, his wife was bugging him to lower the price and get rid of it. They had already bought a retirement home in Florida and she was anxious to move down there. Tyler and I used to shoot the breeze about how we'd operate it if we could own it—that we'd be a winning combination. I had a pretty good portfolio but not enough to invest on my own. Tyler, on the other hand, didn't have a pot to piss in. Whatever he earned, he spent." He made a hand gesture that mimicked the money flying away. "Then he gets this letter from the lawyer representing his uncle's estate." He shook his head and smiled. "It was an amazing stroke of luck. He hadn't seen his uncle for a couple of years, had no clue that he had accumulated such a healthy nest egg—especially since he had been in an expensive nursing home for six years. But the lucky SOB ended up pocketing almost two million." He threw his hands up and grinned broadly, but his expression immediately sobered when he realized what Tony was thinking: Tyler wasn't so lucky after all since he ended up with a knife in his chest. "That was it. We were off and running."

"Tell me about the relationship between Tyler and Suzanne Oliveri. How would you describe it?"

Cody took a long pause, then looked Tony in the eye. "Look, Sergeant, Tyler was my friend. I don't like to say anything against him, especially now that he's dead."

Tony returned a piercing look. "Mr. Griffin, the fact that Tyler is dead is exactly why I'm asking."

"Yeah, right," Cody said. He blew a sigh, reluctant to discuss the matter. "He pampered her … bought her clothes and jewelry, but to tell you the truth, I think he did it more for his self-image than because he cared for her. Once he inherited that money … well, I guess he started living the way he always wanted to live."

"You don't think he had any feelings for her?"

"Oh, I didn't say that. She couldn't make a move without him or without his permission."

"So he kept a tight leash on her, you'd say?"

Cody dipped his head. "That's a good way to describe it. He treated her like a dog—a well-dressed dog, as long as she remembered to obey her master."

"And did that bother you?"

Cody lifted his brows and shrugged. "Not really. It didn't seem to bother her much, so why should I care?"

"Let me back up a little," Tony said. "You mentioned that you and he had the same taste in women. Did you and Tyler ever clash in that regard? Were you ever interested in the same woman?"

Cody waved it off as ludicrous. "No way! I said we had the same *taste,* not the same woman."

Tony remained impassive, but after questioning him another twenty minutes, he concluded that if Lily Santos was to be believed, Cody Griffin's credibility had just taken a nose dive.

Chapter Forty-three

Tony had met Andy Donovan for a quick dinner before heading home to Maine. They had eaten at Patsy's Grille on 53rd Street, which was one of the NYPD's favorite hangouts. He had enjoyed the food, the relaxed atmosphere and the company, but thoughts of the long trip home made him anxious to leave.

They shook hands at the 21st Precinct parking lot, where Tony had left his car. "Don't forget what I said, Tony," Andy said. "Just give me a call whenever you need me. And don't worry about my busy schedule. Hell, if we had to wait for crime to slow down, we'd never get to sack out in our own beds. So don't hesitate to call—got it?" He pointed a finger for emphasis.

Tony gave him a warm smile and a brotherly hug before settling in his car. "Got it. And thanks for squeezing in dinner with me."

Andy laughed. "You paid for it, so I'm the one who should be saying thanks."

"You did already. Twice," Tony said, then threw him a final wave and drove off.

Andy had convinced him to hang around until all commercial and commuter traffic died down before taking off and he was glad he did. Once he got out of the city streets and onto the West Side Highway, it was clear sailing.

He checked with Dispatch again and there were no major developments that would require his attention tonight. He hoped it would stay that way.

Corrine filled his mind again as soon as he was on the open road. He turned on the radio and listened to an all news station for a while. When that failed to distract his thoughts of Corrine, he tried a call-in talk show and that too was no help. Neither the commentator nor the caller had anything to say that Tony considered worth listening to. He couldn't believe the garbage on radio and television that managed to grab audiences. He settled for a soft rock station when Rod Stewart's gravelly voice came on singing, *I've Got a Crush on You,* an old lovers' favorite when Frank Sinatra ruled as king of the music world.

Listening now with no distractions other than the roar of the road, the words got to him like a punch in the gut. He was an ass and he knew it. In retrospect, he realized that jealousy is nothing but an express exit out of a relationship. At his age, he should have been long past that immature crap, but his old temperament sometimes shot up like a blazing fire. He had lashed out at her, particularly for not telling him. Maybe he could have handled it better if she had been honest.

But he remembered her words that night at his house: "Oh, yeah, right! Like you would have given me your permission!"

She was absolutely right. He would have raised hell if she had told him she agreed to have dinner with "an old friend"—and old *boyfriend,* who just happened to be passing through Ogunquit. *What did she expect me to do, give her a kiss and say, Fine, have a good time?*

He felt the heat rising inside him again, then took a few deep breaths. He resolved to shake off the whole incident and bury for good this streak of jealousy that gave him nothing but grief whenever it surfaced.

Tony didn't bother to look at the time when he picked up his phone to call her. Her voice was raspy when she answered and he had a short pang of guilt for waking her out of a sound sleep.

Corrine shook the drowsiness from her eyes when she saw his name on the Caller ID. "Tony?" she said, assuming this was business. "What's up?" When he didn't immediately answer, she tried again. "Tony, what's wrong?"

"Nothing's wrong, except that I've been a Class A ass. I'm sorry, I'm sorry, I'm sorry. And if you want me to say it another hundred times, I will." Then, all in the same breath, he added, "I'm on my way back from New York. I should be home in two hours. Can I come straight there?"

Corrine giggled. "You know, you're absolutely adorable when you're humble. Sure, you can come here. But it'll be about 2:00 a.m. We're both on duty tomorrow."

"Well, you can still catch another two hours. I'll be wiped out, but what the hell—why worry about tomorrow when we have tonight?"

Again Corrine giggled. "Hey, wasn't that a line from an old '40's movie?"

"Probably. But tonight it's mine."

After his conversation with Corrine, Tony no longer minded the long drive home. He was so keyed up and anxious to hold her in his arms again. The memory of their last, albeit brief, reconciliation at his house sent a surge of heat to his groin. This time he'd make sure it didn't end in disaster like that night. He'd lost her twice before, and if he knew Corrine, with three strikes against him, she'd boot him out of her house and out of her life.

His foot leaned a little too heavily on the gas pedal and he had to keep reminding himself to slow down.

He made it to Corrine's house on Israel Head Road by 1:45 a.m. She was at the porch window waiting for him. The outdoor light cast a soft glow on her face. When she smiled at him, the flash of her white teeth rendered him breathless.

She welcomed him with open arms and he barely managed to kick the door closed. His hands wrapped around her bare midriff. The warmth of her body radiated through his.

She made a sudden break away from his kiss and laughed. "Wow! Your hands are ice cold. Look, I'm shivering."

He pulled her closer and nibbled at her neck. "Honey, you've only just begun."

From the porch they worked their way into the living room and never missed a beat. Tony's mouth was so hungry for her that he hadn't even shed his jacket yet. The shrill sound of his cell phone brought the two detectives back to reality. Tony threw his head back and clenched his teeth to hold back the expletives about to spill out. "Damn!" he yelled instead and yanked the phone off his belt. "Would you believe I actually prayed this damn phone wouldn't ring? Just tonight … that's all I asked."

He pulled in a long breath to cool himself off, but the bite remained in his tone. "Yeah, Gerard here."

Corrine fingered her chestnut-colored hair for a fast comb-through and tucked her sports bra and tank top back where they belonged. Drained of the soaring passion that filled her only moments ago, she watched Tony as he listened, trying to read in his face the severity of the call.

He snapped the phone shut and slipped it back in its case. He looked at her like a treasure being offered that he had to reluctantly refuse. For now at least. He held her face again to freeze its image, then ran his fingers through her hair, using the same tracks hers had left. He kissed her again, more gently this time, his lips clinging to the sweet taste of her. As she moved, the stream of light from outside splashed across her face, illuminating her hazel eyes. Tony held her face and looked at her as though he had to be sure this scene was real and not just an image his heart had conjured up. He kissed her forehead and played with the curly wisps along her hairline. "To be continued, sweetheart," he said ruefully.

Her sigh was almost a groan of disappointment. "Why? What happened?"

"A shooting at Scotty's Tavern," he grumbled. "As usual, I seem to be the only guy available. Sometimes I wish I could quit this damn job and get myself a nice, cushy nine to five one behind a desk. Maybe then I can have an uninterrupted private life."

"You'd be bored stiff and you know it."

"Maybe. But I could enjoy the fringe benefits." Tony threw her one of his sexy smiles. "I'd be there now," he said, pointing to the bed, "with no one to bother me but you."

She stood on her toes for one last kiss. "Ah, but these stolen moments are much more exciting."

They stole five minutes more.

Chapter Forty-four

Heather had been fussy half the night. Frannie had given her a bottle which she didn't usually demand during the wee hours, then changed her diaper. And still she cried and fussed.

As she walked the floor with her infant cousin, Frannie couldn't stop thinking about Suzanne. Working full-time and taking care of a baby all by herself was worthy of a lot more credit and respect than she had given Suzanne. She mumbled apologies under her breath to her cousin, promising she'd repeat them over and over again when she opened her eyes again. *If* she opened her eyes again. Despite Dr. Quinlan's assurance, until it actually happened, everyone was apprehensive.

After Frannie paced the floor for another twenty minutes, singing softly in a tired, raspy voice that was in no mood to sing, Heather finally settled down. She tiptoed back to her bed—God forbid the floor should creak—and curled up in her down comforter like a snail in its shell. In seconds, she drifted off to sleep for the two hours she had left.

But a half hour later it was the musical sound of her cell phone that woke her. Her heart pounded as she threw the covers off and ran to grab it. *Only bad news comes in the middle of the night.* Her stomach turned over.

"Ms. Oliveri, this is Nurse Darnell at Maine Medical Center. Our records indicate that you requested we contact you immediately if there's any change ..."

Frannie's breath caught in her throat. "Yes, what is it?"

"Your cousin is coming out of the coma—"

"Oh, my God! Did she? She's awake?" With her mouth open and her eyes widened in surprise, she stopped and listened. Tears fell in a rush and she wiped them with the sleeve of her pajamas. "I'll be there as fast as I can."

"Miss Oliveri, I understand how anxious you are, but it would be foolish to rush here now. Dr. Quinlan can't possibly arrive until about eight o'clock, and the attending physician won't allow visitors. It's too risky to rush her. She might revert. We have to bring her back slowly and cautiously. I suggest you wait until Dr. Quinlan comes in. Let him examine your cousin and I'm sure he'll contact you immediately after."

Frannie blew a breath and hesitated before responding. Nurse Darnell was speaking rationally, without emotions to deal with, but Frannie wished she could jump in her car and race to the hospital anyway. "You haven't notified my uncle yet, have you?"

"No. You and he had agreed that you should be the first contact person if her condition changes in any way."

Frannie picked up on the nurse's clipped, defensive tone. "No, that's okay," she said. "You were right to call me first. My uncle gets confused easily so he wanted me to take charge."

"Fine, then," Nurse Darnell answered, her tone relaxed now. "So sit tight and try to be patient until you get Dr. Quinlan's call."

"Just one thing more, please, before you hang up. Did Suzanne speak or mumble anything at all?"

"Oh, no. It's much too soon to expect that. Sounds yes, but nothing coherent."

Frannie sat on the edge of her bed too keyed up to try sleeping again. It was almost five o'clock anyway. Why bother? She turned off the alarm, went into the kitchen and picked up the phone. Bill Franklin had left clear instructions that he be contacted the moment Suzanne comes out of the coma, no matter what time.

"No, Frannie, don't worry about waking me up," he said in a groggy voice. "That's what I told you to do. Has she spoken any words yet? Did you ask?"

"I did ask. The nurse said just sounds, nothing coherent."

"Good. But I have to hang up now. For Suzanne's protection, I have to call the hospital right now. And when you and your family get there, remember what I told you. No one—and I mean no one—is to discuss anything about the night of the accident. Not with her or with each other in her presence, understand?"

"Absolutely. Since you explained how anything she says can and may be used against her, we understand perfectly how important that is."

When she concluded the call with Bill, she started to call her uncle, but decided she'd better have a cup of coffee first. Or better yet, she'd call her parents now, let her dad handle calling his brother, and then have her coffee in peace.

According to the thermostat, the house was certainly warm enough. Now that she had Heather, she had kept the temperature slightly higher. But she hugged herself while waiting for her coffee to be ready, rubbing her goosebumped arms. No, it wasn't the temperature that chilled her. It was Old Man Fear doing a number on her again. This was the day she had waited for—had prayed for. And yet it was also the day of reckoning. No matter how she tried to chase it away, that thin line of doubt snaked its way into her thoughts again.

What if ... What if Suzanne had completely lost her mind and really did kill her lover?

The thought terrified her. She shook it away and tried to think positively. It's also very possible Suzanne could free herself from all suspicion with a perfectly logical and credible explanation, right? *Sure.*

But all the way through two cups of coffee and a hot shower it was the first image that flashed steadily like a heartbeat and ominously like war drums.

By 6:30 Frannie couldn't wait a moment longer to call Glory. "I'm sorry I woke you, Glory, but I couldn't wait. Suzanne is out of her coma!"

The shocking news silenced Glory momentarily but her elation rang out in a shriek. "Oh, thank God! I've been so afraid that she'd never wake up, even though the doctors expected her to."

"You and me both! When I called my parents, they admitted harboring the same fears."

"So now what?" Glory asked. "You're going to the hospital, aren't you? I can watch Heather for a few hours."

"Actually, Glory, I was depending on that. My parents want to go too. Let's face it, my uncle Jerry, my parents and I are the only family she has. We should all be there when she opens her eyes. But they won't stay long, they said. They'll come back to take care of Heather so you can have a few hours free before you go to Amore Evenings."

"Okay, so let's not waste time talking. Let me get in the shower and—"

"No, Glory, don't rush. The nurse who called said I should wait until Dr. Quinlan comes in and he won't be there before eight o'clock. Until I hear from him, Suzanne can't have visitors. So I'll take Heather to Amore and you can pick her up about nine, okay?"

"Sure," Glory said, glad she could help. "And speaking of Amore, will the staff need help?" Remembering the discussion with her dad, she asked the question cautiously.

"Amore should be fine. We've always had a Plan B in the event of my absence and now, since Heather and Suzanne became my responsibility, we've fine-tuned it."

"Okay, then," Glory said softly.

Frannie could easily visualize the look on her friend's face judging by the tone of her voice. "Glory, I only say that for your sake. Between your column and Amore Evenings—and now with unexpected babysitting thrown in here and there—what kind of friend would I be to ask anything more of you?"

"A good friend. One who knows she can ask for any favor she needs. I might not always be able to accommodate those needs, and if that's the case, I'll tell you."

Frannie heaved a sigh. "I always said you were a glutton for punishment. Okay, then. Stop in today after my parents relieve you with Heather. Just to make sure there are no unforeseen problems." She paused, then added, "You miss hanging out at Amore Breakfast, don't you, Glory?"

Glory smiled at the honesty of Frannie's question. "I guess I do. It's funny, I know Amore Breakfast is yours alone, but I have a sentimental attachment to it. So much has changed in my life since that day I walked in for the first time ..."

"And all for the better?"

Glory paused. "Not one hundred percent on all counts, but for the most part my life is much better, much happier here in Ogunquit. What more could I want? Since I found my father especially, I have everything," she answered, but she stifled the urge to add *Except the man I love a lot and hate a little. And the baby I hoped he would give me.*

Frannie understood that Glory was holding back; trying to sound perfectly content since her problems could not be equated with Frannie's these days. But Frannie couldn't help thinking that if Glory had never come to

Ogunquit, she never would have met Alex and her heart wouldn't be aching now. She also would never have met Carl, who left her with a memory that would haunt her for the rest of her life.

But then again, she found Dan in Ogunquit. The love Glory felt for her father was worth almost any suffering, even losing Alex. She and Dan lost thirty-five years; they were still getting to know each other and she adored him.

Maybe that's the problem between Glory and Alex, Frannie realized.

Chapter Forty-five

Frannie had managed fifteen minutes lead time before Amore Breakfast would be open for business. As she parked her car she was glad to find no one waiting on the porch yet because she wanted to feed Heather herself. Any one of her staff would jump at the chance—Heather had already been unofficially crowned Amore's princess—but Frannie didn't want to share that pleasure unless she absolutely had to. Fruit and cereal had just been introduced this week and Frannie got the biggest kick out of feeding her. She loved how her tiny mouth puckered and quivered impatiently for the next spoonful; how she'd shake her little fists and cry if she wasn't fed fast enough.

Yes, every day was a new experience with Heather. She had to keep reminding herself this was nothing more than a temporary babysitting job. Don't get too attached—Suzanne will get well and take her daughter back.

Yeah, sure. As if Suzanne's physical injuries were the only impediment that could separate this mother and daughter. As if a possible murder charge could be brushed aside like a minor complication to be dealt with and promptly eliminated.

She left Heather in her infant seat on a booth table while she called out to her staff. "Hey, guys. I've got great news. The hospital called. Suzanne is awake—" Frannie held up a hand to stop all the joyous outbursts. "No, hold it. I appreciate how you've all been plugging and praying, but I have to talk fast before the cars start rolling in. Here's the story—I'm expecting a call in the next hour or two from her doctor. They won't allow visitors until he examines her and gives the okay. But I'll be flying out of here the moment he does. I know I can count on you guys to hold the fort and close up for me."

It seemed everyone spoke at once, responding to the happy news and eager to help in any way. Frannie tilted her head to swallow the lump in her throat. Funny, she thought, how you take people for granted. You're never conscious of how much affection you share until you have a problem or a crisis in your life, like this one. Then the love bursts through like sunshine and warms you all over.

She thanked them with tight lips and a brush of her hand, then dug into the diaper bag to prepare Heather's breakfast.

Tracy, the newest young college student to join the Amore staff, called out to her. "Hey, Frannie, how did your uncle react to the news? I could imagine his relief."

A mischievous smile crept around Frannie's mouth. "I'm not sure exactly. I left that call to my dad. I had to rush to get here with Heather. We weren't planning on telling him the call came at 4:30. He'd have a fit that we didn't let him know immediately."

Tracy grimaced, but her look easily translated to *Can you blame him?*

Frannie gave her the yes-I'm-guilty nod. "My dad and I talked about it and decided to wait. He would have insisted that we take him immediately. And as much as we're all anxious to get there, what would be the point if we can't get in to see her? The nurse distinctly told me to wait and I didn't want to appear uncooperative. My uncle taxes their patience enough—and mine!"

*   *   *

Every time the phone rang Frannie jumped for it until her nerves were frazzled, but finally at 9:20 the call from Dr.

Quinlan came through. The immediate family could all come, but for very brief visits. There would be absolutely no questions or discussion about the death of Tyler Keaton or anything else about her activities prior to the accident. Even if Dr. Quinlan would have allowed it at some point later, Bill Franklin had left strict orders that no one could speak to her or conduct any tests without his permission. They could only assure her that Heather was fine, but no details.

Since Sal was driving his brother, Tess and Frannie traveled alone in Frannie's car. They both welcomed the opportunity for a private mother/daughter talk. "But how long can we hold back Tyler Keaton's murder?" Tess asked her daughter.

"Forever as far as we're concerned. Only Bill Franklin will tell her what she needs to know and when. He was adamant about that. And I can certainly understand why, can't you, Mom?"

"Oh, of course I can, but still, once she starts talking—even to her lawyer—and asking questions ... And how can they prevent her from talking to the medical staff? Even without a TV in her room, she's bound to hear something. Somebody can so easily slip and get her talking ..." They both had the same fears and suspicions but neither one dared breathe a word in that direction.

"Mom, we have to trust that her doctor and lawyer will prevent that from happening. We can't start worrying about things that *might* happen. We have enough to deal with, so let's talk about something else."

"With something like this hanging over us, what's there to talk about? Everything else seems unimportant," Tess said. They rode in silence for a few minutes until Tess spoke again. "Your father wasn't too happy when I asked him to take your uncle in his car. It's a good thing we're leaving the hospital earlier, he said, so you can take him home. One trip a day with your uncle Jerry is enough for him, he said." She smiled as she spoke but her face was devoid of humor.

Frannie shot her mother an exaggerated look of annoyance. "Thanks a lot!"

Tess smiled back at her and waved it off. "Oh, you know what he means. You seem to have a better handle on him. Uncle Jerry sort of follows your lead. With your father, he's cantankerous, foul-mouthed and downright obnoxious."

"Oh? And does Daddy think I never heard—was never *mortified* by his foul language and obnoxious behavior?"

Tess lowered her gaze and nodded apologetically. "No, he knows, Frannie—we both know. But it's so much worse for your father to handle him." She drew a deep breath and exhaled. "The plain truth is Daddy's ashamed of him. He made such a mess of his life with that drinking. And Suzanne's. Your father used to try talking to him in the beginning, but how do you reason with a drunk? Even when he wasn't too far gone, Daddy couldn't get through to him."

"Mom, to an alcoholic, the almighty bottle is a crutch—their lifeline. They think they can't survive without it. They need steady treatment and a strong commitment to fight their battle. An occasional pep talk is like spitting in the ocean."

"I know. Daddy knows too but he still feels like a failure. He can't shake the guilt for not keeping after him … for giving up on him. He says as ugly as it gets, it's a sickness and he should have been more patient. Maybe he could have turned him around before he got this bad."

Frannie shot her mother a long look. "Mom, you'd better work on Daddy and his guilt. If you can't convince him, I will. He's not a professional and all the brotherly love in the world can't help Uncle Jerry now. He's too far gone."

Tess heaved a long sigh and crossed her arms on her chest. "Damn shame, though. I remember your uncle way back when." Her fingers waved the years over her shoulder. "To look at him now, it's hard to believe he was such a nice guy; intelligent, sociable and your father's best friend. Now …" She threw her hands out as a gesture of hopelessness.

"You're right, Mom. It *is* hard to believe."

*   *   *

No one said a word as the four of them sandwiched themselves into an already crowded elevator. Frannie wondered if everyone in the silent cramped space could hear her heart thumping.

Dr. Quinlan had obviously been alerted to their arrival because they found him waiting at the doorway of Suzanne's room. He extended his arm to stop Jerry from getting past him. "Mr. Oliveri, let me remind you how very important it is for you and everyone to be extremely cautious," he admonished. "Speak softly and assuringly. She needs to know she has the comfort of a loving family standing by, ready to support her. At this point she hasn't regained full memory yet. She knows who she is and understands there was an accident, but from what I could discern she has no recollection as to what preceded the accident. And let me remind you that Mr. Franklin was emphatic about his instructions. He doesn't want anyone— not even you—to speak to her about anything other than her physical condition. When she's able to, I'm sure she'll ask about her daughter. You can only assure her that the baby is with Frannie and doing fine. Nothing more. Her lawyer will handle the rest. Do you understand that, sir?"

Jerry Oliveri nodded impatiently without meeting the doctor's gaze. When he brushed aside Dr. Quinlan's extended arm, Frannie pulled him back with a yank at his collar. "Hold it, Uncle Jerry. I know you're anxious to get in there, but do you realize how important it is to follow the doctor's instructions? It's all for Suzanne's protection. I know you want to hear what she has to say, but we can't discuss it with her yet. So not a single word—got it?"

She shook a finger in his face; a gesture he would understand, then glanced up at the doctor. She shot him a look that asked *Does that cover it, Doctor?*

Dr. Quinlan smiled and nodded, admiring her take-charge ability with this difficult man who had exhibited several times the typical behavioral pattern of an alcoholic in desperate need of help.

"I hear, I hear," Jerry growled and pulled away from her grasp. He did, however, look at the doctor for his nod of approval before entering the room. Jerry sucked in a long breath to brace himself, then gently pulled aside the bedside curtain.

His agonizing gasp sent them all in to restrain him but when his brother's hand gripped his shoulders, Jerry shook them off. He crossed his hands over his mouth to smother his sobs, but silent tears fell from his red-rimmed eyes.

Frannie whispered to the doctor who had reentered the room with them. "Is it okay if we stay? We need to keep a close eye on my uncle."

Dr. Quinlan fingered his chin thoughtfully. "Why don't you alternate staying with him? That might be better. I can hang around for only another minute or so, but don't worry. They'll page me if there's a problem." He patted her hand, as though to indicate she was now in charge.

The family lounge was directly across from Suzanne's room. Frannie convinced her mom to relax with a cup of coffee. With her father watching from the doorway, Uncle Jerry would be fine, and if not, they'd be only steps away.

"It's so much scarier this time, Frannie," Tess said, blowing short breaths into the steaming coffee. "As much as we've all been waiting for this day, we're all afraid of what she'll say to her lawyer; what she'll remember. God forbid any of those silent accusations are true, she's better off being in a deep sleep. What a horror to wake up to."

"We have to stay positive, Mom. So far that's all speculation. No one has *formally* accused her yet. God only knows how many people have been wrongly accused. And even if it comes to that, now that we have Bill Franklin handling her defense, I feel a heck of a lot better."

"Me too," Tess said, then went silent while she sipped her coffee again.

"What's going on in your head, Mom? I get the feeling you don't share the same confidence in Bill Franklin, am I right? He's supposed to be the best defense attorney."

Tess put her cup down and broke away from her thoughts. "Oh, I'm not disputing that. I know his reputation. His name is always in the papers and even on TV sometimes." Her positive expression faded. "But I'm not always crazy about his clients. From what I read about them, in my opinion, some should be locked away with no chance of parole. The thought of Suzanne being lumped in with those seedy characters makes me sick."

"I understand what you're saying, Mom, but first of all, that's stretching *guilt by association* too far. And besides, not all 'seedy characters' are guilty. That's why we need defense attorneys. And especially when someone in *our* family takes the hot seat!"

"That's for sure," Tess said, but inwardly she couldn't share her daughter's optimistic attitude. Even the very best lawyers occasionally lose cases.

Sal poked his head in the doorway and crooked a finger for them to follow. "She's waking up!"

Her eyes never opened again during the ten minutes they all stood by silently, watching and waiting. Although they had watched her do nothing but sleep for the past ten days, she looked different now. The respirator, the IV, the Foley catheter and surgical bandages were gone now. Her swelling had substantially subsided, but her eyes looked like two sunken black circles. Every visible part of her body was bruised and discolored. Her face appeared peaceful, as though she had enjoyed a full night of deep and dreamless sleep. So unlike the stony coldness all the days before when it seemed she wore the face of death.

Sal quietly placed the visitor chair closer to the bed for his brother. Jerry reached to stroke his daughter's arm, but pulled back and glanced questioningly at Dr. Quinlan, who smiled and simply nodded.

With remarkable restraint that surprised but pleased his family, Jerry ran one gentle finger along his daughter's arm smoothing out the fine hairs.

Tess grabbed the little box of tissues to dab at the corners of her eyes, then handed the box to Frannie, who did the same.

Sal put a hand on Tess's and Frannie's shoulders and led them out of the room. His brother needed a few private moments with Suzanne and he should be the only one at her bedside when she opened her eyes. When he expressed that feeling to his wife and daughter, they both disagreed.

"Dad, I don't like leaving him alone with her—"

"He's not alone. I'll be right here at the door."

"Frannie's right, Sal," Tess argued. "You know how erratic his behavior is. What if she opens her eyes and he scares her to death? What if he blurts out something about the murder?"

Sal rolled his eyes. "Tess, you're overreacting. He's as sober now as he's ever going to get. And he's not stupid—

he only *looks* stupid all the time. My brother may be a drunk, but he loves his daughter, no matter what you think."

Tess's eyebrows curled in indignation. "Who ever said I think otherwise?"

"You don't have to say it. I can see it."

"What you've seen, my dear husband, is *abhorrence* for the way he always talked to her like she was dirt under his feet, but that doesn't mean—"

"No," Sal cut in, jabbing a finger in the air, "that's always been the crux of his problem with Suzanne. *He* feels like dirt under *her* feet and every insult he's ever thrown at her was really his way of lashing out at himself."

Tess folded her arms in defiance. "Oh, so now you're a psychiatrist?"

Frannie heaved a sigh. *Here we go again.* She had hoped the flickering flames of her parents' argumentative discussion would die out, but their voices were rising above the whispers that initiated it.

She slipped between them and put a hand on each. They were a loving couple who would be lost without each other, but this was not the first time she had to step between them and referee. "Time out, guys. This is a hospital. Do you want to get us thrown out? This is just the kind of scene that Dr. Quinlan is trying to protect Suzanne from. So please … *cool it!*"

Tess and Sal realized instantly the wisdom of her words and both lowered their eyes and nodded their agreement.

"Okay, truce," Sal whispered to his wife, then smiled at her without provocation or reason.

"Yes, truce," Tess said, making the peace sign. "Until we get home," she added then covered her mouth to suppress a giggle.

Frannie shook her head and gave them a *what-am-I-going-to-do-with-you-guys* face. As long as they come out laughing, she thought. But this was neither the time nor place for laughter. Although on second thought, maybe these are God's little ways of helping you cope with agonizing situations.

Chapter Forty-six

Dr. Quinlan addressed the family when they arrived. "Suzanne is still out of it for the most part, but her memory and comprehension are slowly returning. Not completely from what I've seen so far, but enough to allow each of you a minute or two with her. Mr. Franklin should be here shortly and I'm sure you'd want to save her energy for him." He lifted a warning finger. "But remember, I said *slowly* returning. She understands where she is; that she was involved in a serious accident a week ago. I explained her condition when she was admitted; the subsequent surgery we performed and why."

"Did she remember how the accident happened, Doctor?" Frannie asked.

Dr. Quinlan lowered his eyes. "I didn't question her about the accident. Any questions I posed were related strictly to her physical condition in accordance with instructions from Mr. Franklin."

Frannie rolled her eyes. "Boy, this is going to be rough for us. Maybe we shouldn't go in yet. Do you think we should wait for Bill Franklin and let him guide us after he sees her?"

"I think that's an excellent idea." He looked directly at Jerry, anticipating his objection.

Bill Franklin stepped off the elevator ten minutes later and Frannie approached him. She introduced him to her uncle and her parents. "We decided to wait for you before going in, Bill, as anxious as we are."

"Good. I had hoped you'd make that choice. So, okay. Here's what I'd like you to do. As her closest family, you and your uncle will go in first, but only for a minute or two. And put on the biggest smile you can manage. The last thing we want is a tearful, emotional scene. That won't help Suzanne. Depending on what she remembers, she's bound to be very frightened."

Frannie understood clearly. She understood more what Bill Franklin *wasn't* saying than what he *did* say. Will she remember that she abandoned her daughter? Will she remember how Tyler Keaton died? Will she have a story to tell that could help Bill Franklin prove her innocence? Is that too much to hope for? And most importantly, what about Bill Franklin? Did he already conclude his client is guilty, shrug it off, and simply plan to give her the best defense possible?

She left the questions suspended and responded to the lawyer. "Dr. Quinlan made that very clear to us, Bill. My uncle and I understand perfectly. Right, Uncle Jerry?" She held his arm and her eyes gave him one last warning. Jerry broke from her hold, but she pulled him back, gripping his arm tighter. She then turned to Bill Franklin again. "Bill, should I break it to her that you're coming in? I'm afraid she'll freak out if she hears *lawyer.*"

He waved off her concern. "Don't say a thing. I'll introduce myself. You two go in first and comfort her. I'll stay in the doorway for a moment or two. Give your cousin a hug. Tell her she's going to be fine. Tell her Heather is fine—healthy and happy. When I come in, you two step out and I'll take it from there."

Frannie stiffened when she walked into Suzanne's room. A shiver rippled through her body. Instinctively, she crossed her chilled arms and rubbed them.

Her uncle Jerry was unusually docile today. Depending on his alcohol consumption each day—or lack thereof—his temperament was subject to change. But her parents had also remarked about the noticeable difference today. They credited it to the fact that he had given Eloise her "walking papers," he'd said, and slammed the door in her face.

Frannie watched Jerry approach the bed and moisture filled her eyes. But she steeled herself not to succumb to them. At least not now. She stared at Suzanne as though she were seeing her for the first time. Her eyes were slitted slightly like a clam shell, but she blinked a few times and managed to open them wider. Seeing her father, she drew back and her lips trembled. She pulled the sheet up, leaving only her eyes exposed.

Jerry forced a smile but his hands began to shake. He tucked them under his armpits first, then settled for the pockets of his pants. "How are you feeling?" he asked blandly.

With a thumping heart, Frannie watched her cousin come back to life. The sight was bittersweet. Suzanne put a finger between her teeth. Tears streamed down her face like icy ribbons. Except for the purplish circles around her eyes, her skin was milk-white. Her long, black hair had been brushed but its satin sheen gone, replaced by clusters of dry, brittle strands fanned in disarray on her pillow. Her blue hospital gown was clean and crisp with a cheerful print of tiny pink flowers, but to Frannie, Suzanne still looked like a character in a horror movie.

Suzanne gave her father a shrug, as if to say how she feels is insignificant, then turned to Frannie with furrowed brows and fear in her eyes. "Heather? Is she okay, Frannie?" Her voice was scratchy and thick. Like a person dying of thirst. She sobbed and buried her face in her hands. "I'm sorry. I'm *so-o-o* sorry …"

Frannie's mouth went dry wondering if Suzanne was sorry for leaving Heather or sorry for killing her lover. "She's fine, absolutely fine. We're all spoiling her and she loves every minute, so don't upset yourself worrying about her."

Suzanne's eyes darted over to the stranger in the doorway. Bill Franklin took that as his cue. He entered with a smile wide as a watermelon slice. He walked up to her bed as if he were about to announce she holds a winning lottery ticket, not that he's been retained to defend her against a possible murder charge.

Jerry stepped back but remained standing alongside the bed. His gaze shifted from his daughter to the gray tile floor. Suzanne, noticing his lowered eyes, yielded an arm from under the sheet. Limply, she extended it towards her father. The gesture stunned Jerry and filled him with remorse, prompting him to grab her hand and bring it to his cheek. He burst into tears and Frannie quietly escorted him out to her waiting parents.

Suzanne glanced at the well-dressed man with the soft smile and assumed he was a doctor. She raised a hand to stop him from speaking. "Where's my daughter? Can I see her? Where did my cousin go?" Her words were drowned in tears and Bill Franklin spoke softly. "Suzanne, Heather is in very capable hands. As your cousin told you, she's happy and healthy. Let's just concentrate on getting you well enough first, then we'll see what we can do. Okay?"

His soothing tone calmed her enough to nod reluctantly, but she looked at him cautiously. "Who are you? I thought Dr. Quinlan was my doctor."

"He is, Suzanne, and I'm not a doctor. My name is Bill Franklin and I'm here to help you. I'm the attorney your family retained to represent you."

Suzanne's eyes went wide. She tried to lift her head but it fell back on her pillow. "Why? Did I hit someone in the accident?" She sobbed at the thought. "Did someone die?"

"No, no. And even if that were the case, it wouldn't be your fault. The overpass collapsed. You happened to have the misfortune of crossing it at the time." He gave her an assuring smile. "But thanks to the fast action of the rescue crew, this hospital and particularly Dr. Quinlan, you'll eventually be good as new. Trust me on that."

Suzanne sniffed and pulled a tissue out of the little hospital-issue box resting on her chest. "I guess I have to trust you. What choice do I have?" She shot a look out the door, hoping to see Dr. Quinlan so she could call him in. The moment she laid eyes on him, and especially after he spoke to her, she knew he was everything she always wished her father to be—kind, caring, gentle, protective. She looked at the lawyer again, still unsure if she could trust him. "Mr. Franco—what was your name?"

"Franklin, Bill Franklin, but you can call me Bill if you'd like."

"Yeah, I do like. I used to know a nice man named Bill, so that'll work for me."

Bill Franklin eyed the doorway to be sure no one was within earshot. "Do you mind if I close the door while we talk, Suzanne?"

"Why? What do you have to tell me?"

Bill recognized the suspicion in her eyes and gave her an easy smile. He closed the door, then pulled up a chair, rather than hover over her. "Suzanne, do you have any idea why I'm here? Do you have any recollection of what happened prior to the accident?"

She turned her head and focused on the bed rail. Telling her story to an inanimate object would be easier than looking into the lawyer's smoky-blue eyes that silently demanded the truth. Her mouth twitched and a breath caught in her throat before another rush of tears flooded her eyes. She used the sheet to blot her cheeks. "Please ... I don't want to lose my daughter." She pleaded with her eyes. "Are you sure she's with Frannie? You wouldn't all lie to me, would you?"

Bill Franklin patted her hand. "No one is lying to you, Suzanne. If we want to get past this, we both have to be truthful. Of course Heather is with Frannie. Where else would she be?"

Her gaze flew back to the bed rail. "With her father?" The image of Tyler snatching Heather out of Frannie's arms made her wince. She covered her eyes as though it would stop the image from taking shape again.

"Suzanne, first of all I'm not here because you left your daughter alone in your cousin's house. Yes, it was an irresponsible act on your part, but I need to know *why* you left your baby. You left a note saying it was an emergency. Please try to relax and tell me what made you desperate enough to leave Heather. Tell me everything you remember leading up to that point and everything that followed up until the accident. Again, remember that you can trust me, Suzanne. I'm your lawyer. You can trust me the way you trust Dr. Quinlan. He saved your life and you're his patient so he's concerned about you. Well, you're my client and I'm just as concerned about you. I'm here to protect you also."

"I *do* trust Dr. Quinlan," she answered without hesitation.

The way she responded told Bill she wasn't ready to equate him with Tim Quinlan. Bill knew he had to work a little harder to gain her confidence; to make her understand that although the doctor had saved her life in this hospital, Bill's job—his equally difficult job—might be to save her life in a courtroom.

"Okay, Suzanne. Let's get back to Heather's father. I'm glad you mentioned him because that's a good place to start. I need to know who he is."

Suzanne kneaded at her thermal blanket. "Why is that important? He doesn't know Heather exists and I've tried so hard to keep it that way." Inwardly, Suzanne knew she'd have to reveal his identity. But she also knew that once she did, she'd be blowing up the protective balloon she had built around them since she first learned of her pregnancy. "He's not a good person, to put it mildly. He's a violent, possessive man, and I can't do that to Heather ..." She burst into tears again. "Besides, he might kill me for not telling him he has a daughter. You don't know him like I do!"

Bill drew a breath and observed the haunting fear in his client's eyes. She had to be told, but it might be the lesser of two evils. He held her hand. "Suzanne, as I said, my presence here has nothing to do with the care or custody of your daughter—not directly anyway."

"Then why *are* you here?"

"Try to stay calm and I'll explain." Bill decided it might be better to help her along rather than wait for her to get the courage to spill it all out to someone she met only seconds ago. "Suzanne, I understand you lived in New York City for a few years before moving back to Ogunquit. And during that time you were involved with—you *lived with*—a man who fathered your child, I assume. Am I correct in making that assumption?"

Suzanne let the question hang between them like a heavy curtain. She didn't want to answer but had a strong feeling he already knew more about her than she cared to share. Lawyer or no lawyer.

Her head throbbed like it was being attacked by woodpeckers but she refused to use that as an excuse to stall this inevitable questioning. It could be worse, she reasoned. At least he's not a prosecutor.

"Yes," she finally said.

"And his name is Tyler Keaton?"

"Yes," she repeated. "But why do I get the feeling you already knew that?"

Bill threw a hand up. "No, that isn't so. I don't know all the answers," he said. "That's why I'm going to need a lot of help from you to prepare a proper defense, if it should come to that."

"I thought you said you were not here about Heather … that I left her at Frannie's."

"Yes, that's true." He took a moment for a long look into her eyes. "Suzanne, there's no easy way to tell you this. You've been in a coma since the accident. But that same night, sometime before your accident, someone murdered Tyler Keaton while he slept in his bed at The Admiral's Inn." He paused to let his words sink in; to watch her reaction. With one mournful shriek and terrified eyes, she told him all he needed to know. Over the years, he had become adept at picking out the liars. They were as obvious to him now as a slimy worm in an apple.

Bill tried to soothe her, whispering softly until her sobs had reduced to a whimper. "Suzanne, I know—and the police know—that you were present in that room. In fact, it's an established fact that you slept in his bed and had sexual relations with him. Is that correct?"

Suzanne's sobs rendered her speechless. She covered her mouth and simply nodded in defeat. Then, as though jolted with the realization, she forgot about her injuries and tried to raise herself up. "But I didn't kill him! No way! He was a sick bastard, yes, but I'm no murderer. All I did is lie about the baby. No—not even lie—I just never told him. After I left him I swore I'd never let him get within two feet of her. She deserves better than a lowlife abusive man like him for a father. I was prepared to make up a real tear-jerking romance story when she's old enough to start asking questions." The word *murder* pounded in her head like something weird she just dreamed. She reached out and grabbed Bill's sport jacket. "This can't be—this murder thing. It's crazy! Yes, I did sleep with him but not because I wanted to, *believe me.* It was all part of my plan." She covered her eyes and cried again, but her sobs sounded more desperate. Every one a plea for Bill Franklin to believe her. "You're my lawyer. You have to believe me, right?"

"I do believe you, Suzanne, but the fact is you were at the crime scene. You could be charged with the crime and your case presented to a grand jury. I'm not saying that will happen, but I must warn you it's highly likely. So believing you might not be enough if you're not completely honest with me. You can be sure the Attorney General's Office will have some very skilled people working hard to win a conviction. But I too engage some very skilled people to see that doesn't happen. We can win this, Suzanne, but not if you lie or withhold any information. I want the absolute truth. I can't stress that enough."

Suzanne nodded emphatically all through his speech. "I understand. I do, I do," but she whimpered the words as if she already felt her world caving in.

"Now let's get back to my original request, Suzanne. I want to hear every single detail that led up to the moment you left Heather at Frannie's house to the moment of the accident." He folded his arms.

Suzanne closed her eyes and tried to concentrate. "I guess I should start when I got home from work. I had Heather in my arms and my nosy neighbor ..." She rolled her eyes upward. "She was waiting for me in the hall ..."

Chapter Forty-seven

Sara's upcoming birthday offered the perfect opportunity to patch up whatever triviality had come between Glory and Alex. Assuming optimistically that it *was a triviality.* But Sara had a hard time believing otherwise. Despite the twenty-year difference in their ages, the friendship she and Glory shared was probably as strong as the friendship between Glory and Frannie. Maybe more so. Glory and Frannie never looked death in the face.

She drove her car along picturesque Shore Road into Perkins Cove, home to Amore Evenings. As much as she loved her job there, she didn't want to go indoors yet. The sun had finally chased away the last of the clouds and spilled its warmth on the walkers enjoying the spectacular views along The Marginal Way. The spring season would officially open with the weekend celebration of Patriots Day later this month. Perkins Cove and all of Ogunquit would be buzzing with activity.

But today shops and restaurants were already open for business welcoming the locals and tourists after the cold and quiet winter months. People walked leisurely along the wooden walkway or relaxed on benches to soak up the scenery and inhale the sea breezes. To add the perfect touch, a scattering of seagulls took their rightful places, either perched on pilings or sharing the walkway nibbling on crumbs. Sightseeing boats, lobster and fishing boats docked in the cove's sun-splashed rippling waters rocked lazily while their crews cleaned and polished them to prepare for the flood of tourists who would visit Ogunquit this year.

When Sara spotted Dan Madison aboard the Finest-kind Scenic Cruise boat, where he worked as captain, she pulled her car into the parking lot rather than drive farther down the cove to Amore Evenings. She had a half-hour to spare and thought she could put it to good use. To get his attention, she waved to him with two hands high above her head. Even from a distance his smile radiated, encouraging her to walk the gangplank and step aboard.

"No work today?" Dan said, and kissed her on the cheek.

"Yes, I'm due in soon, but I wanted to catch you first. I know you're busy, so I'll be brief. Sunday is my birthday and I decided to plan my own little surprise party."

Dan arched a brow and laughed. "Now that sounds like you," he teased.

She laughed with him, then said, "No, wait. This isn't a self-serving idea. It has an entirely different purpose. I plan to have my mom ask Glory if it's okay to have a little celebration late Sunday evening, after most of the diners are gone. I'll act so surprised it might even fool you."

Dan shot her a sidelong glance and grinned. "And what may I ask is the real reason for this celebration?"

"Well, Glory will already be there, of course. But my mom will play dumb, like she has no idea she and Alex broke up, and she'll invite Alex. I don't know for sure, but I'm banking on Alex not refusing to come to a party in my honor. If I know him, he'd come not only for me, but also for the chance to see Glory again." She paused to bow graciously and gave him a satisfied smirk. "And that, my dear captain, is the sole purpose of this invitation. Will you and Louise come?"

Dan laughed and patted the top of her head. "You're crazy, but I like the way you think." The smile fell off his face when he added, "But I hope your little matchmaking scheme doesn't turn out to be a waste of time."

*   *   *

Sara's visit had poured a little sunshine on Dan's gray mood, but soon after she left, it darkened again. He wished he had her enthusiastic spirit. Sara was confident that her little impromptu birthday party would easily reunite Glory and Alex. They would simply kiss and make up, then live happily ever after. *Sure.*

He shook his head and laughed at the innocence of youth. All that blind faith in storybook romances.

He had thought long and hard about his conversation with Glory. His heart ached for her when she confided that Alex didn't want children. But he was surprised as well. Before that day, Dan had assumed Glory was strictly a career woman and raising a family was no longer a consideration. If it was *ever* a consideration. Obviously, his assumption was erroneous.

But something gave Dan a strong feeling that she hadn't told him everything. Maybe her reasons were too private, he thought with a shrug of his shoulders. Not for a daddy's ears.

He remembered how anger had often splashed across her face that day. She'd sort of bite her lip to hold the words back. The more he thought about it, the more convinced he was that the crux of their problem was not whether or not they had children. That sort of conflict would reflect sadness or disappointment, not anger. No, something Alex had said or done had cut deep into his daughter's heart.

And then there was Vanessa. He exhaled a long sigh. He and Louise were still in shock over her startling revelation. Although they had met Wanda Prewitt briefly as Amy's English teacher, Vanessa would be presenting her quite differently next week. They were both nervous about the visit, afraid they might say or do something unintentionally offensive.

229

As Vanessa had made them promise, they hadn't said a word to their other children yet. She feared there might be awkward moments and didn't want to overwhelm Wanda with too much too soon.

And Dan feared Vanessa might be right.

Chapter Forty-eight

Martha Simone had another ten minutes to wait before her ride would arrive. There was nothing wrong with her own car but she hated to drive, especially when she was out for a good time. Earlier this morning she had met Betsy Turner at the hairdresser's. She too had been invited to the retirement luncheon of a mutual friend they had known since high school. "Why don't you pick me up on your way?" she had asked Betsy. "No sense using two cars." It wasn't exactly on the way for Betsy—Martha knew that—but she also knew Betsy was too timid to refuse.

Martha took her hand mirror into her bedroom to check the back of her hair. She was pleased with the job her hairdresser had done. Every hair was in place, stiffened with plenty of hair spray. Sue had teased it to death and although it made Martha feel like she had a bird's nest sitting on her head, she had to admit it was a major improvement over her own daily attempts. It looked soft, shiny and as orange as a setting sun.

She had bought a new black pantsuit for the occasion to wear with the kelly green blouse she wore to the St. Patrick's Day party at the senior center. Stepping back for a final assessment, she smiled smugly at her image. *Not bad for an old broad,* she concluded. *So I'm thirty or so pounds heavier than back in our high school days, but who the heck isn't?*

When she glanced again at her bedroom window, Betsy's car was pulling in. Martha grabbed her black clutch bag, locked her apartment door and went down to meet her.

*　　*　　*

At The Grey Gull Inn at Moody Point in Wells, Martha and Betsy were not seated at the same table, but Martha was pleasantly surprised to see several familiar faces seated with her. Maureen Spencer and Ellie Peterson from the Ogunquit Police Department were seated to her right and after drinking the introductory champagne toast, she polished off two glasses of white zinfandel. Conversation came easily and Martha was in good spirits. Literally. She couldn't have noticed Maureen's subtle but futile attempts to discourage further conversation or Ellie's empathetic smile and eye rolls to Maureen.

"So what do you hear about our big murder case—the guy in The Admiral's Inn? I imagine you two hear plenty that doesn't make the papers, huh?"

Ellie leaned forward and came to Maureen's rescue. Since Martha had grabbed hold of Maureen's ear, she hadn't let up for a minute. "Martha, first of all, that's a State Police investigation, and secondly, we don't hear as much as you think. And even if we did, we wouldn't discuss it in public. We *couldn't* discuss it, I should say."

Martha laughed, then sneered. "Ah, don't give me that ethics crap. I'm a lot older than you guys. Plenty of stuff that's supposed to be confidential leaks through." She reached for the fresh carafe of wine the waiter had just placed on their table and refilled her glass. "I know you ladies have to stick to Diet Coke since you have to go back to work this afternoon. But I got a ride from Betsy, so I'll drink your share. What the heck, it's paid for." She gave them a smirk as if she were a benevolent soul who had done them a favor.

Somewhere between her lobster baked haddock and the parfait dessert, Martha found herself at a loss for words. It sure wasn't for lack of trying, but she was surrounded by a bunch of unsociable stiffs. Sometimes in a hopelessly boring situation, she told herself, the only thing that works is down and dirty malicious gossip.

Maureen and Ellie were having a conversation only between themselves and Martha decided they had excluded her long enough. She nudged Maureen with an elbow. Maureen turned to her with a wide-eyed look of annoyed surprise. "Excuse me!" she said.

"Sorry," Martha said with a laugh. "I didn't mean to poke you so hard but I wanted to get your attention now that these people left." She pointed to the empty chairs across the table.

Maureen and Ellie eyed her curiously but their expressions revealed that they were both losing their patience with this overbearing woman.

Martha cupped a hand over her mouth. "I wanted to tell you two that I bumped into Sergeant Gerard the other day at Amore Breakfast. I told him all about how I saw that Keaton guy right at her door when he came looking for her." Finally she had their attention so she dramatized the two scenarios, embellishing the story along the way. She told them first about her encounter with Tyler, followed by Suzanne's subsequent reaction. "But there's one little detail I never mentioned to him—"

Ellie interrupted. "Martha, I don't think you should be discussing any details about that case. It's a police investigation."

"Don't you think I know that? I'm not stupid." She lifted her brows. "This is not discussing it with just anyone. I'm telling you guys because you *are* the police."

"Not really," Maureen countered.

Martha threw her hands up. "Oh, okay, so you want to get technical on me. So the two of you are not really police officers but you work for the OPD. As far as I'm concerned, it's the same thing. Besides, what I was leading up to—what I never mentioned to the detective has nothing to do with his murder investigation. It's about Suzanne. Her personal life. She's no angel, believe me. I've got a sneaking suspicion she and Greg Haggarty had something going before she left for New York. And who knows? Maybe when she came home, they took up where they left off."

Maureen and Ellie exchanged a look. A mix of disdain and disbelief. "That's disgusting, Martha!" Ellie said, then stood up and grabbed her handbag. "I think it's time for us to leave, Maureen."

Martha shrugged and gave them a thin *your-loss* smile, then gulped down the last of her wine.

Maureen surprised Ellie. "No. That sounds too interesting to resist. I want to hear what Martha has to say." She darted a look that Ellie immediately understood. Under the pretense of a woman thirsting for juicy gossip, she intended to listen to and heed Martha's every word.

Martha smiled triumphantly and edged her chair closer.

Ellie struggled to hold her temper down to a simmer. "Martha, if you recall," she said with a condescending tone, "Suzanne was very much involved with someone she lived with in New York. She was already pregnant when she came back. And that's a pretty disgusting thing to say about Greg Haggarty, too." Ellie was never too crazy about Martha to begin with, but she looked at her now with revulsion. "Can't you imagine what gossip like that could do to the whole Haggarty family if that gets bounced around?"

Martha's hands went up and she pouted as though she was being unjustly harassed. "Hey, hold it! What are you getting excited about? Who said I was going to bounce it around? I told you I'm just telling you guys because you're *police*, as far as I'm concerned."

Ellie opened her mouth to resume the escalating argumentative discussion, but Maureen cut her off and spoke to Martha with feigned detachment. "Okay, Martha, I know you're dying to tell someone—if you haven't already—"

"No, I swear, I didn't!" Martha's hand flew to her heart. She gave Maureen a pained look, as though the accusation was another blow to her integrity.

"Okay, I believe you," Maureen continued in the same calm, disinterested tone. "So talk. We'll listen."

Martha arched her brows. "I'm not sure I want to now. I can see by your attitude that you won't believe me."

With a flash of her eyes, Maureen instructed Ellie to follow her lead. Martha wanted to be coaxed. She had dangled the bait and would wait for her fish to bite.

Maureen pulled her blazer off the back of her chair and sighed. "You're probably right, Martha. And Ellie and I have to get back anyway, so—"

Martha tugged at her sleeve. Her face went serious. "Sit down. This won't take long ..." She cleared her throat. "A long time ago—before she went to New York, Suzanne used to babysit for Kim and Greg Haggarty." She paused and smiled. "It's funny how that reversed—after Heather was born, Kim Haggarty babysat for Suzanne."

"Stick to the point, Martha. We don't have much time," Maureen admonished.

"Right. Well, for a while when Suzanne didn't have her own car, Greg Haggarty used to pick her up and take her home. My recliner, where I watch TV, is right by my window and I'm a night owl, so I saw him drop her off a couple of times." she shrugged. "Nothing unusual. She'd just get out of the car, wave goodnight and that would be it." Martha paused for effect and her expression went grim. "But this one particular night, when she got out of the car, he came rushing out after her. Well, at first I'll admit I watched like a hawk because I thought he was angry, but then I realized it wasn't anger. It looked more like pleading. He held her cheeks and was talking to her a mile a minute and she just kept her head down—shaking it on and off like she was saying no to him, or she wasn't buying anything he was saying. She might have been crying, but that I couldn't say for sure ..." She raised her right hand, attesting to her credibility.

Maureen's brows furrowed. She peered at her with incredulity. "Is that it? Martha, that could probably be explained in a dozen different ways. Maybe she had a problem and confided in him—or in both of them—and Greg was trying to advise her or convince her, or whatever!" Her shoulders lifted in question and she waved it off as ludicrous.

Martha pursed her lips and nodded. "Yes, I'll con-
·cede that you could be right. I myself waved it off like you just did. I came up with a million different explanations too. It was just what I saw those last few seconds that left me stumped then and still does now." Martha hesitated. This was fun at first, but now she was having second thoughts. The image of Kim Haggarty and her two lovely children tugged at her conscience. But Maureen and Ellie were both staring at her expectantly. Maybe it's better to tell the truth, she reasoned, than clam up and let their imaginations fill in the rest.

No, there was no turning back now.

Martha heaved a sigh and said, "She broke away from him—abruptly—not that he was holding her against her will—but she just ran to the door and left him standing there. He didn't look angry, just stunned or maybe disappointed. But just before she went inside, I saw her blow him a kiss. You know—off her fingers." She raised a hand to demonstrate, then shook a finger at them. "And don't ask me if I'm sure. When something shocks you, you remember."

Neither Maureen nor Ellie could disagree and both were momentarily silenced. Then both women stood up to leave and Maureen gave Martha's shoulder an impulsive squeeze. "Martha, please promise me you won't mention this again to anyone. If for some reason you feel the need to talk about it, call only me or Ellie, but not a word to anyone else, promise?"

Martha stood up too and glanced around for Betsy. "I won't if you won't."

Chapter Forty-nine

Maureen let out a frustrated scream and slapped the steering wheel. With her face twisted sharply and her teeth clenched, at a glance, anyone would think she was suffering excruciating pain. "That woman made me so sick to my stomach, I don't know how I controlled myself! I can't remember ever wanting to punch somebody out more."

"Forget it, Maureen. It's not worth getting excited about."

Maureen turned sharp eyes on Ellie. "Yes, it *is* worth getting excited about. How can you brush it off so casually? Don't you realize what devastation that kind of talk can cause? I've known Kim since the day she was born. Her mother was my closest friend. Do you know what she said to me the day before she died?"

Ellie remained silent knowing her friend would answer her own question. Maureen had repeated Marge's dying words many times before, but every now and then she needed to release that grief again.

"She said, 'Will you be there for Kim after I'm gone, Maureen? She always called you her second mother, so now you'll have to be her number one mom.' And I promised Marge I would always look after her daughter."

"And you've kept that promise, Maureen. You know that and Kim knows it."

For a few tense minutes neither one spoke, but Maureen's gaze shot back and forth like a ping-pong ball from the traffic ahead to Ellie's blatant discomfort.

"As the expression goes, Ellie, your silence is deafening. But I know exactly what you're thinking."

Ellie feigned oblivion. She turned to Maureen wide-eyed and innocent. She tried to fake a laugh but failed. "How can you say that? You can't possibly know what I'm thinking. Actually, I wasn't thinking about anything except how I wish I could take a nap instead of working another three hours."

Maureen slipped her a sly smile and spoke slowly. "Ellie, my mother used to have dozens of favorite expressions she'd dump on us. She used them so often, my sister and I used to complete her sentences." She paused and Ellie raised her brows with that discernible questioning look, waiting for the connection she knew was coming whether she asked for it or not. "The one that fits now is *you have to get up three o'clock in the morning to put one over on me.*" Her tone was admonishing but her grin amiable.

Ellie's defeated smile broke through. She crossed her arms. "Okay, I give up. Tell me what I'm thinking."

Maureen sighed and didn't answer. She waited another minute until she turned into Cottage Street and parked the car. She turned to her friend now so that Ellie could read and heed the seriousness of her message. "You're thinking that we should get right on the phone and call Tony Gerard. That it's our *duty* to report what Martha Simone told us." She grimaced with the word *duty* as if it were a bug to be stepped on before it crawled up your leg. "Well, I'm telling you here and now, Ellie, that we're going to let that little story die a swift and fiery death. And we'll *never, ever* fan those flames. We are not going to be responsible for blowing apart the stability of an entire family on the strength of that bitch's malicious imagination."

Ellie resisted the urge to argue the point. The police station was only steps away and they had already pushed the limit of their extended lunch hour. She reluctantly nodded her acquiescence and opened the car door.

Most of Maureen's steamy anger had dissipated by the time they reached the end of the ramp. Just before they entered, Ellie stepped ahead and leaned against the door. "Wait. Before we go in … what if there's a speck of truth to Martha's story? I don't know Greg Haggarty so I can be objective. What if he fits into this quagmire in the worst possible way? And what if Bill Franklin can't prove Suzanne's innocence? How would you feel then? No matter what the consequences will be, we can't withhold this information. Not when it might be pertinent to a murder investigation. Besides, even if we did shut up, you can't really believe that Martha can be trusted to keep her mouth shut. Suppose she says she mentioned it to us? How do we explain our silence?"

"Very simply. We gave no credence to her insinuation. The woman thirsts for gossip." Maureen reached for the doorknob. The steely determination melted away from her gaze and she made one final plea. "Let it go, Ellie. Trust me on this. I've known the guy a long time. Believe me, he's not capable of anything even remotely resembling a *crime*, much less *murder*."

"Well, then, how about infidelity? Do you think he's capable of that?"

Maureen rolled her eyes upward and swung the door open. This conversation will absolutely, positively, be continued, she resolved.

Chapter Fifty

Frannie and Tess had been walking the halls when they saw Bill Franklin step onto the elevator. "Darn! I knew we should have stayed put. Now how are we supposed to know how it went?" Fortunately, Dr. Quinlan was at the nurses' station, talking to another doctor. When he was free, she approached him. "Why did Bill Franklin leave without speaking to us?"

"He's coming back. He said she was cooperating fully but got herself a little too worked up emotionally. I had told him to give her a break if that happened. He said he'll continue sometime this evening."

The doctor had already started walking away but Frannie stopped him. "I have just one quick question, Doctor, then I'll try not to bother you again today, okay?"

"Shoot," he said with one of his smiles that could melt chocolate on snow.

"Did he give you any indication of what went on in there?" She thumbed behind her towards Suzanne's room.

"Of course not. That would violate the attorney/client confidentiality rule." He looked at her as if surprised that she'd ask the question.

"I know," she said, a little embarrassed. "I wasn't asking for a blow-by-blow description, but a generalization, maybe."

He stared down at her with concern. "I can see how stressed out you are. Try to relax and leave it in Bill's hands. He's a very capable attorney." When she responded with an

I-hope-so roll of her eyes, the doctor squinted, as though studying her. "You've been defending her innocence from day one. Are you doubting it now?"

"I'm not doubting her, I'm *terrified* for her. This is why a part of me dreaded her coming out of that coma. To be honest, I wish I could say I believed in her innocence right from the start—one hundred percent—but no one can be absolutely positive about anything they didn't witness with their own eyes. We all know that sometimes a person's mind snaps. One moment of rage or fear is all it takes."

The doctor rubbed at the stubble on his chin. "In my opinion—and this is just my impression—behind that tough shell, Suzanne is a frightened young woman who never got over the loss of her mother. From what I've observed, her father was never able to fill that void and she's been looking in all the wrong places. So, Frannie, suffice it to say that I too believe Suzanne is innocent." He threw his hands out. "That doesn't mean either one of us is right, but if it makes you feel better, I'm in your corner."

Frannie blew out a breath. "Thanks, Doc. Your support does make me feel a hell of a lot better." She smiled at him. "You're a great doctor, but what you have in here"— she touched her heart—"makes you rise above the rest."

*   *   *

That evening, Tim Quinlan found Suzanne sitting up and waiting with her hands clasped. He smiled at her. "Well, you must have had a nutritious dinner because you look very energetic this evening. Like you could jump out of that bed and do a couple of miles on a treadmill."

Suzanne giggled. "Yeah, sure," she said, then quickly sobered. For a split-second she had actually forgotten this whole nightmare. It was like slipping a foot into heaven and having the devil yank it out. "I'm not sure it's energy you see. I'm a little nervous. I know Mr. Franklin is coming for round two."

Tim laughed. "What are we going to do with you? How can we convince you that Bill is not your opponent?"

"I know," she said with a slight smile. "It's all the questions I don't like. But as far as Bill is concerned, for a lawyer, he's a pretty nice guy." She punctuated her words with a bewildered expression and a shrug. Like wasn't it common knowledge you can't categorize any lawyer as a nice guy? Bill Franklin had to be a fluke.

"I just wanted to let you know that I'll be leaving the hospital in about an hour. At least I hope to. Dr. Burke will stop in to check on you, okay?"

"You mean you don't have an apartment in this hospital?" she teased.

"I should. I spend enough time here to earn one." He stepped away to talk privately to a nurse, then returned to Suzanne. "Okay, I'm taking off now, but I'll be here bright and early tomorrow morning. Your family wants a chance to visit before Bill returns, so I'll send them in." He gave her a sidelong glance. "And you remember the rules, right?"

"How can I forget? Everyone keeps reminding me not to discuss anything that happened before the accident."

"Well, it's for your own good, so get that sneer off your face. I know it still hurts to smile, but try anyway."

She laughed and waved him off. "Go, get out of here before they bring in another emergency and you'll be stuck all night."

When Frannie and her uncle came up from the cafeteria, they returned to Suzanne's room. She had liked having her parents around for moral support, but reluctantly chased them home hours earlier to relieve Glory. She tried to keep her cousin's mind occupied with talk and questions related to

243

Heather's care and habits, and every now and then Suzanne's eyes would well up.

"I miss her so much. Why can't you bring her? Dr. Quinlan had said it would probably be okay after a few days. It's more than that now."

Frannie wasn't sure how to answer her. They had been stalling her all week. "Suzanne, it's not easy. My mom and dad would have to come in their own car so they can take her back home. Heather can't stay here as long as I do."

"I don't care if you stay only an hour, as long as you bring Heather."

"Truthfully, Suzanne, we're also afraid that seeing her might upset you. Knowing she's with me now and not you. And the fact that you left her ... you know ... alone, might make you too emotional. But we'll try—maybe after the weekend. Monday or Tuesday."

"Oh, please, Frannie. I need to hold her. To tell her how sorry ..." A rush of tears left the rest unsaid, but she held them back when a knock on the door grabbed her attention.

"How are you feeling tonight, Suzanne?" Bill Franklin said. "Can we continue our discussion?"

"Why not? You're the only one I'm allowed to speak to anyway."

"Oh, so you mean I'm not your first choice? You're just settling for me?"

"Sorry," she said with an apologetic smile. "That didn't come out right."

"No need to be sorry. It takes a lot more than that to insult me, young lady."

He turned to Frannie, who held a hand up. "No, don't say it. We're leaving. We'll be in the lounge if you need us."

"Okay, Suzanne, let's get started." He poured each of them a glass of water and sipped his own. "Why don't you tell me how you met and became involved with Tyler Keaton."

Suzanne's face soured. "I'm ashamed to admit what a stupid, gullible jerk I was. Only God knows how I wish that day never happened. But then, I wouldn't have Heather."

Bill interrupted. "Suzanne, don't make it harder on yourself. You can't undo what's been done. We all make mistakes."

She lifted her brows, doubting that his mistakes could match hers. "Sorry," she said, and continued. "I applied for a job. They had a sign in the window for a waitress." Her laugh was laced with bitter regret. "And I was happy as a-pig-in-you-know-what. I thought it was my lucky day. Little did I know ..."

Bill grinned at her; tried to make light of his reprimand. "Suzanne, you're doing it again. We'll be here all night."

"I'm not going anywhere," she answered and drank half her water. "But okay, I'll cut the editorializing. Where were we? Oh, yes, the job. I was hired on a Thursday, my first week in New York, and started the next night. It was great for a while. I was Cinderella and he was Prince Charming."

"So what happened to change that?"

"His possessiveness. At first I was flattered by it. It made me feel loved again. For a long time no one cared where I went or what I did. When my mom was alive she used to make me report every step I took—where I was going, which friends I was with ... the whole bit. It used to drive me crazy." She closed her eyes but silent tears escaped. She wiped them away like an annoying interruption, then punched her pillow into shape and went on. "As I was saying, I thought my mother was too strict, but after she

245

died, I realized it was all about love. She cared about me, worried about me. And I gave her such a hard time ..." She bit into her bottom lip.

Bill patted her hand. "I'm sure she knew you loved her. Don't torment yourself with old guilts. I doubt that your behavior was much different from any other teenager putting gray hairs on their parents' heads." He laughed but his facial expression clearly suggested he had plenty of his own stories to tell. "Go on, Suzanne."

"Anyway, maybe because all that fussing reminded me of my mom—gave me a taste of that all-encompassing love ... Who the heck knows? I'm no psychiatrist. Whatever it was, I fell for him so fast and hard I never knew what hit me. Until his so-called love—that possessive love—turned physical. And still I let him con me with all his sweet talk. He was always so sorry. It was only because he loved me so much he couldn't bear it if anything or anybody hurt me." She rolled her eyes and her shoulders shivered. "It embarrasses me even to say it. I can't believe what a jerk I was. He could slap me around—punch me around, I should say—but I had to stay glued to him so he could protect me. What bull!"

"Let's move forward a little, Suzanne," Bill said. "I promised Dr. Quinlan I wouldn't wear you out. Tell me about your job; your relationship with both your employers and how you got along with the rest of the staff and the customers."

Suzanne smiled and looked up. Her flashback thoughts relaxed her face. "I loved my job! Met so many great people. Had a lot of laughs with some of the regulars." Her face went taut as the fleeting pleasant memories were swept away. "But the job didn't last long. Once we got involved—seriously involved—when I gave up my flea-bag room and moved in with him, that was the end of the job," she said ruefully, then brightened. "But don't get me wrong. I didn't mind. I understood that as 'his woman' ..." She made a face that mocked the title. "As *his woman* he wanted me with him as close as his car keys. At that point, though, it was still fun. At least I had a social life, but never without him." She made a sweeping motion with her hand.

"When did the abuse start?"

"Right after I fought him on the possessiveness. I mean like *the same day*," she answered, stretching the last three words for emphasis.

"How often did he abuse you physically?"

She pondered that a moment. "Well, that depends on how you measure abuse."

"Any time he struck you in anger. One slap constitutes abuse. Nothing justifies it."

Suzanne crossed her arms. "Then in that case, I don't have to think about it. The answer is every day. Every day or every night. Sometimes both."

"What was it that set him off? Was there one thing that angered him more than anything else?"

She threw her hands up. "Hey, he'd go nuts if he saw a speck of white in his scrambled eggs. He'd grab my arm and whip it around fast to show me how to *properly* beat an egg. He'd be screaming like a maniac and I'd be begging him to let me go."

Bill allowed a short silence to pass, then prompted her. "Go on ..."

"I guess you're going to ask me why I stayed with him. Well, I stayed for the same classic reason that keeps all abused women chained to their men. FEAR. What I just described was typical of what he'd do over something stupid, like that egg incident. Don't ask what he did when he accused me of flirting with someone. Or if some customer talked to me longer than what he considered acceptable." She shook her head remembering.

"But I *am* asking," Bill said gently.

Suzanne sighed. "Then he'd use his fists, mostly on my body. Furious as he was, he usually managed to avoid my face. Not that he was worried about me, but he knew you can't conceal the face like the body."

"So would you say jealousy triggered his anger most of the time?"

"Yes. And it was always unfounded. The guy was plain crazy."

"So you were never unfaithful to him or flirtatious— in his eyes—with another man? Every incident of abuse was all about his abnormal jealousy, is that correct?"

Suzanne wanted to be truthful. Really she did. But Bill had asked a compound question, so he had given her a multiple choice. "Yes, that's correct," she said.

Bill pressed on. "And you were never unfaithful or involved with another man while you lived with Tyler?"

"No," she said, but other words crossed her mind like a news crawler on a TV screen. *Sometimes the truth DOES NOT set you free.*

Chapter Fifty-one

Greg Haggarty was probably the only person on earth who would feel relieved if Suzanne died. It was an awful thought that hung a lot of guilt, but not to be compared to the guilt that caused it. He must have been out of his friggin' mind, he thought, to have let that little spark of attraction blow up like a raging fire.

"Daddy!" his four-year-old son, Scott, called down. "Mommy said time to eat."

"Coming, buddy. In a minute," he yelled back from the basement. He picked up the tangy aroma of Kim's sweet and sour chicken the moment Scott had opened the door. When he got to the top step, he lifted the boy high above his head and sat him on his shoulders. Samantha, his five-year-old, wanted her share of the fun and he scooped her up as well while both squealed and giggled. From the corner of his eye he caught Kim's gaze—the one that needed no words—it was simply a shadow of a smile that revealed to anyone looking how much she loved her family.

There was nothing glamorous or provocative about her at the moment. She stood there in wrinkled flannel lounge pants and his old "Kiss the Cook" tee shirt. Her feet were bare and he could see the shape of her braless breasts under all that excess cloth. Her dark hair was pulled back with a huge clip. Shiny strands that had escaped capture framed her face. When he first met Kim, Greg thought she was the image of Connie Sellecca, the raven-haired beauty he had loved in his teens. Once he had fallen in love with Kim—which he admitted to himself soon after—she had surpassed Connie Sellecca and all other beauties who graced the screen.

He put the children down and put his arms around his wife. She had been standing at the microwave, watching the numbers count down on her green bean casserole. He kissed her neck. "I love when you give me that look."

She smiled wide, savoring his affection. "What look?"

"Oh, the one that shows how you love when I play with the kids. Like you're proud I'm their daddy."

The microwave buzzer went off and she pulled the vegetable dish out with thick red oven mitts. She set it on the stove to simmer down, then turned and put her hands around her husband's neck. "Of course, I'm proud. Why wouldn't I be? They adore you and so do I." She brushed his lips with a kiss and when he reached for seconds, she pushed him aside with a familiar silent expression. *Later*, it promised.

Greg acknowledged her promise with a pat on her behind, then helped her put dinner on the table. A baby food commercial flashed on the TV screen, and when the children sat on their booster seats at the table, Samantha asked, "When is baby Heather coming back, Mommy? I miss her."

Kim cupped her chin. "I miss her too, sweetie," she said ruefully. "But her mommy is pretty sick in the hospital. She'll get better, but it'll take a long time. When she's all better and goes back to work again, she'll bring Heather here so we can babysit her." She gave them both a huge smile and wondered how long she could get away with that optimistic explanation. Between Suzanne's injuries and a possible murder charge looming over her, Kim doubted that life as Suzanne knew it would ever return.

Kim prepared the children's dishes with small portions of chicken, whipped sweet potatoes and a few string beans that they never touched no matter how she camouflaged them. She hadn't yet taken a bite out of her own dish when the phone rang.

"It's Michele," Greg said, checking the caller ID. "Let it go. You can call her back after we eat."

Michele and her husband were their closest friends. Kim and Michele spoke on the phone almost every day, but they never seemed to run out of conversation. Kim knew a return call later would slice a good hour out of her time.

After the dishwasher was loaded and the kitchen tidied up, Greg offered to take the children upstairs for their bath while she called Michele.

"Boy! I hope you appreciate that guy," Michele said. "A lot of men still cling to the outdated attitude that child care is exclusively the woman's job and their only responsibility is to support the family."

Kim laughed. "Yeah, well, they can kiss that one good-bye. That chauvinistic attitude is dying off rapidly. It was part of our grandparents' generation. Today, none of us would let them get away with it. Especially in households with two working parents."

Michele sighed. "I guess that's true ... to a certain degree. Some of us are tougher than others. All I know is I still bathe my kids.

"Anyway, that's not why I called you," she said dismissively. "Haven't you heard about Suzanne Oliveri?"

Thinking the worst, Kim's stomach somersaulted. *"W-h-a-t?"*

"Oh, no, I'm sorry," Michele quickly blurted. "It's good news. She's out of her coma. I thought for sure you would have heard by now."

"No. I was out all day but no one called me. Why? Was it on the local news?"

"Not that I know of, but Frannie Oliveri told her staff this morning and, naturally, word got around."

"Oh, my God! That's such a relief. Do you know how she is? Any other details?"

"No, that's all I heard."

Kim pulled the clip off her head and raked her fingers through her hair. "Michele, can I call you back? This is such great news. I want to run upstairs to tell Greg. He's been worried about her, too."

"Sure. I could use some time myself. Talk to you later."

Samantha and Scott were both out of the tub, wrapped in their Elmo towels. Greg was gently brushing the tangles out of Sam's hair while both chatted away, competing for their daddy's attention. Greg playfully put their heads together and kissed both foreheads.

"Greg, I just talked to Michele," Kim said, slightly breathless. "She said Suzanne is out of the coma! Isn't that wonderful?"

Greg's face went serious for a second but he immediately forced a smile. "It sure is, but the doctor had assured them from the start that she'd come out of it."

Kim bent down and took over drying Samantha while Greg put on Scott's pajamas. "True, but we were all sort of holding our breath until she did. It was a scary situation—still is, maybe. We don't have any details yet. I hope her memory is okay. She's going to need total recall to clear herself from all this—" She stopped herself short avoiding *suspicion of murder*. She had long ago learned that children have sharp ears and amazing memory retention.

"I hope so, too," Greg said ruefully, but he wished it were possible to forever obliterate one particular night from Suzanne's memory.

Chapter Fifty-two

Suzanne couldn't stop thinking about Bill's last question. Once her mother died and she had no one to answer to but herself, she had put a tight lid on her conscience. She was angry with God for taking her mother so young and ignoring her pleas to break her father from the clutches of alcoholism.

But her conscience pounded away. Her head felt like it was being smashed by a gigantic stone mallet. Like the ones those sweaty, muscle-bound guys used in the old biblical movies.

It was her lawyer's admonitions that bothered her the most. The fact that she had left that gaping hole in her story. But her decision had been instantaneous. No matter how many times Bill Franklin stressed the importance of complete disclosure, she knew without a doubt that she'd never budge on this. What good would it do? The fact that she had spent two lousy hours in a hotel room with Greg Haggarty had absolutely no bearing on Tyler's death. In all the time she had lived with Tyler, she never slept with anyone else. Not because no one else ever appealed to her, but the thought of Tyler finding out doused that flickering flame faster than a sand sack dumped on a birthday cake.

So why Greg Haggarty? She had asked herself that question so many times and could never nail down the reason conclusively. It didn't really matter. There were several reasons but none of them justified her actions.

He was so damn nice ... so polite, soft-spoken, congenial ...and married. Did I put my guard down, feel safer, because he was married—to my babysitter, no less? I thought he was just a nice guy who made me feel special, like my mother, like he was completely oblivious to my physical attributes. And let's face it, I know I've always had what it takes to attract men; I have mirrors. But Greg was different. He really seemed to enjoy my company. He laughed at everything I said, even when I didn't mean to be amusing. Still, I never caught him looking at my body with lustful eyes. Most other guys stared with laser beam eyes that wanted to peel off my clothes like the skin on a ripe banana.

So how the hell did I let it happen?

Since that night she had never allowed herself to think about it. She'd shiver and shake it off as if she had a spider crawling up her back. But now, in her hospital bed, she dwelled on those two hours with Greg. If only she could cut them out of her life like a malignant tumor. It had been a living hell of guilt seeing Kim so regularly; being welcomed in her home like family. Kim fussed lovingly over Heather as if she were her own baby. Fortunately Greg usually wasn't home from work when she picked up Heather, and if he was, it didn't matter much. He had already mastered the art of deception.

And so had Suzanne. But if she had confessed to Bill her indiscretion with Greg, the results could be disastrous. If that story could not be suppressed an entire family would be ripped apart for no reason at all. It's not as if it was Greg's child she conceived in New York.

Suzanne allowed all the memories to take shape. Her throat felt dry and thick. She reached for her water and sipped from the straw. The familiar hospital sounds around her faded into her subconscious mind and, with her eyes closed, she relived that brief, bittersweet and forbidden romance …

It had begun so casually. So innocently. She was without a car at the time and Kim eagerly offered Greg's services. "I hate to bother your husband," Suzanne had said. "He'll have to pick me up and drive me home. But I guess if he doesn't, you guys can't go out."

"Right!" Kim answered. "So don't give it another thought. Greg won't mind at all. See you later."

"You shouldn't have such a low opinion of yourself, Suzanne," Greg said one night. "This is the third time I'm driving you home and you're always down on yourself for some reason or another."

Suzanne wrinkled her nose and swept it away. "You take me too seriously. I kid around a lot."

"Yes, you do. You're witty as hell and those wise-cracks come shooting out of your mouth like fireworks. But under that façade I see a very bright and personable young lady who sneaks out only once in a while."

She laughed off his compliment. In the car's darkness, the whites of her eyes and flash of her teeth were luminous.

Greg took a second look. "And you're a beautiful girl, too. You have a lot going for you."

She stretched her legs. "Hey, while you're dishing out compliments, what do you think of these? Any good?"

Greg pulled over on the shoulder of the road, threw the car in park and in one wild moment, he forgot all about her intangible attributes.

Suzanne shoved him away. "What are you doing? Are you crazy?"

He stared at her, too stunned to find his voice. He pulled out into the stream of traffic mumbling incoherent apologies. They rode home in total silence, both not daring to exchange a glance.

When they were close to home, Greg turned to her, calmer now but contrite. "Suzanne, please, I just want you to know how sorry I am. I can't believe I did that."

Suzanne put her hands over her ears to block it all out. "Forget it. Let's not talk about it again. It was my fault as well as yours. I was only fooling around about my legs … I thought you were immune." She snarled. "Stupid of me. I should have known better. Men are men. They all come from the same mold."

"That's not true, Suzanne," he said softly.

"Yes, it is. At least when it comes to sex it is."

"That's a cynical attitude. You're too young to be that bitter. I suspect you're carrying a lot of baggage." He raised a hand before she could object. "I'm not prying, but I feel for you. And please understand that I don't know what the hell happened back there. It was a crazy impulse. I never did anything like it before since I met Kim. *Never.*"

"Greg, let's try to forget this ever happened. It's not as if we can ask Kim to drive me next time. So let's just agree never to discuss it again. It'll go away like a bad dream." She extended a hand. "Shake?"

He smiled and shook her hand. "So, you like baseball? How do you think the Sox look this year?"

It amazed Suzanne how the subject of sports had smothered the effects of their earlier encounter. But it was only temporary. For that short time until they reached her parking lot, they had managed to fool themselves. Without looking at him, she mumbled a short "Thanks, good night," and got out. But before she realized he had stepped out too, his hand was on her arm, then her face. She yanked it away and ran for the front door while he was still pleading. She wasn't afraid of him; only afraid of how these inexplicable feelings had developed out of nowhere. Like being caught in a thunderstorm with no shelter in sight. He looked so sad standing there when she turned a last time. Her heart swelled. She brushed a kiss on her fingers and waved. The gesture had been impulsive and she instantly regretted it. But she worried more about the message it conveyed than the innocence of the kiss.

Years later, in New York, their intimacy was completely unplanned, or at least Suzanne had thought it was. Greg had come across her new cell number in Kim's phone directory. He battled with the temptation but lost. He'd be in New York on business for one night and he hated to eat alone. Why should he, he reasoned, when he could dine with an old Ogunquit friend? He took the plunge and called. Strictly dinner, he promised when they spoke.

Ordinarily, there would have been no chance. But Tyler claimed to have business in Boston for two days. "No sense you hanging around alone in a hotel room," he told her. "And I don't want to worry about you wandering around in a strange town. It's only two days, so you might as well stay home. But watch your ass," he'd warned, pounding a finger in her forehead, "I'll be calling to check."

She only half-believed him. Her first clue was when he feigned concern about her being bored. That wasn't Tyler. No, he probably had some chick lined up and waiting for him in Boston. And if so, Suzanne wished she could thank her for the two nights off.

Suzanne thought long and hard while Greg waited for her answer. Recalling Tyler's warnings moved her to defiance.

"It's just dinner, Suzanne," Greg coaxed.

"I know. I'll meet you. I'm just trying to think of a safe place. My boyfriend is out of town but so many people know me through him."

"Then I suggest my hotel. They have a good restaurant that's used mostly by the guests."

"Fine," she said.

*   *   *

She arrived at his hotel with butterflies in her heart and a rumbling stomach that couldn't digest a morsel of food. Greg was in the lobby, all smiles, waiting to greet her. He gave her a friendly kiss on the cheek. "What a pleasure to see you, Suzanne! I'm so glad we were able to work this out. After I spoke to you, I had a better idea about dinner. I didn't want you to be tense; to keep looking over your shoulder. So I ordered room service. Stupid of us. We should have thought of it sooner. Besides, wait till you see my suite. My company takes good care of me," he said with a laugh and led her to the bank of elevators.

Suzanne's tongue felt like it was glued to the roof of her mouth and her legs hadn't felt this rubbery since the first time she got drunk.

But she followed him into the elevator with its elaborate mirrors and gleaming brass. When he took her hand, she offered no resistance when his fingers laced through hers.

For a while she thought it might be remotely possible he was sticking to his promise. *Strictly dinner.* And maybe he did decide on room service to make it more relaxing for her. Maybe he had come to his senses and felt there would be no danger. Nothing and no one was worth the risk of losing his family.

They talked for a long time over dinner. Suzanne sipped her wine and her appetite returned once she started to believe Greg had no other motives. They covered so many topics, serious and humorous, and Suzanne was so pleased she had taken the chance and accepted. He got to talking about his children—how much work they were but how much fun as well, and she was quick to agree. "You're both lucky to have them. When I babysat for them, I enjoyed them too. Someday I'd like to have a dozen just like them." She laughed. "No, make that two or three."

Greg covered her hand with his. "Well, don't wait too long. Find the right guy and start your family. I would have liked one or two more."

He left the question wide open so she went for it. "So why didn't you? Too much for Kim?"

"No. I wish she hadn't wanted more, but she did. I'll always feel bad about that, but I had mumps awhile back. Never had them as a kid. When we tried for our third child we found out that the mumps had done me in." He shrugged, still unable to label himself *sterile*. "What are you going to do? That's what was meant to be. But Kim and I are both grateful it hadn't happened in the early years of our marriage. At least we have two children."

What happened immediately after that was still hazy in Suzanne's memory. All she remembered clearly was that bed. That huge, round bed. She had no idea how they went from a totally G-rated conversation like two old friends who hadn't seen each other in a long time to two lovers who *hungered* for each other after a long time. But it happened and it would never go away.

Much as she hated to admit it, Tyler was Heather's father. So there was absolutely no reason to breathe a word. about her one night with Greg Haggarty. The whole world didn't have to know about their affair, most particularly his family. And even if, hypothetically speaking, Greg hadn't been left sterile and had fathered Heather, that would only strengthen Suzanne's reason to remain silent.

Never would she do anything to destroy that family. She had hurt them enough.

Chapter Fifty-three

Rob stopped at the florist and picked up a dozen roses for Wanda Prewitt. He was so glad they were able to spend this night together, face-to-face, in a relaxed atmosphere. After high school, they had bumped into each other occasionally at games and other local events, but their conversations were brief.

He turned the key in the ignition and smiled remembering their phone conversation two nights ago. She had been so delighted to hear from him, and even more so when he invited her to dinner. But her spirits deflated faster than air out of a balloon when he told her why. Like everyone else, Ms. Prewitt was proud but frightened for his safety. She had adamantly declined his dinner invitation, insisting that she wanted to prepare a home-cooked dinner—whatever meal he desired. As long as he didn't request something too exotic, she had added. They settled on a small-scale Thanksgiving dinner and his mouth was already watering.

He hugged her and lifted her off her feet the moment she answered the doorbell, then stepped back to look her over. "Hey, did I get taller or did you get shorter?"

Wanda laughed. "Well, I didn't get shorter, that's for sure. I'm still too young to start shrinking." She broke away to look him over. "You look wonderful, Rob! What ever happened to that tall, skinny kid I used to know? Maturity has certainly turned you into a handsome young man." She picked up the box of roses he had set aside and gave him a disciplinary frown. "They're beautiful, Rob, but why did you spend so much money? One rose would have been enough."

"Ms. Prewitt, I can afford it, believe me. I'm not a teenager anymore. Besides," he said with a shrug, "I'll be getting room, board and three squares soon, all on our government, so who needs money?"

All traces of humor faded from Wanda's frown. "That's not one bit funny, Rob." She took his hand and brought him to her kitchen where she pulled out a vase and handed him a pair of scissors. "Here, you handle the roses while I open the wine."

Rob wrinkled his nose. "Why don't I do the wine and you do the roses?"

Wanda laughed. "Deal," she said, handing him the corkscrew.

"I hope you're not opening this for me. A Coke would be fine, if you have one."

"You can have both. Open it. I'll drink a glass with you."

Rob took a long, deep breath. "Man, this place even smells like Thanksgiving." He looked over the stove top and the island counter. She had a golden brown turkey breast on a wooden board waiting to be carved. He eyed a casserole dish of candied sweet potatoes prepared just the way he loved them—glazed and baked with tiny marshmallows melted into its crusty peaks. To whet his appetite further, there were platters of broccoli patties, asparagus wrapped in bacon and a stuffing creation topped with drizzled cheese and chopped nuts. A fresh-baked apple pie with a glazed crust was cooling on the rack. Rob wished he could bottle the delicious aromas and take them with him. "Wow! This is not what I'd consider *small scale,* but if you promise to repeat this meal when I come home, that'll give me all the incentive I'll need to make it back!"

They sat for dinner in her dining room where Wanda's huge oak table could have comfortably seated twelve, but tonight it was set for two with candles flickering between them as they ate. They spent the first hour catching up. They played the what-ever-happened-to-so-and-so game. Their conversation never waned and laughter spilled over it often as they reminisced and recalled some memorable moments. Some of the old stories hadn't amused Wanda then, but now, after surviving all her students' formidable years, she could look back with affection. She shook her head and laughed. "Yes, now I can appreciate the humor in it all, but back then you all made me crazy sometimes. Many a day I went home frustrated and nursing a splitting headache."

A lull hadn't fallen between them until Wanda served the coffee and apple pie. Rob's stomach was already so full that he looked at the cinnamon-sugary pie as though it were a mountain to climb. It would be a challenge to eat the huge slice, but he'd be sorry tomorrow if he didn't try it tonight. Besides, Wanda had on that proud anticipatory grin, waiting to see if he liked it. How could he refuse? He speared the crust, releasing all the plump apple wedges and sweet juices. One bite and his full stomach was forgotten. He consumed every last crumb.

"What?" Wanda asked when she caught him staring at her. "I must look like hell, huh? I wilt easily."

"On the contrary, Ms.—can I call you Wanda? Now that I'm 'a man' as you say, the formality seems awkward."

"Of course. I meant to tell you that before." She waved it off and concentrated on her succulent pie, glad she had opted to make it herself. Nothing compared to homemade apple pie.

Rob helped himself to a second cup of coffee. "As I was saying, *Wanda* ..." He grinned. The use of her first name would take some getting used to. "You don't look like hell— far from it. Now, don't think I'm getting fresh, but you're a very attractive woman. A little short, maybe," he teased, "but still attractive."

Wanda rolled her eyes, then laughed. "Ah, *attractive*, yes. Such a cautious word. It takes a giant step over ugly, homely and plain, then gets stuck somewhere between pretty, beautiful and gorgeous."

Rob knew she was teasing him, but nevertheless felt a little embarrassed. He lowered his eyes. "I meant it as a compliment, Wanda."

She patted his hand. "Oh, don't feel bad. I know you did. And I know what you were leading up to. How come an attractive—short, but attractive—thirty-five-year-old woman like me is still unattached? No husband, no live-in lover."

Rob felt the flush rise from his neck and splash over his cheeks. "I'm sorry, I didn't mean to pry into your private life, but as long as you brought it up, I must confess my mind did wander in that direction. You're not only *attractive*," he said with a short laugh, "but you're intelligent, a great conversationalist, you have a beautiful home, and you can cook! What more could a guy want?"

She shrugged and pretended to give the question serious consideration. "A woman with all those attributes who won't need a stepstool to kiss him?"

Rob roared with laughter, but quickly sobered when he met Wanda's gaze. She stared at him with one of those classic dead-serious faces. Nonplussed, he stared back wondering why her jovial mood had stopped short. His brows furrowed. "Is something wrong?"

Wanda drew a breath. "Well, you may think so, Robert, but I don't. Actually for me, something is very right, not wrong." She picked an apple out of her fruit bowl, then used a napkin to buff its shine. She had no desire to eat it, but she didn't want to deal with the disappointment she expected to see reflected in his eyes. "I do have someone special in my life, Rob. A wonderful person who's made me happier than I ever dreamed possible. If you find the time before you leave Ogunquit, I'd love for you to meet her."

Rob felt like a tree struck by lightning. He never had the slightest inkling that Wanda was gay. Hell, she was just their teacher and neither he nor any of his friends had ever given thought to her private life. He searched for the right words to say, but nothing came to him. When he stumbled through an apology, Wanda helped him out.

"I'm sorry, Rob, if I made you uncomfortable. That certainly wasn't my intention. I had hoped you'd understand."

"Oh, I do … no, I've got to be honest, I didn't understand, but only because it hit me like a ton of bricks." Another embarrassed laugh spilled from his lips and he avoided her gaze. "Give me a minute to switch gears and see you—"

Wanda stiffened. "No, don't say that. I don't want you to *see me* any differently than you did before. I'm the same person you loved and respected eight years ago. You came here tonight with that same love and respect. Why should my sexual orientation have any effect on that?"

Rob lifted his gaze to meet hers. Now that the initial shock had subsided and his thinking cleared, he felt low enough to crawl under a worm. Wordlessly, he stood up, walked around the table and sat next to her. He covered her hand with his. "It doesn't. Believe me, it doesn't. You've been a very special person to me since I was seventeen and you still are. *Nothing* can change that." He tilted his head and gave her his old boyish grin. "Can you forgive my stupid reaction?"

"There's nothing to forgive." Her smile widened and broke into laughter. "It was my fault, I guess. I did dump it on you too fast in that one little word—*her.*"

"That you did! But now that I've recovered, I want you to tell me all about her, okay?"

Wanda beamed with relief. She couldn't exactly define the reason, but Rob's acceptance was particularly important to her. Maybe because she had always favored him among her students. He was an exceptionally decent kid with a gregarious personality and a mentality with great potential.

"Her name is Vanessa Madison, and if I start telling you all the good things about her, I'll never shut up. As I said, I'd like you to meet her and draw your own conclusions."

"It would be my pleasure, but we'd better make it soon." He gave her a dubious smile.

Worry lines creased Wanda's forehead. She turned her head away. "Oh, please, don't remind me. You'd better be very, very careful, you hear me?"

"Is that an order, teacher?"

"It sure is!" She looked him in the eye, then sighed. "I know this is what you want to do, Robbie, and I couldn't be prouder. But I still hope and wish that between now and next week, something will make you change your plans."

*   *   *

Rob's mood was high as he drove home. His evening with Wanda Prewitt had been even more pleasant than he anticipated, despite her shocking revelation. But he was totally comfortable with it now and looked forward to meeting Vanessa. Those were his last pleasant thoughts before racing headlights blinded him.

Wanda didn't know it yet, but her wish came true.

Chapter Fifty-four

That evening, after she had slept off the effects of all the wine she consumed at the luncheon, Martha was restless and fraught with guilt. At the time she told her little story to Maureen and Ellie, guilt never came into play. The wine helped justify her actions. And it wasn't as if she had told just anyone. After all, those two women are Ogunquit Police Department employees, she reasoned. They, of all people, should be trusted to keep their mouths shut. Or maybe that very fact will compel them to contact Tony Gerard, sending the detective straight to her door.

Oh, dear God, what did I do? And did I really see what I told them I saw? Or did my bored and lonely mind embellish it into something more than it was? She couldn't sweep the faces of the Haggarty family from her mind. What she had done could have a devastating impact on all of them. And why? Because she grew bored at a luncheon and decided to spice it up with gossip?

While Martha agonized trying to make a decision, the time kept ticking away. Nine forty-five. Too late for a social call, but not too late for an emergency. And Martha deemed the weight of her conscience an emergency. She picked up the phone with a trembling hand. A sleepy voice answered. "Maureen? I'm sorry if I woke you, but it's important."

Maureen was now wide awake. She sat up on her sofa and muted the TV. "What's important?"

"I needed to talk to you about what I told you today. Ever since I came home, I've been worried that you or Ellie might feel obligated to call Tony Gerard."

"We did discuss it, but I haven't called and I doubt that Ellie has yet. I think she would have told me."

"Oh, God, I hope not because to tell you the truth, I've been trying so hard to recall that night—to separate what I saw from what I think I saw—that I'm totally confused now. It was a long time ago. Do you think you and Ellie can just forget the whole thing? Just erase it from your minds?"

"It's funny, Martha, how sure you were this afternoon and how doubtful you are now." She paused, waiting for Martha's response, but all she heard was a mumble. "We can keep it to ourselves, maybe, and never discuss it again, Martha, but that's why gossip is so deadly. It's like a cancer cell that hides until it's ready to attack and kill you. You never forget it's there."

"Look, what can I say? I'm sorry. I made a stupid mistake, but I can't put the words back in my mouth. If I were positive what I said was the absolute truth, it would be different, I wouldn't feel so bad, but I'm not positive, and that's the bottom line. So can you and Ellie just forget it?"

Maureen went silent again. Martha deserved to suffer a little. "For the Haggartys I can, Martha, but I can't speak for Ellie."

"Oh, but can't you talk to her? She looks up to you. You can convince her if you try. Look, this is not for me. I'm thinking of the Haggartys."

"If you were concerned about that family, Martha, we wouldn't be having this conversation." Maureen heaved a sigh. "But yes, I'll talk to Ellie."

Chapter Fifty-five

Dr. Tim Quinlan looked at the blood-soaked patient and cringed. In less than a week, two accident victims with serious injuries had been admitted to his care. Both in their twenties and both from Ogunquit.

Nurse Darnell stood by, waiting for his attention. "His parents just arrived, Doctor. They're pretty shaken up, so as soon as you can ..."

He acknowledged her polite plea with a nod and continued his examination.

Later, as he walked towards the family waiting room, he easily recognized the young man's parents. Both were pacing restlessly in the corridor. A familiar scene for a trauma surgeon, but one that has yet to lose its emotional impact.

Catherine and Jim Butler froze when they saw the doctor approaching. Catherine burst into tears and her husband grabbed her. He held her glued to his chest, anticipating her collapse. Dennis Butler had been sitting behind them, with his elbows on his knees and his head cradled in his hands, making promises to God. He cut short his prayers when he too spotted the doctor. He sprang from his seat and stood behind his son and daughter-in-law, resting heavy hands on their shoulders.

Dr. Quinlan raised his left hand. To anxious loved ones, the simple gesture was a hopeful sign. Compared to a sympathetic gaze and a barely audible "I'm sorry," it symbolized the fragile space between life and death. Plenty of buts hung on that word *life*.

The doctor never tired of approaching a family with a raised hand. He loved seeing agony disappear from their faces like a rubber mask they had yanked off and replaced with wide-eyed hope. In the twelve years he had been a surgeon, he didn't want to count the times he had approached families with a somber expression that needed not a single word to convey its message. One faint tilt of his head never failed to trigger agonizing screams. The sound ripped through his heart every time. Contrary to the common misconception, Tim Quinlan and most of his colleagues were not immune to the pain of grief. They had families too. *There but for the grace of God go I,* flashed through his mind once again as he ushered the family back into the privacy of the waiting room.

Catherine Butler clenched a finger between her teeth. Her breaths were short and labored. Her husband whispered the words she couldn't speak. "How's our son, Doctor? Will he be okay?" Grandpa Dennis Butler stood behind them. His fingers clamped down harder now on their shoulders. But Dennis's legs were so weak and rubbery that he feared they would surely buckle under him any minute. Silent tears streamed down his face.

For a second too long, Dr. Quinlan hesitated and was instantly sorry he did. In that one moment, the look in their eyes had elevated from fear to terror and Catherine gasped. The doctor's hand shot up once again, more forcefully this time to allay her worst fears. "Robert had a serious accident, as you know. He's lost a lot of blood, and we're treating him for shock. Now, I *do* feel confident that we can pull him through this crisis…" He paused again at their sighs of relief, then continued. "But I'm afraid we have another serious situation to face. Robert's right foot sustained severe injuries. It was crushed on impact." A mournful cry came from Catherine's lips and Jim tightened his grip while tears welled in his eyes. "I'm sorry," the doctor said gently. "Would you like to sit down?" Catherine waved it off and steeled herself to listen carefully to the doctor's words. "No, please, continue, Doctor."

"I need to perform surgery immediately on Robert. A surgical team is being called in as we speak. Rest assured he's getting the very best—the top specialists in their fields. Among those who will assist me is Dr. Elliott Morgan, an orthopedic foot and ankle reconstructive surgeon. All I can tell you at this point, though, is we'll do everything we possibly can to save his foot."

"Oh, no, Doctor! Are you saying he could lose it?"

"That's a strong possibility, I'm afraid. You'll have to prepare yourselves for that. But even if we can save it, your son has a long road ahead. He'll need all the love, support and help his family can give him." He smiled softly. "I can see by looking at the three of you that he'll never be lacking that."

Dennis spoke up. "Doctor, if love can save our boy, our Robbie won't have a thing to worry about." He got the words out, then broke down until he crumbled. Jim led him to a seat and handed him a cup of water. Dennis sipped it slowly with choppy short breaths in between. His son and daughter-in-law held their emotions locked inside until Dennis's breathing had calmed.

Sitting between them, he took a hand from each of them and kissed the tips of their fingers. "You know how we say, *God works in mysterious ways*?" he whispered. "Well, who knows? Maybe this was His way of keeping our Robbie safe. Maybe he wasn't meant to come back from Iraq. Now, God forbid he should lose his foot, that's how we have to look at it. Better his foot than his life."

Dr. Quinlan walked away silently. He couldn't have said it better.

*   *   *

The next morning, Rob woke to excruciating pain and unfamiliar sounds. He blinked his eyes. His vision was obstructed by dust motes dancing in strips of sunlight that beamed from the window. He squinted and his face cooled. When he was able to focus, he saw his father adjusting window blinds. A flash of memory chilled him. He suddenly realized where he was and why. And the three grim faces at the foot of his bed frightened him. His parents and his grandpa were looking down at him with red-rimmed eyes and lips that struggled to smile.

A hard cast covered his right leg and his chest was bound with bandages. "What happened?" he asked, his breathing labored, his teeth clenched.

Catherine gasped and lost control. Seeing the pain in her son's face stabbed at her heart. "I'm sorry, Rob. I'm crying because I'm so grateful that you're alive, but I hate to see you in pain like this …." She turned to her husband who wrapped an arm around her.

"How bad is my leg? Guess I won't be dancing for a while," Rob said to his father.

"They had to do surgery. Your doctor will explain it all. His name is Timothy Quinlan, a great doctor. He's been wonderful since they first brought you here—to you and to us."

His grandpa let out an anguished cry and quickly fought for control. "I'm sorry, Robbie. Like your mother, I'm so relieved to hear your voice again, but it hurts to see you in pain. I wish I could bear it for you." He glanced out the doorway hoping to see Dr. Quinlan, but he was nowhere in sight. "I'll be right back," he said to Robbie. "Your doctor wanted to be paged as soon as you were awake."

"How did it happen … the accident … do you know?"

Jim welcomed the question. It allowed him to stall and steer away from the extent of Rob's injuries until the doctor showed up. "They think the other driver fell asleep at the wheel. He veered into your lane. You swerved, but …" He threw his arms out and bit down on his lip.

"Did he die … any passengers?"

"No, no passengers. And as far as we know the driver is still alive, somewhere in this hospital."

Dennis Butler reentered the room, relief evident on his face. "They found him. He was with another patient right on this floor. He'll be here soon."

In the next two minutes Rob watched the tension, the heartaches in the faces of his family. He wanted to question them further, but their silence told him plenty. A strong feeling came over him. He suspected that under the cast was more than a broken leg.

Jim and Catherine stepped aside when Dr. Quinlan finally arrived and introduced himself. Catherine stared out the window, unable to bear seeing her son's face when he's told. His dad and grandpa continued to avoid his gaze.

"What's going on, Doctor?"

"You had a very serious injury to your lower leg, Rob. The front part of your foot—the forefoot—was severely crushed in the accident. We had to amputate part of it. The remainder of your foot and ankle are saved, though, and you will be fit with a prosthesis. You'll need to begin physical therapy immediately and after a period of adjustment, you'll be able to walk again. You should be able to handle most of your normal activities once everything has healed."

His parents were huddled together, forming a picture he'd never forget. Trying to look brave and optimistic for his sake while their hearts were breaking.

"It's okay," he said to them. "You can cry. I might join you in a minute." He tried to smile but couldn't fake one. He turned again to the doctor. "But all those 'normal activities'—I'll only be able to handle them with a prosthesis, right? I'll have to wear it for the rest of my life? Isn't there any surgical procedure that could rebuild the part of my foot you had to cut away?"

"Nothing that can work for you like a prosthesis. It'll take time and a strong resolve, Rob, but it'll become part of you. You should be able to do everything you did before."

"Like run and play ball?"

"With some limitations, I don't see why not."

"Like, for instance?"

"Well, I understand you run miles every day. You will run again, but not for long distances, I'm afraid. Maybe a mile should be your target now. Dancing might be a problem without toes. You won't be able to kick a ball with that foot, or wear open-toed beach sandals."

A long moment passed while Rob digested the doctor's information. "It could be worse, I guess, but the running and the dancing will hit me hard. I'm good at both—I *was* good, I should say."

"You'll be able to run, Rob. You'll just have to accept your limitations. And as far as the dancing is concerned … well, maybe you'll develop a brand new style that'll work for you."

Rob faked a laugh, then lowered his gaze. In the presence of his family he stopped himself from asking another question that came to mind. *When I'm alone with a woman, what do I say? "Oh, excuse me a minute, I have to remove my prosthesis."* Or can I leave it on and hope she ignores it?

Dr. Quinlan had a good idea what Rob was thinking, and said, "Rob, once you get through with your physical therapy and you're comfortable with your prosthesis, everything will work out, you'll see."

Rob swallowed hard. "I hope so."

Chapter Fifty-six

Wanda was pleased to find herself with twenty minutes to spare before she had to leave for work. She had dragged herself out of bed a little earlier to straighten out the last of last night's clutter and her sacrifice paid off now. She sprinkled her oatmeal with a generous coating of cinnamon, then stirred in a splash of milk and a spoonful of raisins. She had a contented smile on her face as she ate, thinking back to last night. All her work had been worth the effort because the entire meal had been successful.

Rob came with a huge appetite and a slightly matured version of his innate lovable personality. They had talked and laughed for hours. Even later, when their mood made a sudden, serious turn with the introduction of Vanessa in Wanda's life, Rob couldn't have been more understanding and supportive. Recalling all they had discussed, it amazed her now that she was able to forget for a while the real reason she had invited him. The image of Rob thrown to the lions in Iraq chilled the grin off her face.

Wanda was halfway through her oatmeal when the door chimes pealed. Its melodious church bell sound contrasted sharply with the simultaneous heavy knocking. She was surprised to see Vanessa at her door and welcomed her with a perplexed smile. "What the heck are you doing here at this hour? I have to leave for school soon."

Vanessa walked in wordlessly and hugged Wanda, then gently pulled her down to sit on the couch. The corners of Vanessa's mouth quivered, and although she hadn't shed a tear, her eyes were glazed like crystal.

"Oh, no. I can see in your eyes that this is no spur-of-the-moment visit ..." A lump shot up in Wanda's throat and her mouth went dry. "Who is it ... who died?"

"Nobody died, thank God. But there's been an accident ... with serious injuries." Vanessa grabbed Wanda's hands as if she feared they'd go flailing wildly. "It's Rob, Wanda. Last night, on his way home—"

"No! No! No! Don't tell me this ... not my Robbie—he's like my son ... I love that kid!" She pulled her hands out of Vanessa's grip and put them over her ears while she rocked her entire body. Her tears fell in a rush and Vanessa lost control just watching her friend's grief. "What kind of injuries? How bad is he? Tell me, I have to know ..." Wanda's sobs were heart wrenching and Vanessa hesitated, unsure of how much she should say.

"Tell me, Vanessa, and tell me the truth! I'm going to find out anyway."

Vanessa lowered her voice to a whisper. "All I heard is he lost a great deal of blood—" She stopped suddenly, hating to go on, then blurted it out. "They had to amputate his foot."

Wanda's mournful cries broke Vanessa's heart. All she could do was hold her until her tears were spent. But she had no doubt this would be the first of many heartaches to follow. She had never met Rob Butler, but Wanda had a deep and sincere love for the young man. The guy had to be special.

Long minutes of silence passed during which all that could be heard were birds chirping in trees—reminders of sunnier days ahead, and Wanda's sobs, reminders of human vulnerability to tragedy.

Wanda blew her nose, then raked her fingers through her hair. "How did it happen? Not that it matters ..."

"I don't think anyone knows for sure. Supposedly witnesses said the other car veered into his lane and hit Rob head on. They're assuming the guy fell asleep or lost control for some other reason." Vanessa sighed. "You're right, though. What the heck does it matter how? All that matters is that it did happen and poor Rob and his family will have an uphill battle for a long time."

Wanda nodded and stared into space silently, deep into her ruminations. "It does matter, Vanessa. It matters a *great deal* ..." She had begun speaking with an eerie calm, but her last words slid off her lips an octave higher, as though she were falling off a cliff.

Vanessa asked the question *why* with only a curl of her eyebrows.

"Because I'm thinking I might have caused his accident." She paused, knowing Vanessa would fight her on this and was waiting for a plausible explanation. Wanda recognized that her friend was ready to reject it before it was offered. "No, don't give me that analytical look, Vanessa," she said. "I'm not some hysterical person caught in the throes of grief. It's true. I might be responsible for what happened to him ... my God ..." She swallowed hard and sniffed away her tears. "Rob brought me *roses* last night—those beautiful roses—" She pointed to the vase on her dining room table. "*Roses,*" she repeated, "not wine. But I took it upon myself to give him my own bottle to open. He didn't even want it ... he asked for a Coke, but I poured it for him anyway. Now that I think about it, he probably took it just to keep me company. I hate to admit it but I never even gave thought to the fact that he had to drive home. All I thought about was how a good bottle of wine would complement my dinner." She cringed with regret.

"Oh? Did you hold his nose and force it down his throat?"

Wanda frowned at her reprimanding tone. "Vanessa, please. I can do without the sarcasm right now."

Vanessa melted; went instantly contrite. "I'm sorry. I guess that was insensitive of me, but it has to be shock making you think that way. It's totally irrational. If the situation were reversed, you'd be preaching the same sermon to me. The plain truth, Wanda, is the accident was tragic enough. Don't exacerbate it by hanging guilt on it too. You'll make yourself sick carrying that weight on your shoulders."

Wanda cocked her head. "Vanessa, the last person I'll be thinking of now is myself. The simple truth is Robbie neither brought wine nor asked for it. I pushed it on him by pouring him a glass because I didn't want to drink alone, I guess."

Vanessa blew an impatient breath. "Okay. So how much did he drink—do you remember? Did you and he finish the bottle?"

"No, not even close." Wanda jumped up and retrieved the wine bottle, happy to be innocent on that count. She slammed the bottle down like proof positive.

"Look at that," Vanessa said when the wine settled. "It's not even half-finished, so just put that far-fetched thought out of your head. It's no one's fault. Not even the guy who crossed into his lane and hit him. Not if the poor guy fell asleep. It's frightening when you think about it, but it can happen to anyone."

Wanda agreed silently with a nod. "What about the other driver? Was he killed? Did he have any passengers?"

Vanessa shrugged. "He was alive when they got to him but I haven't heard anything about his condition. No news is good news so I guess he's still alive. I hope so. And no, he was alone in his car too."

Wanda seemed somewhat calmer and Vanessa studied her. "Are you going to be okay with this now? I don't mean Rob, I mean this stupid wine thing. I want you to just erase the thought from your mind every time it shows up. And definitely don't talk about it—not to me or anyone else. Let it die, okay?"

Wanda lifted her brows, gave her a sad smile. "The way you phrase it, it sounds worse—like a cover-up."

Vanessa threw her head and hands upward.

"Okay, okay. Don't get excited. I can't undo what I did but it happened and I'll have to live with it." She shot her friend a glance. "Yes, silently, I know. I will let it die, I promise."

Vanessa's cell phone rang and Wanda was left with her thoughts about the wine. Vanessa's reasoning was probably right. It wouldn't do anyone any good to mention the glass of wine. But she would never shake off the feeling that she was at least partly responsible. Would Rob have acted seconds faster and avoided collision if he were truly alcohol-free? Did his one glass of wine make him sleepy or slower? She'd never know for sure. What she did know for sure, though, is Rob's foot had been amputated, and that glass of wine might have been a contributing factor.

Chapter Fifty-seven

Weather permitting, Dan and Louise Madison routinely started their days with a walk along The Marginal Way. But today their hearts were heavy after getting that early morning phone call. Friends had called to notify them about last night's tragic accident. Catherine and Jim Butler were one of the couples Dan and Louise socialized with every Friday night for potluck dinners and card games. They had met their son Rob and the whole group took an instant liking to him. Everyone was concerned when the Butlers said they couldn't talk him out of enlisting. Yes, they were proud of him, they said, but until he came home—all in one piece, they added—they would never rest.

"Let's skip our walk, Dan, and go to Amore Breakfast. We should let Frannie know about Rob and ask how Suzanne is doing."

"I'm sure everyone at Amore already knows. Bad news travels fast."

"True," Louise answered, "but bad news also makes you want to surround yourselves with friends who feel as badly as you do. And we always find friends at Amore Breakfast." .

At Amore, Frannie greeted them both with a kiss and her usual bright smile. "How are you guys doing?" She gave Dan an *everything-will-be-okay* pat on the arm thinking only about the breakup of Glory and Alex.

"Any changes with Suzanne?" Dan asked. "Glory's been keeping us posted."

Frannie sighed. "She's awake—technically, but she hasn't spoken a word yet. Sounds, yes—or moans might better describe it. God only knows how much pain she's feeling." She interrupted her brief conversation to call the next people on her waiting list. "Excuse me. I'll try to catch you guys later."

Dan gave her a quizzical look. "Don't tell me you didn't hear?"

That line caught Frannie's attention like a fire alarm. "Hear what?"

"Oh, gee," Dan mumbled, looking around at the crowded restaurant. This was not a good time to drop the bomb about Rob. But if she hadn't heard it yet, someone would surely mention it this morning.

Louise said it for him. "Dennis Butler's grandson, Rob—the one who was planning to enlist next week—do you know him?"

Frannie felt a skip in her heartbeat. "I just met him days ago. Dennis brought him in for breakfast. Why?" Her hands clutched her cheeks. "Oh, God, what happened?"

"An accident last night. He's alive but in pretty bad shape, we hear. Lost a lot of blood and his right foot was crushed." Louise hesitated too, her eyes scanning Amore Breakfast's full dining room. "I'm sorry, Frannie, to give you this news now in the middle of all this, but we assumed you'd know by this time. They had to amputate Rob's foot."

The shock momentarily silenced Frannie, but an involuntary cry soon followed. She covered her mouth to muffle its sound but sorrow veiled her widened eyes. She lowered her head and took a deep breath to control her emotions. Rob Butler was a total stranger to her before this week, but he was the kind of guy you warm up to the moment you meet him. Dennis had spoken about him several times with love and pride in his eyes, but Frannie assumed it was talk typical of any grandparent. Once she met Rob, it was easy to see he really was something special. A genuinely decent young man with a huge smile and a heart to match.

"How did you find out? Someone called you?"

"Early this morning, yes," Louise said. "Rob's parents, Catherine and Jim, are friends of ours. They're part of our dinner party group that meets every Friday night. Their next-door neighbors belong to it too. They called us."

"So then you'll be getting word on his condition, right?" She ripped a piece of paper off her clipboard, scribbled her cell phone number and handed it to Louise. "Do me a favor, Louise, Dennis is a friend of mine, but I wouldn't want to bother him with phone calls. Can you call me whenever you hear anything new? I'll be at the hospital this afternoon and I always turn off my phone, but leave a message, okay?"

"Absolutely," Louise answered. "As soon as we hear, you'll hear."

Frannie started to walk away when she had a sudden realization. She stepped back, meeting Dan's gaze. "I forgot to ask—where is he? What hospital?"

Dan nodded, reading her thoughts. "Yes, Frannie, don't be surprised if you run into the family. They rushed him to Maine Medical Center."

Chapter Fifty-eight

Sara drove into Perkins Cove, parked her car and walked towards the water's edge. Now with Amore Evenings built high atop the black rocks like a beacon for land and sea travelers, the sight was even more captivating than before. From that vantage point, she would have an unobstructed view of Glory's private driveway. It would have been nice, she mused, to see Alex's Mercedes parked alongside Glory's Lexus, but that romantic vision soon faded when the driveway came into view. The Lexus stood alone gleaming in the sunlight. Sara got a freaky impression looking at it. As if it were palpable representation of Glory's new persona— total independence, emotionally and financially, from the men in her life, both of whom had smothered her with love, then sucked it away with the speed of a tornado.

Sara flipped open her cell phone and called Glory. "Hey, it's me. I'm here in Perkins Cove. I thought I'd browse through the shops for an hour or so and check out their new spring stock. Are you busy? Can I stop by for a quick cup of tea?"

"Sure. I look like a slob—haven't taken my shower yet—"

"Oh, stop, Glory. With your face and figure, if you wanted to wear a burlap bag it would become high fashion."

Glory laughed. "That's a gross exaggeration, but it's still nice to hear. Drive yourself down. I'll put the kettle on."

They split a corn muffin to enjoy with their tea and sat out on the balcony. Sara closed her eyes and let the sun warm her face. She inhaled deeply and smiled as though breathing the sea air was a first-time pleasurable event. "What a spot! I never get tired of looking at this view, but when we're working who can relax and enjoy it?"

Glory turned to her and smiled. "I know what you mean. Back in New York we had some breathtakingly beautiful spots along the Hudson River, but never right outside our door, like this." She spread her arms out as if everything within sight belonged to her alone. "This apartment is definitely one of the greatest perks Amore Evenings has given me." She paused for a pensive moment. "It's better when you can share it with someone, though."

Sara cleared her throat and sat up straight, pretending not to have noticed the sadness in Glory's last line. She was dying to ask her what caused the split between her and Alex, but wouldn't dare. If Glory wanted to talk, she had to be the one to open up that subject.

"Did you hear about that horrible accident on Route 1 last night?"

"Oh, yes, I did. Frannie called me this morning, but Amore was so busy, she couldn't say much. I do know the poor guy lost his foot. What a tragedy!"

"I don't know Rob Butler, but I served breakfast to his grandfather several times last summer at Amore Breakfast. What a nice man he is! He must be heartbroken." She sipped her tea and thought about Dennis Butler, wondering how he was. She couldn't imagine his face without that adorable smile.

"Yes, I'm sure he is. His parents too must be going through hell." She pursed her lips thoughtfully. "Stories like that make you rethink your own problems. You realize you should be counting your blessings instead of drowning yourself in self-pity."

Sara glanced at her cautiously. "Glory, if you need to talk, I'll listen. But if not—" She made a sweeping motion with her hands. "I know I'm much younger than you, but when it comes to matters of the heart … well, I'm not too young to relate to that."

Glory grinned at Sara. "Now what do I always tell you when you mention our age difference?"

Sara mimicked Glory's familiar words. "Yes, I know. 'When two people face death together, they're bonded for life.'" She laughed. "Isn't it amazing that we can resurrect that horror and find something to laugh at?"

Glory sighed. "It keeps us sane." For a minute they stared at the ocean and listened to its rapturous melody. Sara's gaze shifted to the arm of Glory's chair. She watched her long red fingernails drum on its arm. Its steady tapping sound was lost by the crashing surf but Sara kept a close eye on it.

"Okay," Glory said, slapping her hands on her thighs. "I guess this is as good a time as any to get it off my chest. It's so hard to talk about. Frannie tried to give me an opening once or twice, but how could I bother her with my stupid love life while her problems are monumental?"

"Frannie's the type of person who somehow manages to find time for everyone. If she gave you the opening, maybe you should have talked to her. I can understand why you wouldn't want to bother her now, but look at it this way: maybe as your closest friend, she feels shut out."

Glory pondered that a moment and sipped at the last of her tea. "In a different situation I might agree, but when it concerns your love life, a friend might steer clear, considering it private territory not to be invaded."

Sara stood up, grabbed her bag. She tried to smile but it wouldn't stick. "Never mind, Glory. Maybe I should leave and let you take your shower. I honestly wasn't trying to *invade your private territory*," she said, her tone putting imaginary quotations on Glory's words. "I just thought that when people are hurting, they might want to talk to someone close. I know you have your dad and Frannie, but if for some reason you can't talk to them, I like to think I'd be the next best thing."

Glory gave a scolding grin and pulled at her denim jacket. "Where are you going? Sit down. Before we go any further, Sara, get it through your pretty little head that you *are* one of the people closest to me. That special circle will always include my dad, Frannie and you. Of course, Alex was in there too, but ..." Her shrug and rueful smile completed her sentence. She drew a breath and opened her mouth to speak again but didn't know where to start or how much she should say. "Are you sure you don't want a sandwich or something? Half a corn muffin isn't much of a lunch."

Sara stared her down and grinned. "You're stalling, aren't you?" She shot up out of her chair again. "It's okay, Glory. I'm not insulted in any way. I just wanted to make it clear—"

"Shut up and sit down," Glory answered with a friendly smile and a finger pointed at the chair. Sara complied and sat with her arms crossed.

"My whole problem with Alex can be summed up in a few words. First—this is going to sound crazy to you, maybe—but I'd like to have a baby and Alex is dead set against it. The other part of our problem is that—believe it or not—he's jealous of my father!" She glared at Sara, waiting for her reaction.

Sara let it swim around in her head a minute, blew out a long breath, then said, "First of all, why would I think wanting a baby would sound crazy? You're certainly still young enough to have one—or more, if you want."

"Maybe so. But Alex is pushing fifty, remember, so he's not all wrong."

"Not exactly young, I admit, but the chances are good that he'll still be alive and healthy when the child grows to adulthood. Did he tell you that in the beginning of your relationship?"

Glory tried to answer honestly, thinking back. "He did mention it in a joking way, but I didn't realize how strongly he felt against it. I thought I'd be able to convince him. I assumed if he loved me as much as he claims to, he'd want to make me happy. And I'm sure—without a doubt— that once the baby is born, he'd forget all those fears and be deliriously happy." She turned her gaze to Sara. "Am I being too Pollyanna?"

"Not at all. I agree totally. My only thought is do you think you can handle running Amore Evenings, writing your column, and a baby all at the same time?"

Glory waved it off. "Absolutely. I'm home all day. Amore Evenings is right here. It's not as if I have to commute to work. And we can afford a good sitter; one we can screen carefully."

"And the nights? Are you assuming Alex would sit home alone every night with the baby?"

"Well, with the baby he won't *be* alone. But I know what you're driving at. No, I won't expect him to assume the role of house husband. Not that it doesn't work for some people, but Alex has been an active businessman for decades, and he intends to continue when he moves back to Ogunquit. To pin him down at this stage of his life would be like cutting off his legs."

"Again, I agree. But between the two of you and a reliable sitter, I can't see why it won't work."

"It *can* work. But Alex has this obsession about his age. He says he can't see himself taking his child to kindergarten when he's fifty-five years old and coaching Little League when he's past sixty. Men are grandfathers at that age, he says, not fathers." She threw her arms up in defeat.

"So, okay. As you said, Alex is not all wrong. I can understand his trepidation, but I think you can make him see it through your eyes. Why don't you try talking to him about it again. Stubbornness has no rewards, Glory."

Glory stood up, leaned on the railing and kept her gaze fixed on the ocean. "Maybe you're right. Maybe I *can* convince him, and maybe he'd give in for my sake, but that's no way to bring a baby into the world. Both parents have to want it and love it."

Sara frowned. "Glory, you can't change what he's feeling inside him now, but you can't possibly believe he won't adore his child once it's born. No way! I guarantee you'll laugh at yourself later recalling that you once entertained that thought." She laughed and shook her head as though Glory's fears were ridiculous. "Tell me why you think Alex is jealous of your dad," she asked, then joined her at the railing. "That was hard for me to swallow, I must confess. I've seen them together many times and they always seem like bosom buddies. Are you sure you're not imagining that or blowing something out of proportion?"

Glory grimaced. "I wish," she said and repeated for Sara the words exchanged between her and Alex that fueled their breakup.

This time Sara could find no gray area. If it happened just as Glory told it, she had to agree. Alex may sincerely like Dan and enjoy his company, but he damn sure wouldn't like it if Glory demonstratively put her father before him.

A while later, when they had squeezed the matter dry, Sara and Glory hugged and parted. Glory thanked her for listening and Sara thanked her for confiding in her.

As soon as Sara was back in her car, she called her mother. "Mom, I know you already invited Alex to my surprise party. Is there any possible way you can tactfully uninvite him?" She cringed, anticipating her mother's unfavorable reaction.

"Uninvite him! Sara, how can you expect me to do that? This was your idea, Little Miss Cupid. It's too late to chicken out."

"Okay, Mom, forget it. We'll just have to let the pieces fall where they may."

"And, Sara, before you hang up, you should know we'll have one more guest at your 'surprise' party. Glory called me earlier this morning and asked if she could bring a friend because she had already made plans for a late dinner at Amore Evenings Sunday night. The guy's name is Steve Lynch. Who is he? Do you know him?"

Sara sighed. "No, I haven't the vaguest idea who he is or what their relationship is, but I'd better find out fast."

Chapter Fifty-nine

The east wing of the hospital had its own share of tragic cases. Robbie Butler was one of the luckier ones.

Frannie had her arms open wide for Dennis Butler long before she reached him. He cried the moment he saw her. She sat down with him in the lounge. While he sobbed, she stroked his back, and all she could say was "I know, I know," like it was useless to try to comfort him with any clichéd or superfluous words. Do you say "Thank God he's alive" when a part of him actually did die? Do you tell the family not to mourn that missing part of his young body? Not to mourn for all the day-to-day functions he could no longer perform or pleasures he could never again enjoy?

"Robbie was such an athlete. Rain or shine, he never failed to run his five miles a day. He loved softball, swimming, bowling—you name it, he did it. He coached Little League for years." He slammed his head. "Jeez, those poor kids. They all love Robbie. They must be heartbroken too, like us." He stopped to blow his nose. "I'm sorry, Frannie. I got so wrapped up again I forgot to ask about Suzanne. How's she doing?"

"She has a lot of healing to do and probably months of physical and occupational therapy, but she'll be okay in time, we hope. That's physically, though. But we're more concerned with her other problem." She threw her gaze up and smirked. "I hope He's willing to throw another miracle down to Bill Franklin like the one He sent to Dr. Quinlan. Suzanne's going to need it."

Dennis had pulled himself together now and put an arm around Frannie's shoulder. "We have to keep the faith that everything's going to work out." A grin spread across his face and the pink fullness of his cheeks returned. But his grin was tinged with sorrow. "I wish I could practice what I preach. Without two feet to stand on, life's going to be tough for him. Why? Why, I ask God." He sucked in a breath. "I get so angry. Then I remember that eventually he would have been sent to Iraq, and that shuts me right up." With two fingers, he pretended to zipper up his lips.

"We all get angry," Frannie said. "We all blame God." She stared at her feet and smiled gently. "Poor God. He only stands for everything good, but until our anger passes, we blame Him for everything."

Their conversation was cut short when Catherine and Jim came out of Rob's room. Catherine let get of her tears and Jim looked as if he wished he could too.

Dennis whispered the introductions. "Frannie, this is my son, Jim, and his wife, Catherine."

"Oh, I'm sorry," Catherine said, "but Rob just fell asleep and we don't want to disturb him. He's in so much pain."

"No, no, don't be sorry. I didn't mean to intrude, and I certainly wouldn't be here to visit Rob so soon," Frannie told Catherine. "I came to see Dennis, my dear friend, and also to tell him that Rob and Suzanne have the same doctor. I just met your son last week. What a great guy he is. You can't help liking him once you meet him." She lowered her eyes. "Everyone is so shocked about this." She wanted to say *but thank God he wasn't killed,* but Frannie had a feeling they'd be hearing that so much from now on that it would grate on their nerves. Although it was certainly something to be thankful for, no parents want to hear the loss of their child's foot being discussed dismissively like a spare part he could live without. Like tonsils or an appendix.

"And your cousin? How's she doing?" Catherine asked with only half-interest. Before last night she had cared very much about Suzanne's progress. Now she inquired only as a courtesy. "We don't know Suzanne, but Dan and Louise Madison have been keeping us informed. They're good friends of ours."

"She's coming along," Frannie said. "But you have your own troubles now." She patted Catherine's shoulder. "We'll talk another day. Suzanne and Robbie will both be here awhile, I imagine."

Frannie walked away from the Butlers feeling awful about her thoughts, but she almost felt a pang of envy. The loss of Rob's foot was indeed a tragedy that would impact the rest of his life. Suzanne's injuries would all heal in time, hopefully, but if she's charged and convicted of murder ...

*   *   *

Wanda Prewitt was nearly numb by the time she reached Robbie's floor, but she was determined not to fall apart. Her eyes were already red and swollen from all the crying she had done since Vanessa's morning visit.

She swallowed a lump that felt like a golf ball when she saw Rob's parents watching every breath he took. Only last night he had been sitting in her home, healthy and happy, talking, laughing and eating nonstop. He had talked about his enlistment plans like something he felt compelled to do; something that would merely interrupt his life, not put it in harm's way. Now all his plans would be sharply altered. Now he was safe from the threat of losing his life fighting the war, but lying helplessly in a hospital bed, connected to an EKG monitor, with an IV in his arm. His elevated leg was covered with dressing from the knee down. Mercifully, medication eased his pain and for a while he'd be able to sleep.

Catherine could barely remember what Wanda Prewitt looked like. She hadn't seen her since Rob was in high school. They had discouraged all visitors except immediate family, but made an exception for the teacher.

Catherine hugged her like a long-lost loved one. "He called me yesterday all excited. He was looking forward to having dinner with you and enjoying your company after such a long time." She sobbed into her hands, still shaking her head in disbelief. "He asked me what he should bring you—wine, flowers, cake ..." she shrugged and smiled forlornly. "I said, 'How should I know? I don't even know her. But chances are,' I said, 'she might already have wine and cake.' I teased him and said, 'She was your teacher. How about a basket of apples?' He laughed; said '*Corny, Mom.*' So I told him to go for the flowers."

"And he did. And they're beautiful—still on my dining room table." She didn't add how she had to avoid looking at them because every time she did, the tears would turn on again like an open faucet.

Wanda exchanged a few whispered words with Jim and Dennis, but her gaze remained fixed on Rob—in a deep sleep, machines monitoring him constantly. So peaceful now, she thought, but how horrible it had to be for him this morning when he was told. How do they break such news? *Oh, you're awake now. Good for you! You had a rough time there, Robert, but you came through with flying colors! And oh, by the way, we had to amputate your foot.*

Her gaze fell on his parents. She watched them watch their son. Suddenly she was relieved that she never became a parent. She'd never have to wait for her son to wake up to tell him a part of his body was amputated.

Later, when she couldn't hold back her emotions any longer, she thanked the family and left, tears still streaming down her face as she waited for the elevator. The only comforting thought she took with her was Catherine's mention of the wine. It eased her conscious ever-so-slightly to learn Rob had considered bringing it himself.

Chapter Sixty

With mixed emotions, Louise and Dan gave Wanda Prewitt a warm welcome when she and Vanessa arrived.

"Oh, gee," Wanda said, looking at the attractive display of fruits and sweets spread across the table. "I didn't want to put you to all this trouble. "I thought we agreed on only coffee and cake so we could sit and talk without you fussing. You have so much here and I brought you more." She handed Louise a Jello creation made with cranberry sauce, pineapples and chopped nuts.

"Don't sweat it, Wanda," Vanessa said. "If we met in your house, you'd fuss even more."

"Actually, Wanda—" Louise began, then stopped and forced a laugh. "We'll have to get used to calling you by your first name. You've always been 'Ms Prewitt' to us since Amy's high school days."

Wanda's gaze looked troubled, but she quickly lowered her eyes. "Ah, yes. I'm a little apprehensive about facing Amy when she hears. I imagine it'll be awkward for her. You haven't told her yet, have you?" She looked at both Louise and Dan when she asked the question.

"No, we haven't said anything to Amy or Todd yet. Vanessa wanted just the four of us for the first time," Dan said. "I'm sure they'll be okay with it once the shock settles. If there is any. People are not easily shocked these days. They're more accepting of other people's lifestyles. Don't worry."

"To be honest, I have been worried. I remember how my parents reacted years ago when I told them. It was not a pleasant scene." She raised a hand and thinned her lips. "But I'd rather not get into that. They're okay with it now, I think. I don't see them too much since they moved to South Carolina. Just holidays and special family occasions. It's better, I guess."

Dan saw the hurt in her eyes and wondered if Wanda's parents' move to another state had been prompted by their daughter's revelation. Would they have taken such drastic action? "Have you told them about Vanessa?" he asked.

"Not yet. They're still uncomfortable with the fact that I'm gay. Whenever I visit, I always go alone and they try to pretend that night I told them never took place."

"What Wanda means, dad, is that her parents would never accept us as a *couple.* I would never be welcome in their home. And truthfully, knowing they have that attitude, I wouldn't want to be there anyway."

Louise reached for Wanda's hand and held it between hers. "That's a heartache for you, I can see. So let it go. We don't ever have to discuss it unless you feel the need. I just want to assure you that as far as Dan and I are concerned, you'll always be welcome in our home. And I'm sure our children will welcome you into theirs."

Vanessa's heart swelled with love and she couldn't hold back her tears. She hugged her mom first, then her dad. "See, Wanda? Didn't I tell you my parents are very special people?"

Wanda smiled and looked at Louise and Dan when she answered. "You did. And they certainly are!"

Dan picked up the cake knife. "Does this mean we can attack these great desserts now?"

Vanessa laughed. "Go for it, dad. Do the honors. A little of everything for each of us. I'll pour the coffee." She winked at him. A silent simple gesture replete with thanks and love.

Chapter Sixty-one

Tim had worked out the details with Glory to set up Sara's birthday celebration. He played along, making suggestions to ensure her surprise, although he was uncomfortable about the underlying plan.

"I hate lying to Glory," he told Sara when they arrived for work at Amore Evenings. "And even though I haven't spoken to Alex since you schemed this up, we're lying to him too. Everyone has to work out their own problems, Sara. If it's meant to be ..." He let it go and made a hand gesture, like slamming a lid on a box. It was too late to cancel anyway. Sara's *surprise* had been arranged for tonight.

They both emerged from the car, but Sara stopped him from walking towards the restaurant. "Wait. Don't go in yet. First of all, don't make it sound like we're doing something deceitful. And secondly, don't give me that *if it's meant to be* stuff. Sometimes a relationship *is* meant to be, but both parties are too stubborn to make the first move. All we're doing here is giving them a little push."

Tim pointed a warning finger. "It could backfire and embarrass them now that Glory invited Steve Lynch as her guest. That threw a monkey wrench in your plan, Cupid."

Sara blew a sigh. "I know. Don't remind me. She keeps stressing he's just a friend, but I'm not so sure about that. They certainly enjoy each other's company. I've seen them together a few times." She scrunched her face and paused. When she opened her mouth to speak, she stopped short and gave him a *never mind* hand wave.

"What?" Tim probed.

She crossed her arms. "Okay, I'll go for it. I'm thinking maybe it's just a harmless friendship between Glory and Steve. Maybe he has no other interest in her?"

She posed it as a question and Tim laughed. He tickled the back of her neck. "Are you trying to ask me if I think he's gay?"

Sara exhaled the breath she held and smiled. "Yeah, I guess I am. If he is, then naturally he poses no threat. He could end up being a good friend to Alex too. But what if he's bisexual? That would definitely present a problem." She paused, furrowed her brows. "You know, you'd think that we'd be able to instinctively recognize sexual orientation in a person. But since we've always had such a strong gay presence in Ogunquit, we don't pay much attention. Who really cares? We're all lumped together in a big pot and simply pick and choose people by their personalities. At least I do."

Tim pursed his lips. "Me too, but we can't speak for everybody. As for Steve Lynch—do I think he's gay? I think so, but I'm not sure. You can't always tell. And as far as whether he's bisexual—well, I wouldn't even try to guess. That's his business." He lifted his shoulders dismissively.

"Yes, ordinarily I would agree, but not in this case. I *want* him to be gay but not bisexual."

Tim rolled his eyes and laughed. "You are a real wacko, Sara."

"And that's what you love about me, huh?"

*   *   *

The plan was for everyone to gather in Glory's apartment until they could spring their "surprise" on Sara. But when Glory stopped in with a tray of hors d'oeuvres, she returned to the restaurant in a huff. She grabbed Tim's shirt sleeve and pulled him into the kitchen. "What's Alex doing here?" she asked.

He looked at her, feigning surprise at her question. "He's here for the party, I guess. Ask Sara's mom. She only asked me to handle inviting her friends. She did all the others. Maybe she didn't know you and Alex aren't talking."

Glory clucked her tongue and eyed him suspiciously. "If she didn't know, I think she would have sent an invitation to me for both of us."

"Not necessarily. This is your restaurant. You're arranging the party. She might have thought you didn't need an invitation. Maybe she felt sending a separate one to Alex was the proper thing to do. What do I know? I don't get into that stuff. Besides, I have to get back to the dining room." He flashed her a playful grin, the kind that usually worked with Sara. "If my boss sees me idle, she might fire me!"

Glory tried to hold a stern face, but melted. "Wise guy," she said. "Go, get to work or I *will* fire you!"

Amore Evenings was doing its usual weekend business—full to capacity and a long wait. It killed Glory to see how many grew impatient and left, but she couldn't stretch the place like a piece of taffy candy. Not that she was complaining. Riding on the tails of Frannie's excellent reputation and a waterfront location, success was almost guaranteed. She laughed to herself thinking of all the anxiety attacks she had prior to opening.

Later, when the last round of diners had been served their dessert and coffee, Glory asked Sara to help her prepare two tables for the private party of twenty-four. It amused Glory to watch her set up for her own party.

Sara, also amused by Glory's sincere attempts to keep it a secret, played her part well. "Well, I guess I won't get to celebrate my birthday for a while. Not with Tim and me still in college for the next three years and working here every weekend."

"I'll try my best to get you out a little earlier, but it depends on how long these people linger," she said circling a finger over the party tables. "Unless Frannie comes back. When she was here early this afternoon, before she left for the hospital, she said she'd try. But she's been like a crutch to Suzanne. Hates to leave her sometimes. The poor girl tries to pretend she's not scared, but Frannie says she breaks down when her father's not around."

"Hey, forget it. We have no plans—just a birthday cake when I get home. My mom insisted—didn't want to skip it entirely."

When Glory left her to complete the tables by herself, Sara was feeling sorrier by the minute. She never should have talked her mother into this stupid party. It had gotten out of hand. A few people had mushroomed into twenty-four. And even though she made her mom write "no gifts," on the invitations, chances were great everyone would ignore the request. And she knew Frannie was definitely coming back to join the "celebration." The more she thought about it, the more she regretted it. Seeing the two tables set up for twenty-four people for the sole purpose of hoping two of them would talk to each other was insane! She cringed thinking of all the people in Glory's apartment waiting to surprise her.

She wondered where Glory would send her so every-one could scramble in. And with Steve Lynch at Glory's side, Alex will probably grab a chair at the other table. So why bother?

"Too late now," she mumbled as she headed back to the kitchen. *I must have been out of my mind.*

An hour later, sure enough, Glory sent Sara over to Spoiled Rotten, supposedly to pick up her gift for this spurious "farewell" party. She knew the guest of honor only slightly, she said, but thought it would be nice to present a gift from her and Frannie. Sara struggled to keep from laughing while she listened to Glory's incessant chatter. She tried hard to sound convincing, but failed.

When Sara returned from Spoiled Rotten, her stomach went queasy. Faking this wasn't going to be as easy as she had thought. As soon as she opened the door, she bumped into Frannie, who had frowned on the idea initially. Sara glanced around to be certain no one was within earshot. "They're all in there, aren't they?" She made a face that begged for a way out.

Frannie laughed, but swept her hand towards the dining room with a *no-sympathy-from-me* expression. "After you," she said.

With Frannie behind her, she walked into a burst of applause. Except for the select few who knew, her shocked look fooled everyone, but she caught Tim's telltale grin.

"Happy nineteenth birthday," her mom said. "This really *is* a farewell party since this is your last year as a teenager." Her mother seemed completely at ease. Probably because once the planning had begun, she decided it was a good idea, after all.

"Oh, my God!" Sara cried out when she found her voice. What appeared as genuine surprise to some and an Academy Award performance to others was actually embarrassment. She cringed thinking how she alone was responsible for bringing all these people together under false pretenses. Bearing gifts, no less. A back table was piled high with wrapped boxes, balloons, and streams of curled ribbons.

Tim, her parents, Frannie and Glory were first to welcome her with the customary hugs and kisses. Sara put a hand up to stop the others. "No, don't get up. I'm coming around to say hello to every one of you." Since there was no turning back now, she ignored her guilt pangs by reminding herself this deception was planned for good reason. Before circling the tables to greet her guests, she grabbed Glory's arm. "So I guess that little trip to Spoiled Rotten was a wild goose chase to get rid of me, huh?"

"Yes, but it was only a half-lie," Glory answered with a grin. "I said it was my gift for the guest of honor, and it is. That's your birthday present from me."

Sara's friends were all smiles with outstretched arms waiting for her. She was about to oblige them when something at the other table caught her attention. "I love you guys, and I want to sit with all of you, but let me say hello to my relatives first." She cupped a hand over her mouth. "You know how my parents are about the respect thing. I'll be right back, promise."

It took her awhile to reach her target—she really did have to greet her relatives first, but when she finally approached Alex, he was still engaged in animated conversation with Steve Lynch. Not polite conversation like two strangers who are thrown together, but like two people who've been friends for years.

She kissed Alex and offered a hand to Steve. "Hi. I know who you are but we've never been formally introduced."

Steve stood up, shook her hand and treated her to one of his knock-'em-dead smiles. "Well, it's my pleasure, pretty girl. And a very happy birthday to you. Nineteen, is it?" He sighed. "Ah, I'd give my eye teeth to be nineteen again."

Sara laughed. "And I'd gladly take them if I could. You have the most gorgeous teeth I've ever seen!"

He blinked his blue eyes feigning modesty. "Oh, I bet you say that to all the boys!"

"She does," Alex said with pouted lips. "She probably doesn't remember, but she gave me the same compliment when we first met."

Sara patted his cheek and gave him a rueful look. "Oh, I'm sorry. I guess I took your crown away. Yours are gorgeous too." Then to Steve she said, "He's right. I did say that and I didn't remember. But don't pay attention to me," she said dismissively. "I have a thing for teeth ... should become a dentist, I guess."

"I hope you don't mind me crashing your party," Steve said. "Glory simply adores you and your Tim and she assured me you wouldn't mind. Actually she said you'd be delighted, but that was pushing it, I'd say."

Sara laughed. "Not at all. I *am* delighted. You not only have great teeth but a great personality, too." The more she spoke with him, the more she considered the possibility that he might be gay. She wished she could just ask him, explain why she needed to know, and be done with it. Hell, if he is, he might even help her!

When the wait staff began serving the soup, everyone took their seats again, including Glory, who had no choice but to face Alex. She intended to take the seat on Steve's right, but he jumped out of his chair and with a gallant sweep of his hand, offered it to her. Reluctantly, she sat down between them, acknowledging this man she loved with merely a nod of her head.

Seated with Tim and their friends, Sara loosened up and enjoyed herself. But she kept glancing over to watch the action or inaction at Glory's table. From a distance, and constantly distracted by everyone around her, she wasn't able to observe too closely. What she did notice, however, was that although Glory did not appear uncomfortable, she spoke only to Steve. Alex had made one attempt at conversation, but Glory responded to whatever he said with only an affirmative nod. It was Steve's head that kept popping forward trying to include Alex in their conversation.

Well, at least that's a good sign. If he had any romantic interest in Glory, would he encourage conversation between her and Alex? Or was he just a nice guy trying to be polite? On second thought, maybe he had been enjoying Alex's company too much, wishing he had found him first.

Tim held his party smile when he bent down to whisper in Sara's ear. "You're being too obvious," he said, barely moving his lips. "Let it go."

"I can't," she whispered back. "I have to try at least. I'm getting up. Don't follow me."

Tim rolled his eyes and gave up.

Steve stood up when Sara approached the table again. "Well, aren't we lucky! Our birthday girl is back. Did you miss us already?"

Glory sneaked her a piercing look.

Oh, Jeez, Sara thought. *She sees right through me.* She ignored Glory's look and tugged at the sleeve of his blazer. "I'm sorry, Steve, but when I went back to my table, I realized you don't know anyone here. Let me introduce you—"

"No, that's not necessary," he answered with a smile that did not mask his reluctance. "I'm fine. Go enjoy your party."

"Oh, don't worry. I'm not going to drag you around to everyone. Just Tim and my parents."

"Fine," Steve said amiably. "It'll be my pleasure to meet them. As long as you keep your promise not to drag me around."

"You guys won't mind if I borrow Steve for a few minutes, right?"

Glory gave her a taut *I'll-get-you-later* smile while Alex winked his thanks.

After a fast introduction to her parents, she took Steve to her table. Tim sneaked Sara a disapproving look but there wasn't much he could do to stop her. She carefully positioned her chair so that she wouldn't have to lock eyes with Glory again.

Steve gave her a bewildered look. "Am I missing something? What's going on?"

Tim cut in before she could answer. "Before she gets into it, I just want you to know that I tried to talk her out of this." He swept a hand to Sara for her to do the explaining.

Looking at the curious but guarded expression on Steve's face, Sara knew she'd never get away with chucking the whole idea. "Okay, here goes. I'm sure you know that Glory and Alex were engaged to be married. Well, Tim and I were supposed to maid of honor and best man for them, and of course, we were honored to be asked. We were also devastated to learn they broke up."

Steve listened with his arms crossed while she struggled with her speech. He could spare her the torture of getting through it, but it was becoming fun. His smile widened as she went on.

"Look, you have every right to tell me to mind my own business, but as her maid of honor, I feel I should try to help patch things up between them." Her hands went up. "But I don't know what's going on between you and Glory—or *if* something is ... this is so embarrassing ... I really don't want to pry into other people's personal affairs—"

"You could have fooled me!" Tim said. He had resolved to let her sink or swim on her own, but couldn't resist throwing that in.

Steve burst into laughter. "Oh, please stop, Sara. I can't let you put yourself through this discomfort any longer. Let me help you out. What you want to know plain and simple is whether Glory and I have anything more developing other than a good friendship? Well, the answer is yes, in a way. She pours her heart out to me about her lost love and I cry on her shoulders as well for mine. We're good therapy for each other."

Relief washed over Sara's face. "Oh, I'm sorry for pushing you to tell me that. And I'm sorry your relationship broke up. Was it recently, like Glory and Alex?"

"Yes, John moved out just before I came to Ogunquit." He smiled at her. "So you see, Glory may be an extremely attractive woman, but what I find most attractive is what she feels in here." He patted his heart. "Feel better now?"

"Very much so! And thanks, Steve, for being so nice about it. I've been a jerk for trying to interfere into everyone's personal business."

"On the contrary! Those two stubborn mules are miserable without each other. What kind of friends would we be if we didn't try to help them out?"

Sara beamed. "You mean we can scheme something up together?"

Steve gave her his card. "Call me on my cell whenever you get a chance. We'll see if we can knock any sense into those two."

Sara turned to Tim with a complacent smile. "See? It wasn't such a bad idea after all!"

Chapter Sixty-two

Suzanne watched Rob Butler being wheeled into the physical therapy room for the first time. Judging by the strained look on his face, the pain had to be unbearable. Having been there herself, and already familiar with the torturous regimen, she empathized.

She waited for the opportune time and wheeled herself over. "At first it'll seem like you'll never be able to do it, but you will. These therapists are relentless, but they're good. Don't tell them I said that, though," she whispered. "I keep telling them I hate them. That they get a perverse pleasure out of watching me suffer."

Rob laughed and no one was more surprised than he. He would have bet anything that his smile muscles would lie dormant for a while. It seemed unbelievable that he could laugh with pain so severe it compared to nothing he had ever felt before. And without his right foot.

Yolanda, his therapist, returned with some equipment and paraphernalia to get him started. She grinned at him.

"Is that for me?" Rob asked.

"Exclusively yours, Robert," she said, as if it were a prize he had won.

"I think I'll pass. Looks too challenging to me." Then he turned to Suzanne, woefully. "You may be right about that perverse pleasure theory."

Suzanne laughed. "See you later. My guy is giving me the eye too. Back to the torture chamber." She waved back as she wheeled away. "Good luck!" she called out.

When Suzanne was a safe distance away, Rob whispered to his therapist. "Was that who I thought it was?"

Yolanda nodded. "Suzanne Oliveri, yes." She didn't add *murder suspect*, but it was implied in her facial expression. Rob gave no verbal response but countered with his own implied facial expression. *No way!* it said. *She's no murderer!*

Later, nearly breathless from the exertion, Rob gazed pleadingly at Yolanda. "Would it help if I beg for mercy? I don't think I can take any more—"

Yolanda cut him off and smiled. "You won't have to beg. You've had enough for day one. Someone will be here soon to take you back to your room."

He blew a sigh of relief and let his gaze fall on Suzanne again, who was still working with her therapist. He watched her struggle through with her eyes squeezed tightly closed and her teeth clenched. But she was a trouper. She did some deep breathing and persevered even when her therapist said she could stop.

A few minutes later, while she was helped back into her wheelchair, Suzanne caught Rob watching her. She waved to him and wheeled herself over. "How did it go?"

Rob gave a *don't ask* roll of his eyes. "Painful, bordering on agony, I'd say, but I survived," he said with a smile that came easily now. "I'm not looking forward to going through this every day, though. Is this your regular time slot for therapy?"

"Afraid so. If I could run and hide from them I would but ..." she shrugged and smiled. His face was sweaty and one side bruised and discolored, but Suzanne got a funny tingling sensation in the back of her neck. *God, he's gorgeous!* But the moment passed and reality set in. Her face dropped the friendly smile. "Do you know who I am?" she asked.

Rob stared at her a few seconds before answering. Her long dark hair was pulled back in a ponytail, accentuating high cheekbones set in satiny skin with doe eyes reflecting an innocence that belied the web of suspicion surrounding her. "Yes," he said softly, "You're Suzanne Oliveri, Frannie's cousin, who's going through a rough time right now."

The kindness emanating from his voice touched her so profoundly that her voice cracked when she spoke. "It's nice of you to say that. Sometimes people around here gawk at me with that *did-she-or-didn't-she* look."

"That's awful."

"No, not really. What's worse are the ones who've already closed their minds. They just assume I'm guilty. You can tell the difference. But you're a refreshing change. Like my family, I think you believe I'm innocent. Am I right?"

"Absolutely."

"Good. You're my new friend for life."

Rob laughed. "I certainly admire your attitude. I wish I could be as courageous."

She lowered her eyes. "I'm not. It's a front." She lifted her gaze to meet his. "Hey, I'm sorry. I got so wrapped up in my own troubles, I never asked how you're doing. And I'm *so* sorry about your foot."

"It's okay. They're making me a new one."

Suzanne looked at him, in awe. "And you call *me* courageous?"

Rob turned when he heard his name called. "This is Charlie, Suzanne, my personal driver. He'll wheel me anywhere I want to go, he said. Within these hospital walls, of course."

Charlie laughed, gave Suzanne a mock salute. "Ready, boss?" he asked Rob.

"Guess so," Rob answered, then turned to Suzanne again. "I'm out of here. See you here tomorrow?"

"Sure. Unless you're feeling stir crazy later, like I do when everyone leaves. I'm a pro already with my chair, so I can whiz on down for a short visit if you want. We can drown our troubles in pretzels and ginger ale." She lifted a finger. "If I don't get arrested before that, of course."

"Don't even *think* that."

A sob caught in her throat but she didn't give in. "It's hard to think about anything else."

Rob shook his head, wishing he could think of some encouraging words. "You come see me later, after visiting hours." He threw a finger out, like a reprimand, before Charlie wheeled him away.

Chapter Sixty-three

Tony was in his office with Pat Carney when Corrine arrived at the station house. He waved her in.

"What's up?" she asked.

"Plenty. Have a seat. You came back at just the right time. I was about to give Pat this latest piece of interesting information, so now that you're here too, I won't have to repeat myself.

"Both of you already know that I asked the NYPD to apply for a warrant to seize the computer at The Bird's Nest, the lounge formerly jointly owned by Tyler Keaton and Cody Griffin, now solely owned by Griffin, of course." He paused and smiled. "You guys will love this ... I talked to the guy from the forensic computer lab this morning. He said he'll send his written findings later today or tomorrow. But here's the highlight: Someone there in The Big Apple did. some interesting research." He paused again for a drink from his water bottle.

"Look at him," Corrine said to Pat. "He's enjoying keeping us in suspense."

Tony laughed. She was absolutely right.

"If we did that to him, he'd say 'cut to the chase,' and give us that annoyed and impatient face he's famous for."

Tony went palms up in surrender. "Okay. I won't fight both of you, so as I was saying, our computer guy discovered that someone did a Google search for whatever." He leaned forward. "Now you know how when you start to feed something in for a search, if there were any common characters that were used in a recent search, that previous search will pop right up. Follow me?"

Both women nodded, their interest piqued.

"Well, apparently Tyler Keaton had done some Ogunquit research—probably to get a room somewhere—and he chose The Admiral's Inn. Sometime after, murder suspect number two comes along, fools around with the computer, hoping to discover where Tyler went or what he's up to. Needless to say, by doing so, that murder suspect number two might advance to the number one spot, taking the heat off Suzanne Oliveri."

Corrine raised a hand to interrupt. "But wait a minute, Tony. Stop right there. If this murder suspect number two discovered that Keaton had chosen The Admiral's Inn, how would he or she have known where to find him when he or she got there?"

Tony pointed a finger. "I'm getting to that. On the computer desk was a little yellow stick-on note with 'TAI, RM3' written on it in red ink—Tyler Keaton's handwriting. The red pen was also still on the desk."

"Damn," Pat said. "It's almost like Keaton unknowingly gave the guy a written invitation to come get him."

"Exactly. I think I want to pay Mr. Cody Griffin a surprise visit. Corrine, you'll come with me because Pat's tied up here today."

Pat gave each of them a sly smile. "How convenient, huh? Did you dump that file on me before or after you decided a New York City trip was necessary today? Nothing like mixing business with pleasure if you can." She stood up. "So okay, good luck, guys. And call in from New York if you uncover anything really hot."

Tony gave her a devilish grin.

"I meant hot on the murder investigation, wise guy."

*　　*　　*

Cody Griffin shook Tony's hand vigorously. "Sergeant Gerard! This is a surprise. If you came to see me, you took quite a chance driving all the way down from Maine. Suppose you didn't find me here today?"

Tony had already handled that through his friend, Lieutenant Donovan of the NYPD, but he didn't share that with Cody. He introduced Corrine and the three of them sat in Cody's office.

"So what brings you here this time, Sergeant?"

"I'll get right to the point and save us both time, Mr. Griffin. We learned that someone used Tyler's business computer after he arranged for a room at The Admiral's Inn in Ogunquit. That person easily obtained that information— his exact location in Ogunquit and even his room number."

Cody peered at Tony with blatant indignation. "Now wait a minute, Sergeant. Don't you think for one second that you can hang this on me. I told you before that I was right here when Tyler was killed and I can give you a dozen witnesses to prove it."

"Relax," Tony said softly. "I'm not accusing you of anything. I simply need your help. Now I want you to think carefully and give me the name or names of people who had the freedom to use Tyler's business computer. Freedom or opportunity, I should say, not necessarily authorized."

Cody's forehead creased as he pondered the question. "Well, no one is authorized, I can tell you that. Opportunity is something else. If an employee tried that and we caught him, he'd be fired on the spot, so that would be very risky."

"What about your off-hours employees—the kitchen help or maintenance crew who worked when you and Tyler were not here?"

"Impossible. We always locked our office doors at night and no one else has a key."

"Did Tyler have any friends or girlfriends maybe who had the freedom to hang around often?"

"Not since Suzanne, no."

"And what about you—same question."

Cody sighed. He didn't even want to think about that bitch, much less talk about her. But he wasn't about to cast suspicion on himself by withholding information. "There was someone, yes, but she's long gone." He looked across his desk at Tony, hoping he didn't have to go any further. But Tony merely stared back, waiting for more. "Her name is Adrienne Fox. I met her through Tyler. It was just a fun thing for a while, but we got serious. I never thought I'd be considering marriage, but I did. We were great together—I had never been happier and same for her, so she said." He hooded his face with his hands and lowered his gaze. "Then the night I told Tyler how serious we were—that we wanted to get married—everything hit the fan."

"I can see this is unpleasant for you, Mr. Griffin, but I need to know more. Tell me why 'everything hit the fan,' as you put it. What happened when you told Tyler?"

"Tyler *enlightened* me," he said bitterly, "about why I should reconsider proposing to Adrienne. You see, Tyler never bothered to mention to me where he had met her. He argued that he had no idea our relationship was that serious. He then revealed that she had a very successful profession for a few years—earned tons of money. As an escort, entertaining the visiting male clients of various companies." His grin was laced with sarcasm. "Of course, she never mentioned it either. Adrienne explained—and felt perfectly justified, mind you—that that part of her life was past tense and we should never look back, only forward. Those were the words of wisdom she expected me to swallow. In this day and age, it was no big deal, she had the nerve to say." He stood up and extended a hand dismissively. "So does that cover it, Sergeant? As you observed, yes, it is unpleasant for me to discuss and I'd rather not continue, if it's okay with you."

"I understand, but I'm not quite finished, sorry. First, tell me what story she gave you about her past. I'm sure she made up some other job or profession. Secondly, tell me what transpired between you and Adrienne that last day. I assume you argued and broke up. Did she threaten you with anything? More importantly, did she throw out any wild threats concerning Tyler? I imagine she had to be furious with him."

"She cursed him out left and right, used words I never thought would come out of her mouth. But I think she was angrier with me. She took the defensive; like I was making a big fuss over nothing. Can you imagine?" He raked his fingers through his hair. "But actual threats? Maybe she did, maybe she didn't. I was so upset I can't remember. As for your first question, she told me she was manager in a high-priced gift shop somewhere in New Jersey, but the owner died and the place closed."

"Okay, one more and I'll let you go. Do you know where Adrienne is now?"

"I don't know and I don't care. She's totally out of my life."

"Fine, no problem. We'll find her."

Chapter Sixty-four

Suzanne stopped at Rob's doorway. His eyes were closed, his lips slightly apart. Disappointed, she turned to wheel herself away.

Rob jumped to attention at the sound. "Suzanne, wait. I wasn't sleeping. Come in, please."

She hesitated. "Are you sure? If you're not up to company, I understand."

"Are you kidding? Your company is the highlight of my day. I was looking forward to your visit."

Suzanne giggled. "Well, I don't know how flattered I should feel, considering the choices in a hospital setting." She pulled out a plastic bag tucked in the corner of her wheelchair. "I brought our party supplies. Two ginger ales, pretzels, and my private stash of apple sauce—four servings!" She arranged it all on his tray table, playing it up like an unburied treasure. "All compliments of our hospital kitchen. And now in this corner," she said, reaching behind her back, "the grand prize: one large bar of Hershey's chocolate, compliments of my uncle Sal."

Rob eagerly reached out. "Good. Let's start with the chocolate."

While they munched and sipped their ginger ales, they talked about their hospital routines, the doctor they both respected and admired and their injuries. After a while it went from serious to humorous once they had begun poking fun at hospital procedures, like how all rules of modesty or vanity must be temporarily waived. "I'm sure if given the opportunity," Suzanne said, "I could design a hospital gown that would allow easy access to all parts subject to examination and would please the patients as well. Look, I'll show you." She ripped a piece of paper off his pad and scribbled a rough design. "Here, something like this," she said, handing him her creation.

Rob laughed. *Really* laughed. "I don't mean to quash your creativity, Suzanne, but I was just imagining the over-eighty patients struttin' their stuff in this."

She grinned and wiggled her eyebrows. "Never know. They might get the greatest charge of all. Like a last hurrah."

When their light-hearted banter subsided, a brief silence sobered them. Rob cleared his throat. "Suzanne, are you okay? Do you need someone to confide in? I'm an experienced listener. It's a prerequisite for bartenders."

Suzanne made a woeful face as she opened her mouth to speak.

Rob's hand went up. "No, don't get me wrong. I'm not pushing. But sometimes we need to vent, to get it out of our systems."

"How right you are! You have no idea how right you are, Rob. The whole friggin' mess is stuck here, like a rock," she said, touching her breastbone. "But I can't let it out. I'm not allowed to discuss anything with anybody except my lawyer."

"Oh, I should have realized that, sorry." He hadn't known she already had legal representation. "I can understand how frustrating that must be, Suzanne, but it's for your own protection. I'm sure you know that."

Suzanne blew out a breath. She looked at Rob, their eyes locked and he gave her a gentle smile. She felt the smile cross her lips. It amazed her how he warmed her insides, allowing an inexplicable calm. "I do know that, of course, but it *is* frustrating. *And* frightening."

"We won't get into it—I know we can't—but I just want to say it'll all work out. You'll see. Investigative techniques are so advanced these days, it's a lot easier to solve a crime than it used to be. Criminals unknowingly leave evidence everywhere."

"And so do innocent people who then *look* like criminals." She threw a hand up. "Forget it. I'd better stop right there. Are you sleepy?"

"Not at all. Why?"

She pulled out the last of her surprises. "I have this travel Scrabble game my father brought. I couldn't believe he remembered how my mom and I used to love playing Scrabble." She looked at him with a polite but pleading expression.

"I'd love to play! Let's clear up this mess."

They both laughed as they cleared the tray. But when their hands accidentally touched, their eyes met like magnets.

Chapter Sixty-five

"Today, more than ever, I can't wait to get out of here," Suzanne told Rob at their break in physical therapy. "I'm so excited about finally seeing Heather and holding her in my arms. I know people might think I don't deserve her— oh, forget it—I can't get into that. It's so hard to bottle up everything. There's so much I want to say."

Rob leaned forward, bringing his face inches from hers. "You have to hang tough, Suzanne," he whispered. "You'll get your chance to clear it all up. Even if the worst happens, your lawyer will handle it for you. But there's a good chance it'll never come to that. And stop worrying about what people think about you. That's the least of your worries."

Suzanne nodded and blinked away the tears that crept up. It was not the subject matter that made them surface, it was the gentleness, the kindness of this prince of a man. His words were no different from any her family might have said, but coming from Rob, they had a tranquilizing effect. No sugar-coated words to lift her spirits, but sincere words he truly felt. Despite what he knew about her, by word-of-mouth or media coverage, he *believed* in her. She could read it in his eyes every time their gazes met.

"Your faith in me is amazing, Rob. I can't tell you how much it means to me," she said, then smirked and added, "considering all the stuff we can't talk about."

"No, Suzanne, it's not amazing at all. It's simply another skill you sharpen as a bartender. You develop a keen ability to recognize a person's true character. Very often the image they try to portray is not who that person really is inside, here." He tapped his heart. "You learn to sift through. Sometimes you don't like what you find and other times, you find ... how can I say this?" He looked away for a moment, then stared straight into her eyes. "And other times you find someone really special."

Suzanne let out an involuntary gasp, overcome by the words he said and the words he left unsaid.

"I'm sorry. I didn't mean to make you cry."

She pulled herself together and smiled. "Oh, that wasn't crying. You just choked me up. It's been a long time since anyone ..." she avoided his eyes and made a *forget-it* hand wave.

Seeing Suzanne's struggle with her emotions, Rob switched his tone to light and playful. "So, let's get back to Heather. What time is she coming? Can I see her? Do you mind?"

"Mind? Are you kidding? I can't wait to show her off. I'll call you as soon as she gets here, so you can get Charlie to wheel you down."

*   *   *

Suzanne chose to stay in her room rather than the lounge so she could have totally private moments with her baby. She burst into tears the moment Frannie carried her in. "Oh, hurry, give her to me," she said, her arms outstretched.

"Give me a minute to unbundle her, and she's all yours," Frannie answered.

"Oh, my precious sweetheart," Suzanne cried, kissing her daughter repeatedly. "Mommy is so-o-o sorry. So, so, sorry ..."

It was impossible to watch and remain dry-eyed. Frannie and her parents stood at her bedside, making no attempt to hide their tears. If Jerry's eyes had filled up too, no one noticed. He turned away and sat in the chair behind them, his head cradled in his hands.

"See, Suzanne? This is what we were afraid of," Frannie said. "Try to stop sobbing, for goodness sake! You might scare her. And how many times are you going to tell her you're sorry? She's fine, thank God, and she hasn't a clue about that night, so stop torturing yourself."

Suzanne blotted her tears with a tissue and managed a smile. "I know, but I think I'll be doing that for the rest of my life. It won't be easy to forget."

Tess put a finger on her lips. "That's enough, Suzanne. Remember that discussion is taboo. Just enjoy your baby."

"Mom, why don't we all sit in the lounge for a while so she and Heather can have a nice private reunion," Frannie said, then looked at Suzanne.

"Yes, if you don't mind, I'd like that. It'll be only for a few minutes anyway, 'cause Heather and I are expecting company." She paused and looked up at their questioning faces. "Rob Butler is coming down to meet Heather," she said with a radiant smile.

Frannie arched a brow. "Oh, that's nice! I'd like to see him again and ask how he's doing. So it seems you and he are becoming fast friends, huh?"

Suzanne wrinkled her forehead as though in disbelief. "That guy is an absolute saint. I think he fell off a cloud or something!"

Frannie laughed. "That seems to be the general consensus about Rob." She lowered her eyes. "I feel so bad for the guy."

"So did I, at first. But he has an attitude like you wouldn't believe! He'll be fine. I'm sure of it."

"I think you're right. I hope so," Frannie answered and led them all out of the room.

Seated in the lounge, she asked Tess, "I wonder if, under different circumstances, Suzanne and Rob Butler would have been more than friends?"

"Why 'under different circumstances'? They already have a lot in common; their accidents, their injuries; their doctor; their uncertainties about what lies ahead for them … plenty to form a friendship, or more, if it's meant to be."

"True, Mom, but as serious as Rob's injury is, he's not threatened with arrest for murder. My heart skips ten beats every time I hear footsteps coming into her room. I keep visualizing her in handcuffs."

Tess heaved a sigh. "You and me both."

*   *   *

"Oh, my goodness!" Rob said when Suzanne placed Heather in his arms. "Now I know what *love at first sight* means. This baby is beautiful—look at those eyes—and a dimple too! And look, Suzanne, she's smiling at me."

"Oh, sure! She hasn't smiled for me since she got here, but you show up and charm it right out of her."

Rob stroked Heather's hair with gentle fingers. "So, little princess, you're one lucky girl. Everyone adores you and your mommy is a very, very special person. Do you know that?"

Frannie and Tess stood against the wall near the foot of the bed. Tess poked her daughter and tilted her head towards the doorway. "Let's leave them alone," she mouthed.

Frannie gave her a wide smile, but it was shaded with sorrow.

Chapter Sixty-six

Wanda decided to wait a few days before going to the hospital again. It had been insensitive of her to go there the very next day. True, she did want to show Dennis and Rob's parents how sorry she was and tell them how much she adored Rob, but her motivations were also self-serving. Guilt about the wine had begun to torment her, despite Vanessa's sermonizing. She was determined to deal with it, though, because the more she thought about it, the worse she felt. She wanted so much to talk to Rob about it, to apologize, but wouldn't dream of burdening him. How could she equate the weight of her conscience with the challenges he's facing?

"I'm going to the hospital straight from school today," she told Vanessa. They routinely enjoyed a brief telephone conversation every morning before their work day began. "I stayed away for three days to give the family some privacy, but I can't wait any longer. I have to see him—talk to him. He was asleep that first time I went."

"Fine. You should go. He'll probably be very happy to see you."

"Maybe. But maybe he shouldn't."

"Wanda Prewitt! Don't tell me you're still on that wine thing! Do I just waste my breath on you?"

Wanda let a little laugh escape. "No, I'm much better most of the time, but when I think too much, it gets to me." She winced, anticipating the reprimand.

"Well, don't think so much!" Vanessa yelled into the phone. "What's wrong with you? This is so unlike you."

"Be patient. I'll shake it off. I've never had to deal with something like this, where my actions or inactions affected another person's life so profoundly."

"It wasn't your action or inaction. It was that guy who fell asleep and crashed into him. And let this be the last time we discuss this."

"Okay, okay. You're going to puncture my eardrum."

* * *

Wanda found Rob sitting up and alert when she walked in. She brought him a plant and chocolate chip cookies she had baked the night before.

He thanked her, unwrapped the cookies and bit into one. "So, should I say you shouldn't have spent the money on this plant, like you did?" he teased.

Wanda laughed. "Your roses are still alive. I enjoy looking at them."

"I'm glad that worked out. I was going to bring wine, but I didn't know what kind you'd prefer, so when my mom suggested flowers, I went with that." He beamed at her. "Boy, what an unexpected surprise. I'm so glad to see you. I heard you were here the day after the accident. Why didn't you wake me?"

"Oh, no way," she said with a hand wave. "You had just dozed off and we wouldn't dare disturb you. You were in so much pain. How is it now, Rob? Still that bad?"

"Only when the medication starts to wear off. And when they put me through physical therapy."

Wanda winced. "Oh, I can imagine. How often do you get it?"

"Every day, and it'll go on for months, I think."

"Oh, you poor thing," she said sympathetically. "That has to be tough."

"There's a bright side, actually. I made a good friend there. A girl with some pretty bad injuries herself, along with plenty of troubles and heartaches, but you'd never know it. She has a great sense of humor."

Wanda was truly elated. "Rob, that's fabulous! Tell me about her. Is she from the area?"

"Her name is Suzanne Oliveri."

The smile dropped from Wanda's face. "Oh, Rob," was all she could say.

"No, Wanda, don't believe everything you read and see. That girl is absolutely innocent, I'm sure. She had to fight her way through life for years—especially since her mother died—but she's strong, a fighter. She's not the type to drown herself in self-pity."

"Well, if you think she's innocent and as nice as you say, then that's what I think too." She paused, not sure of what to say next. "Do you want to talk about your foot, Rob? It's difficult for me—and I guess for everyone—to know what you'd prefer. You tell me. If you don't want to talk about it, we won't."

Rob forced a laugh. "Well, it's not as if it'll suddenly grow back if we ignore it."

Wanda's laugh came naturally. "You're an amazing guy, Rob. No wonder everyone loves you, including me, of course." Her eyes grew watery, but the smile remained stretched across her face.

Rob repeated everything Dr. Quinlan had explained and Wanda drew a deep breath. "It's wonderful the things they can do these days …" She thinned her lips, couldn't verbalize the rest of her thought. *But they can't replace your foot.*

Rob saw Wanda struggle to rid herself of the grim look on her face, so he helped her. "So when are you going to bring Vanessa? I want to meet her."

Wanda's face lit up. "Really? You want me to bring her here?"

"Absolutely. First chance."

A knock interrupted their conversation.

"Hey, c'mon in," Rob said.

"Oh, I'm sorry. I didn't know you had company."

"Wanda's not company. She's practically family." He shifted his gaze to Wanda. "Wanda Prewitt, meet Suzanne Oliveri."

Wanda and Suzanne exchanged a smile. "Actually, we've already met. Suzanne was one of my students too."

"Probably one of your greatest challenges," Suzanne said.

"Not even close," Wanda answered with a laugh.

The three of them fell into comfortable conversation and Wanda studied her two former students with a keen eye. There was something about their looks, Wanda observed, the light in their eyes, maybe. But whatever it was reminded her of Vanessa.

After an hour she left, promising to return with Vanessa soon. She felt as if she had lost a hundred pounds of anxiety as she drove home. Rob had relieved her guilt about the wine, and seeing his marvelous attitude inspired her to emulate his spirit.

She couldn't wait to tell Vanessa.

Chapter Sixty-seven

Sara and Steve didn't reach each other by phone until four days later. They met for an ice cream on Main Street that evening. Neither one had come up with a single idea all week.

"I thought for sure throwing them together at my birthday party would work, but that was a dumb idea," she confessed.

"Not really. Everyone had a good time, you got loads of gifts—"

"Oh, don't remind me. I feel awful about those gifts, knowing I schemed up the party myself. And all for nothing."

"No, not necessarily. Let me finish what I was saying. Once Alex and I started talking, we hit it off like that." He snapped his fingers. "He knows I'm gay and therefore my friendship with Glory poses no threat. If anything, it could help."

"That's exactly what I told Tim."

"Also," Steve continued, "through this conversation with Alex, I do know that Alex will do anything to get her back. The guy is crazy about her."

"And she with him. That's why I'm sticking my nose in their business. Some day they'll thank me."

Steve laughed. "Don't be so sure. I'm not wishing it on them, but many marriages and relationships go sour."

Sara wrinkled her nose. "Nah, I think they passed over that danger zone. They both had first marriages that left them a lot wiser. They'd enter this one with their eyes wide open. Maybe *too* wide." She paused on that thought, then asked, "Steve, did Alex confide in you the reasons why they argued and broke up?"

Steve took another mouthful of his sundae before he answered. "Yes, he did, but since he told me in confidence, I can't bring myself to share that with you. Sorry."

"Well, Glory confided in me, too. So let me help you. Whatever Alex told you, does it concern parents and children?"

Steve's hearty laugh resonated, causing heads to turn.

"What's so funny?" Sara asked.

"You," he said. "You're such a conniver. I don't mean to poke fun at you. It's just so amusing, really. But seriously, I understand what you're trying to pull from me, and yes, since you already know, he told me about Glory wanting a baby, and how he feels about it—or felt about it— and he also told me she accused him of being jealous of Dan." He made a face that reflected his disapproval. "I'm not sure that's entirely true. Maybe she was too hard on him."

"Maybe. But hearing it from her, I'm inclined to agree." Her hand went up. "Now I'm not saying he dislikes Dan. On the contrary. But Dan and Glory are so affectionate with each other. You can see the love on their faces. I can believe Alex might feel left out."

"Ludicrous!" Steve said, with a vigorous hand wave. "The love between parent and child bears no resemblance to the love between two people in love. As far as the baby goes, I'll side with her on that one. She's too young to be denied a baby and he's not too old to give her one. And I'm sure once it happens, he'll be thrilled."

"Did you tell him that?"

"Absolutely. And I think I convinced him."

"Good. So that leaves only the Dan issue. They're both wrong, so I say she should apologize for accusing him so harshly, and he should apologize for being a little jealous in the first place. Like you said, they're two different types of love. He has no right to deny her the freedom to love her own father. Especially since she just found him less than two years ago!"

"I agree wholeheartedly. So now what?"

"So now you talk to him and I'll talk to her. We'll negotiate. And if that doesn't work, I'll pull her by the hair if I have to."

Steve roared with laughter again. "I'll tell you what. If you succeed, will you try it on John and me?"

Chapter Sixty-eight

Adrienne Fox wasn't through with Tyler yet. Killing him wasn't enough. The anticipation during that long drive to Ogunquit had excited her more than shoving the knife in his chest. It happened too fast. His eyes had opened as she stood at his bedside staring down at him for one last hateful look. Oh yes, he had sensed her presence. Had seen the crazed look in her eyes. And she had seen the terror in his. But he lunged at her. Poor Tyler. He never had time to notice the knife in her hand. With incomparable pleasure, she watched his gasp while blood exploded from his chest like a gushing oil well.

She lifted her wine glass in a triumphant salute and talked to the air. "Too bad, Tyler, you pushed me too far. Don't you know what they say about a woman scorned? Well, that's me." She pounded a fist against her chest and said it proudly, like it would fuel her determination. "Yeah, that's me ... woman scorned!" A fit of laughter ripped through her until she could barely breathe. She sunk herself into the recliner Cody had bought her and popped up the foot rest. Laughter and sorrowful tears melded together into cries of despair. She yanked out all the magazines from the chair's side pocket and flung them across the hardwood floor, screaming his name. But she could scream until the roof flew off. Cody wasn't coming back. He wanted no part of her. Tyler, the king of all sonsofbitches, had seen to that. Not everyone knew it, and few would believe it, but Tyler was a vengeful and evil man. *A street angel and a house devil,* Suzanne had called him.

How well Adrienne knew that. She moaned thinking how close Cody had come to proposing marriage. What a beautiful life she had to look forward to—finally. True, it had started out as a simple physical attraction. One that would ignite like a roaring fire and burn out to cold ashes. But they never expected to *like* each other, to become close friends. They never expected the *love* word to pass between them. But it had and Cody had begun spending more and more time at her condo than his. He had given her money to redecorate, adding things for his pleasure. He talked about his plans for the future, what he wanted to accomplish, places he wanted to visit. All those plans included Adrienne.

She had never been happier, nor had he. Until Cody told Tyler that he planned to surprise her with an engagement ring. When everything exploded.

But now that her final revenge was well-planned, she felt confident she could pull it off. It would be like burying him deeper. She caught her reflection in her living room mirror and smiled, pleased by the images her mind formulated. *You may not be able to see me from Down There, Mr. King Sonofabitch, but I'll know. And that's revenge enough for me. You take from me and I take from you. Fait accompli.*

Chapter Sixty-nine

Adrienne checked into The Admiral's Inn as Julianne Baker, enjoying her whole new look, including her mother's engagement ring. She used a false address and paid cash for a two-night stay. She had planned to stay at one of the larger motels on Route 1 so her face could get lost in the crowd, but had a sudden change of mind. Why not go directly to the scene of the crime where she could enjoy her celebrity status—albeit silently. She could sit at the bar and mingle with the guests, acting shocked and horrified, like everyone else, while they all played amateur sleuth.

"My fiancé thought I was crazy for wanting to stay here," she told Ken when she checked in. "Not only because someone was murdered here, but the killer is still out there!" She shivered for effect. "It *is* scary, I admit, but too exciting to pass up."

Ken laughed. "Well, you can be sure the guy isn't going to show up here again. That only happens in the movies." He opened the door to her room and turned on the lamp lights. "I hope you're comfortable here. It was our last availability when you made your reservation."

"I guess I'm lucky, then. I expected things to be slower here in early April." She grinned. "That killer did you guys a favor, huh?"

Ken cocked his head as though the thought had never occurred to him. But it had. "Maybe so," he said.

*   *   *

Early that evening she strolled into the village, browsed through the shops and checked the menus displayed outside the many restaurants. Like any other tourist. She even made some purchases and chatted amiably with the shop owners. On Shore Road she found a realtor, Ogunquit Sunrise Properties, and sauntered in, all smiles, asking questions about summer rentals and condos for sale. The agent she spoke to, Bob Poliquin, was very accommodating and offered to arrange for showings.

"No, not yet. I'd like to explore the area a little more before I commit to—"

"Well, you certainly won't have to commit, Julianne, but you can get a general idea of what's available so you can make choices with a clearer picture."

"You've already helped me a great deal, but I'm only here for the weekend. My fiancé was supposed to make this trip with me to check out Ogunquit—we had heard so many great things about it. But he got stuck again on business—" She sighed and rolled her eyes, playing out her role. "So I decided rather than sit home alone, I'd check it out myself first. No sense making a return trip with him if Ogunquit disappointed me. But now that I've arrived and looked around a little, I'm sure there's no chance of that. From what I've seen so far, it's absolutely delightful." She stood up. "Look why don't I just take your card. Once we know which weekend we'll be back, I'll contact you to set up appointments, okay?" She didn't wait for an answer, just reached for the doorknob and smiled. "Thank you so much. I'm sure we'll see each other again real soon."

"I hope so," Bob said. "It's been a pleasure talking to you. Why don't you leave me your phone number and e-mail address? Once in a while something really special opens up and it's sold so fast you'd never get a chance to see it."

Adrienne Fox, a/k/a Julianne Baker, wrinkled her nose. "Don't bother. I'm bad about responding to e-mails. I get so many. You'll hear from me, believe me. I'm very impressed with Ogunquit."

Bob Poliquin smiled amiably. "It'll be our pleasure to have you, I'm sure."

That's what you think! Adrienne thought as she closed the door behind her.

*   *   *

After enduring the discomfort of eating alone and aching for Cody, her hatred for Tyler grew stronger and her need to avenge his betrayal obsessed her. If she managed to pull it off, she'd be hunted down by every law enforcement agency in the country. Fine. What's the difference? she thought. After premeditated murder, kidnapping an infant didn't seem so bad since she had no intention of harming the baby. Tyler Keaton would surely turn over in his grave if he knew she would become mother to his daughter. It seemed a surreal kind of justice ... Tyler had bombed out her chance to become a mother to Cody's child—a dream she had so foolishly entertained. The bastard *owed her* a child.

After a two-hour nap, Adrienne took a shower and changed into jeans and a turquoise stretch top that made her look *classy* sexy, not *flashy* sexy. Her jet black wig was razor-sharp straight with blunt-cut bangs that nearly obliterated her eyebrows but called attention to the huge green eyes she had resurrected from the old days. She had several pairs of contacts in different shades to match her clothes and/or her mood.

She hoped the bar was crowded tonight and that she'd find the right person with the right information. Ogunquit was not around the corner from New York and she didn't want to make another trip if she didn't have to.

Vic the bartender kept her entertained with conversation and answered all her questions about the area. Too bad it was all a farce, concocted only to give credence to her solo weekend trip. By the time he served her second Cosmo, she hadn't yet been able to steer him unobtrusively towards the information she needed. She sipped the fresh drink and licked her lips. "I'm a scotch drinker usually, but I heard your Cosmos are terrific, and they are," she said, raising the glass.

Vic smiled wide. "I'm glad you like them. That's always nice to hear. Who gave me the plug?"

"Oh, I got into a little conversation with someone in one of the shops this afternoon. When I said I was staying at The Admiral's Inn, she mentioned your name and your Cosmos, but sorry, I didn't ask her name."

But later, when the bar got so crowded Vic no longer had time for lengthy conversation, Adrienne had to seek out other sources. When she overheard a piece of conversation between two women who had come in together, she found her opening.

"Excuse me," she said. "I couldn't help but overhear part of your conversation. I read and saw some TV coverage about that grisly murder and the girl's accident that night. I know she was his girlfriend and had a baby, but I always seem to get the story in bits and pieces. Naturally, since it happened here, I admit to being fascinated in a way. I couldn't resist staying here. Can't deny murder is a great conversation piece!" She followed it with a laugh and they joined right in.

The two women introduced themselves and were happy to fill her in on the details she claimed to have missed.

Adrienne bought them a round of drinks. "My goodness," she said, shaking her head and munching on trail mix, "You've got to feel bad for that poor baby, though. It doesn't look good for the mother. The relative who's taking care of her—I forget her name—does anyone know her? Is she a local? Sometimes those relatives waiting in the wing put on a good front, but turn out to be abusive or neglectful—just in it for the money." She made a worried face that could fool the most skeptical mind.

Her two newfound friends, Erin and Patricia, were quick to ease her concern. "Oh, no, don't worry about Frannie Oliveri. That baby couldn't have fallen into safer hands," Erin said. Patricia cupped her mouth and whispered, "Truth be told, that baby is probably better off with her mom's cousin than her mother."

Adrienne eyed them curiously. "Oh, really? Do you guys know this cousin?"

Patricia creased her brows. "Oh, sure," she said, making the *long time* hand gesture. "She invited us to her housewarming party when she moved into her new place. It's beautiful—right on the ocean. You can sit on her porch and watch the sun rise every morning. You should take a quick ride down to see it. Just make a right on Beach Street—"

"Hold it," she said with a friendly laugh. "I haven't been here long enough to be familiar with street names."

"Oh, true. I'm sorry," Patricia answered. "Well, if you'd like, Erin and I can ride you around tomorrow to see some of Ogunquit's highlights. Too bad the Ogunquit Playhouse isn't open yet. They put on some fantastic productions. But you'll come again, I'm sure. Everyone does."

Adrienne struggled to keep the grin off her face. She thought she'd have to fish—and very subtly—to find Frannie Oliveri's house, but Patricia and Erin not only volunteered the information, but would give her a guided tour!

As their conversation progressed, Adrienne learned— without probing—that Frannie Oliveri went to the hospital every day after closing her restaurant. Her mother usually babysat while she was gone, and occasionally her friend and business partner, Glory English. *How cool is that?* And she couldn't credit herself for anything more than striking up a conversation with them.

She spent the entire night with Erin and Patricia and actually enjoyed herself. Even after their conversation drifted off the murder. She never thought herself to be the type, but she was making new discoveries lately. *If you can get away with it, crime can be fun!*

Chapter Seventy

It hadn't taken long for Tony to compile a full profile on Adrienne Fox. She might have climbed all the way to the top if she hadn't been impatient for the fast buck. Why would she spend four years working for an escort service when she had degrees in journalism and political science?

The big question today was still the same. Where is she now? He had assigned several detectives to track her down and had again put a call in to Lieutenant Andrew Donovan of the NYPD.

"We're coming up empty, Tony. She left her job at Morgan & Greeley without a word, without a hint that she didn't plan to return the next day. Or ever. We talked to everyone there. They say she was not particularly close with anyone. Polite and amiable, yes, but only on a professional basis. As far as we could tell, she never talked to anyone there about her private life."

"And her residence? Any luck there?"

"Well, we didn't connect with all the residents, but it seemed no one knew her. Maybe just by sight. And if anyone did know something, they weren't talking."

"Thanks, Andy. Appreciate it. But don't knock yourself out. I have a feeling she's not in New York anyway. For her to disappear like that ..."

"Maybe she's not on the run. I hate to say it, but maybe her body will turn up in a garbage dump somewhere. She has no relatives here that we know of, but if anyone reports her missing, I'll be in touch. Sorry we can't help you any more."

Pat had been standing in the doorway waiting for Tony to conclude his call. When he hung up, she walked in and sat down. "I have the same feeling, Tony. It's been bugging me."

He gave her a quizzical look. "What's been bugging you? What feeling?"

She looked up at the ceiling, feigning impatience. "The feeling you told Andy Donovan about. I was listening," she said, eyeing the doorway.

"Oh? And what did you conclude, Sherlock?" he asked, bowing his head.

"Don't give me that condescending crap, Tony. I helped you break cases several times when you were boxed in." She frowned and stuck her tongue out.

He tried to keep a straight face, but couldn't. "True, and you'll throw it up to me for life. And P.S., that wasn't 'condescending crap'; that was banter, so knock that chip off your shoulder."

"Okay, I concede," Pat said. "So let's cut the banter. I have calls to make. I just wanted to ask what your thoughts are about the elusive Adrienne Fox."

"I think she's a player in the Tyler Keaton whodunit. A principal player. I haven't figured out yet how or why."

"Me neither." She scrunched her face thoughtfully. "But on the other hand, Tony, we could be way off base. If the split between her and Cody had left her as angry and bitter as we suspect, she might have said 'F it all,' walked out on her job, and hooked up with an old client from her escort years. Possible?"

Tony sipped his coffee, made a sour face and put it in the microwave. "I hate cold coffee."

"Well?"

"Well, I'm thinking." He sipped the reheated coffee, burned his tongue, and put it aside. "It's possible, but not probable. Now you know the facts—according to Cody Griffin, that is—so tell me, Pat, wouldn't you agree she might want vengeance and go after Tyler for screwing up her life?"

Pat gave him a dubious look. "I don't know ... revenge is something a normal person might pursue to satisfy whatever hurt the other guy inflicted, but to imply that so-called normal person would stoop to murder ... well, that's a stretch."

Tony pointed a finger. "But not when the person suddenly vanishes. And I have a pretty good idea where she is or where she's headed.

"Let's take a ride. I want to flash her DMV photograph around, just for the hell of it."

"Around where? Here? Ogunquit?"

"Don't look at me like I'm crazy. Yes, Ogunquit first, but she could be holed up anywhere in Maine."

With a smirk and a shrug, Pat said, "Sounds like a long shot to me, but you're the boss."

They were on their way out when Tony's secretary called out. "Tony, wait. Don't leave."

"I'm in a hurry, Joan ..."

She unfolded a sheet of paper and handed it to him. "The DNA results you were waiting for." She gave him a *cat-that-ate-the-canary* smile.

Tony's eyebrows shot up as he read the report. "Well, isn't this interesting ..." he said, his smile growing wider and wider.

Pat leaned closer to read it. "No match! Tyler Keaton is not the baby's father? That's a hell of a switch!"

"It sure is. If Keaton is not the father, that takes a lot of heat off Suzanne Oliveri. We assumed since she never told him he had a daughter, she had strong motive. So now this takes a lot of weight off motive."

"Not if she hated him enough. And not if she *thought* he was the father."

Chapter Seventy-one

"I had a very pleasant weekend here," Adrienne told Ken and Jake when she checked out of The Admiral's Inn. "You've both been wonderful—made my stay relaxing and comfortable. I can't wait to come back! Thank you so much."

"It'll be our pleasure. And we hope you can stay longer next time," Ken added.

Jake carried her bag and walked her out to the parking lot. "Have a safe trip home and come back soon."

"Oh, I will," she said. "As soon as possible." She buckled her seat belt and looked up at him. "But I'd feel a whole lot better if they arrested that girl. At least I'd know the police are keeping a close eye on her. Even though she's confined to a hospital, it still gives me the creeps to imagine her standing over me with a knife in her hand."

"I guess the police have their doubts. If they had enough conclusive evidence, I think they would have arrested her once she was out of the coma. I'm sure the investigation is still ongoing because the detective in charge was here earlier showing a woman's photograph, asking if anyone recognized her." He shrugged. "But no one did."

Adrienne's stomach turned over. She wanted to ask what the woman in the photo looked like, but she didn't want him staring at her face while he tried to remember.

*　　*　　*

Later, she did the tourist thing again, in and around the village, waiting until past noon to eat at Amore Breakfast. She wanted to see Frannie Oliveri, check out what kind of car she drove and keep her ears tuned for any information that might upset her plan.

Adrienne was thrilled to find more than she expected when she got there. Frannie Oliveri had the baby in her arms, feeding her a bottle, while people gathered around to admire the infant girl. Soon to be *my* infant girl, she thought.

"Yes, her mom is coming along," she heard Frannie say. "She's been through a lot of surgery, and the physical therapy every day is no picnic, but she'll be okay in time."

"It's a good thing she has you to care for her baby in the meantime," the woman said.

"Well, a lot of credit has to go to my parents—my mother, mostly—and Glory—they babysit while I'm there. As a matter of fact, since Amore Evenings is closed on Monday nights, Glory's coming with me to the hospital while my mom babysits."

Perfect. And everything I need to silence the babysitter is right here in my tote bag. She took her time eating her breakfast, saved the kiwi slice for last, then paid her check.

Next, she returned to one of the secluded spots she had discovered Saturday. Off came the black wig, the green contacts and the gray sweat suit. She replaced them with jeans, a navy crew neck polo, pale blue windbreaker, an ash blonde wig and blue eyes. On her head she wore a denim hat with *Ogunquit* stitched across its brim.

She left the car in the parking lot of one of the larger Route 1 motels and simply walked out, strolling along like any tourist on her way to the village. But this time there would be no browsing through the shops. She turned onto Beach Street instead and walked towards the ocean. Her large tote bag now contained only the bare essentials required to get the job done.

She maintained a slow and easy pace while her heart thundered in her chest. A little fear and a lot of anxiety. She couldn't wait to get her hands on that baby.

The driveway had only one car. A Camry, not a Volvo. The babysitter's car. Adrienne was pleased that thick clusters of weeds and shrubbery bordered most of the house. They would facilitate her first, and hopefully last, home invasion. Now that she would become a mother, she would have to behave more responsibly.

She entered the property at the same slow pace and, to the best of her knowledge, no one had seen her. With the sun in hiding, the day was cool and slightly windy, reducing the number of walkers. As she headed towards the front of the house, she nearly jumped out of her skin. When she, Erin and Patricia had driven near the house yesterday, the dog pen was not visible. Now the sound of the dog's barking took her by surprise. Observing that he was well-secured, however, she ignored the golden retriever and rang the doorbell.

"Who is it?" the voice called out.

"Child Protective Services, ma'am."

Tess hesitated. "Was someone supposed to come today? No one told me," she said through the speaker.

"No, ma'am, the temporary foster parent was not notified, but we routinely make unscheduled visits to be sure the child is okay."

Tess opened the door. "Oh, she's fine. Come see for yourself," she said, welcoming her in with a sweeping hand gesture. "What's your name, miss? You have ID, I assume?"

"You assumed correctly," Adrienne answered and shot the spray straight into her eyes.

Tess screamed, coughed and spit into her hands while blinded by burning eyes.

Adrienne laughed as she watched the reaction. She had no idea the stuff worked this well when she bought it for her own protection. She made no move other than to observe while the woman struggled to breathe and stay on her feet. "Okay, that's enough," she said as though Tess could control it if she chose to. "Now listen to me and don't give me a hard time, lady, because I'll kill that baby right before your eyes. No problem for me. So either you get on that floor and don't move a muscle or you get this." She pulled out the knife and snapped it open. "Wherever you want it. Your choice, lady."

Still sightless from the burning in her eyes, Tess crumpled her trembling body to the floor. "Please, please, don't hurt the baby. What do you want? I'll give you whatever I have … *please* …"

"I don't need your money, lady. I'm no petty thief. All I want is that pretty little girl over there." Heather had been asleep in a swing in the living room, but the sound of Tess's screams had startled her and her cries were frantic now.

On the hardwood floor, face down, Tess pleaded with her assailant, gasping for air and coughing through every word. "Please, I'm begging you—not the baby. Please don't hurt her."

Adrienne looked down at her victim, oblivious to the fact that Tess couldn't see her sinister smile. "Not to worry," she said, while she worked to tape her up like a mummy. "That baby will be just fine. *I'll* be her mommy now. Why would I want to hurt my own baby?"

"But she's *not* your baby! Who are you?"

"It's none of your damn business who I am. And you know what? I'm sick of listening to you. So if you don't shut up, you'll *really* be struggling to breathe, 'cause I'll tape up your mouth too! Just keep in mind that I don't have to go through all this trouble. I could just as easily use this." She lifted the gleaming blade. "I'm experienced now. A seasoned killer," she said and laughed.

After completing the job to her satisfaction Adrienne looked down at Tess and giggled. "You look like something straight out of a horror flick," she said and went for the screaming baby. She struggled a few seconds to unlock the infant seat strap, then cursed and cut it away. She put the baby's pacifier in her mouth and picked her up. A calm came over Adrienne when she held Heather in her arms. All the anger, the hatred for Tyler, her obsession for vengeance, melted away in that first fleeting moment. "You're my baby now. I'll be your mommy. And I'll be a good mommy, you wait and see."

While Tess's muffled cries filled the silence, Adrienne picked up the unfinished formula bottle and sat on the couch, Heather cradled in her arms. "Now you drink up and go back to sleep, baby, because you have to be very quiet for a while. Just until we get back to our car, okay?" She kissed the baby's forehead and hummed a lullaby until the bottle was empty.

Conscious but helpless, Tess's tears helped wash the sting from her eyes. She didn't dare struggle to free her body. While this madwoman had Heather in her arms, she would do nothing to provoke her into any maniacal action.

Chapter Seventy-two

Benny's barking could still be heard as Adrienne strolled once again along Beach Street, this time headed for the Route 1 motel where she left her car. Before she left the Oliveri house, she had shoved into her tote bag the baby's bottle, a stack of disposable plastic inserts and two cans of ready-made formula. From the dressing table she grabbed a supply of diapers, three stretchies, three undershirts and a thin baby blanket. Heather would have to survive on that modest wardrobe until they were out of Maine and settled elsewhere.

The baby's stroller was on the porch and Adrienne had been tempted to use it. But it would be too chancy, she decided. What if someone spotted a strange woman walking off the property wheeling a baby stroller? Would that arouse curiosity? It would have eliminated one problem and created another. If Heather cried in her stroller while her "mommy". walked her, who would notice or care? If she cried while inside her "mommy's" tote bag, well, that would surely draw attention. She opted for the tote bag, put the baby's pacifier in her mouth, hoping that would keep her quiet until they reached her car.

The uphill walk from Main Street to the motel parking lot was already giving Adrienne second thoughts. Maybe revenge was not so sweet after all. She couldn't believe a little infant could weigh her down like this. Twice she had switched the bag from one shoulder to the other, but she was still short of breath and tempted to yank the hot and itchy wig off her head.

Every now and then she sneaked a look into the bag to make sure the kid wasn't dead. It seemed unbelievable that she could sleep so soundly in a tote bag, although it was well-lined with five thousand dollars in cash cushioned by baby clothes.

"Just stay quiet five minutes more, baby, and we'll be out of here," she whispered. "Once we get in our car, you can cry your heart out."

As she entered the motel parking lot, one of her imagined fears was taking place. Right next to her car, a family was loading their trunk. There was no way she could approach her car. One sound from her bag would ruin everything. She had no choice but to sit on one of the benches on this cool and windy day as though she were basking in sunshine. To make matters worse, Heather began to squirm now that the rhythmic motion had stopped. Pretending to be searching for something in her bag, Adrienne reached in and replaced the pacifier in the baby's mouth. From behind, she heard the sound of a trunk closing and car doors slamming. She stole a look, then inhaled deeply, relieved to see the car pulling out.

"We're almost there now, baby," she whispered through her teeth. "In two minutes, we'll be safe in our car. And you won't be Heather Oliveri anymore. You're getting a new name and a new life. Your daddy left us and we're on our own. That's the story and we'll take it from there."

With Heather snugly tucked in a cardboard box on the floor in the front passenger side of her car, Adrienne sang along with the radio, trying to con herself that all was well. She had been driving south for almost two hours now and feeling safer with each passing mile. From all that Erin and Patricia had casually mentioned about Frannie's routine, she wouldn't return until seven or eight o'clock tonight. If there were no unforeseen mishaps, she would have a good head start. The babysitter was certainly in no condition to cause trouble. She had taped her mouth before she left and with her hands tied behind her back, she could neither scream nor make a phone call.

Phone call! "You stupid, ignorant sonofabitch!" she screamed. "How could you have overlooked something that obvious? What about incoming calls? What if someone doesn't get an answer and keeps trying?"

A voice cut through the music. "Breaking news in the Tyler Keaton murder case regarding the paternity issue. DNA results have just been released revealing that Tyler Keaton is not the child's father. This information leaves authorities faced with the following question: If Tyler Keaton is not Heather Oliveri's father, then how much credence can be given to the theory that Suzanne Oliveri might have murdered Keaton to deny him knowledge and therefore custody rights to his child? Stay tuned to this station for further developments in this case."

Not his child? Stunned, Adrienne looked down at the baby whose eyes were open wide, captivated by the blue sky and colorful scenery whizzing by. "You're not Tyler's daughter, kid? Well, if that doesn't knock the wind out of my sails, I don't know what does!"

She kept her eyes on the road, shooting occasional glances back to Heather as she reassessed her situation. From the moment she had pulled out of the parking lot and onto the highway, she had felt a surge of confidence. There had been no sirens, no flashing lights racing up behind her, as she had feared. She had laughed at her paranoia. How could anyone possibly be on to her? No one knows the baby is missing and won't know for hours, so relax and enjoy your triumph, she told herself.

But that was before she realized what an unanswered phone call could trigger off. A damn manhunt! And before that news broadcast that shocked the hell out of her.

"So now what?" she said aloud. A strange feeling enveloped her. Like a new mother who discovers that the baby in her arms is not hers. A mistake. "Sure, it's still cute and cuddly, this mistake, but I can get a kitten or puppy if I want cute and cuddly," she reasoned. "I got away with murder, so why push my luck?"

Adrienne grimaced as she caught a whiff of unpleasant odor. "Oh, don't tell me you messed up!" she said, looking down at Heather. "You don't expect me to just pull over somewhere and change your diaper, do you?" She gritted her teeth when she realized that in her haste to get out, she had forgotten the baby wipes.

It suddenly all tumbled down on her like a landslide. "All this insanity! For what? For revenge on a dead man I have to live the rest of my life looking over my shoulder?" She peered down at Heather. "You know what, baby? It's been fun and exciting, and real satisfying to know I could pull it off, but you're just not worth my freedom or my life. I suddenly lost my taste for babies—Tyler's, Cody's or any other bastard's baby. I'm thinking if I can get rid of you, I can cut my chances of getting caught by fifty percent. They haven't got a clue about Tyler—if they did they would have grabbed me already. So as soon as I figure out how and where to dump you, you're history, angel face."

Chapter Seventy-three

In the hospital cafeteria, Frannie pushed aside the second half of her tuna sandwich. "I'm getting a little worried now," she told Glory. "I called my house almost two hours ago and my mother didn't answer. This has happened before, so I wasn't concerned at first. She loves to sit in my rocker with the baby. If she falls asleep in her arms, she doesn't disturb her and won't answer the phone if it's not within reach. But now I called again and she still doesn't answer."

"Wait a few minutes and try again. Maybe she's in the bathroom, or changing Heather's diaper, or out for a walk."

"I doubt it. I know my mother. She won't walk if it's too cool and especially if it's windy, like today."

Frannie tried three times more in the next ten minutes with the same results.

Maybe she went out with the car somewhere," Glory suggested. "What about your dad? Why don't you call him? Maybe he knows."

"My dad had a golf outing today. I can try his cell, but it's not always on and anyway, I don't want to scare him unnecessarily. Let me try my neighbor, the young woman behind me. Her house looks down on mine."

Frannie tapped her foot while she waited, hoping the woman was home. "Camille? This is Frannie," she said when she answered. "I hate to bother you, but I haven't been able to reach my mom and I'm a little concerned. Can you just tell me if her car is in my driveway?"

"The car is there, Frannie, but Benny is still in his pen, barking like crazy. Your mom doesn't usually leave him in there so long." Camille hesitated, then said, "Look, Douglas went in for his nap ten minutes ago, but I guess I can wake him and go check on your mom."

A sick numbing feeling gripped Frannie. "No, don't bother, Camille. I can have someone else there in minutes. Thanks."

Glory watched Frannie's face freeze in silent panic. "Let me try Steve. He can be there in no time." She pulled out her cell. "Damn! Voice mail."

"Maybe I should call the police. I hate to panic, but–"

"No, wait one second," Glory said, raising a finger with her phone pressed to her ear. "Alex? Thank God you're home. It's me. Listen, Frannie and I are at the hospital and we need a favor ..."

Seconds later she slipped the phone back in her pocket. "He's on his way to your house, Frannie. We should hear from him in minutes, so let's just wait right here."

"Oh, my God! Oh, my God!" was all Frannie could say. She visualized her mother collapsed on the floor while Heather was screaming, injured or dead, after falling from Tess's arms. "This is like the night Suzanne was missing. We spent all night saying 'maybe this, maybe that,' and look what happened!"

"But this time we won't have to wait so long. Alex was flying out the door when I told him and I'm sure we'll hear from him the second he gets there."

There was nothing they could say to each other that could possibly distract them, so neither one tried. Glory went for coffee refills which neither one wanted but sipped at them anyway to occupy their restless hands.

When the phone rang minutes later, Glory answered and the color drained from her face. "We're on our way!" She grabbed Frannie by the arm. "Let's go!"

"Why? What happened? You're scaring me to death!"

"Your mom looks okay, Alex said, but he called 9-1-1. Paramedics will check her out."

"What happened to her? What did he say?" Frannie's voice resonated through the hospital corridors as they both raced to the exit. "Answer me, dammit!"

Glory waited until they were outside, then held her friend by the shoulders. "Someone tied her up and sprayed her with something, he said. He couldn't talk. Just said to get home fast."

"Oh, my God!" she cried again. "Is she hurt bad? What about Heather? Did they hurt Heather?"

Glory hugged her tight and the words came out in sobs. "Frannie, he can't find Heather."

Security personnel ran to the sound of Frannie's screams.

Chapter Seventy-four

The house was swarming with uniformed police, detectives, EMS personnel and CSI technicians. FBI agents were expected momentarily to join forces with local and state police to search for the kidnapped baby and her abductor.

Frannie ran to her mother and embraced her. Tess rocked with sobs in the arms of her husband and could barely speak coherently when she saw her daughter.

"They gave her a sedative. She was worse when I got here—couldn't stop trembling," Sal told his daughter.

Tess struggled for control so she could communicate. "I couldn't stop her, I couldn't stop her ..." she cried.

"Who is *she*, mom? Did you know her? Was there anything about her that looked familiar? *Think*, mom."

Tony Gerard put a gentle hand on Frannie's shoulder. She stood up and hugged him. "Oh, Tony, I'm so glad you're here. I didn't see you. What can you tell me? I'm sick thinking not only of the baby, but Suzanne too. Has anyone told her? She'll go out of her mind!"

"No, she hasn't been told yet, but we can't hold that back too long. I'll handle that myself, but I first had to contact her doctor at home. He's on his way back to the hospital to be with her when I break that news."

"Oh, that sounds like him. He's an angel, that doctor. Suzanne loves him. But she still won't have family around when she hears. Not that there's a person on earth who can soften that blow!" Frannie burst into tears again. "Oh, God, I wish I could wake up and find this is all just a bad dream ..."

Tony put a finger to his lip. "I know it's hard, Frannie, but try to keep your voice down. We're trying to calm your mom so we can question her further. We found her tied up, hands and feet, with tape wrapped all around her body. It's a good thing the tape over her mouth had moistened enough to loosen, because the spray her assailant used causes severe discomfort—lots of coughing and spitting. With her mouth sealed ..." He shook his head.

"She could have died! What did the guy spray her with—Mace?"

"Or its equivalent."

"Was she able to see him? Did she give you a description?"

"All we know so far is that the assailant was a woman—or dressed to look like one. Blonde, wore sunglasses, tall and thin, she said. But she only saw her a second or two before the woman attacked her with the spray. That stuff not only blinds you temporarily, but the victim has a hard time breathing."

"Did the bitch say anything? Make any demands about money?"

"She said she was from CPS, making an unscheduled visit to check on Heather. Your mom fell for it and made the mistake of unlocking the door. She did ask for ID, but the woman was already in the house at that point. That's when she sprayed her, straight in the eyes. And no, it wasn't about money. Your mother offered her anything she had to give, but the assailant was insulted. 'I'm no petty thief,' she told your mom."

"And that's it? She just grabbed Heather and took off like one of those crazies who steals babies out of hospitals?"

"At this moment that would be my guess. Especially since she told your mother, 'I'll be her mommy now.' I know it's no consolation, Frannie, but it might be better if she *is* one of those crazies. If she's been desperate for a baby, chances are she won't harm Heather. We just have to find her. And now, with the FBI coming in, we'll have plenty of manpower."

Tony didn't mention it to Frannie, but they already had uniforms and detectives in the field and computer experts searching through myriad databases for any information that could lead them to Adrienne Fox. He had suspected her the moment he learned she had vanished, but the pieces had been connecting faster than a child's puzzle.

He hadn't given much thought to the colors of hair and eyes, aware that both could be easily disguised, but Tess had said *tall and thin.* Andy Donovan was on his way to see Cody Griffin to squeeze out everything he knows about Adrienne Fox. He'll start by asking about height and weight. If Cody says *tall and thin,* that'll be a start. If they're real lucky, he might even have a recent full-body photograph, but after witnessing his bitterness, Tony strongly doubted that. He sorted out and tossed around the facts he had so far:

So let's say Cody tells Andy Adrienne is tall and thin.

Cody already told me Adrienne hated Tyler Keaton.

Cody also said he dumped Adrienne because of Tyler Keaton.

If they had married—or even if they hadn't married—Adrienne could have had Cody's babies someday. But Tyler killed all those plans. So Adrienne kills Tyler and takes his baby for herself.

Or Adrienne kills Tyler's baby.

Tony chased that last thought out of his head.

Chapter Seventy-five

Adrienne took the exit for Providence, Rhode Island. The sooner she got rid of the baby, the better off she'd be. Not that they'd stop hunting for the abductor, but it would certainly be easier to escape capture without her. Once an Amber Alert is activated, a woman traveling alone with an infant girl would grab more attention than blinking neon lights in a cemetery.

Well, you should have thought about that before, girl.

She had no particular destination in mind. Wherever her instincts led her would be the drop-off point. The small part of her that regretted all she had done and what she was about to do hammered away at her conscience. She used Heather as her sounding board, her confessor, who would understand it was love for one man and obsessive hatred for another that fueled her actions.

"I'll try to find a spot where they'll find you, baby, but not where they'll find you too soon. I need a little lead time, right?"

Heather's intermittent whimpers escalated to red-faced, nonstop cries. It had been hours since she had fed her that last ounce of formula. "You're hungry, aren't you? You're hungry and your diaper is dirty. Sure, I can pull into any one of these parking lots and feed you. Mothers feed their babies anywhere, anytime. But once word gets out that you're missing, someone might remember seeing us. And they might remember our car, so we have to be real careful, right?"

Adrienne winced and cupped a hand over her right ear. "Stop that crying, damn you! How can I think straight when you're screaming your lungs out?"

On impulse, she pulled into the parking lot of a medical building rather than a supermarket where people come and go constantly. One pressing question took precedence in her mind. *To feed or not to feed.* "If I feed you, will you shut up for a while? I need to put some distance between us." The conscience she had thought was lost forever now gripped her. She circled the lot and chose a spot in the back that faced nothing but shrubs, grass and trees.

While Heather drank her bottle, Adrienne's head throbbed, denying her the ability to concentrate. The odor from Heather's diaper wasn't helping. "Sorry, kid, I can't handle that too. At least I fed you."

With eyes that squinted from her blinding headache, she looked in all directions. There were no windows facing the back, so she couldn't be seen from the building, but there were plenty of parked cars. She had to be sure no one was walking to one near her.

When she felt safe enough, she put Heather back in the cardboard box, threw her blanket over her, and stuck the pacifier in her mouth. She then opened the door slowly, lifted the box and placed it carefully between her car and the SUV parked on her left.

"Good luck, kid," she said aloud as she backed up. "I wish I could say it was fun…"

But as she drove away feeling a thousand pounds lighter, she realized it *had* been fun, but only in the planning, not the doing. Just before she reached the front exit, she passed a receptacle. Instinctively she backed up to it, grabbed the clothes, diapers and one remaining formula can and tossed them in.

The gentleman standing in a doorway behind her smoking his cigarette wondered what she had discarded that was so important she had to back up. It wasn't fast food containers or coffee cups like the stuff most people dump in there. It looked like cloth of some kind. Pink cloth.

When he finished his cigarette, the Saab was long gone and he was about to go back upstairs. But they said his wife wouldn't complete her tests for about forty-five minutes so he was in no hurry. He decided to enjoy the fresh air and walk a little around the front parking area. When he passed the receptacle, curiosity made him take two steps back to peek in.

Chapter Seventy-six

Despite Frannie's reluctance to leave her mother, Tess insisted that she and Jerry ride with Tony Gerard to the hospital. Although Dr. Quinlan would be at her side when she's told, she still needed family.

"I knew I shouldn't have let you talk me into skipping the hospital today," Jerry said, banging his fisted right hand into the palm of his left.

"Uncle Jerry, stop. What difference would it have made? Glory and I were there. It's not as if she had no company. The important thing is you'll be with her now, when Tony tells her. But you'd better prepare to be strong. This news is going to rip her heart out."

Jerry couldn't answer. Just thinking about telling his daughter had his eyes filling up already. He bit his dry lip and stared out the window.

*   *   *

"You didn't say anything, did you, Doc?" Tony asked.

"No, not a word. I didn't even mention that you were coming. I was hoping for a miracle—that the baby would be found before she had to be told. Once it gets on the TV news, it would be impossible to keep it from her."

"I know," Tony said. "That's why I had to make this a priority. And who knows? Maybe she can tell us something that might help."

Suzanne's eyes went wide with fear when she saw Tony. "My lawyer said I'm not supposed to talk to you."

"Forget all that for now," Frannie said. "Sergeant Gerard needs to talk to you about something else. Something much more important."

"Suzanne, I brought Frannie and your father with me and Dr. Quinlan was kind enough to come back when I called him at home. I'm afraid I have some bad news. As far as we know, Heather is alive and safe, but she's been kidnapped."

She stared at him a few seconds, just shaking her head in denial, then screamed. "Kidnapped! How can you say she's alive and safe if she's kidnapped?" Her hands flew to her mouth as if she could keep the screams locked inside and hold back this horror. She rocked her body side to side as she moaned and sobbed through her words. "What are you talking about? What happened?"

Tony told her what they knew so far. "Suzanne, I know how very difficult this is for you, but if you can hold yourself together, I'd like to ask you a few questions that might help us find Heather. And I said that we feel she's alive and safe because we strongly suspect that she was abducted by someone who desperately wanted a baby and decided to take yours."

"What someone? Do you know who she is?"

"We think we do. Tell me, Suzanne, when you lived in New York with Tyler, did you ever meet an Adrienne Fox?"

"Adrienne Fox! Sure I remember her. Don't tell me you're wasting time chasing after her!"

"What did she look like? Can you describe her?"

Suzanne tried to visualize Adrienne. "Nothing that would make her stand out; brownish-red hair, pretty if you like the type."

359

"What type is that?"

"Classy looking, like one of those tall skinny models."

"How tall would you say she was? Your best guess."

"Well, she used to tower over me, so I'd say about 5'10"; maybe taller and rail thin. At least she was when I knew her. She used to come in once in a while, then more often later. Had her eye on Cody, Tyler's partner. But the last thing that one wanted was a baby. She was strictly a career woman. Trust me, she was not the type to sit home and change diapers. You're wasting precious time, Sergeant. You need to find Heather, not Adrienne Fox!"

"Bear with me, Suzanne. I believe if we find Adrienne, we'll find Heather. But as you said, I don't want to waste precious time explaining. So tell me, if you can remember, did you ever have a conversation with Adrienne when she might have confided or just casually discussed anything about her private life? Maybe people she might have discussed ... friends, family or anyone in particular?"

Suzanne put her head in her hands and tried to concentrate. "This is so hard ... how can I concentrate knowing my baby is missing?" She paused a few seconds, then said, "All I remember is she lived in the city, the Gramercy Park section. But I don't remember any specific conversation where she told me something I'd recall now. I left not too long after she starting coming around often." She looked up at him. "Can't you tell me why you suspect she took Heather?"

"Well, briefly, after you left she and Cody started seeing each other. Eventually their relationship became serious—marriage plans and all—until Tyler told Cody about her past. Apparently she had worked for an escort service entertaining male clients for various businesses. They fought when Cody confronted her and we have strong reason to believe she had a vendetta against Tyler. His life and his baby."

"Oh, my God! Then how can you say she's alive and safe?" She broke down again. Tony and Frannie stood by while Dr. Quinlan whispered to her. Suzanne sniffed away her tears and nodded. "I'm okay now, Sergeant. I'll try to stay calm so you can get out of here and look for my daughter."

"Suzanne, we have scores of law enforcement officers looking for Heather. Don't think for one minute that because I'm here, the search is at a standstill."

"I know; I realize that. But are you saying you think she killed Tyler?"

"We believe she did, yes."

"In a way, I should be glad. That would clear me as a suspect, but if she's a murderer and has my daughter ..." She steepled her fingers over her face again.

"No, don't think that way. It was Tyler she hated, not the baby. We think she wants Heather for herself, especially since she thought Heather was Tyler's baby."

Suzanne glared at him. "What do you mean *thought*?"

"Well, before all this happened, the DNA results came in today. Tyler Keaton is not Heather's father. Were you aware of that?"

Jerry punched the air. "Jeez! You lived with that creep and slept with someone else? What the hell were you doing with your life, Suzanne?"

"Ruining it. Like you, Dad."

Tony put a hand up. "Let's hold it right there. Otherwise I have to ask you to leave the room," he said to Jerry, then turned again to Suzanne. "Is there anything you'd like to say to me alone, Suzanne? I can ask your cousin and father to step out. Dr. Quinlan too, if you want."

"If you're going to ask me who the father is, don't bother."

"But the baby's father can be an important missing link here. I'd like to rule him out as a possible suspect."

Suzanne remained silent, thinking. Investigating her daughter's kidnapping superseded all else, of course, but disclosing that Greg Haggarty is the baby's father could not possibly serve any useful purpose. She opted to cast another dark shadow on herself rather than hurt his family. She gave her cousin the eye.

Frannie took her uncle's arm and said, "We have to cooperate in every way we can, Uncle Jerry. The faster Tony gets the information he needs, the faster they'll find Heather."

She waited until they left the room, then said, "I have no idea who the father is, Sergeant," she lied. "When Tyler was out of town one night, I went to a bar uptown. I met a guy, drank way too much, and took him home. An hour later he was gone and I never saw him again. End of story. But I never considered the possibility that he could have made me pregnant. Supposedly it wasn't the right time of the month, but I guess those DNA results prove all those ovulation statistics wrong."

Tony fingered his chin and studied her. She hadn't once made eye contact during that explanation. "You took him home to Tyler's place? You took quite a chance, I'd say."

"Alcohol makes you do crazy things. Ask my father."

"Why don't I believe you?"

"I have no idea why because that's all I'm going to say on the subject. Don't you think if I had any information that could help you find Heather I would tell you? Now please get out there and find my baby!"

After everyone left, Dr. Quinlan stopped in again. "Are you going to be okay? Is there anything you want to tell me before I say goodnight?"

"No, I don't plan on getting any sleep tonight, but I'll be okay. I'll call Rob and see if he can keep me company awhile."

She watched him as he walked away. *He's such a gentleman. A gentle man. He didn't believe my story either.*

The doctor wasn't gone for a minute when Suzanne burst into tears again. Images of Heather with a woman gone mad horrified her. She picked up the phone and called her friend. "Rob, something awful happened. Can I come down?"

"Something awful! No, you wait right there. I'll come to you."

Chapter Seventy-seven

On his way back from the hospital, with Frannie and her uncle in the car, Tony got a call from Andy Donovan. Thirsting for any information about Heather, Frannie tried to pick up the gist of the conversation, but Tony wasn't talking much; just listening.

"Thanks a million, Andy. I'll buy you a steak dinner next time."

"Make it a Maine lobster. My wife and I are coming up to Ogunquit this summer."

"You got it. And you can meet Corrine. I chewed your ears off about her that night."

"Looking forward to that. And Tony, good luck. I hope that baby turns up tonight. *Alive.*"

Tony thanked his friend and paraphrased Andy's words for Frannie. "He said, according to Tyler's partner and also Adrienne Fox's employer, she's tall and thin, as your mom described. We can't put too much emphasis on hair and eyes because that's easily disguised. We have people at her condo right now and they already learned the lady uses wigs and contacts. With no distinguishable markings—like a visible birthmark would be nice—she can change her appearance daily if she wanted. But she drives a black Saab. If she used her own car, that'll narrow down the search. There were no car rentals made in her name recently."

"Why would she drive her own car?" Frannie asked. "Once you have the make, color and plate number, how can she hide?"

"She can't. Unless she has a good place to hole up. And she'd have to get there before word gets out and we hunt her down. As for a rental, she probably figured that can be easily traced too, so why bother."

Frannie pursed her lips. "It doesn't make sense to me. Even a person with half a brain would do a better job covering their tracks. It's like leaving crumbs in the forest."

Tony smiled. "Birds and animals eat crumbs in the forest."

"What about walking off her job without telling a soul? That certainly raises a red flag. Why would she call attention to herself like that?"

"Who knows? Sometimes they think they have it all figured out and can get away with it. They love the excitement of living life on the edge. And then there are those who want to get caught. They hate their life and what they're doing, but can't stop. They're not—"

Tony's phone interrupted again just as he approached Frannie's driveway. Again Tony listened and Frannie watched. From his attentive look, she could only tell that it was important, but not whether the news was good or bad.

"I'm going to drop you two off. There are plenty of people inside your house, Frannie, to help you out till I get back."

"What? What happened, Tony? Anything bad?"

"No, but it could help. That was Corrine. I have to get over to The Admiral's Inn."

*   *   *

"Sergeant, I'm in shock," Ken said. "When Corrine came here a few minutes ago, she showed me that same photo again—the one you brought earlier. Well, it still didn't ring any bells in my head until she mentioned the car. Then it all meshed together. That woman just checked out this morning! Said she and her fiancé wanted to buy property, Supposedly she was here to check out the area." He slapped his forehead. "I noticed the New York plates but we get thousands of New York tourists—you know that—so I never gave them a second thought. And she paid us in cash; no credit card transaction. But that's not unusual either. She was so pleasant ... I'm so sorry."

"There's nothing to be sorry about, Ken," Corrine said. "None of us knew enough at that point." She turned to Tony. "I fooled around with the computer and changed her appearance. This shot did it." She showed him an image of Adrienne with long black hair.

"When I think that we had the actual murderer here as a guest in our inn ... it blows my mind!"

Jake came in and joined them on the porch. He shook Tony's hand. "Did you tell him about the girls, Ken?"

"I'll tell him," Corrine said. "Tony, Saturday night Adrienne Fox, who registered as Julianne Baker, did a nice con job on two women she met here at the bar; Erin Crowley and Pat McGovern—"

"Erin and Pat are regulars here," Ken said. "Corrine asked me to call them—oh, here they come now," Ken said, looking out the window. "They can tell their own story."

*   *   *

In Providence, Rhode Island, while Arthur Wilkes waited for the red light to turn green, the radio announcement jolted him like an electrical shock. He made a sharp turn, drove back into the medical building lot and parked by the receptacle.

"What the heck are you doing?" his wife asked, annoyed by his swift and unexpected moves.

"I have to make a phone call. And while I'm talking, don't let anyone go near that garbage receptacle. This could all be nothing, and I'll feel like a jerk, but I can't ignore it."

She peered at him. "Arthur, I think you're losing it!"

Arthur ignored her and spoke into the phone. "My name is Arthur Wilkes and I'm calling about that Amber Alert." He repeated what he had observed, then described the woman and her car. "It was baby clothes I saw in there. And diapers—clean diapers, you know, like folded from the package." He paused to listen, then said. "No, we're not going anywhere. My wife and I will wait right here. But wait—one more thing before I forget—there was something else I realized after I discovered the baby things—there was no car seat in that Saab. If she had a baby at home or somewhere, wouldn't her car have a seat?"

Arthur and Anabelle Wilkes got out of the car and paced. "I'm so scared, Arthur. What if that baby is in there?" She pointed to the receptacle.

"Take it easy. The police will be here any minute."

"I can't stay still. I have to walk," she said.

But Anabelle hadn't walked more than fifty feet when she stopped short. "Arthur! Arthur! Come here!" she cried out.

When her husband reached her, he heard it too. A wave of dizziness came over him. "Walk with me, Anabelle. It might be nothing. Maybe another baby in its mother's arms."

"And what if it isn't?"

"Then at least we know she's alive."

Sirens and screeching tires were welcome sounds to the Wilkes. They embraced each other, but both were trembling. When the first officer approached them, Arthur pointed to the back of the building. "Go … hurry!"

367

Chapter Seventy-eight

When Adrienne checked in at The Rise & Shine Motel in Providence, Rhode Island, Harry, the clerk, suggested that she move her car to the immediate left of the office, which would place it right outside her room.

"No, thanks anyway," she said. "I don't have much to carry. I can walk."

"Whatever you prefer, miss. Would you mind filling this out, please?" He handed her a vehicle ID form. "We have problems with people who aren't guests here using our parking area. When you complete that, I'll give you a sticker for your car."

"Oh, do I have to bother with this now?" She put a hand on her forehead. "I have such a headache. I need to get in my room and sleep it off."

"I apologize, miss. Certainly it can wait." He handed her the room key. "Can I get you something for your headache?"

"No, I have it, thank you."

Harry went about his business but noticed the woman as she passed the office headed for her room. True, she had only a small suitcase on wheels and a tote bag on her shoulder, but she walked briskly, her demeanor generally alert. Her eyes were wide open, not squinted by the headache she complained of.

He might have brushed her off entirely if the car hadn't piqued his curiosity. Why would she park so far from the office when she checked in? And if she had faked the headache, was it about the car? Maybe it was stolen?

He shrugged it off and returned to his computer. Minutes later, his fax machine came alive and Harry went to pick up the paper from the tray. His mouth remained open as he read a State Police notification asking motel personnel to look out for a 2004 black Saab, bearing license plate number …blah, blah, blah …

With the paper in his hand, he closed the office door and walked around the bend. His heart raced when he spotted a black Saab. With his cell already in his hand, he walked closer to check the plate number.

He cursed the woman who called herself Julianne Baker and dialed 9-1-1.

*   *   *

When the police surrounded the motel and received no response to their warnings, they broke the door down and stormed in.

They found Adrienne Fox hunched over on the floor, legs crossed, rocking back and forth. She moaned repeatedly only one word:

"Cody … Cody … Cody …"

Epilogue

A month later, Ken and Jake hadn't received a single negative response to their invitations. Everyone was thrilled and excited about The Admiral Inn's celebration party. Tyler Keaton's alleged murderer was under police custody but hospitalized for mental evaluation. With little Heather safely back in her mother's arms, it was a joyous occasion to celebrate.

Since Suzanne and Rob were the guests of honor, Ken and Jake had insisted on picking them up. They brought Suzanne in first and she burst into tears as soon as she entered. "Oh, I knew I shouldn't have worn mascara tonight!" She kissed both her hosts when she saw the entire dining area and bar full of familiar faces. Everyone applauded and came up to kiss her and Rob. In one corner of the room there were two fully decorated pedestal chairs, hers trimmed with pink ribbons and Rob's with tiny American flags.

Rob swallowed hard, filled with emotion. "You guys are amazing ..."

"No, we're not," Jake said, waving it off. "We love this stuff, especially fussing for happy occasions. And this one beats all!"

Heather was wide awake in Kim Haggarty's arms and Suzanne laughed at the surprise. "You were supposed to be babysitting for me tonight!"

"Well, we all had to do some lying," Kim answered. "You look wonderful, Suzanne. We're all so happy for you." She turned to her husband. "Right, Greg?"

"Absolutely," Greg said. "You had plenty of prayers from plenty of people."

Suzanne laughed. "I did a lot of praying myself, more than I ever did in my life!" *Especially for you and your family. That none of you would ever find out that child in your wife's arms is yours.*

Glory and Alex came up together for their congratulatory kisses. Suzanne had met Glory for the first time at the hospital, that horrific day when Heather was kidnapped, but had seen her many times since. "It's so great to see that ring on your finger. Make sure it stays there," she teased with a pointed finger.

"Oh, it's there to stay, don't worry," Alex said. "And it'll have company real soon."

"*Really?* Did you guys set a date?"

"We're shooting for late September, after the summer rush," Glory answered.

Suzanne was genuinely thrilled. "That's only a few months. How wonderful!"

"I wish it were sooner," Alex said, then cupped a hand over his mouth. "We have to get busy making babies."

Suzanne nudged Rob who was talking to another guest. "Rob, did you hear this? Glory and Alex are getting married in September and hope to get pregnant right away."

"Sounds good to me," Rob said and squeezed her shoulder.

Sara, Tim and Steve Lynch sat on bar stools watching the festivities. "What a pleasure to see all these happy faces—especially Suzanne and Rob, of course." Steve said. "Who would have believed we'd be here celebrating after all that's happened to them?"

"And what about those two?" Sara said, gazing across the room at Glory and Alex. "They're cause for celebration too."

"Yeah, and with no help from you. See, didn't I tell you they'd have to work it out themselves?"

"Yes, you did," Sara answered, "but I never dreamed it would be that poor baby's kidnapping that would bring them together."

"Sometimes in the aftermath of tragedy comes joy," Steve mused. "Take another look at Suzanne and Rob. They went through hell and their faces are lit up tonight like Christmas trees—especially when they look at each other. Talk about chemistry!" He sighed, reminiscing about happier days he left behind.

"I don't mean to sound insensitive," Tim whispered to Sara, "but when does the food come out? I'm starving!"

"Be patient. It had to be heated. You should be glad we don't have to serve it tonight. We can relax and be guests."

Dan and Louise arrived next, along with Vanessa and Wanda. The two women's first public appearance together as a couple raised some eyebrows, but only to reflect surprise, not objection.

Wanda embraced Rob and couldn't let go. Rob laughed and released her arms from his neck. "Hey, I know you're glad to see me, but I can't bend down that long!"

"I'm sorry. I didn't expect to cry, but they're happy tears. Every time I look at you, I thank God for saving your life."

"And what about her?" he said, smiling at Suzanne.

"Oh, this one, this lovely young woman. What you survived—the accident—the way your car was crushed ..." Wanda winced, recalling the photos. "Then the baby. How much can a person go through and still survive? It has to be some kind of miracle."

"We all agree on that, Wanda," Suzanne answered softly.

Later, when Glory introduced Steve to Vanessa and her partner, Steve congratulated them, then pouted. "I'm jealous," he said.

Although he tried to pass it off as playful pretense, Sara had been saddened by Steve's two simple words. They had so clearly reflected his aching heart. She went to him and politely apologized to Vanessa and Wanda for interrupting. "If you don't mind, ladies, I need to borrow this gorgeous guy for a few minutes. Come with me, Steve. I have a surprise for you."

"My! How suggestive," he teased. "But I'm afraid you're wasting your time, my friend."

She took him by the hand and led him to a back room. Steve looked at her curiously. "You're taking me to a *bedroom?*"

Sara giggled. "Shut up, Steve." Without another word, she opened the door. Seeing nothing but an unoccupied room with the TV on, tuned to Larry King, Steve gave her a perplexed look. "Is he my surprise—Larry King?"

The bathroom door swung open. "No, I am!"

"John!"

The two men laughed and embraced. "What the heck are you doing here? I'm so shocked and totally confused."

John pointed to Sara. "Your friend here hunted me down. She's very persuasive. Quite a salesperson, this girl." He pinched Sara's cheek. "I was still mad as hell—didn't even want to talk about you, much less *see* you. But she wouldn't let go, melted me like butter." He shrugged. "And here I am."

Sara beamed. "I had to try, Steve. Since I couldn't take credit for Glory and Alex's reconciliation, I had to work on you two. And anyway, you asked me to, remember?"

Steve hugged her. "So I did, pretty girl." He brushed the hair away from her ear and whispered. "And thank you, Sara."

"Where did you disappear to?" Tim asked when she returned to the party.

"Oh, Tim, that felt so-o-o good," she said, then told him about Steve's surprise and how she had arranged for John's arrival in Ogunquit.

"You *what*?" he said, a little too loud.

Sara plugged her ears with her fingers and gave him a puppy dog look. "You mad at me?" she asked, laughter tugging at her mouth.

Tim couldn't hold his stern expression any longer. His laughter exploded.

Tony and Corrine didn't arrive until ten o'clock and apologized to Suzanne and Rob.

"Forget it," Suzanne said. "The party's in full swing now that the food came out. But what happened, Tony? Work problems again?"

"No, not this time," Tony said, flashing his sexy smile. "Corrine and I needed some time at Perkins Cove."

"At this hour? Wasn't it cold?"

Corrine answered for Tony. "It was when we got there, but not after this." She held out her left hand. "Now we're not just engaged to be engaged. This will take us straight to the altar!"

Suzanne screamed and hugged them before spreading the news.

Frannie and her parents shared a table with Rob's family. "What a difference tonight is from that night we first met at the hospital!" Frannie said to Catherine. "And it wasn't only about Rob. Watching you, Jim and Dennis was heartbreaking, too. I felt your pain. Everyone did." She erased the memory with a hand wave. "But thank God, he's doing so well now, and always smiling, that boy of yours! To watch him and talk to him, no one would believe what he went through. Never a word of complaint."

"How true," Catherine said, her face lighting up with pride. "My Robbie always had a good attitude. Never lets anything get him down. He's always more concerned about the other guy's problems than his own. Even now, since the accident."

Dennis, who had been talking to Jim, leaned forward. "I'm listening to you guys," he said to Frannie, "and of course I agree with everything you said. No man could be prouder of his grandson than I am. He's a gem, our Robbie." He raised a finger. "But Frannie, what you said about Robbie always smiling ... I just want to say that although that's his nature, he seems happier now than before. So enthused about life in general."

"I think you're right," Frannie said. "Maybe when he thinks about all that happened and how much worse it could have been, he appreciates life more than ever."

"Yes, maybe," Dennis said, his gaze shifting to his grandson. "But I think your cousin and little Heather had a lot to do with it." He looked at his son and daughter-in law. "We talked about it, and even Jim and Catherine get that same impression."

Frannie held back her smile while she glanced at Catherine. Suzanne's history is not exactly what you "bring home to mother," but Catherine and Jim both smiled warmly, relieving Frannie's apprehension. "That's nice of you to say, Dennis. And I'm inclined to agree."

"So where's your uncle?" Dennis asked to change the subject. "I never got to say hello."

Frannie took a fast look around, then curled her brows. "I don't see him," she said, imagining him drinking at the bar. He had joined Alcoholics Anonymous only two weeks ago and getting through this party would be challenging. "Excuse me, guys, let me take a look around."

She found Jerry sitting on a leather sofa in the TV room behind the bar. The sight was so wonderfully out of character for him that she burst out laughing.

"What's so funny?" he asked, looking highly indignant.

"I'm sorry, Uncle Jerry. I'm not laughing *at* you. It's just that I was surprised. Very pleasantly surprised to see you with Heather in your arms, feeding her a bottle, no less!" Frannie knew for a fact that he had never held his granddaughter, except when he yanked her from Glory's arms. And that certainly didn't count.

"You think I never fed a baby before? I figured let her mother enjoy herself. I can't sit at the bar anyway, so I'm good here, with the TV and my Diet Coke."

She sat down and put a hand on his shoulder. "I'm proud of you, you know. I think you're going to make it."

He gave her a long look. "And what about you? Are you going to make it?"

"Make what? My restaurants are doing fine."

"I'm talking about your personal life. Practically everyone here has somebody. And all you have is that dog, Benny."

"Yes, as much as I complain about him, I love my Benny. But he's not all I have."

"You mean you *do* have somebody? Who is it? Someone we know?"

She gave him one of those *wouldn't-you-like-to-know* grins and rejoined the party.